Christ...
with Him

Three charming romances
from favourite authors

Would he propose this Christmas?

Christmas

Christmas
with Him

JACKIE BRAUN
CHRISTINE RIMMER
SHIRLEY JUMP

First published in Great Britain 2012
by Mills & Boon, an imprint of Harlequin (UK) Limited,
Eton House, 18-24 Paradise Road, Richmond, Surrey TW9 1SR

CHRISTMAS WITH HIM © by Harlequin Enterprises II B.V./S.à.r.l 2012

The Tycoon's Christmas Proposal, *A Bravo Christmas Reunion* and *Marry-Me Christmas* were published in Great Britain by Harlequin (UK) Limited.

The Tycoon's Christmas Proposal © Jackie Braun Fridline 2008
A Bravo Christmas Reunion © Christine Reynolds 2007
Marry-Me Christmas © Shirley Kawa-Jump, LLC 2008

ISBN: 978 0 263 89710 4
ebook ISBN: 978 1 408 97079 9

05-1212

Printed and bound in Spain
by Blackprint CPI, Barcelona

THE TYCOON'S
CHRISTMAS PROPOSAL

BY
JACKIE BRAUN

Jackie Braun is a three-time RITA® finalist, three-time National Readers' Choice Award finalist, and a past winner of the Rising Star award. She lives in Michigan with her husband and two sons, and can be reached through her website at www.jackiebraun.com.

'In 1991 I was sure I was getting an engagement ring for Christmas. So were all of my sisters. The first thing they did when Mark and I walked in the door for dinner was grab my left hand and look. But I didn't get a ring. Mark thought that was too predictable. He proposed to me a few days into the New Year when I least expected it. I've never regretted saying yes.'

For my late father, Walter Braun.

Thanks for sending down a little inspiration in the wee hours of the morning, Dad.

I miss you.

CHAPTER ONE

DAWSON BURKE was used to people doing things a certain way. *His* way.

For that reason alone he found the telephone message he'd just retrieved from his voice mail annoying. He flipped his cell phone closed and tapped it against his chin as he stared out the limousine's windows at the fender-to-fender traffic fighting its way into Denver. What did Eve Hawley mean she would be *popping by* his office later today to discuss his gift needs? What was there to discuss?

He'd only met his previous personal shopper on a handful of occasions during the past several years. All other dealings with Carole Deming had been accomplished by telephone, fax, e-mail or proxy. Dawson provided a list of names and the necessary compensation. In return, Carole bought, wrapped and saw to it that his gifts were delivered. Mission accomplished. Everyone happy.

Well, he wasn't happy at the moment.

Eve said she needed to ask him some questions about the intended recipients on his list. Eve said she preferred to meet with her clients face-to-face at least once before setting out to do their shopping. She said it gave her a feel for their tastes and helped her personalize the purchases she made. Eve said…

Dawson scrubbed a hand over his eyes and expelled a ragged breath. This was the third voice mail full of comments and requests that he'd received from the woman. He didn't have time to deal with this bossy stand-in any more than he cared to make time for Christmas. He couldn't help but wonder what had possessed Carole, who was recuperating from knee surgery, to suggest this woman as her replacement.

Maybe he should call Carole and see if she could recommend someone else. Someone who didn't ask unnecessary questions. Someone who simply did his bidding and required no hand-holding.

The limousine pulled to the curb in front of the building that housed the offices of Burke Financial Services. His grandfather, Clive Burke Senior, had started the company, which specialized in managing stock portfolios and corporate pensions. Clive Senior had been gone nearly a dozen years and Dawson's father, Clive Junior, had retired the spring before last. These days, Dawson was the Burke in charge. And he believed in running a tight ship.

His secretary rose from behind her desk just outside his office the moment the elevator doors slid open on the eleventh floor. Her name was Rachel Stern and her surname suited her perfectly. She was an older woman with steel-gray hair, shoulders as wide as a linebacker's and a face that would have made a hardened criminal cross to the opposite side of the street before passing her. In the dozen years Rachel had been in his employ Dawson couldn't recall ever seeing her crack a smile. Stern. That she was, but also efficient and dedicated. He swore sometimes she knew what he wanted before he did.

This morning was no different. She fell into step beside him, prepping him on the day's itinerary even before he had peeled off his leather gloves and shrugged out of his heavy wool overcoat.

"The people from Darien Cooper called. They got held up in traffic and are running about fifteen minutes late. I've put the information packets in the conference room and the PowerPoint presentation is ready to go."

"And my speech for the Denver Economic Club this evening?" he asked.

"Typed, fact-checked and on your desk. The television stations are looking for a preview since their reporters won't be able to get anything back before the late night news. I've taken the liberty of highlighting a couple of points that might make for good sound bites."

"Excellent."

"Oh, and your mother called."

Dawson gritted his teeth. He reminded himself

that the only reason she called him so often was because she loved him and was worried about him. Of course that did nothing to assuage his guilt. "Does she want me to call her back?"

"No, she just asked me to remind you to have your tuxedo dry-cleaned for the ball this weekend. She's reserved a seat for you at the head table and won't take no for an answer."

He bit back a sigh. The annual Tallulah Malone Burke Charity Ball and Auction was the see-and-be-seen-at event for Denver's social elite. He'd hoped to send a generous check along with his regrets. But the ball was celebrating its silver anniversary this year, and he had little doubt his mother would show up at his door to personally escort him.

The cause was worthy, raising funds for the area's less fortunate. At one time Dawson had been happy to do his part by suiting up like a penguin, shaking hands and making small talk with Denver's movers and shakers. But for the past few years he'd made excuses not to attend the event, which always fell the second Saturday after Thanksgiving. It was a bad time of the year for him. The absolute worst, in fact. He'd been grateful that his mother, who was a stickler for appearances, had been willing to let him shirk his responsibilities as a Burke. Apparently his amnesty had run out.

And she claimed he had inherited his stubborn streak from his father.

He consulted his watch. "My housekeeper should be in by now. Give her a call. Ingrid will see to it that the tux gets cleaned. And when you get a minute—"

"A cup of coffee and a toasted bagel, light on the cream cheese, with a side of fresh fruit," Rachel finished for him.

"Please."

His efficient secretary could all but read his mind, whereas Eve Hawley apparently was unable to make sense of a simple list of names, even when it included particulars like sex, age and how they were acquainted with Dawson.

"Will there be anything else?" Rachel asked.

"Actually, yes." He retrieved the cell phone from the inside pocket of his suit coat and handed it to her. "Call Miss Hawley back for me. Hers is the third number down. She's the personal shopper Carole recommended. Tell her I'm too busy to see her today and, though it should be completely self-explanatory, see if you can answer the questions she claims to have about the list of names I had you e-mail her last week."

"Very well."

"Thanks." He reached up to massage the back of his neck as he said it, grimacing when pain radiated all the way down his spine. It had been a frequent visitor for the past three years, ever since the car accident that had claimed the lives of his wife and daughter. Tension made the pain worse. This time of the year, when memories and regrets swirled their thickest, it became almost unbearable.

"Is your back bothering you again?" Rachel inquired in a tone devoid of the syrupy concern he so detested. The last thing he wanted was to be the object of pity. Yet he knew that's precisely what he had become in many people's eyes.

Poor Dawson Burke.

"A little."

"I'll call Wanda and see if she can come by for a session between your afternoon meetings today," she said, referring to the masseuse he'd kept on retainer since leaving the hospital after the crash.

That sounded like heaven, but he shook his head. "No time. I ran into Nick Freely on my way out last night. I promised I'd go over some stock options with him."

"I can call him, reschedule," she offered.

"No. I tell you what. Ask Wanda to come by my house this evening. That way I'll be nice and limber for my speech."

When Rachel was gone, he made a mental note to increase the amount on her holiday bonus check. She had it coming.

Eve Hawley had something coming, too, he decided later that evening. And it wasn't monetary compensation.

He was lying on the portable table his masseuse

had set up in the center of his den, only a thin white sheet standing between him and immodesty, when his housekeeper tapped at the door.

"Excuse me, Mr. Burke," she said from the doorway. "There's someone here to see you."

He wasn't expecting company. He had barely an hour before he was due to leave for his speech. As Wanda kneaded his knotted muscles with hands that would have done a lumberjack proud, he asked between gritted teeth, "Who is it?"

"Eve Hawley."

He lifted his face from the donut-shaped rest and gaped at the housekeeper. "She's here now?"

"Yes."

The woman was relentless and obviously incapable of doing the job if, even after talking to Rachel, she was still hounding him.

"Tell her I'm indisposed."

"I did, Mr. Burke. But she's insisting on seeing you," Ingrid said.

"Insisting? Well, if she's insisting…" He figured he knew a surefire way to get rid of her. "Send her in."

"Right now?" The housekeeper gaped at him.

"Yes. Right now." If Eve Hawley wanted to see him, Dawson would give her an eyeful.

Ingrid's gaze cut to his bare back and the sheet that rode low across his hips, covering the essentials and then leaving his legs exposed. She was old enough to be his mother. In fact, it was at his mother's suggestion that he'd hired her. Her pursed lips told him exactly how inappropriate she found his suggestion to be. But, like all—or at least the vast majority—of the people in his employ, she minded her own business and did as he asked.

"Very well," she said, withdrawing from the room without further comment.

"Carry on," he told Wanda, before lowering his face back into rest. The masseuse was chopping down his spine in karate fashion when he heard the door open a moment later. The person who entered sucked in a startled breath. Though it was small of him, Dawson grinned at the floor.

"Oh. You're…"

"Busy," came his muffled reply.

Feminine laughter trilled. "Actually, I was going to say naked."

"Not quite." But he frowned at the same floor he'd smiled at a moment earlier. She didn't sound nearly as distressed by that fact as he'd hoped.

"I'm Eve Hawley."

"Yes, I know," he snapped. "Even if my housekeeper hadn't announced your arrival, I would recognize your voice from the many messages you've left on my phone."

"Messages that went unreturned," she had the audacity to point out.

"They were returned. My secretary called you back," he said.

"Ah, yes. Mrs. Stern. If I'd wanted to talk to your secretary, Mr. Burke, I would have dialed her direct. I need to speak to you."

Dawson felt the muscles in his back beginning to tighten again despite Wanda's competent ministrations. "Look, Miss Hawley, surely Carole Deming briefed you on what I'm looking for. This is gift shopping, not rocket science. If you can't do the job—"

"Oh, I can do the job. I just believe in doing it well," she replied in a voice that was stiff with pride. Another place, another time, he might have admired it. He had no patience for it at the moment. "I won't take up much of your time," she promised.

Dawson relented with a sigh, but he didn't raise his head from the padded hole. He was being rude, insufferably so. But then that was the point. The woman already had strained his patience.

"Fine. Shoot."

"You want to discuss this right now?" Her tone was incredulous.

"Right now is all the time I have. My schedule is very tight and will be for the next several days."

"I see." He thought she might object and leave. That had been his goal. But he heard a pair of heels click over the parquet floor. They stopped just outside his limited field of vision.

"I have some concerns," she said, her tone that of a professional who apparently was not the least bit concerned about discussing business with a nearly naked man. Perhaps like the housekeeper, she, too, was old enough to be his mother.

"What are these concerns?"

"Well, in addition to business associates and acquaintances, your gift-giving list includes friends and several family members."

"My parents, sister, her husband and their two children," he said. "I'm well aware of who is on the list, Miss Hawley. After all, I'm the one who made it out." Well, his secretary had done that, but he'd approved the final version.

"I do things a little differently when family members are involved."

Heels clicked on the floor again and Dawson was forced to revise his opinion of her age when a pair of lethal-looking pumps came into view. They were red and made of faux alligator skin. But those weren't the reasons that had Dawson subtracting a few decades from her age. Women of his mother's generation generally didn't have little butterflies tattooed on their ankles.

Curiosity got the better of him. He brought his elbows up and levered partway off the table so that he could see her. Then he sorely wished he hadn't. The rest of Eve Hawley, from the curves that filled out her knit dress to the long dark hair that snaked over her shoulders, was every bit as sexy as her legs and those shoes. Suddenly, the fact that he was nearly naked didn't give Dawson the advantage he'd sought. No.

That had shifted squarely to the black-haired beauty who at the moment was eyeing him with her arms crossed, brows raised and unmistakable amusement glimmering in her eyes.

He sent a glance over his shoulder in the direction of his masseuse. "Wanda, that will be enough for now."

"I don't know, Mr. Burke. You still feel awfully tense to me," she objected.

Out of the corner of his eye, he thought he saw Eve's full lips twitch.

"I'm fine." To Eve he said, "Give me fifteen minutes and we'll go over your concerns."

"Sure."

This time he was positive she was holding back a smile when she sauntered from the room.

Eve waited in a sitting room that was tucked just off the kitchen. The housekeeper had thoughtfully brought her a cup of hot tea. She sipped it now as she stared into the flames of the fire that was flickering cheerfully in the hearth and contemplated her client.

Dawson Burke was a surprise, and not because he'd been clothed in nothing more than a bedsheet at their introduction. He was not the paunchy, middle-aged workaholic who so often relied on her services. God bless those men since they had been helping to pay her bills for nearly a decade, but she hadn't expected Dawson to be quite so young or handsome or—she sipped her tea—physically fit.

As an unattached woman of not quite thirty, there was no way details such as those were going to escape her attention.

Eve was relatively new to the Denver area, and the state of Colorado for that matter. The beauty of her job was that she could do it anywhere. She'd been looking for a fresh start after a particularly nasty breakup the previous spring, and after some Internet research she'd decided that anyplace with a view as pretty and panoramic as the one the Mile High City boasted just might provide it.

So she'd been settling in, building up a client list and sinking down roots. She'd caught a lucky break when she'd met Carole Deming while shopping in a boutique a couple of months back. The two women had hit it off right away. The fact that Carole was fifteen years older and they were technically competitors hadn't stood in the way of their friendship. Indeed, Carole had been kind enough to toss some of her clients Eve's way while she recuperated from surgery.

What was it she'd said about Dawson Burke? "I think you'll find him a challenge."

At the time, Eve had assumed Carole was referring to his gift needs, not his personality. Now she suspected she understood perfectly why the other woman had laughed while saying it. A challenge? Just getting past his pit bull of a secretary had taken an effort, which was why she'd decided to drop by his home unannounced.

Eve didn't mind difficult clients. She'd worked for plenty of them in the past, picky people who gave her cart blanche to buy presents for others or clothing for themselves only to veto her every choice later. But this was different. She simply couldn't do what Dawson wanted her to do without gathering more information, gaining more insight. It wasn't right. As far as Eve was concerned, family members deserved more thought when it came to gifts. She had no qualms about buying for them, but she wouldn't allow the purchases to be impersonal.

She set the tea aside and stood, walking closer to the fire when memories left her chilled. Her mother had died when Eve was eight years old. Suicide, or so it had been rumored. The alternative, an accidental drug overdose, had carried nearly as much stigma, especially since her mother's family blamed her father. Growing up, she'd been shuttled from one relative's house to another's. Her dad had hit the road, ostensibly to try to turn his pipe dream of being a musician into a bona fide profession. More accurately, though, he'd been running from a reality he could not accept.

The last she'd heard, he had a gig at a pub in Myrtle Beach. At nearly sixty, Buck Hawley was no longer waiting for his big break. But he was still running.

He'd missed out on more than two decades of Eve's life, though he always managed to send her a gift to mark another birthday and Christmas. She hated those gifts. They were always impersonal things that Eve knew upon opening he hadn't picked out. For that matter, even the signatures on most of the cards hadn't been his.

While growing up, that had pained her. All these years later it still hurt. She'd needed her father's time, craved his attention as a child. At the very least, she'd wanted to know he thought about her while picking out gifts. So, when clients asked her to buy for their loved ones, she required more than the name and age Dawson had provided on his list.

"Would you care for more tea?"

She turned to find the man in question standing in the doorway. His dark hair was combed back from his forehead, lean cheeks freshly shaved. He was wearing an expertly cut charcoal suit with a white shirt and conservatively patterned tie, yet her heart did the same little somersault it had upon seeing far more of his skin.

"I'm fine." Eve spoke the words for her own benefit as well as his.

He nodded. "Well, not to rush you, but I do have someplace I need to be. I believe you said you wouldn't take much of my time."

"Right." She retrieved her briefcase from the side of the chair. "I do things a little differently than Carole."

"So I gathered," he said dryly.

"For starters, when I shop for close relatives such as those on your list, I need to know something about them." He opened his mouth, but before he could speak Eve added, "Something beyond their sex and age and your price range. For instance, what are their hobbies? Do they have a favorite color? Do they collect something? For the children, are they into video games, sports? Who's their favorite recording artist? And for the record, I don't believe in gift cards, fruit baskets, flower arrangements or the like. Anyone can purchase and send those. They don't take any effort or require any thought. I won't buy gifts like that."

"Maybe I have the wrong person for the job."

Dollar signs flashed in neon green before her eyes. This was a big account, the biggest by far of the ones Carole had fed her. The commission it was likely to bring would go a long way toward fattening up the bank account her cross-country move had depleted. Still, Eve crossed her arms, blinked the dollar signs away and said, "Maybe you do. It's a matter of principle for me."

He studied her a long moment before sighing. "What do you need?"

Eve opened her case and pulled out a folder, which she handed to him. "Given how difficult it's been to reach you, I decided that instead of conducting an interview I would give you this questionnaire. Fill it out at your convenience, but if I could have it back to me by next Monday, that would great."

"Anything else?"

She didn't miss the sarcasm in his tone, but she chose to ignore it. "Actually, there is. While I don't mind flying blind when it comes to buying gifts for business associates and clients, if you have any insights or personal anecdotes about any of the people on your list, I'd welcome them. Feel free to jot down anything that comes to you on the line I've provided next to their names."

"Maybe I should go shopping with you."

Again, she ignored his sarcasm. Smiling sweetly, she replied, "It's kind of you to offer, but that won't be necessary. Unless you really want to. I can always use someone to carry the purchases out to the parking lot."

She wasn't sure why she had just baited him, other than the fact that his arrogance rubbed her the wrong way.

"Excuse me, Mr. Burke?" the housekeeper said from the doorway. "The driver has brought the car around."

"Fine." He turned his attention back to Eve. "I believe we're finished."

"For now," she affirmed and had the satisfaction of watching him scowl.

CHAPTER TWO

DAWSON prided himself on being the sort of man who thought outside the box when finding solutions for problems. It was one of the things that had helped make him a success in business. So, when adversity knocked Friday afternoon, he let opportunity answer the door.

"Your mother is on line one and Eve Hawley is on line two," Rachel informed him.

"I'll take the call from my mother. Tell Miss Hawley I'll call her back." As he said it, he glanced in the direction of his in-box, where the questionnaire she'd given him remained untouched. He had a good idea of the reason behind Eve's call. He also knew why his mother was phoning. The charity ball was Saturday.

"Hello, Mom."

"Dawson, darling. How are you?" she asked.

"Fine."

"So, you always say," she chided. "But I still worry about you."

"There's no need to, really."

But she disagreed. "It's a mother's job."

"I'm an adult, Mom. Thirty-eight last month," he reminded her.

"Your age doesn't matter. Nor, for that matter, does mine." Tallulah was quiet for a moment. Then she said, "I know this is a difficult time of year for you."

"Mom—"

"It's a difficult time of the year for everyone," she went on. "We all miss Sheila and Isabelle."

Hearing the names of his late wife and daughter spoken aloud turned his voice unintentionally crisp, "Don't. Just...don't." He softened the command with "Please."

"Dawson—"

But he held firm, even if he did moderate his tone. "I prefer not to talk about them. I've made my wishes on that very clear."

"What is clear," Tallulah began, "is that you've locked yourself inside a prison of your own making for three very long years. You've always been a fairly rigid individual. But in that time, you've become overly controlling, overly driven. You don't make any time for friends or family, let alone yourself. You spend every waking hour at the office."

"Yes and Burke Financial has thrived as a direct result," he replied. "The last quarter's earnings were the best in the company's history."

"Your father and I don't give a damn about the

business," she snapped. The fact that his mother had used even a mild curse had Dawson blinking in surprise. This was a woman who rarely raised her voice let alone lost her temper. Neither had ever been necessary. She'd always had more effective ways of getting her children to toe the line. She pulled out one of the big guns now. "I hate to say this, Dawson, but I'm very disappointed in you."

He sank back in his chair and closed his eyes. Whether he was eight or thirty-eight, that particular weapon never failed to hit the mark.

His tone was contrite when he said, "I'm sorry you feel that way, Mom. That's certainly not my intent."

"I know." But, of course, she wasn't through. "Have you made plans for the holidays?"

It was a Burke tradition to gather for dinner at his parents' estate on Christmas Eve. In fact, that had been his destination the evening of the crash. Ever since then, he hadn't been able to make it. He expelled a ragged breath. "You know that I have."

"San Tropez again?" she inquired, dismay obvious in her tone.

He'd gone to that tropical paradise the past two years, unable to remain in snowy Denver for the anniversary of that fateful night. This year, however, he'd decided on a different destination. "Actually, I thought I'd try Cabo. I've rented a condo 'til just after the new year."

Like San Tropez, it was warm and sunny with

gorgeous beaches and, most importantly, no one who knew him. People wouldn't ask how he was doing, tilting their head to one side in sympathy as they spoke, or regard him with an overly bright smile that failed to camouflage their pity.

"Alone?" his mother asked.

"Mom—"

But she talked over his objections. "You know, it wouldn't bother me so much that you refuse to spend the holidays with loved ones in Denver if I at least knew you were spending them with someone special."

"I'm fine." He repeated the old saw.

But she threw him a curve. "Are you seeing anyone, Dawson?"

"I've gone out a couple times," he admitted. The dates had been unmitigated disasters, from the stilted conversations at the beginning to the awkward goodnight kisses at the end. Both attempts had left him feeling guilty and angry at fate all over again, but he didn't see any reason to divulge that information to his mother.

She apparently figured it out, though, because she said in a quiet voice, "Oh, son, at some point you need to move on with your life."

"I have," he insisted. He got up each day, didn't he? He went to work. He'd turned the company into an even bigger success than it had been under his father.

As usual, though, his mother cut to the chase. "But you haven't forgiven yourself."

No. He hadn't forgiven himself. He couldn't do that. He closed his eyes, only to see it all happening again. He'd been the one behind the wheel of the car on that snowy Christmas Eve, the one firmly in control of all their destinies until a patch of black ice had changed everything.

Dawson had been the only one to survive the impact with the bridge abutment. He'd walked away with a nasty gash on his forehead and a busted arm. His wife had died instantly, while his daughter had hovered on the brink for several more hours with internal injuries before a surgeon had come out of the operating room to deliver news Dawson still wasn't ready to accept.

"Sorry, Mr. Burke. We did all we could, but we couldn't save her."

How could Dawson forgive himself for that?

His mother's voice snapped him back to the present. "I want you to be happy," she said.

He opened his eyes, rubbed them with his free hand. She didn't get it. No one did. For him, happiness had ceased to be relevant. "Don't worry about me, Mom," he told her for the second time.

But she was saying, "You know, the Harrisons' daughter recently moved back from California."

At that an alarm bell began to sound in his head. He silenced it by saying, "The one who got married a couple of years ago?"

"Yes, but she's divorced now." The alarm sounded

a second time as his mother continued. "I ran into her at the club a couple weeks ago. She still has that same lovely, bubbly personality. She'll be at the ball tomorrow evening. I was thinking of asking her to sit with us. That would give us an even number at our table. And you know how I like an even number."

Dawson straightened in his seat. This was the last thing he needed. The last thing he wanted.

"Mom, I'd really rather you didn't do that."

"She's nice, dear. You'll both have a good time. It doesn't have to lead to anything. In fact, I'm not sure she's ready for a relationship yet herself. Her divorce was final only a few months ago. But at least it will give you both an opportunity to get your feet wet again." Sounding pleased with her plan, she added, "I'll phone her after I hang up."

Good God! His mother setting him up on a date with a newly divorced woman who probably was every bit as unenthusiastic about the matter as he was.

"No!" His gaze caught on the questionnaire Eve had left with him and inspiration struck. Perhaps there was a way he could kill two birds with one stone. His lips curved with a smug smile. "What I mean is, there's no need to do that. As it happens, I already have a date."

Eve was on her way to Boulder, the rear of her Tahoe already laden with the morning's finds in Denver, when her cell trilled. Normally, she didn't like to operate a vehicle and talk on the phone at the same time, but when she saw the number of the person who was calling, she decided to make an exception.

"Hello," she said.

"Hi. It's Dawson Burke."

"Well, this is unexpected."

He sounded confused when he asked, "Didn't my secretary tell you I would be calling?"

"Mrs. Stern? Yes, she did. Which is why I'm in a state of shock. I mean, if I had a dollar for every time your secretary has told me you'd get back with me…" She let her words trail off.

"Very funny," he muttered. "Are you this flippant with all of your clients?"

"Nope. You seem to bring it out in me." But she moderated her tone and added, "Thank you for returning my call."

"You're welcome."

"The reason I phoned you earlier is that I'm on my way down to an art gallery in Boulder to pick up some pieces by a local artist for another client of mine. Buying artwork for someone is like buying clothes. It has to fit the recipient's style."

"Which makes it personal," he said.

"Exactly. So I was wondering if art might be something that would appeal to any of the friends or family members on your list?"

He made a humming noise, then said, "My parents' walls are pretty full at this point and I wouldn't presume to know my sister's taste in art as she's made a hobby out of redecorating her home. My friends...I don't know."

"Oh, well, it was just a thought." Her exit was coming up, so Eve shifted her vehicle to the right lane. "How's the questionnaire coming along?"

She heard him clear his throat. "Actually, I wanted to talk to you about that."

"You haven't filled it out," she guessed.

"Not yet, no."

"Mr. Burke—"

"Dawson, please."

"All right. And you can call me Eve. But I really want that information. I need it, as I explained to you the other night," she said.

"A matter of principle, I believe you said."

"Yes."

"And if I refuse?" he asked. The question sounded almost like a dare.

The dollar signs flashed again, but Eve thought about her father and she remembered her disappointment and heartache. She wasn't willing to pass on those emotions to someone else. Her tone was firm when she replied, "I'd have to ask you to find another personal shopper. So, are you refusing?"

"No, but I have a better idea," he said. "Do you have plans for tomorrow evening?"

"As a matter of fact, I do." Since moving to Denver, Eve had spent nearly every Saturday night alone. But as it happened, she did have something going on. She'd told Carole she would stop by with Chinese food, a bottle of wine and some Christmas movies for the two of them to watch.

"I see." Then he surprised her by asking, "Would it be possible for you to change them?"

Her curiosity was good and stoked. "Why? What do you have in mind?"

"Each year around this time my mother throws a really big to-do. Perhaps you've heard of it? The Tallulah Malone Burke Charity Ball and Auction."

She put on her blinker and maneuvered the Tahoe onto the exit ramp. "No, sorry, but I haven't been in Denver long."

"That's all right. Stick around and you will." There was pride in his tone when he added, "It's been an annual event for the past twenty-five years, drawing in the well-heeled and well-connected to raise money for the area's less fortunate."

"How nice," Eve said and meant it.

"Yes, well, the party is tomorrow night."

Comprehension dawned and something Eve didn't want to admit might be interest danced up her spine. After all, the man wasn't her type at all. Too arrogant. Too domineering. "Are—are you asking me out?"

"Not exactly," he said. "I need an escort for the evening. And you will be compensated."

Indignation blasted along with the horn of the car

behind her, and she realized she'd come to a full stop even though she had the right of way. She sent the other driver a wave of apology and turned into the nearest parking lot.

"Eve?"

She waited until the vehicle was in Park before she let loose. "Maybe I wasn't clear about the nature of the services I provide. I'm a personal *shopper*, not a personal anything else."

She heard Dawson cough. Actually, he sounded as if he might have choked a little, which suited her just fine. He deserved it. Then, he said, "I didn't mean to imply otherwise. Compensation was a poor choice of words. What I meant by it was that many of the people on my gift list will be in attendance. In addition to my parents, sister and her family, a number of business acquaintances and longtime Burke Financial clients attend."

"Oh."

It was on the tip of her tongue to apologize when he added, "I thought seeing them, meeting them, might help you do your job more effectively. You know, live up to those high principles you speak of."

"Are you mocking me?"

"No." He expelled a breath. "For the record, Eve, I admire you for taking a stand. I haven't met many people in business whose principles can hold up under pressure from the bottom line."

He sounded sincere, which went a long way toward soothing her temper. "So, this would be sort of like a business function."

"It would be *exactly* like a business function," he corrected. "But with better food. No rubber chicken or cheap champagne. My mother doesn't believe in doing anything halfway."

As Eve was privy to Dawson's gift budget she decided it was a trait he had inherited.

"It sounds very fancy."

"Black tie required. Do you have something to wear?"

"I think I can find something suitable in my closet," she replied blandly. She sucked in a breath and let it out slowly between her teeth. "Where and what time?"

"Does that mean you'll come?" He sounded surprised and maybe even a little relieved.

She was probably going to hate herself for it later, but she said, "Yes."

"And your other date? I trust that the last-minute change in plans won't cause any…problems."

Eve nearly laughed out loud as it dawned on her that he thought the plans she'd mentioned earlier were with a man. She saw no reason to enlighten him.

So she said, "Don't worry. I can reschedule it. After all, this is work."

CHAPTER THREE

DAWSON cursed and yanked at his bow tie as he stood in front of the vanity mirror. This was his third attempt at tying it and it still had turned out lopsided. He wasn't sure why his hands wouldn't cooperate, any more than he could put a finger on the origin of the nerves fluttering in his stomach.

He hadn't felt keyed up before either of the other dates, disasters that they'd wound up being. And his evening with Eve wasn't a date at all. It was business, he reminded himself, as he finished with his tie, checked his watch and called for his driver to bring the car around.

Business was forgotten, however, the moment Eve opened her apartment door. She was wearing red, her lips and nails painted the same dangerous shade. She'd done something different with her dark hair, pulling it back and up to reveal the slim line of her neck. Diamond studs caught fire on her ear lobes as she tilted her head to one side and regarded him with a smile that he was pretty sure dated back to the original Eve.

"Hello, Dawson."

"You look…" Words failed him. For a moment, he thought his heart might fail him, too. The woman should come with a cardiac arrest warning.

"This works for the occasion, right?" She did a three-hundred-and-sixty-degree turn that made him wish he had a defibrillator handy. "I wouldn't want to stand out."

"You'll stand out, but for all the right reasons," he replied with more honesty than he'd intended.

Her smile bloomed again. "That's quite a compliment. You look pretty good yourself. It's a sin there are so few places for a man to wear a tuxedo nowadays."

"I doubt you'll get many men to agree." He pulled at his collar as he said it. The damned thing seemed to have grown too tight.

Eve laughed. It was a husky sound, entirely too provocative for the mere reason that it wasn't intended to be. "Come on, a tuxedo can't be as uncomfortable as my shoes. My arches are going to hate me by the end of the night."

Dawson allowed his gaze to skim down, which he regretted almost immediately. He'd already known she had a pair of killer legs. Tonight they were accentuated by black pumps that added a good three inches to her already respectable height. His pulse took flight along with the little butterfly tattooed on her ankle. He didn't particularly care for the reaction. Business, he reminded himself.

"Ready to go?" he asked. "While I have no problem arriving fashionably late, my mother is a stickler for punctuality."

"Ah. Right. So, exactly what have you told her about me?"

"Your name."

"A man of few words," she said on a laugh. "Just let me get my coat."

He glanced around while she did so. Her apartment was a loft in a former commercial building that had been converted to residential use. Its exposed ductwork, distressed wood floor and battered brick walls gave it an almost industrial feel. It was small, its total square footage probably not equal to that of his master suite, but Eve certainly had made the most of every inch.

Her taste was as bold and uncompromising as the woman. Vivid colors were splashed against neutrals and a rather eclectic mix of artwork adorned the walls. At the far end of the room, he spied a slim staircase that led to the sleeping loft. A horizontal chrome railing defined the space up top and allowed a tantalizing glimpse of a platform bed beyond. He saw more bold colors there, rich crimsons, plums and golds. For a moment, he allowed himself to wonder what one might interpret from her decorating choices.

"Dawson?"

He turned to find her standing directly behind him. She held a small clutch in her hands and was already wearing her coat, a long wool number that was cinched in at the waist with a belt. Even covered up with not so much as a scrap of red showing, she still exuded far too much sex appeal for his comfort.

He glanced away and cleared his throat. "Nice place you have here."

"Thanks. I like it."

"Excellent location given your job." He made a circular motion with one hand. "Close to shops and all."

"Yes." She smiled. "But work wasn't the only reason I chose it. I like being in the thick of things."

She would. Though he didn't know her very well, he'd already figured out that Eve was the sort of woman who grabbed life with both hands and held on tight, even when the ride got wild.

"Well, we should be going." As he followed her out the door, Dawson wondered why he felt both eager to leave and disappointed that they couldn't stay.

He knew the answer to at least half that question when they arrived at the Wilmington Hotel twenty minutes later. The large ballroom could accommodate seven hundred guests. Only a fraction of that number had arrived, as it was early yet. But his mother gave him a pointed look when she spied him. Dawson sent her a wink and purposely steered Eve in the opposite direction. He needed a little fortification before he faced his family and began fielding their questions. He also needed to clue Eve in on a few pertinent facts.

"How about a glass of wine?" he suggested.

"I suppose that even though this is technically a work function for me a nice glass of Chardonnay wouldn't be out of line," she replied.

"Not at all."

As he ordered their drinks from a bar that had been set up in one corner, Eve said, "I guess you weren't kidding when you said your mother doesn't believe in doing things halfway. I wasn't expecting the party to be quite this large. This room must be set up for at least a few hundred people to dine."

"Seven hundred, actually."

She blinked in surprise. "Is everyone in Denver on the guest list?"

"Sometimes it feels that way," he said. He swept an arm out to the side. "But what you see here are the people with the deepest pockets. My mother's specialty is getting them to reach in, grab a wad of bills and make a donation."

"She sounds like a formidable woman," Eve said.

He merely smiled. She could be, he thought, recalling the previous day's conversation. At times, Tallulah could be downright relentless. The bartender handed them their wine.

"So, is your family here?" Eve inquired, taking a sip. "I'm eager to meet them."

"Some of them are, I believe." He cleared his

throat. "Before I introduce you, though, I need to ask a favor of you. I would prefer that they didn't know what it is you do for a living."

"Ashamed of me?" She tilted her head to one side, sounding more amused than insulted, although he thought he saw something akin to vulnerability flicker briefly in her dark eyes.

"Of course not. It's just that I don't want them to feel…" He groped for the right word.

"Like you brought in a designated hitter because you couldn't be bothered to shop for their gifts yourself?" She smiled sweetly before taking another sip of her wine.

Because his conscience had delivered a swift kick to his nether region, he replied, "You know, you can be annoyingly blunt at times."

Her shoulders lifted in a delicate shrug. "I know. It's a gift."

"It's something," he muttered. "Maybe you should sign up for a Dale Carnegie course."

"I already took one. Passed with flying colors, as a matter of fact. A star pupil." She smiled at him over the rim of her glass. "So, who exactly do they think I am?"

Dawson felt as if he had been dumped back into junior high school when he admitted, "They think you're my date."

"Ah. Your date." She was enjoying his embarrassment. Of that much he was sure. "And how long have we been an item?"

"We're not an item," he groaned.

"First date. Got it." She grinned. "Well, I promise I'll try not to be obvious while I'm plying them with questions to get an idea of their likes and dislikes."

Eve wouldn't be the only one with questions, Dawson thought. Out of the corner of his eye, he spotted his mother. She was homing in on them with the precision of a heat-seeking missile, not even stopping to chat with the people who greeted her along the way. There would be no avoiding her this time.

He put his arm around Eve, leaned close and whispered, "My mother is headed this way."

"Uh-oh. Should I bat my eyelashes at you or something?" she asked.

"This was a bad idea," he mumbled, not quite sure if he felt that way because of her glib reply or because he'd caught a whiff of her perfume. It was sexy, sinful. He ignored the tug of lust it inspired and pasted a smile on his face as his mother reached them.

"Dawson, darling," Tallulah called. "I thought I saw you come in a moment ago."

He kissed her cheek. "Hello, Mom. You look as radiant as ever. Is that a new dress?"

"It is, though I doubt you could give a fig," she replied on a chuckle, letting him know that his attempt at flattery had not sidetracked her in the least. Indeed, speculation lit her eyes even as her lips curved into a smile. "And who might this lovely young woman be?"

Eve knew she was being inspected from head to toe even if Tallulah Burke was smiling and greeting her in as gracious a fashion as she did it.

Dawson performed the introductions, all the while looking uncharacteristically uncomfortable. All of his usual cockiness was gone. Eve liked him all the more for it.

"Mom, this is Eve Hawley. Eve, my mother, Tallulah Burke."

"Eve, it's very nice to meet you." Tallulah shook Eve's hand, covering it with both of hers, which were fine-boned and heavily bejeweled. She didn't let go immediately afterward. No. She held on as she added, "I have to say, I was a little surprised when my son mentioned yesterday that he would be bringing a guest to the party this evening. I wasn't aware he was dating anyone. I guess the mother is the last to know."

Even as she said it, Eve got the feeling that very little got past Dawson's mother. This was no flighty society maven. Her blue eyes were keen with intelligence and, at the moment, a great deal of curiosity.

"Eve and I haven't known one another very long," Dawson hedged.

"Oh?"

"First date," Eve supplied. She didn't quite bat her eyelashes, but came close. Dawson scowled.

"Really? How exactly did you meet?" Tallulah asked, her gaze never wavering from Eve.

"A mutual friend got us together." Since it wasn't exactly a lie, Eve had no problem supplying the information.

Out of the corner of her eye, she saw Dawson nod, apparently pleased with her response. Then, before his mother could probe any further, he added, "It was no one you know, Mom."

Someone called her name then. Tallulah turned and waved. "Well, I need to mingle. You should do the same, Daw. It's expected."

"Right."

She turned to Eve then. "I'll look forward to getting to know you better over dinner."

Oh, I bet you will, Eve thought.

Will I measure up?

The question had her stomach knotting and some of the old insecurities managed to sneak in, despite the fact that her relationship with Dawson wasn't the romantic one his mother had been led to believe.

"I have a feeling that the salmon won't be the only thing grilled here tonight," she murmured once she and Dawson were alone.

"Don't worry. My mother is harmless."

Eve decided to reserve judgment. Admittedly, her first impression of Tallulah had been a positive one. The woman seemed kind, and the very fact that she threw an annual ball to raise funds for charity elevated Eve's opinion of her. But Eve had had enough negative experiences in her past to know better than to trust first impressions.

Pot calling the kettle, she thought, since she did her best to make a stellar first impression. It was important to her.

Thanks to her penchant for sniffing out sales and spending her pennies on quality pieces, Eve knew what to wear. She also had no problem holding her own in social settings. One of the great aunts she'd lived with had been a stickler for etiquette. Eve knew how to sit with her legs crossed demurely at the ankle. She knew how to walk—head up, shoulders back. She knew which fork to use for the various courses served at dinner. And when it came to the art of small talk, she could hold her own with the best of them.

But she was a fraud. An absolute and utter fake underneath all of her props and polish.

She had not been born into money, and, as she'd learned with her last boyfriend, when it came right down to it, for some people it was the pedigree that made all the difference.

Eve notched up her chin, crooked her arm through Dawson's and in her best haughty voice, asked, "Shall we go forth and mingle?"

He heaved a sigh. "I'd rather not, but yes. Just let me do most of the talking."

"Oh, don't worry about me. I'm a regular chameleon," Eve assured him. "No one will ever suspect that I don't belong here."

He sent her a questioning look, which she ignored. Despite those noxious self-doubts, she continued to smile brightly.

Everyone with whom they stopped to chat seemed surprised to see Dawson and, oddly, a little tongue-tied around him. Eve might have thought that was because he was the sort of man who exuded power. Some people found that intimidating. But it was more than his importance. She felt an undercurrent here, something just below the surface of the polite conversations that seemed almost like sympathy. It didn't make sense. Why would anyone feel sorry for Dawson Burke? The man had it made: a high-powered job, wealth, exceptional good looks and a body that appeared to have been chiseled from granite.

Yet for all that, he couldn't manage a real date for an evening. *Hmm*…

As they made their way over to the tables where the items for the silent auction had been set up, Eve said, "I'm curious about something."

"Yes?" he replied absently.

The first item they came to was a gift basket full of aromatherapy bath products. The opening bid was far more than the actual value of the individual components and yet several others had already topped it. Dawson scrawled his name down along with an outrageous amount. She added generous to his list of attributes.

"I'm trying to figure out what's wrong with you," Eve stated bluntly.

He straightened and regarded her from beneath furrowed brows. "Excuse me?"

"Well, you're obviously successful and you're attractive." She gave one bicep a squeeze through the sleeve of his tuxedo jacket. "Your body's definitely all male, even if you do have a penchant for lavender-scented bubble baths."

"It's for charity," came his dry reply.

"Right." She winked because she knew it would annoy him. The man seriously needed to lighten up.

"Charity," he muttered a second time.

"So, why couldn't you get a real date for tonight?"

Dawson looked perplexed by the question. "Aren't you having a good time?"

Surprisingly, she was and so she admitted as much. "All things considered, I'm actually enjoying myself. I'm just, you know…" She motioned with her hand. "Curious."

"Curiosity killed the cat, Eve."

She merely shrugged. "Cats have nine lives. So, why aren't you dating?"

"Who says that I'm not?"

She settled a hand on one hip. "Everyone we've met tonight seems shocked to see you out at a social function." She paused for effect before adding, "Especially in the company of a woman."

"I have a very demanding position as the head of Burke Financial." The excuse was weak and he knew it based on the way his gaze slid away after he said it.

"Okay, got it. Work is the love of your life, so you have no room for a flesh-and-blood woman," Eve deduced, being purposefully blunt.

His gaze snapped back. "I enjoy what I do. There's nothing wrong with that."

"I agree wholeheartedly." She crossed her arms. "I enjoy my job immensely. I'm paid to shop and that's not a bad way to spend the day, in my humble opinion."

Dawson snorted. "Name me a woman on the planet who doesn't like to shop?"

Her eyes narrowed. "Got a pen and piece of paper handy? The list is long, which is why I've remained gainfully employed twelve months of the year since I started doing this. Not everyone who hires me is male or in need of someone to buy their holiday gifts."

His smile was tight when he conceded, "Point taken."

"Actually, my point is that while there's nothing wrong with liking what you do for a living, you also need to enjoy, well, living. That's hard to do when what goes on at the office sucks up nearly every waking hour."

He frowned and said nothing, but for just a moment, when she'd spoken of enjoying life, his expression had turned grim and almost haunted. She'd struck a nerve, of that she was sure. Which nerve, however, remained a mystery.

They moved to the next item up for auction. When Eve saw what it was, she squealed in delight: two tickets to the stage production of *Les Misérables*. Its limited run at the Denver Center for the Performing Arts was scheduled to come to an end just before Christmas. The set of seats being auctioned were prime, a fact that was reflected in the most recent bid. Even so, she snatched up the pencil and jotted down a sum that topped the previous one by twenty-five dollars.

Dawson was rubbing his chin when she straightened. "Your line of work pays very well."

She laughed ruefully. "I'll be eating salad for a month, but I'm dying to see this show. Tickets for seats this good are impossible to get at this point. I've checked. And checked. And checked."

He tapped the paper with the tip of his index finger. "Well, if you really want them, you're going to have to bid higher than that."

"You think?"

"I know. The evening's young yet and the people with the fattest wallets tend to arrive fashionably late to these things."

"Great," she muttered.

"You can always buy the soundtrack."

"I have the soundtrack." She listened to it so often she could sing every song from memory. Sucking a breath between her teeth, she leaned over to erase her first bid. Then she raised the previous amount by fifty dollars. Afterward, she sent him a weak smile.

"I like salad and I've been meaning to lose a few pounds anyway."

His gaze detoured south and his brows rose right along with her pulse rate. Though he said nothing, his eyes communicated something quite clearly. She knew that look. It was all male and interested. Her heart thudded in response, which struck her as outrageous since she wasn't even sure she liked Dawson Burke. Of course, like and lust weren't mutually exclusive.

Then he shrugged and his expression once again turned aloof and arrogant, leaving her libido feeling duped.

They moved on. Standing before the next auction item was a couple Dawson apparently knew well.

"Hey, look who's here," the man said, smiling as he reached out to clasp Dawson's hand.

"Hi, Tony. Christine," he added, leaning over to buss the woman's cheek. "It's been awhile."

"That's because you haven't returned any of our phone calls," Tony reprimanded lightly.

Apparently he made a habit of that, Eve thought.

"We've been worried about you," Christine added.

Dawson cleared his throat as he sent a fleeting glance in Eve's direction. "There's no need to worry about me."

The couple followed the direction of his gaze, spied Eve and attached a far different meaning to his glance.

"So we see. We're glad for you, Daw," Christine said. "Really, glad."

"Yeah," her husband added. "It's about damned time you returned to the land of the living."

Because he hadn't actually introduced her, Eve did the honors herself. She recognized their names from Dawson's gift list, so she discreetly sized them up during the brief conversation, trying to concentrate on the kind of item that might suit their tastes, rather than their curious comments that Dawson had already made clear related to something that was none of her business.

"Well, we probably should make our way to the head table," he said, winding up the conversation just after Christine mentioned running into the parents of someone named Sheila at the theater recently. "It was nice seeing you both again."

"Yes. We'll be having our annual party weekend after next. The invitations go out on Monday. Do you think you might make it this year?" Tony asked. "And, of course, Eve is welcome to come, too." He sent a smile in her direction.

Uh-oh.

But she was saved from having to answer. Dawson was shaking his head. "Sorry. Other plans."

"Oh." Tony shrugged, though he was clearly disappointed. "Maybe we can get together for dinner one night between Christmas and New Year's. Christine and I have been meaning to try out that new steak house."

"Sorry," Dawson said again. "I'll be in Cabo from Christmas Eve 'til the first of the year."

"Cabo?" Tony glanced at Eve and then back at Dawson. "I guess I thought that maybe this year…" His words trailed off awkwardly.

"We should head to our table, too," Christine said, taking her husband's arm and sending a tight smile in Dawson's direction. "It was nice meeting you, Eve. Hopefully we'll see you again."

Though it was the other couple who moved away, Eve was left with the distinct impression that Dawson was the one who had gone somewhere else.

CHAPTER FOUR

"Dawson?"

He blinked twice and seemed to snap out of whatever fog he'd been in. "Yes?"

"You mentioned something about taking our seats," Eve reminded him.

"Right." He put a hand on the small of her back, guiding her away. He didn't sound irritated, but weary, when he said, "I've done just about all of the mingling I can stand."

The head table was at the front of the ballroom just to the right of a raised stage, presumably for easy access to the podium and microphone. The table was round and had place settings for eight. A woman with two young boys was already seated there. The boys were slouched down in their chairs, looking sullen and subdued, but their expressions brightened considerably when they spied Dawson.

"Uncle Dawson!" they squealed in unison.

"You're here!" the older one said.

To which the younger one added, "Mom bet Dad that you'd find an excuse not to show up, even though you promised Nana you'd come this year."

"You're not supposed to tell him that," the other boy said, rolling his eyes in disgust.

"Why not? It's true."

"You're so lame."

"Boys, no name calling," their mother warned. Then she said, "Hello, Daw."

"Hello." But he returned his attention to his nephews. "Nice suits." Like all of the men in the room, the boys were outfitted in black tuxedos. The only difference was that their ties were askew and their white shirts were looking wrinkled and coming untucked. Eve found them adorable.

"Mom made us wear them," the younger one grumbled, pulling at his collar.

"I know how you feel," Dawson said on a chuckle. He put his hand behind Eve's back and drew her forward. "I'd like you to meet my guest, Eve Hawley. Eve, these are my nephews, Brian and Colton. Brian is eight and Colton is ten."

"I'm nine, Uncle Dawson," Brian corrected.

"And I turned eleven over the summer. Remember? You couldn't make it for dinner, but you sent me that chemistry set." The way Colton's mouth twisted on the words told Eve exactly what the boy thought of the gift. She'd bet someone else—Carole, perhaps?—had purchased it.

"Ah. Right. Nine and eleven," he repeated on a nod, looking slightly embarrassed. Was that because he'd forgotten their ages or because the gift had obviously been "lame," to use the boy's vernacular.

"Well, it's nice to meet you both," Eve said and she meant it. She was determined that by the end of the evening she would have a good idea of the kind of gift they would cherish from an uncle they clearly adored.

"Are you going to introduce us, Daw?" the woman asked. Dawson's sister shared his dark coloring, with the added bonus of having their mother's startlingly blue eyes. She was a striking woman—a striking woman who at the moment also looked openly curious.

"I'm not sure I should," he said.

"Fine, then I'll do it myself." She stood and smiled at Eve. "I'm Lisa Granderson, this ill-mannered buffoon's younger sister."

"Hello, Lisa. It's nice to meet you." That seemed to be Eve's stock phrase this evening…and the evening was young yet.

The other woman studied her a moment. Eve felt herself brace. But all Lisa said was, "I love your dress, by the way. That color looks incredible on you." Her gaze slid to Dawson. "Don't you agree?"

"Incredible," he said stiffly.

"Thank you."

"Why don't you sit next to me?" Lisa invited. "We can talk fashion and you can tell me how you were able to drag my reclusive brother out of his cave for the evening."

"Sorry. Mom has the seating arranged," Dawson said before Eve could respond. Picking up a small place card, he told his sister, "Eve is next to Colton. It looks like Mom's put you next to David." He glanced around then. "Speaking of your husband, where is he?"

"He and Dad are out by the coat check." Lisa rolled her eyes as she added, "They're listening to the last period of the hockey game on David's iPod."

"The Avalanche are playing the Red Wings," Colton supplied.

Dawson snorted as he shook his head. "Does Mom know what they're doing?"

"What do you think?" Lisa said.

"I think if she catches them, there's going to be hell to pay." Dawson chuckled after saying it. The sound was a bit rusty at first, but it wound up rich and inviting.

His reaction surprised Eve. She hadn't been aware the man knew how to smile let alone give in to mirth. Apparently, she wasn't the only one in shock. All eyes at the table had turned to him. But it was his sister's expression that caught Eve's notice. Lisa looked wistful and…hopeful?

"God, I've missed you," she said, her eyes turning bright. "I'm so glad you came tonight, Daw."

He unbuttoned his jacket and tucked his hands into the front pockets of his trousers. Though his shrug was intended to be casual, Eve saw the discomfort he tried to hide. "You know Mom. She wouldn't take no for an answer since this is the silver anniversary of the party."

"Well, whatever the reason, I'm glad you're here. And it's good to hear you laughing again," Lisa said.

Dawson glanced Eve's way, but then his attention was diverted by an older man, who slapped his back before pulling him in for a bear hug.

"Dawson! You made it."

The man was the same height as Dawson, although his build was a little thicker and less muscled. He was handsome, distinguished in the way men get from the same crow's feet and silver hair that women paid big money to diminish and conceal. Eve would have figured out his identity even if Dawson hadn't said, "Hello, Dad. How are you?"

"Better now that you're here."

Was Dawson the black sheep of the family? The prodigal son returning? Eve couldn't help but wonder given all of the comments.

"So, what's the score of the hockey game?" Dawson asked.

The older man shook his head in disgust. "The Avalanche are down by two. They should have traded that goalie when they had the chance."

"Actually, they're down by three now," inserted a younger man Eve assumed was Lisa's husband, David. "Detroit just scored during the power play."

At this, Lisa stood. "That's it." She settled one hand on her hip and held out the other. "Give me the iPod before Mom gets to the table and pitches a fit." She nodded in Eve's direction then. "And before Dawson's date gets the impression that his family is completely backward."

"Dawson has a date?" David asked as he handed over the iPod, earpiece and all.

"Yes, he does." This comment came from Tallulah as she joined them at the table. Eve felt her stomach knot. And that was before the woman smiled brightly and said, "Why don't you introduce Eve to everyone, Daw, and then we can all sit down and start getting better acquainted."

After he made the introductions, Tallulah said, "Eve, dear, why don't you tell us a little bit about yourself?"

She smiled easily even as she straightened in her seat. "What exactly would you like to know?"

"Anything you wish to share. This isn't an inquisition, dear." Tallulah laughed, intending to put her at ease.

"No, that comes later," David inserted sotto voce. Lisa slapped his arm and the boys giggled. Dawson's expression softened.

"Why don't you start with where you're from?" Tallulah said. "I detect an accent of sorts in your speech."

"Actually, I was thinking the same thing about all of you," Eve replied without missing a beat. Then she added, "I'm from Maine originally. I was born in Bangor. I guess to folks here it probably sounds as if I flatten my vowels."

"Maine? You're a long way from home," Tallulah said.

"Do you have family here?" Lisa asked.

"No. No family here." At least she didn't think so. But her father tended to get around. In college she'd gone into a Daytona Beach bar while on spring break only to discover her dad was the opening act for the band.

"What brought you to Denver?" Dawson asked.

"I came here for the view."

"That's an interesting reason to pull up stakes and move across the country," he said.

"I was ready for a change of scenery."

"What about a job?" his father asked. "Did you have something lined up here?"

"Not exactly, but I had no problem finding employment once I arrived."

"What line of work are you in?" his mother asked.

Eve felt Dawson's foot nudge hers beneath the table. He needn't have worried. She'd told him she wouldn't lie and once again she didn't have to. "I specialize in sales," she said.

"Well, if you ever need any investment advice, go see Daw. He's got the Midas touch when it comes to picking stocks." Tallulah beamed with pride.

Eve eyed him speculatively. "Really? The Midas

touch." She wondered what other things could be said about the man's touch. "I'll keep that in mind."

For the next several minutes, while his family subtly grilled Eve, she returned the favor. And not just for work purposes. They were an interesting and likeable bunch. Despite their obvious curiosity about her, they were warm and inviting. They were not in the least what she'd expected. Given Dawson's wealth, she'd figured his family for upper crust, emphasis on crust. She'd been prepared for them to be distant or act superior. Drew's family had been outright judgmental of those who came from less affluent families.

The Burkes were anything but.

Dawson was turning out to be a surprise, too. There was far more to the man than first met the eye, which was saying a lot given how little he'd been wearing at their first meeting.

At first she'd pegged him as a workaholic who was too busy to buy gifts even for his family. Then she'd thought that maybe he was a self-absorbed CEO who was indifferent to everyone around him and estranged from his loved ones.

But his family obviously adored him, and though he wasn't overly demonstrative, it appeared the feeling was mutual.

"Eve?" He leaned over to say it.

"Hmm, yes?" When she turned, their cheeks brushed.

"Come to any conclusions?" he whispered.

"No," she admitted. Then blinked. "Oh, do you mean about gifts?"

He frowned. "Of course I mean gifts. What were you referring to?"

She shook her head and worked up a smile. "Nothing." Because he was still frowning, she added, "I might not have actual gifts in mind, but I'm definitely getting a good idea of personalities."

With that she reminded herself that her reason for being there this evening wasn't to probe into Dawson's motivations for hiring her or to delve into his past. She was at the charity ball to find out more about the people on his list, in particular the members of his family. So, after Tallulah took the stage to welcome everyone and ask them to be seated for dinner, Eve took her assigned seat next to Colton. In between making polite conversation with the adults, she began to subtly pump both boys for information about their hobbies and extracurricular activities. By the time the salad plates were being removed to make way from the main course, she was pleased to have already come up with some excellent leads.

While the waitstaff brought dishes laden with pork tenderloin, grilled salmon, chicken marsala and an assortment of steamed vegetables, rice and boiled red-skinned potatoes to each table, Dawson pretended to follow his father's lament over the Fed's decision to raise the interest rate a quarter point. In truth he was listening to Eve and his nephews discuss videogame strategies.

She was talking them through level six of what was apparently one of the hottest games among prepubescent boys if his nephews' reactions were any indication. Brian and Colton were absolutely enthralled.

Dawson was, too. But in his case it had less to do with her tips on how to defeat a dragon and secure extra lives than the effect her laughter was having on him. Though she had a job to do, she obviously liked kids.

Eve glanced up and caught him staring. "What?" she mouthed.

He shook his head and mouthed back, "Nothing."

How could he tell her that he hadn't expected someone who looked as glamorous as she did to be such a natural with kids?

She'd probably be insulted, though he considered it a compliment. A lot of women he knew weren't overly fond of kids. Even his late wife hadn't been comfortable around children. Oh, she'd adored their daughter, and Dawson had been close to persuading Sheila to try for a second just before the accident. But she hadn't been the hands-on sort, preferring to relinquish what she called "the minutia of child-rearing" to a nanny. That had been a source of friction in their marriage, since their opinions of what constituted minutia differed greatly.

Like Sheila, Dawson had grown up with every

advantage and luxury at his disposal thanks to his parents' wealth. But while his mother had been practical enough to delegate certain responsibilities such as cooking, cleaning and, at times, carpooling to the hired help, she'd been integrally involved in all aspects of her children's lives.

That hadn't changed even though they'd grown up and moved out. Across the table, he heard his sister and mother arguing over the current length of hemlines.

"There's nothing wrong with showing a little more leg," Lisa said.

"If you're young and have long, slim legs like yours or Eve's, no," Tallulah agreed. In the dim light, he thought Eve flushed. "But women my age or who have put on a few too many pounds, shouldn't show so much skin. It's not attractive."

"You could show a little more skin for my taste," Clive said, sending his wife of forty years a bold wink.

Tallulah wagged a finger in his direction. "Stop flirting with me in front of the children."

Laughter erupted. Eve joined in. Dawson did as well. Afterward, his chest ached. He'd missed this, he realized. The good-natured bickering, the teasing, the laughter.

He'd always been the most serious of the Burke bunch, a trait his father claimed had skipped a generation and come directly to Dawson from Clive Senior.

Grandfather had been an imposing man, downright rigid in some ways. Dawson's father had called the older man Sir until the day he died. Perhaps that was why he insisted that his own children call him Dad and his grandkids call him the more informal Grandpa or Gramps. So, the comparison to Clive Senior wasn't exactly a compliment. These days, Dawson supposed, it was more apt than ever.

He glanced around the table at the smiling faces of his family and then finally at Eve. She was smiling, too. Looking radiant, lovely and so…alive.

For the first time since the accident, Dawson's regret was not that he hadn't died with his wife and daughter, but that he'd forgotten how to live.

CHAPTER FIVE

WHEN the meal was finished and the servers began clearing away the dishes, Tallulah once again took to the stage. This time, as she stood at the podium, she reminded her guests why they had come.

"Thanks to your past generosity, a lot of lives have been changed for the better. I know I can count on that generosity again tonight. The silent auction will close in another hour. If you aren't lucky enough to take home one of the incredible items supplied by our various sponsors, you're welcome to make a donation.

"In the meantime, please enjoy yourselves. We have a wonderful DJ, Dan Williams, on hand. So, let the dancing begin."

After Tallulah exited the stage to applause, the music began to play. The DJ kicked off with a slow number in deference to the fact that people had just finished their meals. Dawson leaned back in his seat, biding his time. Another hour or so and he could leave, his duty to his family fulfilled as well as his duty to Eve. Surely by then she would have enough information to do her job.

She had turned sideways in her seat so that she could see the stage. Now that the music was playing, one of her feet had begun to tap. The polite thing to do would be to ask her to dance. His mother was giving him pointed looks in that regard. But he didn't. Dancing required entirely too much physical contact for his comfort.

He should have known Eve wasn't the sort of woman who would wait to be asked. Bold, he thought again, when her gaze locked with his and she smiled.

"Do you dance?"

He made a dismissive sound. "It's been awhile."

And it had. The last time he had been on a dance floor, he'd been here. With his wife. While their daughter slumbered safely at home under the watchful eye of a sitter. The realization caused him to frown.

"No need to look so distressed," Eve assured him, misinterpreting his pained expression. "I hear it's like riding a bike. You never forget how."

"I'm not—"

But she was already laying her napkin aside and rising to her feet.

"Come on. It will be fun."

Fun? He doubted that. But his family was watching, his mother nodding in approval, his sister's eyes growing misty again.

"Very well."

He and Eve were the first couple on the dance floor. The only couple, in fact. They might as well have had a spotlight shining down on them. The music was too loud to hear, but Dawson imagined the murmurs coming from the crowd as he took Eve in his arms.

In addition to feeling conspicuous, he felt wooden and awkward as the past and the present intertwined, making way for comparisons that he didn't particularly like. Sheila had been petite, her build small and delicate. Eve was tall for a woman and her heels made them nearly the same height. He rested one palm just above her hip and grasped her hand, determined to keep a respectable distance between his body and her dangerous curves.

As soon as they began to move to the music, however, that space began to evaporate. Thighs mingled. Their hips bumped. Sheila had been pliant in Dawson's arms, going in whatever direction he chose. Not Eve. It was clear almost immediately that he was not the one in control.

A tendril of her hair tickled his nose when he turned his head to whisper, "You're leading."

"Yes, I am." She said it without a hint of apology. Then she asked sweetly, "Do you have a problem with taking instruction?"

"A problem? No. Not really. I simply prefer to give it." He attempted to back away, but the scent of her perfume followed right along with the rest of her. Before he knew it, she was close enough to his body that he swore he could feel the vibration when she made a tsking sound.

"And here I thought you were original, Dawson. But that's such a typical male response. It's a good thing I'm wearing high heels or I'd be drowning in testosterone."

"Funny."

Eve executed a turn that Dawson wasn't prepared for and he stepped on her toes. She grimaced.

"I should apologize for that, but I find myself wanting to say it serves you right. I'm a far better dancer when I'm allowed to take the lead," he said meaningfully.

"Funny. I feel the same way."

That had him frowning. "Do you mean to tell me you always lead?"

"For the most part. You could say it's a habit." Her shoulders lifted in a delicate shrug.

"Just what kind of men do you date that leading while dancing has become a habit for you?" he asked.

"The kind who are secure in their manhood," she replied. She leaned back as she said it. Amusement glittered in her dark eyes. She knew she had him. There wasn't much he could say in response to that without impugning himself.

Dawson exhaled slowly and shook his head. He felt irritated, frustrated and, God help him, invigorated. "You're something else."

"Thank you."

"I'm not sure I intended that as a compliment."

"No? Well, that's all right." She brought her cheek close to his and he felt her breath caress his ear when she added, "I'm going to take it as one anyway. Lemons from lemonade, that's my motto."

Dawson gave in and let Eve lead for the rest of the song. It was either that or he was going to continue to knock knees with her and step on her toes. He preferred not to make an even greater spectacle of himself, even if it meant handing over control.

Thankfully, by the time the song ended, they weren't alone on the floor any longer. Several other couples had joined them, including his parents. Clive and Tallulah were smiling at him. He could only imagine what conclusions they were reaching, especially when, as another slow song started, Eve was still in his arms.

"Care to do this again?" she asked. She sweetened the deal by adding, "I'll be good and let you lead."

Because he felt just a little too tempted, he shook his head and released her. "Maybe another time."

They stayed at the ball for another hour and a half, which was long enough to hear the results of the silent auction. Eve didn't win the theater tickets, but then Dawson had known that her bid, generous though it was given her means, ultimately wouldn't be enough. Indeed, the winner had outbid her by nearly five hundred dollars. This was for charity, after all.

"Oh, well," she said when the winner was announced. "I've got the musical's soundtrack."

"Maybe you can listen to it while you dine on lobster," he said, referring to her earlier mention of having to eat salads if she won.

But she was shaking her head. "Lobster? I'm from Maine. Once you've had it there, where it's caught in the morning and on your plate that afternoon, you're pretty well spoiled. I'll have a steak. A nice, juicy T-bone cooked so rare that it melts in your mouth."

His own mouth began watering when she made a little humming noise. To his mortification, her benign talk of red meat was whetting far different appetites. He glanced at his watch. It was just after ten. He was relieved that the evening was almost over, and not just because of his unexpected attraction to Eve.

Even though the point of bringing her had been to introduce her to his family and some of the other people on his Christmas list, he wasn't sure he appreciated the way she'd been received. Everyone liked her. No surprise there. She was a likeable woman, not in spite of her outspoken nature, but in some ways because of it. But it was more than that. He saw the speculation in their gazes and read between the lines in their comments. He knew what they were thinking: he had finally moved on with his life.

Nothing illustrated this more than his mother's question while he and Eve were saying their goodbyes.

"Will you be coming to dinner tomorrow afternoon?" Tallulah inquired.

Sunday dinner with his parents was a tradition, or at least it had been until the accident. He, Sheila and Isabelle had rarely missed it. In the intervening years, however, he could count on one hand the number of times he'd shown up.

So he shrugged. "I don't know, Mom. I have a lot I want to wrap up."

Tallulah nodded, not quite able to hide her disappointment. "Before you leave for Cabo."

He swallowed. "Yeah."

She forced a smile to her lips and sidled closer. "Well, if you change your mind, I hope you'll bring Eve. She's delightful, Daw."

He cleared his throat. "It's not what you think, Mom. Eve and I aren't…serious."

"Maybe you should be."

Dawson thought about his mother's remark during the ride home. Eve was seated next to him on the limousine's plush leather seat. She was wrapped up in her long wool coat. Even so, the scent of her perfume kept drifting to him, just as it had on the dance floor. It was sexy, dangerous. It slipped over and around him and cinched like a lasso. He found it a small consolation that the woman was completely unaware that his insides were being trussed up like a rodeo steer. She was talking business.

She had pulled a personal digital assistant from her clutch and was entering in some notes as she talked. "I couldn't help but notice your mother's jewelry. She's obviously very fond of gemstones."

He snorted at the understatement. As far as he knew, it was his mother's one weakness. "If it sparkles, she's got to have it."

"There's a boutique in town that carries one-of-a-kind pieces from a Venetian artisan. His work is quite remarkable and of the highest quality. I was in the shop last month to purchase something for another client and remember seeing some lovely rings. I'll pay him a visit first thing Monday and let you know what I find."

She shifted in her seat, undoing the top button of her coat and loosening the silk scarf beneath it. Her perfume wafted to him and once again had him thinking about sex—the act itself and how long it had been since he'd engaged in it. He'd work out when he got home. Thirty minutes with the free weights should do it. Followed by a cold shower, he amended when she began to suck on the end of the PDA's stylus.

"Okay," he managed.

"As for the boys, that's easy. They're salivating for that new gaming system."

"Every kid in the country is," he said on a snort. "It's the hot toy this year."

"I know. When we were in the ladies' room, your sister admitted to me that she hasn't been able to find one anywhere. All the stores she's tried have been sold out and they can't guarantee they'll get another shipment in before Christmas. She was thinking of going online and paying a private seller whatever price it takes. I talked her out of it. I told her I was pretty sure you'd already gotten them one. You should have seen the look of relief on her face."

"Great. How are you going to track one down if she's been unsuccessful?" he asked.

She sent him a wink. "I have my ways."

He meant it when he said, "If you pull this off, they'll be in heaven."

"Yes, and you'll be their hero, Uncle Dawson." She sent him a grin.

He glanced away, uncomfortable to be cast in that role. "I'll just be happy to redeem myself for the chemistry set fiasco."

"Did you pick out that gift yourself?" she asked.

"No. Actually, Mrs. Stern was the one who bought and sent it."

"Why am I not surprised?" she muttered.

"What?"

"Nothing." She waved a hand and then went on. "During dessert I heard Lisa say something to your mother about a Misty Stark dress she bought recently. I was thinking that a handbag from the designer's new collection might be a winner."

"She likes handbags," he said. "She probably needs a walk-in closet just to accommodate the ones she has now."

Eve smiled at him. "I knew I liked her."

He folded his arms. "What is it with women and purses? How many do you need?"

"One to go with every outfit and to suit every mood. In other words, you can never have too many. Handbags are like shoes that way."

"God, you sound like my wife." The words were out and, judging from Eve's stunned expression, he wasn't going to be able to pretend he hadn't said them.

Nor was he going to be able to change the subject, he realized, when she said, "Do you mean as in ex-wife?"

"No. As in late wife. She…she and my daughter died in a car accident." He swallowed the bitter memories and absently rubbed a hand over the raised scar that was partially hidden in his hairline.

"My God, Dawson. I had no idea. I'm so sorry."

She rested a hand on his forearm and gave it a squeeze. He nodded stiffly to accept her condolences and then moved slightly, forcing her hand to drop.

"When did this happen?"

"Three years ago." He cleared his throat. "Look, no offense, but this isn't something I care to talk about. Mind if we change the subject?"

She nodded. "Of course."

Even so, the remainder of the drive to her apartment was accomplished in silence.

* * *

Well, Eve thought, some things about the man—not to mention the interesting reactions he'd received all evening—finally made sense. But far from alleviating her curiosity, this new bit of information stoked it more.

Three years was a long time. But not when tragedy was involved. Tragedies changed people. Eve knew that firsthand. As young as she'd been at the time of her mother's death, it had shaped her life. In a way, she'd lost both of her parents—her mother to an overdose, her father to the road. Her mother's death had certainly changed her father.

How had tragedy changed Dawson? And she had little doubt it had, especially after meeting his family. What had he been like before the accident?

When they arrived at her apartment building, he walked her to her door. She expected that. He was a gentleman, and having met his mother, Eve knew good manners had been drilled into him.

"Tonight was very productive," she said.

He was standing on the opposite side of the small elevator, studying her. "That was the purpose."

"Yes. But I had a nice time anyway. You have a great family," she told him.

His head jerked down in what resembled a nod. He said nothing.

They arrived at her door. Eve wasn't sure what prompted the invitation, but she asked, "Would you like to come in for a drink?"

His jaw clenched. "It's getting late."

Because she felt foolish, she teased, "Worried that you'll turn into a pumpkin?"

He snorted. "Worried that my driver might."

"Jonas, right?" She'd forgotten about him.

"Right."

She pulled the keys from her small clutch. "Well, I'd offer to invite Jonas in for a nightcap as well, but I wouldn't want to give you the wrong impression about me."

Dawson laughed at that remark. The sound was rusty but pleasing. "Since the first moment I met you, Eve, I've formed all sorts of impressions. I don't think I've figured you out yet." He sobered, leaned against the doorjamb and studied her in the hallway's dim lighting. "You have a lot of layers."

"If you compare me to an onion you'll ruin what is otherwise a fairly interesting compliment."

His eyes narrowed. "Why do I get the feeling you like to keep me guessing?"

She batted her lashes. "Maybe because mystery is half of my allure."

He straightened and she thought he might turn to leave. In fact, she swore he started to, but then he was closing the space between them.

In that brief moment as his mouth hovered just above hers, Dawson whispered, "Don't sell yourself short."

As kisses went this one shouldn't have rocked

Eve's world. It was brief, close-mouthed and nearly perfunctory. Yet her knees felt weak afterward.

She credited Dawson's expression for that. She'd seen the man nearly naked, but at the moment he was far more exposed. Emotions played over his face in rapid succession, so many that she could barely keep track of them. But a couple stood out. He definitely looked angry and he most certainly was turned on.

We're even, she thought, as he stalked down the hall and she closed the door.

CHAPTER SIX

"You might have mentioned something to me about Dawson's having lost his wife and child," Eve said.

She was at Carole's comfortable home just outside Denver, making good on the movie, wine and Chinese food night that she'd previously had to cancel. Carole's leg was propped up on a pillow on the couch and an old Cary Grant movie was playing on the television, though neither one of them was watching it.

Between bites of sweet and sour pork Carole admitted, "I thought about it. In fact, I nearly did when you said he wanted you to come to the charity ball. But I wanted you to form your own impression of the man without being prejudiced by his tragic history."

"Why?"

Carole shook her head. "We'll get to that in a minute. First, I want to hear what you think about him, especially after spending an entire evening in his company."

"You make it sound like it was a date," Eve said dryly. "It was work."

Her gaze slid away. Well, it *had* been mostly work. The big exception of course was the kiss he'd given her at her apartment door. While it had ended well before turning into anything remotely passionate, it had been on her mind ever since. Were Dawson a different sort of man, Eve might have thought that was his intent.

Keep her guessing...

Keep her wanting...

As it was, she doubted he'd meant to lock lips with her in the first place. Afterward, he'd barely managed to bid her a curt good-night before stalking away.

"Are you going to tell me you didn't enjoy yourself?" Carole asked.

"No. I enjoyed myself." It was easier to concentrate on the event rather than the man, so she said, "It was a first-rate affair. You wouldn't believe the food that was served, or the dishes it was served on, for that matter. It was like being at a five-star restaurant. And the dessert? Sin on a plate."

"Chocolate?" Carole asked.

"You got it."

Carole made a humming sound, but then she was back to the subject at hand. "Okay, so tell me what you thought of the man."

Eve poked through the white takeout carton with a pair of chopsticks, coming out with a peapod.

"Let's see. He can be incredibly overbearing and arrogant. Oh, and he definitely needs to be in control all of the time," she added as she recalled their dance and the jolt it had given him when she'd taken the lead.

She still wasn't sure why she'd done that. She only knew that for some reason she'd felt the need to push him outside the rigid confines of his comfort zone.

"Anything else?" Carole's smile turned knowing. "What did you think of him physically?"

Eve heaved a dramatic sigh. "Okay, he's also seriously gorgeous and just about as sexy as they come."

Carole laughed. "That was what I thought, too. Of course, he was married at the time and I'd just gone through a very ugly divorce. In fact, landing the Burke Financial account helped pay for my lawyer fees among other things," she said wryly. "Officially, Clive hired me, but I worked mainly with Dawson via Rachel Stern."

"Mrs. Stern. That woman needs a hobby."

"She's really not so bad. She's just very protective of Dawson, almost like a second mother," Carole said. "And speaking of mothers, what did you think of Tallulah and the rest of his family?"

Eve grinned. "I liked them all. Very much. They're nice people. Normal. Not at all hoity-toity, if you know what I mean."

"I know."

"Dawson is different around them. He's less...

stuffy. They obviously love him. That much came through loud and clear."

"The Burkes are a close bunch," Carole agreed.

Eve frowned. "Yes, but he won't shop for them. And he told a friend that he'll be heading out of town at the end of the month to spend the holidays in Cabo San Lucas. From the various comments I overheard, I couldn't help but feel he's avoiding them."

"He's avoiding life and has been since the accident," her friend replied. "In fact, it wasn't until the accident that he added his personal shopping needs to my duties. Before then, I just took care of the business end."

"Sounds like he's really changed."

"Oh, he has." Carole nodded. "Do you feel sorry for him, Eve?"

"Well, of course I do. How can I not? The man lost his wife and daughter."

"Yes. In a car accident on Christmas Eve three years ago." Carole's expression turned grim. "Dawson was the one driving at the time."

"And he was the only one to survive," Eve finished. She closed her eyes, imagining his horror. Her chest ached. "Oh, God."

"Exactly. The Burkes are highly regarded in the community not just because of the business, but because of their overall involvement. In addition to the charity ball, they've got their finger in just about every philanthropic venture that comes along. Dawson's late wife's family is well-known, too, so the accident received plenty of media coverage. There was even some ugly speculation about drunken driving before police revealed that his blood alcohol level had been well below the legal limit."

"How horrible," Eve said.

"Yes," Carole said. "He also was cleared of any negligence. He was driving within the speed limit at the time and, with the exception of that patch of black ice, road conditions were fine."

"It was an accident."

"Yes. An accident. And it could have happened to anyone. Still, from what I've seen and from what those who know him well say, Dawson blames himself."

Of course he does, Eve thought. He was that type of man. Duty, responsibility, family—he took such things very seriously. They were his foundation and in one fell swoop that foundation had been reduced to rubble.

"I really wish you had given me a heads-up, Carole. I'm the first to admit I can be too blunt at times. I might have been a little more diplomatic, a little more sensitive if I'd understood why he needed a personal shopper to purchase gifts for family."

"Actually, that's one of the reasons I didn't tell you," her friend surprised her by saying. "I won't presume to know Dawson well. He's more of a give-orders sort than the sit-down-and-chat kind. But I've always liked him and respected him. And from what I've seen since the accident, he doesn't want coddling or pity. In fact, I'd say those are the last things he needs."

"What does he need?" She hadn't intended to ask that question. In reality, what business was it of hers?

But Carole was smiling coyly when Eve glanced in her direction. "I'm not sure, but maybe someone as resourceful as you will be able to figure it out."

It was half past midnight and though Dawson had gone to bed nearly two hours earlier, he was wide awake. There was nothing new about that. Since the accident he'd had a hard time falling asleep and an even harder time staying asleep once he had. The only time he actually slumbered straight through until morning was when he relied on prescription medication. He didn't like taking that, though. So, instead, he used the wee hours of the morning to make lists of things he needed to do and to catch up on his reading. Sadly, not even the boring article he was scanning in a business journal was making him heavy-eyed this night.

He laid the magazine aside on an oath, turned off the bedside lamp and rolled over. Giving his pillow a couple of punches, he admitted that the insomnia from which he'd suffered for the past several nights was different. He blamed Eve for that.

He also blamed himself.

"I never should have kissed her," he muttered.

Why that mere peck should haunt him, he wasn't sure. At the end of his two dates, he'd kissed both women and with far more intimacy than he had Eve. Yet neither encounter had left him wanting. Quite the opposite.

In the dark, he pictured Eve, her dark eyes wary and going wide as he breached her personal space and settled his mouth over hers. Her lips were soft, inviting. They were tempting, which was why Dawson had ended things quickly. Despite the brief contact, though, he'd felt something he hadn't felt in a very long time: sexually interested.

And alive, his subconscious whispered.

He rolled over and ignored it. "I never should have kissed her," he mumbled a second time.

Yet when he finally drifted off an hour later he dreamed of doing it again, and properly this time.

Eve was preparing to leave for the day when a courier knocked at her door with an official-looking envelope from Burke Financial. She tipped the young man who delivered it and went back inside her apartment to peel back the seal. Then she nearly fell over.

Inside was a pair of theater tickets for the same, sold-out musical that she'd bid on in the silent auction the previous Saturday night, only these were for better seats.

The note read:

Eve,
Burke Financial keeps a box at the theater. No

one was going to this Saturday's performance.
It seemed a shame to let them go to waste.
Enjoy yourself.
Dawson

She called him at his office immediately, and of
course got his secretary.

"He has a meeting in half an hour and he's prepping for it," Mrs. Stern informed her. It sounded like
a brush-off to Eve. "Can I take a message?"

She's like a second mother, Carole claimed. Eve
decided to play on that. Mothers liked nothing better
than women with good manners.

"He was kind enough to send me a pair of theater
tickets. I just need a moment of his time to thank
him properly. Do you think you could put me
through?" she asked.

"Just a moment," Mrs. Stern said. Eve was still
congratulating herself when Dawson came on the line.

"Hello, Eve."

"Hi. I know you're busy, but I just wanted to call
and say thank you."

"I take it the tickets arrived."

"Yes. Just a moment ago. For once I was glad to
be running a little behind schedule." As she spoke,
she paced the length of her living room in front of the
big windows that brought some of the city's skyline
inside. "It's incredibly generous of you, Dawson."

"They weren't being used," he replied.

"So you mentioned in your note."

"It seemed a shame for them to go to waste when I knew how much you wanted to see the show."

"Still, I'm grateful, but I find myself in a bit of a quandary." She nibbled her lip.

"And why is that?" he asked.

"Well, I know what these tickets go for. I feel a little awkward accepting something so valuable from a client." Which was partly true.

She pictured Dawson shrugging as he suggested, "Consider it a bonus."

"Thanks, but my commission is all the bonus I require." Eve twisted a lock of hair around her index finger as an idea took shape. "Perhaps you would consider coming to see the play with me?"

The invitation was met with deafening and prolonged silence, making her regret her haste in issuing it.

"Okaaaay. Apparently not. It was just a thought. You've probably already seen the show," she said in an attempt to save face. Not that that was actually possible at this point. "I'll let you get back to work now. Bye." She hung up without giving him a chance to say anything, although she thought she heard him call her name just before she did so.

"God, I'm such an idiot." She groaned in mortification and shuffled backward a couple of steps so she could flop onto the couch.

What had she been thinking, asking him out? The man was probably seriously regretting his generosity right about now. The cordless phone was still in her hand. It trilled to life as she lay amid the throw pillows mentally berating herself. Eve answered it from her prone position.

"Hello?" Home of the Perpetually Foolish, she almost added, and was mighty glad she hadn't when she heard Dawson's voice.

"You hung up awfully fast. I didn't get a chance to give you an answer."

She straightened to sitting, ran a hand through her mussed hair. "I guess I took your silence for an answer."

"Yeah. I'm sorry about that. I was just a little… surprised," he told her.

"I got that," she said. Indeed, it had come through loud and clear.

"When I sent the tickets I assumed you'd have someone else in mind for the second one," he said.

"Such as?" she prodded.

"Such as the date you had to cancel on the night of the ball," he replied.

"Oh, that." Because he couldn't see her expression, she let her grin unfurl. "It was nothing serious. I was just getting together with a friend."

"A friend." He cleared his throat. "And would this friend be male or female?"

"Female."

"Ah."

He was quiet again. Too quiet. Eve began counting. When she got to ten she said, "You're doing it again."

"What?"

"Not saying anything, which forces me to draw my own conclusions."

"And what might those be?" His tone held what sounded like amusement.

Pinching her eyes closed, she gave in to impulse once again. "You're trying to figure out which restaurant you want to take me to for dinner before we head to the theater Friday night."

While Eve held her breath, she heard a mild oath and then strangled laughter. Her lungs felt close to bursting by the time Dawson finally got around to saying, "You're a mind reader."

CHAPTER SEVEN

THE telephone rang as Eve reapplied her lipstick in the mirror that hung by her apartment door. Though it wasn't her style to appear eager, she was wearing her coat and trying not to watch the clock.

"Eve, it's Dawson. Sorry, but I'm running a little behind," he said unnecessarily. She'd expected him to arrive twenty minutes earlier. Their dinner reservation was for six o'clock and that time was fast approaching.

"Everything…okay?" she inquired.

"Wondering if I've changed my mind?"

"I'd understand," she said. And she would, given everything she now knew about his past.

While Eve wasn't considering this a full-fledged date, neither would her conscience allow her to classify it as mere business. She found Dawson interesting, handsome and definitely sexy. Generally speaking, she'd made it a rule not to become personally involved with male clients. But since the Burke account was hers only temporarily courtesy of Carole, she felt safe making an exception.

"I'm not going to stand you up, Eve." His tone was resolute. "Something came up at the last minute."

"Okay. How about I meet you at Tulane then?" she suggested. The restaurant wasn't far from her apartment and it would save him from having to backtrack, as the place was located between them.

He hesitated and Eve was reminded of the fact that he preferred to lead. But then he said, "All right. But give me another fifteen minutes before you leave."

"Okay."

"And, if I'm not there when you arrive, order an appetizer," he added.

"Should I start dinner without you, too?" she asked dryly.

"No. I'll be there."

Dawson walked through the doors at Tulane just as the waiter brought the artichoke dip. He'd shed his overcoat, beneath which he wore a tailored charcoal suit, white shirt and muted print tie. He looked sophisticated, sexy and a tad arrogant as he scanned the tables. When he spotted her, he didn't smile exactly, but his intense expression relaxed even as it brightened. Eve sucked in a breath and exhaled it slowly between her teeth.

"Sorry I'm late," he apologized again as he slipped onto the chair opposite hers.

Her heart rate back to normal, she offered an easy smile. "That's okay."

"I see you ordered an appetizer."

"Yes, hope you like artichoke dip and toast squares," she said.

"You won't hear me complaining."

"I also took a chance and had the waiter bring us some wine." She nodded toward the glass that was in front of Dawson on the table.

He picked it up and took a sip. His brow beetled as his gaze connected with hers. "Pinot noir?"

"It's what you were drinking the other night."

"You certainly pay attention."

Eve picked up her glass and shrugged. "I tend to remember details."

Dawson studied her over the rim of his glass. He remembered details, too. When it came to Eve Hawley, he recalled far too many of them for his own peace of mind.

Details such as the golden flecks that could be teased from her otherwise brown eyes. The candlelight was accomplishing that. And the paleness of her skin that contrasted with a trio of beauty marks at the base of her throat.

She was wearing black tonight. The dress's cut was simple, elegant, and though it sported three-quarter-length sleeves and a rather demure neckline, it was every bit as sexy as the siren-red number she'd had on the other evening. As for her hair, she'd left it down. It hung in a glossy dark cloud of curls around her shoulders. Dawson wondered if it would feel as soft as it looked. If it would smell…

"You're staring at me and not saying anything," Eve said, snapping him out of his stupor. Her full lips bowed when she added, "I'd wonder if I had a piece of artichoke stuck in my teeth, but I haven't tried the dip yet."

Ah, yes, Dawson thought, and then there was that—the woman's surprisingly direct nature. It was another detail, another characteristic, that made her stand out in a crowd. His late wife had been much more reserved and…

He sipped his wine to wash away the memory before it could fully form. No, he wouldn't think of Sheila tonight. He'd done that on his other dates, he realized, spent the time making comparisons, and finding his companions lacking. Both of them had been nice women, but it struck Dawson now how much they had been like his late wife, resembling Sheila in both looks and temperament. Had he unconsciously been seeking a substitute?

Eve was no stand-in. She and Sheila were polar opposites in everything from their personality to their physical characteristics. In fact, he couldn't recall ever being attracted to a woman who was quite so outspoken, independent and vivacious. Making comparisons wouldn't be fair to either woman. Besides, what purpose would they serve? Beyond making Dawson feel guilty.

He took another sip of his wine and swore he felt a couple shackles from the past fall away when he said, "I'm staring because you look lovely this evening."

"Oh." She smiled. "Thank you."

"Actually, I should thank you. I'm glad you asked me to accompany you to the theater tonight."

Her brows rose at that. "Really?"

He set his wine aside. "Yes. I haven't been to the theater in ages."

Her expression turned incredulous. "Do you mean to tell me that your company has access to a pair of choice seats and you don't bother to go?"

"I've been—"

"Busy," she supplied for him, but her overly bright smile told Dawson exactly what she thought of his long-standing excuse.

"I have been busy," he insisted. When his conscience delivered a sharp kick, he admitted, "All right, the truth is I don't get out much these days."

"No, the truth is you don't make *time* to get out much these days," she told him.

Yes, direct.

"They're sort of the same thing."

He thought she might argue, but she let it go and smiled instead. "Well, I suppose I should feel flattered then that you accepted my invitation."

"You're a hard woman to turn down, Eve."

He meant it. He'd spent the past few days wondering why he'd agreed to go. Even amid his many doubts and regrets, though, he hadn't considered canceling on her.

Her smile widened. "I like that answer."

He chuckled. "I thought you might."

The waiter came by to tell them about the evening's dinner specials then. Eve gave the young man her undivided attention, nodding and making appreciative noises as he described the pressed duck.

"Ooh. It sounds wonderful, Danny," she said, flashing a smile that was warm rather than flirtatious.

The woman had a way with people, Dawson thought. It was more than the fact that she treated them with respect. Eve made them feel singled out, special.

After they'd placed their orders and the waiter had gone, Dawson said, "You know, you're very good at that."

"At what?"

"At making people feel like they're important," he replied.

Her brows rose at the same time her chin dipped down. "That's because people *are* important."

He gave a dismissive wave with one hand. "You know what I mean."

"No, I don't. And I'm going to be very disappointed if you suddenly turn into a snob," she informed him. Though she said it lightly, he didn't doubt that she would be.

"I'm not a snob." When she remained silent, he raised a hand palm up as if making a vow. "On my honor, I swear that I'm not. My mother wouldn't allow it."

Eve's expression softened then. "As I've met your mother, not to mention the rest of your lovely family, I have no choice but to believe you."

"Good. And for the record, I intended my observation to be a compliment. A lot of people wouldn't bother to make eye contact with a waiter much less call him by his given name."

"Oh, Danny and I go way back."

"You know him?" Dawson asked, surprised.

She grinned. "We met when I ordered the appetizer." Then she blew out an impatient breath. "Besides, his name was on a badge that was pinned to his shirt. How should I refer to him? 'Hey, you?'"

"Sadly, I know some people who might not refer to him with even that much courtesy."

She shook her head and frowned. "You need to start hanging around with a better class of friends."

"I didn't say they were my friends. I just said I knew such people. They think they're better than everyone else simply because they were born into money."

"Ah, yes." She twirled her wineglass by its stem before taking a sip. Then she surprised him by saying, "I was in a relationship with one of those people for a couple of years, though it took me a while to figure it out."

A couple of years? "It sounds like the two of you were pretty serious."

"I thought so at the time." She selected a piece of toast and scooped up some dip. Before popping it into her mouth, she said, "It turned out that while I was good enough to spend time with, neither he nor his parents felt I had the right pedigree to carry on the bloodlines or some such nonsense."

"Sorry." The evening of the ball, Dawson had sensed vulnerability. Despite her cavalier attitude now, it made an appearance again, and he thought he understood the reason for it.

"Drew did offer to keep seeing me provided that we met discreetly. He said that he had a lot of fun whenever we were together and he hated for that to end."

I bet. "Good for you that you turned him down."

"Well, he made it pretty easy. He'd already announced his engagement to a debutante that it turned out he'd been dating on and off since grad school. Hence the need for discretion." She made a tsking sound and in a rueful voice asked, "Why is it that the other woman is always the last to know?"

"Sorry." He half meant it when he said, "Does this Drew character live around here? Maybe I could go to his house and beat him up for you."

"A tempting offer, but he's back in Connecticut making the rounds with his bride."

"Connecticut?" Dawson frowned. "I thought you said you were from Maine?"

"I said I was born in Maine," she replied. "But I actually grew up in that state and a few others along the eastern seaboard. I ended up in Hartford after college."

"It sounds like you moved around a lot."

"I did." She selected another piece of toast, and he got the feeling that no more information on her childhood would be forthcoming.

"So, I'd have to travel to Connecticut if I wanted to beat up your ex?"

"Nah. He's not worth the price of airfare. Besides, I'm over it."

Over it? Dawson thought as he helped himself to that appetizer. Perhaps Eve was over the man—and he chose not to examine too closely why he hoped that was the case—but she was not over the slight. No, that wound definitely had not healed yet.

"Well, if it's any consolation, it doesn't sound like his marriage will last very long let alone be very happy," Dawson told her.

"No. Probably not." She dabbed her mouth with her napkin, pulling it away to reveal a devilish smile. "I know it's incredibly small of me, but I hope she takes him to the cleaners when they divorce."

"It would serve him right," Dawson agreed. "In my opinion, a man who can't be faithful to a woman deserves to lose something even more, um, personal than money."

Head tilted to one side, Eve grinned at him. "I knew there was a reason I liked you…well, besides your penchant for bubble bath."

"Charity," he replied on a long-suffering sigh, but then he was grinning back.

He liked her, too. She not only made it easy to carry on a conversation, she made it easy to joke. He'd almost forgotten that he possessed a sense of humor. It resurfaced now as he asked, "Do you mean my wit and charm weren't reasons enough?"

"*Witty* and *charming* were not exactly the two adjectives I would have used to describe you at our first meeting." Her eyebrows bobbed. "Even if I did appreciate the view."

Dawson grimaced. "Is it too late to apologize for that?"

"As far as I'm concerned it's never too late to apologize for anything," she replied.

"Very magnanimous of you. In that case, I'm sorry." He decided to come clean. "The truth is I wasn't in the best mood that day. I was hoping to get rid of you."

"I see." She picked up her wine and sipped. "And, what, you thought I'd run screaming in the opposite direction at the sight of a naked man?"

Unfortunately, the waiter picked that exact moment to arrive with their dinner salads. The young man cleared his throat and glanced from Dawson to Eve as he set them on the table.

"Would you care for freshly ground pepper on your salad, miss?" He held out the wooden mill.

"Please," Eve replied, looking not the least bit embarrassed. Dawson, on the other hand, was pretty sure he'd turned the same color as the raspberry vinaigrette dressing that was drizzled over his plate of mixed baby greens.

"And you, sir?"

Dawson cleared his throat. "No. Thanks."

"Can I get either of you anything else?" the young man inquired.

"No, Danny." She glanced across the table at Dawson and winked. "I think we're…covered."

When they were alone again, Dawson said, "Just as a point of clarification, I was not naked when we met."

"Oh, that's right." But Eve caused him to blush all over again when she added, "You were wearing a sheet. I guess I let my imagination fill in the parts it concealed."

On a strangled laugh, Dawson replied, "I hope your imagination did me justice."

"I don't think you need to be concerned on that score."

"I guess we'll see."

His response and what it implied had both of them sobering. By the time Danny returned with their entrees they had returned to far safer topics of conversation than Dawson's anatomy.

As they left the restaurant an hour later, Eve got an idea.

"You know, my Tahoe is in the parking ramp. Why don't you give your driver the rest of the night off? I can take us to the theater." She sent him an angelic smile. "I promise to be a perfect gentleman and drop you at your home well before you turn into a pumpkin."

Dawson glanced toward the curb where the limousine was waiting. His omnipresent driver had already hopped out to open the rear door for them.

She braced for his protest, but he agreed.

"All right. I guess that makes more sense than taking separate vehicles to the theater."

Even more surprising than his agreement was the fact that Dawson didn't insist on getting behind the wheel when they reached her Tahoe. Without a word, he got in on the passenger's side...after opening the driver's door for her, of course. If she saw his mother again, Eve would be sure to compliment Tallulah on her son's fine manners.

"I'm not sure I've ever met a man who was willing to relinquish the driver's seat, especially to a woman," she joked after starting the vehicle.

She glanced over at Dawson in the Tahoe's dim interior. Far from smiling, his face was drawn, his lips compressed. He was a man who preferred to be in control at all times, yet not only was he willing to let her drive, but it also dawned on Eve that he paid someone else to do the driving for him on a regular basis. Before, Eve had considered that a wealthy man's preference. He could afford such a luxury and so he enjoyed it. It struck her now that, as the survivor of a harrowing crash, hiring a driver really was more of a necessity.

To fill the awkward silence, she said, "Well, just to put your mind at ease, I've never had so much as a traffic ticket."

"Good to know," came his clipped response.

Out of the corner of her eye, she watched him buckle his seat belt and then pull on the strap as if testing it. Afterward, he rested the palms of his hand on his thighs, hardly the picture of relaxation. In the rear of a limo it was probably easy to forget about oncoming traffic. That wasn't the case with a front seat view.

"It's nice to leave the driving to other people once in a while, isn't it?" she said in an effort to make small talk.

Dawson responded with a tight-lipped, "Yes."

"You probably get a lot done on the morning commute."

"Yes." Another laconic reply.

"I'd love to be able to while away my drive time reading or whatnot. I try to time it so I'm not on the roads at the height of rush hour. Traffic can be a killer, especially on the area highways." As soon as the words were out she wanted to snatch them back. If Eve hadn't needed to keep her foot on the gas pedal, she would have used it to kick herself. Talk about a poor choice of words.

Dawson, however, answered with an honest, "Yes. The highways can be a real killer."

"My God, Dawson. I'm sorry. That came out badly."

"No need to apologize."

"You told me before that you don't like to talk about the accident." She refrained from adding that he probably should, rather than keeping all of that pain and self-blame bottled up inside. Her thoughts turned to her father, a perpetual man-child who had been emotionally stunted by his grief. It wasn't healthy, Eve knew.

"We weren't talking about the accident," he said. "And we're not."

"Dawson—"

"We're talking about driving. I prefer to leave that job to other people, which is why I pay a driver."

She allowed him the out, though they both knew he was lying. "Ah. Right. Well, I live for the day I can not only afford to hire a driver but also pay someone to clean my toilets. It's a nasty chore."

"I'll have to take your word for it," he replied blandly.

"Do you mean to tell me you've never scrubbed a commode?" she asked.

"Never."

"Well, I take care of mine every Saturday morning if you ever feel the need to rack up another life experience," she offered.

As she turned onto Curtis Street, she glanced over in time to see his lips loosen with the beginnings of a smile.

"Thanks, but no," he said.

CHAPTER EIGHT

WHEN they left the theater a few hours later, Eve was humming one of the musical's more upbeat tunes.

"I take it you enjoyed the show," Dawson said as they made their way to her Tahoe.

"I loved it." She sighed. "Thank you again for coming with me."

"You're welcome. You know, that's the third time I've seen *Les Miz*. The first two times were years ago when it was on Broadway."

"You're kidding."

He shook his head.

"You must love it."

Actually, he hadn't really cared for it in the past. Tonight, he had. Dawson credited Eve for that. She had a way of making him loosen up and let go. She'd laughed at the ribald antics of the Thénardiers and cried as Jean Valjean made his passionate plea to God to spare Marius's life. At times, he'd found himself more interested in watching her than the stage.

"Do you own the soundtrack, too?" she asked, pulling him from his introspection.

"No."

"You should have bought a copy tonight. I can lend you mine, if you'd like," she offered.

"Thanks, but I'll pass. The music is outstanding, don't get me wrong. But it's not my style."

"Oh?"

"I'm more a vintage rock fan. You know, pounding bass and wicked guitar riffs. Something to get the blood pumping."

Eve smiled at him and he swallowed as the phrase took on a new meaning.

"Blood pumping, right." She nodded as if in agreement, but shattered the illusion by adding, "Don't forget men with seriously bad hairstyles wearing spandex and screaming out indecipherable lyrics at the tops of their lungs."

She had a point about the bad hair and spandex. He tucked his hands deep into the pockets of his overcoat. "I can figure out the lyrics."

When she tipped down her chin and arched her brows, he amended, "Most of the time."

As they started walking again, Eve mused, "I once dreamed about a career on Broadway. My goal was to be cast as Belle in the stage production of *Beauty and the Beast*. I had all of the songs memorized, and I rehearsed them daily in front of the bathroom mirror."

"So, you have a good singing voice?"

She shook her head. "I can't carry a tune, which is pretty much what killed that choice of careers for me."

Dawson chuckled. "I suppose that would nip things in the bud. How old were you at the time?"

"Eleven. My dad's a musician."

It was one of the few references she'd made to her family, he realized. He found he wanted to know more. "Really? What kind?"

"The wanna-be kind. He plays old-school rock," she replied. There was an edge to her tone he hadn't heard before.

"Hence your objection to the genre."

She merely shrugged.

"So, you wanted to follow in your dad's foot-steps," Dawson said.

Eve snorted indelicately. "Only if they led me right to him. He was away. A lot," she added. "Actu-ally, my goal was to become a major stage star, an unrivaled success. I wanted my name in lights, as the saying goes."

It was pretty easy for Dawson to read between the lines. "You wanted your father's attention."

"Sure I did. Sometimes I still do. There's noth-ing unusual about that. All kids want their parents' attention," she stated matter-of-factly, but he noted the stiff set to her shoulders, the furrow in her brow.

Yes, all children wanted their parents' attention, but not all of them got it. Dawson had been lucky in that regard. He'd had it in spades. Still did, come to think of it. Eve? Apparently not.

They reached the Tahoe and she redirected the conversation. "So, what did you want to be when you were growing up?"

Dawson opened the driver's door for her before heading around to the passenger side. Once seated, he replied, "Do you mean before I figured out that I didn't look so good in long hair and spandex, or after I accepted the fact that the National Football League wasn't going to come recruiting?"

Her lips twitched as she started the ignition. "Either-or. Surprise me."

He scrubbed a hand over his chin, thinking. "Well, I pretty much always knew I'd go into the family business. It suited my personal interests, not to mention my academic strengths. I didn't feel pressured to do it or anything." Dawson leaned back in his seat, relaxing a little as he recalled the advice his father had given him just before he'd gone off to college. *Do what makes you happy, son. Not what you think will make me happy.* "My dad would have understood if I had chosen a different career. My grandfather would have been livid, but Dad…he would have understood."

He smiled after saying it, feeling warm even though the Tahoe had yet to heat up.

"The two of you seem really close," Eve noted.

"We are. Yes." He cleared his throat, a little embarrassed to have been lost in nostalgia. Memories had been his nemesis for the past few years, proving so hurtful that he'd blocked out the good along with the bad.

Ahead, a traffic light turned red. After stopping, Eve turned to face him. "I know this is none of my business, but I'm going to ask anyway. If the two of you are so close, why are you estranged?"

The question left Dawson staggered. "We're not estranged," he said.

Eve's gaze remained steady as she said, "Then why are you spending the holidays in Cabo rather than with your family here?"

I don't have a family, he thought. Sheila, Isabelle, they were gone and he was alone. But he knew they weren't the family to which Eve was referring. "It's…complicated."

"I don't doubt that," she replied. "Life tends to get that way from time to time for everyone. That's especially true after a tragedy. But it sure seems like you're punishing them."

"You're wrong. Way, way off base." He shook his head vehemently as his throat seemed to close. Eve was mistaken in her assessment. If he was punishing anyone, it wasn't his parents and sister. He was punishing himself.

"That's the way it seems."

"That's because you don't understand," he said.

Nobody did. They hadn't been trapped inside that crumpled-up car while emergency workers tried unsuccessfully to revive his wife. They hadn't been the ones pleading with firefighters to hurry as they finally managed to free his daughter from her safety restraint in the mangled backseat.

In the Tahoe's dimly lit interior her expression radiated sincerity when she invited, "Then help me understand, Dawson. Better yet, help *them* understand."

"I..." But the words remained stubbornly lodged in his throat. The only ones to finally make it free were, "The traffic light is green."

Eve parked the Tahoe in the circular drive in front of Dawson's home. The rest of the ride from the theater had been accomplished in strained silence. She accepted the blame for that. She shouldn't have pushed him so hard.

She wasn't sure exactly why she'd done it, except that she'd hoped by talking about the accident he would finally see that it was just that—an accident. She wanted him to accept what everyone else knew. Dawson was as much a victim, a casualty, as his late wife and little daughter.

"Here we are," she said. "I know I've already thanked you for the tickets, but I want to do so again. I had a nice time tonight, Dawson."

"You're welcome. I did, too."

"I'm glad you're still able to say that. I'm sorry about..." She waved a hand, opting not to plow that rocky ground a second time.

He caught her fingers and gave them a gentle squeeze. "Let's forget about that, okay?"

Eve didn't think forgetting was wise. Indeed, it was at the crux of his problem. But for the moment she agreed. No more pushing tonight. She smiled. "All right."

Dawson had yet to release her hand. Though they both wore gloves, she swore she could feel the heat from his skin warming hers through two layers of lined leather.

His thumb began to rub the palm of her hand. She'd never considered her palm or any other place on her hand to be an erogenous zone. It turned out she was wrong. Way wrong.

Eve swallowed a moan and stammered, "S-so, should I walk you to your front door? I promised to be a gentleman, after all."

"No need for that."

The palm caress continued. "Mmm-kay," she managed to say.

"If you walk me to my door, I'd only feel obligated to walk you back to your car afterward." One side of his mouth lifted. "Can't let you be the only gentleman."

"Well, I guess I'd better stay here then. Otherwise it sounds like we could pass the entire night walking back and forth between my Tahoe and your front porch."

"That would make for a long night."

"Very long," she agreed.

"And it's cold outside."

"Below freezing." She shivered, though the reaction had less to do with Denver's current temperature than the ministrations of his thumb.

"We'd have to move fast to stay warm," he said. In contrast the smile he offered was slow, seductive.

"If we jogged, I suppose it could be considered aerobic exercise."

"Exercise, hmm?" His thumb stopped moving and Dawson released her hand. Gaze steady, expression serious, he removed his gloves, tugging one finger free at a time. Anticipation hummed until he reached for her across the vehicle's console. Big, warm hands framed her face, drew her forward.

"I can think of more interesting methods of increasing my heart rate while in the company of a beautiful woman," he murmured just before kissing her.

Soft. That was Eve's first thought. Though so much of the man was hard and uncompromising, his lips were soft, their pressure gentle. She thought he might end things as quickly as he had the night of the ball, leaving her to wonder and to want. He didn't.

"Eve." Dawson whispered her name as he changed the angle of their mouths.

His hands were in her hair now, fingers weaving through it. Slow? Soft? Nothing about the man's demeanor fit these descriptions now. *Urgent* was the word that came to mind as he fumbled with the fat buttons of her wool coat. She shifted in her seat to improve his access, her elbow catching on the steering wheel. The horn blasted loudly, blowing a hole right through the intimacy of the moment. Romance took a backseat to reality.

Eve sucked in a breath as Dawson pulled away. Her body was sizzling, snapping like an exposed electrical wire. Had she ever been this turned on? A glance in Dawson's direction had her swallowing the suggestive remark she'd been about to make. He was slumped back in his seat, scrubbing a hand over his face.

Regrets.

She could see them as clearly as if they had been tattooed on his forehead, hear them even though he had yet to say a word. Eve closed her eyes, mentally kicked herself. To think for a moment she'd thought the only thing that had come between them during that passionate exchange had been the vehicle's console and their layers of clothing.

"You're not ready for…this. Are you?"

His laughter was brittle, bitter. "That's not exactly the issue at the moment."

"I'm not talking physically, Dawson."

"No." He swore, stared straight ahead and admitted, "I don't know."

"It's okay," she assured him, even as her own heart began to ache a bit.

"It's not okay!" He cursed again, this time with more force, and turned to face her. She saw anger and frustration, neither of which was directed at her. "None of this is okay, Eve. None of it."

His strident words seemed to echo in the vehicle. She remained silent, waiting for him to continue. After a long moment, he did. His tone was missing its angry edge. Now Dawson just sounded tired and a little lost when he told her, "Some people are able to just go with the flow. Not me. I had my life all figured out, you know? I made plans and then I followed through on them."

"You're talking about before the accident?"

"Yes. I made plans," he said a second time.

Of course, he had. Dawson was the sort of man who needed to take charge, to be in control. But tragedy and grief wouldn't follow orders. On the contrary. Once they were on the scene, they called the shots.

"It's time to make new plans," Eve said softly.

He faced her, his gaze glittering hard in the meager glow cast by the landscaping lights. "I did. After the accident I made new plans. I've been living my life according to them ever since."

She swallowed. "And?"

"You seem to be botching them up, Eve."

Her mouth fell open. Before she could ask what he meant by that potent statement, however, Dawson was opening the door and getting out of the Tahoe. He slammed it shut without another word.

It was several minutes after he disappeared inside the house before she felt steady enough to drive away.

The weekend proved long, as did the following week. Dawson had plenty of work to keep him busy and he finalized his plans for his trip to Cabo San Lucas. Eve called a couple times, but he made excuses not to speak with her.

You're not ready for this, are you?

That damned question seemed to taunt him.

He was glad when Friday dawned. Another week down. Just two more to go until he boarded that plane and left everything familiar. Then he glanced out the window, saw the snow and cursed. The forecast had called for it, so the accumulation blanketing his lawn hardly came as a surprise. Even so, he didn't like it. After showering and dressing in more casual clothes than he would wear to the office, he headed downstairs to his study. As he always did on days when the weather turned inclement, he would work from home.

As a child, he'd loved the white stuff and not just because if enough of it fell he got the day off from school. No, he'd loved playing in it, making forts out of it and packing it into balls for fights with his friends. Even as an adult he hadn't minded it, though it often presented a headache during his commute to or from work.

What had turned him off completely to winter

weather, of course, was the accident, which is why he'd opted to work from home this day.

It came as an absolute shock then when, halfway through the afternoon, his housekeeper tapped at his door to announce he had a guest.

"Eve Hawley is here," Ingrid said.

Leather creaked as he settled back in his chair. He didn't want to see her and yet he did.

"Send her in, please."

She appeared in the doorway a moment later, smiling apologetically and looking lovely enough to snatch his breath away.

"Sorry to disturb you."

"That's all right." He rested his elbows on the desk blotter and steepled his fingers in front of him. "Did we have an appointment?" he asked.

"No. Actually, I wasn't expecting to see you at all. I figured you would be at your office."

Once his ego had absorbed the blow, he replied, "I decided to work from home today."

"So I see."

"What can I do for you, Eve?" he asked curtly.

He saw hurt flash in her dark eyes just before she blinked, and hated himself for it. This wasn't her fault. None of this was her fault.

"I have some gift ideas as well as some actual things that I purchased for family members. I was planning to leave them for you to look over."

"Okay."

At that single, sparse word, she backed up a step, nodding. None of the spunk she'd exhibited on her first visit to his home was evident when she said, "Well, I'll just leave them with Ingrid. Thanks."

She'd already turned and gone before Dawson managed to launch himself from his seat. He caught up with her in the front foyer just as she was pulling on her jacket.

"Eve, wait."

She turned, a manufactured smile tilting up her lips. "Yes?"

He closed his eyes and shook his head. "Don't go. Not like this."

"Like what?"

"Angry."

"I'm not angry. Why in the world would I be angry?" she asked, tossing the end of her scarf over one shoulder.

"Because I was being a jerk."

She stopped in the process of pulling on her gloves. "Yes," she agreed with a considering nod. "You were. A rude jerk to be precise."

Dawson's laughter was strained, even though the ice had been broken. "You don't believe in cutting a guy any slack, do you?"

"To what purpose?"

He ran his tongue over the outside of his top teeth. "Okay, how about this? Do you have any plans for dinner?"

"Tonight?" she inquired.

The woman was definitely playing hardball.

"Yes, tonight."

"Hmm. Let me think." She tapped her lower lip with the tip of one gloved index finger. "Not exactly, although I did take a chicken breast out of the freezer to thaw."

It was a bit of a blow to learn he could lose out to poultry. "I believe Ingrid is making a pork roast."

"Ah, the other white meat," she said, repeating the industry's slogan.

"Yes. She's a very good cook," he added in the hopes of aiding his cause.

Eve eyed him stoically. "Is that an invitation, Dawson?" she asked.

"It is."

"I see."

She was silent for so long that he was forced to ask, "Does that mean you accept?"

She tilted her head to one side. "Depends."

"On what?"

"On what else is on the menu," she said.

He cleared his throat. "I'm not sure. Probably some sort of rice or potato dish and a vegetable. Maybe a salad. Do you have a preference? I can let Ingrid know and I'm sure she'll try to accommodate it," he offered.

"Actually, I meant in the way of conversation."

"Oh."

She folded her arms over her chest. "Are you going to talk to me?"

"Of course I am," he replied, somewhat indignant.

"I mean an actual conversation, Dawson. No chitchat about the weather or diatribes on the economy. I can get that watching the news while I eat Chinese takeout."

He blew out a breath. "Good God, Eve. You're a hard woman to please."

She unzipped the quilted down jacket she wore and laid it over his arm. Her smile was purely female when she replied, "You don't know the half of it."

CHAPTER NINE

SINCE they had some time to kill before dinner was served, Dawson suggested they sit in the great room where a fire blazed cheerfully in the hearth. Eve agreed and he helped her carry in the purchases she'd made.

In the past, he'd given Carole carte blanche to buy his family's gifts. Afterward, he hadn't wanted anything to do with them. Eve, of course, insisted on running everything past him.

"At the very least you should know what you bought so that when they thank you, you won't appear baffled."

"I'm never baffled," he responded. Her brows rose fractionally as if to say, "Right."

"Another one of your principles?" he asked.

"Exactly."

As they sat on the sofa and went through the goods she'd brought with her, Dawson was impressed. The woman had a good eye. She'd pegged his mother's taste perfectly with a specially designed amethyst ring that was surrounded by smaller stones. Tallulah was going to love it. He told Eve as much.

She smiled, looking pleased. "That was my thought, too. As for your dad, he was difficult. I went out on a limb with this since it cannot be returned, but since Clive seemed to be a real hockey fan, I thought he might appreciate it."

She pulled a red game jersey from the bag that was on her lap.

"That's Gordie Howe's number," Dawson said as he reached for it. "He was one of the all-time greats."

"It's a vintage National Hockey League sweater and it's signed. I know the Wings aren't your father's favorite team, but the Avalanche wasn't around back in the day." Her tone turned wry. "I know this because I made a fool of myself in a sports memorabilia store downtown."

Dawson chuckled. "Dad's going to love it. He'll argue, of course, that Ted Lindsay was actually the better player, but he'll love it. Thank you."

She rifled through another bag as he folded the jersey and set it aside.

"And here's the Misty Stark purse I mentioned getting for your sister. I went with something medium-sized from the designer's spring collection."

"This spring?"

"I know someone who knows someone who owed

that someone a really big favor." She let out a sigh that was purely feminine. "Lisa's going to love it."

The handbag reminded Dawson of a pastel-colored sausage with handles. "I'll have to take your word for it," he said dryly.

"I'm still looking for something for your brother-in-law. Suggestions at this point would be appreciated. Christmas is only two weeks away."

"I'll give it some thought," he replied.

"Maybe you could call your sister, pick her brain a little," she suggested. "Or you could go to Sunday dinner this week and talk to her there."

"I…I'll see what I can do."

"Okay. Thanks." She leaned forward then to pull a large and very heavy shopping bag across the Turkish rug. "And now for the coup de grâce."

"What is it?"

"Take a peek."

He felt a bit like a kid himself when he did. Inside was the gaming system Brian and Colton had been raving about the night of the ball.

"No way!" Dawson said on a startled laugh. "I know you said you could get this for the boys, but… How on earth did you manage it?"

"Trade secret." She offered a cagey smile. "I can't give you specifics, but I can assure you that no laws were broken."

"The boys are going to love this." He grinned at her. "You're something else."

Eve focused her attention back on the bag. "I also picked up a few age-appropriate games to go with it that I think they will enjoy."

Of course she had. The woman was nothing if not thorough. "You think of everything."

"It's my job," she said lightly. "Besides, after the chemistry set fiasco I felt you needed to really go all out to reestablish yourself as a 'cool' uncle."

He rubbed the back of his neck and offered a sheepish, "Thanks."

Though he'd known it all along, it hit him suddenly that he wouldn't be there to watch the boys open this gift. He wouldn't be there to see any of his family members open their gifts. Just as he hadn't been at his parents' house on Christmas Day last year or the year before or…

As if she'd read his mind, Eve said, "It's a shame you won't be in town to see the boys tear into this. They're going to be so excited."

While his family gathered around a decorated Douglas fir tree, joking, laughing and exchanging presents, he would be alone in Cabo, as far away from snow and holiday merriment as he could possibly manage. Dawson pictured himself sitting poolside at the condo he'd rented, a tall glass of something chilled and fortified in one hand to help blot out the memories.

Eve was watching him, apparently waiting for him to say something in response. He gave a negligent shrug. "I'll catch up with them after the holidays."

"Okay. Terrific." She nodded. He didn't trust her easy agreement and for good reason. "You can see them at a Sunday dinner at your parents' house."

"Eve—"

She cut him off by slapping her knee in exaggerated fashion. "Oh, wait, I forgot. You don't go to Sunday dinners at your parents' house any longer."

"Are you trying to make me feel bad?" he asked tightly. "I can assure you, there's no need. I already do."

Instead of apologizing, Eve said, "Good, then you understand exactly how your loved ones feel when you shut them out and stand them up not just on the holidays but on a regular basis throughout the year."

On an oath, he launched to his feet. Irritation and guilt blended together, proving to be a volatile mix. "Didn't your mother ever tell you that it's not polite to poke around in people's private affairs?" he snapped.

"No. She didn't." Eve stood as well. "My mother died of a drug overdose when I was eight."

He blanched. "God. I…I'm sorry."

"No." She kneaded her forehead. "I'm sorry. I played that like a damned trump card and it was a lousy thing to do. But I'm not sorry for poking around in your private affairs, as you put it."

"Why does this matter to you?" he demanded.

"Because…because it…" Her next words nipped his anger in the bud. "Because *you* matter to me, Dawson. Okay? You matter."

"Eve." He closed his eyes and shook his head,

unable or unwilling to process the emotions her words evoked. Or maybe he was just too afraid. After all, it was hard to cling tightly to the past when a part of him wanted to start reaching for the future.

"I probably shouldn't tell you that," she said quietly. He opened his eyes in time to watch her swallow and cross her arms over her chest. The move struck him as defensive rather than defiant, especially when she added, "Unfortunately, I have a very bad habit of leading with my heart where men are concerned. Just don't let it go to your head."

"I don't know what to say," he replied, though the truth was that Eve mattered to him, too. Indeed, in a very short period of time, she'd managed to thoroughly shake up the status quo of Dawson's otherwise rigidly ordered life. He still wasn't sure he liked it.

"Don't say anything. I prefer to do all the talking anyway." She pushed the hair back from her face and expelled a deep breath. "As my bombshell of a moment ago should make perfectly clear to you, I don't come from the kind of family you do. After my mother died, my father took off and I was shuttled around from one relative to another, all of whom made it plain that they disapproved of my dad, had been disappointed in my mother and didn't have very high hopes that I'd amount to much."

"Aw, Eve."

"Don't feel sorry for me. That's not the purpose

behind my words. You're lucky, Dawson. Very lucky to have people who care about you and who want to remain close."

"I'm sorry."

"Don't be sorry for me. I've accepted my family for what it is and my father for what he isn't. He's let grief and regrets rule and ruin his life. I don't want to see you make the same mistake." She blinked a couple of times in rapid succession and managed a smile. "Okay, that's all I'm going to say on either subject."

Dawson didn't quite believe her. But before he could think of anything to say in response, Ingrid arrived in the doorway.

"Dinner is ready, Mr. Burke."

Dawson's formal dining room sported vaulted ceilings, a crystal chandelier and an oval cherry table that could comfortably accommodate a dozen guests. A gas fireplace and glowing candle centerpiece made the large room cozy. But it was the framed family portrait hanging over the mantel that made it personal.

Eve had never seen photographs of Dawson's late wife and daughter, but even if he hadn't been included in the shot, she would have known who the other two people were. In an odd way, she recognized them, even if she did not recognize the happy, relaxed man who was seated with them.

As Ingrid set out serving dishes heaped with enough steaming food to serve a small army, Eve discreetly studied the photograph. Sheila was blond-haired and blue-eyed with the delicate beauty of a porcelain doll. Isabelle was lovely, too. Eve glimpsed mischief in the little girl's light eyes and a hint of her father's stubbornness in her small jaw. She'd expected them to be beautiful and they were. But what truly surprised Eve was the odd connection she felt to Dawson's loved ones and the disappointment that they would never meet.

The dinner conversation started out stilted and strained thanks to the emotionally charged discussion that had preceded it. She blamed herself for that. What had she been thinking, provoking the man and then essentially baring her soul to him?

No matter, the deed was done and she wouldn't waste her time or energy regretting it now. Besides, she'd only spoken the truth. Dawson *did* matter to her. Eve hadn't realized how much until the words had tumbled out.

Oh, well. She was who she was…though it seemed she never learned. No, she picked up stakes and started over, but she never learned.

She was fussing with her napkin when Dawson asked, "Would you care for some wine?"

Eve pushed her glass closer to his side of the table. "Yes, but just a little, please."

Once he'd poured the chilled pinot grigio, dinner

became a far more relaxed affair. It had nothing to do with the loosening effects of alcohol, but the fact that Dawson spilled his wine down the front of his shirt when he went to take a sip.

It was an accident, of that Eve was sure. He wasn't the sort of man given to slapstick comedy, though he had loosened up considerably since their first meeting. Had that been a mere two weeks ago?

"I can't believe I did that." He dabbed at his shirt front with his napkin. "I'm rarely so clumsy."

"It's my fault," Eve said.

He stopped wiping and glanced over at her. "How do you figure that?"

Face straight, she replied, "It's the effect I have on men. They become blundering fools in my presence."

Dawson snorted. And though he was smiling, he sounded somewhat serious when he replied, "You certainly do have an effect on me, Eve."

Half an hour later, Eve pushed back from the table on a contented sigh. "I probably should have passed on that second helping of pork tenderloin, but it was too good."

"Irresistible," he agreed as he watched Eve dab her mouth with a linen napkin.

Heat curled inside her at the suggestive remark. Just over his right shoulder, Sheila and Isabelle smiled down at Eve from the portrait, dousing any flames before they could start. Just as well, she decided. Just as well.

During the meal, while they'd talked companionably, steering clear of weighty or emotionally complicated topics, the candles on the table had burned low and the sun had set outside. Though Eve had planned to leave as soon as good manners would allow once they'd finished eating, she glanced out the window and reevaluated.

"Let's go for a walk, work off some of these calories," she suggested instead.

"A walk? It's snowing," he said.

"Yes, I hear it does that in Denver. No need to worry. I won't melt." Her eyebrows arched. "Or are you afraid that you will?"

"It's getting dark, Eve."

Dawson's home was surrounded by a private, almost parklike setting with mature trees and meandering paths. "The landscape lighting looks adequate for a leisurely stroll."

"The paths haven't been shoveled recently. A good three inches have fallen since the grounds crew went through last."

She batted that excuse aside, too. "That's all right. I've got boots."

Of course, the boots in question were unlined and made of supple Italian leather with three-inch heels that hardly made them suitable for a hike—or even a stroll—in inclement weather, but she was willing to take her chances.

"I don't know."

Like a veteran poker player, Eve upped the ante. "I promise to protect you."

But it was Dawson who called. "Maybe I'm not the one who needs protecting."

"Is that a threat?" she inquired.

He set aside his napkin and pushed back from the table. Gaze direct and challenging, he said, "There's only one way to find out. Are you still game?"

"Please." She snorted. "That question is insulting. I've never backed down from a challenge."

"I didn't think you had." One side of his mouth lifted, tugging her pulse rate right along with it. "I'll just get our coats."

Outside, the air was crisp. It stole Eve's breath, making her glad for the scarf that she'd wound around her neck. She tucked her chin into it now.

"It's lovely here," she commented. And it was. Winter had wrought its magic, covering everything in a pristine layer of white that sparkled like diamonds in the moonlight.

"The grounds were what attracted me to this property in the first place," Dawson admitted.

"I can see why."

"If you think it's lovely now, you should see it in the spring or summer. The flowerbeds are incredible."

"I wouldn't have taken you for a green thumb."

"Oh, it's black, believe me. I know my limits, which is why I hired the services of a professional."

She chuckled. "The economy loves people who know their limits since it helps create all sorts of job opportunities."

"Like professional shoppers?"

"Exactly."

"Well, I'm glad to do my part for my country." His voice grew soft. "I haven't walked out here in the winter in…a long time."

Eve figured she knew exactly how long, so she remained silent.

After a moment, he added, "I used to love the winter. I looked forward to the first snowfall."

"Me, too." She scuffed her foot along the walkway, ruffling the blanket of white, before bending down to scoop up a handful. "Snow made everything seem so clean, so perfect," she said as she compacted the snow into a ball.

"And your life wasn't perfect."

"No. But whose is?" She shrugged off the melancholy of childhood memories and changed the subject. "You know, this is really good packing snow."

"So I see. Are you thinking of making a snowman or something?"

"Or something." When she smiled his eyes narrowed.

"You wouldn't."

"Wouldn't what?" she asked innocently.

He backed up a couple of steps. "You wouldn't throw that thing at me."

"And if I do?"

He folded his arms. "You do and you'll be asking for trouble."

"Dawson, Dawson," Eve said, shaking her head. "What did I tell you about me and challenges?"

"That you never back—" The snowball hit him in the chest before he could finish. He gaped at her. "I can't believe you just did that."

Eve bent down and scooped up a second handful. "Then this is going to come as a complete shock," she said, tossing the snow right into his face.

Her laughter followed the ball's flight path, but her mirth was short-lived. Dawson didn't even pause to wipe it off before he launched himself in her direction. She feinted right to avoid him and managed to get a full ten feet up the path before he caught up with her, grabbing her around her waist. Eve skidded on the walk, betrayed by her boots. Both she and Dawson wound up going down. Snow cushioned her fall. Snow and man. Somehow she wound up partway on top of him.

"Are you okay?" he asked.

"I think I broke my heel."

"Are you in pain?"

She laughed as she clarified, "The heel of my boot. It got caught on something. What are you doing, anyway? We were supposed to be having a snowball fight."

"We still are." And with that he brought up his

snow-filled hand and rubbed it over her cheek. It wasn't only the cold that had her shivering. Dawson had shifted so that he was now mostly on top of her.

"You know, when I was a kid I didn't believe in taking any prisoners. But I've decided to make an exception in your case. You're too pretty to annihilate."

"So, I'm your prisoner."

"Yes."

"Hmm." She pulled a considering face. "I guess this isn't so bad."

"That's because the torture hasn't begun yet." His gaze was on her lips.

"Torture?" she repeated in a husky voice she barely recognized as her own. "What kind of torture?"

"This," he whispered just before his mouth met hers.

CHAPTER TEN

DAWSON could think of a million reasons why he should stop the kiss before it progressed any further. First among them was the fact that he and Eve were outside lying on the snow-covered ground. She apparently didn't mind. When he started to pull away, she wrapped her arms around his neck and held him in place, taking where a moment ago she'd been the one giving.

Her arms weren't the only thing wrapped around him. Her legs were, too. One was hooked over his calf, the other angled over his thigh, anchoring him in place. Their bodies fit together perfectly. He could tell that despite the layers of their clothes, and it fueled both his imagination and his desire.

It had been a long time—a very long time— since he'd lain atop of woman. His body had no trouble remembering the pleasure. Need surged through him with tsunami force, shredding his control until it hung by a thread. Though Dawson knew he was playing with fire, he rocked forward slightly anyway.

Eve moaned.

He did it again.

This time they both moaned, and that last frayed thread of his control snapped. It was only when Eve's icy hands moved beneath jacket and sweater and came into contact with the bare skin just above the waistband of his jeans that reality came slamming back.

"This is insane," he said as he came up for air.

There didn't seem to be enough of it, especially when he glanced down at Eve. She was still lying in the snow, dark hair fanning out around her head. In the moonlight her eyes glowed with an arousing mix of awareness and humor.

"Absolutely insane," she agreed on a chuckle. "My butt is numb."

Parts of Dawson had lost all feeling, too. Unfortunately, his back wasn't one of them. He discovered this when he levered away from Eve and rolled to one side. Long into the night, and in more ways than one, he would be paying for this spontaneous and very sensual tussle.

Grimacing as he rose, he reached down to help Eve to her feet.

"Are you okay?" she asked.

"I will be." After a couple or four painkillers. He'd also be calling Wanda for a therapeutic massage first thing in the morning.

They entered the house through the French doors that led from the patio directly into the kitchen. Dawson always hated entering the house in the evening when his staff had gone home. The place was so quiet and seemed so…lifeless. Eve chased away the gloom by stamping her feet and giving her damp hair a toss.

"Ingrid has gone home for the night, but I can make some coffee or a cup of tea, if you'd like."

"Your housekeeper doesn't live here?"

"No."

"What about your driver?" she asked.

"His rooms are over the garage."

"And that masseuse I saw the first day?" she asked as she removed her scarf and unzipped her jacket.

He chuckled ruefully. "At the moment I wish she lived here, but no. I prefer my privacy."

"Nothing wrong with privacy," she agreed. After tucking her scarf into the sleeve of her jacket, she draped it around the back of one chair. "Do you have any hot chocolate?"

"I…don't know. Possibly."

"I'd prefer that to tea or coffee if you have it. Chocolate in any form trumps all else," she said.

"My sister has made the same claim."

"Ooh, and little marshmallows. I love those little marshmallows."

"I can't make any promises, but I'll do my best to accommodate your request. In the meantime, we probably should get out of these wet clothes."

"Hmm." She tapped her lips with an index finger.

"What?" he asked as he put his coat on the back of another chair.

"I'm trying to decide if you're being chivalrous with that suggestion or merely clever," Eve said.

He smiled. "A man can be both."

"Okay, you can prove that by helping me out of these boots. The leather is wet and they feel like they've become a second skin." She took a seat and smiled up at him, managing to look prim and provocative at the same time.

He knelt because it was warranted and pushed up the damp hem of one pant leg so he could find the zipper on the side of the boot. The leather was high quality and soaked. He had a bad feeling her boots might be ruined.

"These aren't exactly practical footwear for Denver winters," he said.

"No, but they're sexy as hell."

She had a point. It took a little effort, but Dawson managed to free the boot from her foot. Though she hadn't asked him to, he peeled off the damp stocking beneath it, revealing a set of chilly pink toes whose nails were painted fire-engine-red. He rubbed the foot between his hands, chafing some warmth into it and hoping to cool down his libido in the process. Since his first days of dating, he'd had a thing for red toenails on members of the opposite sex. He wasn't sure why. Something about them screamed sexy.

That was especially true in the winter when no one else was likely to see them. It made this glimpse more intimate and almost like a secret.

He groaned.

"Is your back giving you trouble?" Eve asked, sounding concerned. "I wasn't thinking when I asked you to help me. Sorry. I can probably do this myself."

"Oh, no." He moved on to the other foot. "I'm fine."

Dawson was one hundred and eighty degrees the opposite of fine, but he didn't want to deny himself a single second of this sweet torture. So he performed the same ministrations on the second foot as he had on the first. And, even though he knew the nails on its toes would be painted red also, he felt a potent kick of lust upon seeing them.

Afterward, he put her boots over a heat vent on the floor and straightened. "I have a robe you can put on while your clothes are in the dryer."

"Not offering to help me off with those, too?" she asked, arching a brow.

"Would you return the favor?"

She gave him a considering look, but said nothing.

Sweeping his arm, he said, "Right this way."

Eve followed him down the hall, past the formal dining room, great room and study. She'd seen some of the rooms earlier today and on a previous visit, but she couldn't help but be curious about the rest of the house. People's homes said a lot about them.

Dawson's told of a fondness for fine things. All of the rooms were large and lushly appointed. She wouldn't call the furnishings fussy or ornate, but they definitely were of the highest quality.

The bedrooms were located on the second floor, up a staircase that curved dramatically around the two-story foyer. Her nerves were humming along on high by the time they reached the master suite.

To one side of the room was a fireplace with its own cozy sitting area. She chose to concentrate on it rather than the king-sized bed. With the touch of a couple buttons, flames shot to life and soft lighting illuminated the room's periphery.

"I think your bedroom is bigger than my entire apartment," Eve remarked as Dawson disappeared into a large, walk-in closet. He emerged a moment later with a sumptuous terry cloth robe in one hand and a fresh change of clothes for himself in the other.

"Here you go," he said, handing her the robe. "You can change in here. The bathroom is right through that door." He backed up a step, looking endearingly flustered when he added, "I'll just…uh…use one of the rooms down the hall."

"Shall I meet you downstairs afterward?"

"Sure. I'll start the cocoa."

"Don't forget the marshmallows," she called as he was closing the door.

Alone, she made fast work of changing her clothes. She was shivering now, gooseflesh puckering her skin. Cold was the culprit rather than pent-up need. Still she wanted to blush when she recalled the wanton way she'd clung to him out in the snow. She hadn't wanted to let go, knowing that once she did he would retreat again to that isolated prison he'd constructed out of guilt and grief. He hadn't withdrawn completely, though his emotions were once again firmly in control.

The robe was too big. No surprise there, but the fact that it smelled like him had her insides curling. Eve turned up the sleeves and cinched the belt as tightly as she could, knotting it just to be on the safe side before gathering up her damp garments and returning downstairs. She found Dawson in the kitchen, standing in front of the six-burner gas stove. He was stirring a pan of milk. He glanced up at her arrival.

She felt suddenly shy. "Hi."

He was dressed in jeans and a chamois-cloth shirt, which he'd left untucked. It was the most casual she'd ever seen him, and by far the most domestic. The wealthy and resourceful Dawson Burke was heating milk to make hot cocoa.

"Hi." His gaze meandered down to her bare feet and she saw him swallow before he looked away. "I should have thought to give you a pair of socks."

"I'll be fine, especially if I can prop my feet in front of a fireplace. There doesn't seem to be any shortage of those in this house."

"No. It has four. All of them gas." He motioned

for her to come closer. "Here. Why don't you take over stirring while I throw your things in the dryer?"

"Are you sure you know how to operate one of those?" she asked dryly.

"I think I can figure it out." Tongue in cheek, he added, "Of course, that's assuming I can remember where the laundry room is."

On a chuckle, she handed over her jeans and socks. "Only the back hem of my sweater was damp and since it's cashmere, I left it to dry in front of the fireplace in your room along with some of the, um, more delicate items."

His Adam's apple bobbed a second time. "Okay."

When he continued to stand rooted in place staring at her, Eve added, "The regular setting on the dryer is fine for those."

Dawson cleared his throat. "Regular setting. Right."

When the cocoa was ready they moved to the sitting room where Eve had sipped tea on her first visit to Dawson's home. After he started the fire, she lowered herself to the rug just in front of the hearth. Making every effort to preserve her modesty, she put her feet as close to the flames as possible.

"Mmm," she said on a sigh. "This feels wonderful." Dawson was still standing. Eve glanced up at him. "Aren't you going to sit down?"

"I was planning on using a chair."

"Why would you do that when there's a perfectly good patch of floor right here?"

She patted said patch of floor. Her smile turned the benign gesture into a dare. Grabbing a couple of throw pillows off the sofa, Dawson joined her. Eve wasn't the only one who refused to back down from a challenge.

"So, how's the cocoa?" he asked.

"Good." She sipped it as if to back up her pronouncement, leaving a fine layer of froth on her upper lip, which she then licked off.

He resisted the urge to groan, but not the urge to touch her. "You've still got a little…" He traced her top lip with the tip of his index finger.

"All gone?" she asked.

"I think so." Still staring at her mouth, he said, "Sorry that I couldn't find any of those little marshmallows to go in it."

"That's all right." Her lips curved. "It was a tall order. You don't strike me as the sort of man who drinks hot chocolate with little marshmallows."

He shook his head. "Not often, no."

"Of course, you didn't strike me as the sort who would tackle me in the snow, either."

"I didn't tackle you. I tried to break your fall," he said.

"Yes, but I only fell because you chased me."

"I only chased you because you threw a snowball at me. Two, in fact," he reminded her. "And I did give you fair warning before you fired a second time."

She took another sip of her hot cocoa and gave

him a considering look. "Okay. I'll give you that. Of course, I'm going to want a rematch. And the next time I can promise you I won't be wearing a pair of high-heeled boots that are far more suited to fashion than they are to function."

"Too bad. I really like those boots." He tortured himself with a glance at her bare feet.

"I loved them." Her lips pursed. "They're probably ruined now."

"I'll buy you another pair," he offered magnanimously.

"That's nice of you, but no need. It was my own fault."

"Agreed," Dawson said and enjoyed watching her scowl. "So, what will you wear for our rematch?"

"A pair of waterproof hikers and my ski bibs and down parka."

"You ski?" he asked, marginally surprised.

"Not really, but I look absolutely amazing in the outfit. Like something out of a magazine." She winked.

Dawson didn't laugh, though she'd obviously intended the words as a joke. "I don't doubt it. I'm beginning to think you'd look amazing in just about anything."

He allowed his gaze to skim over the curves that were partially obscured by thick folds of terrycloth.

"I…I…hmm."

He rather liked knowing that he'd made Eve tongue-tied since the woman had had that effect on him more than once in the past couple of weeks. Though he knew he was playing with fire, he said, "I like what you have on at the moment."

She coughed and recovered enough to joke, "What? This old thing?"

"You know, I never really cared for that robe… until now." He knew he'd never put it on again without thinking of Eve and remembering just how provocative she looked with firelight and curiosity reflected in her eyes.

"I'll take that as a compliment."

He set aside his mug. She followed suit.

"You should," he said.

The space between them diminished fractionally with each breath they took until their faces were mere inches apart. He smelled chocolate, was eager to taste it, but he knew that wasn't the reason he suddenly felt so starved.

"Your hair is still damp," he murmured, reaching up to run his fingers through the loose tumble of curls.

"Dawson." Eve sighed his name and closed her eyes, and just that fast he knew he was doomed. But as he followed her down onto the fire-warmed rug, it felt far more like a resurrection than it did an execution.

He started at her neck, nibbling the spot just below her jaw where he could feel her pulse beating.

Life. It was right there under his lips, inviting him, enticing him.

And so he moved lower, alternately kissing and

nipping his way down to the curve of her shoulder. Her skin was soft and as smooth as satin. When he pushed the robe off her shoulder, it all but glowed in the firelight.

He glanced up to find Eve watching him. Her expression was serious. Her dark eyes were wide and still filled with questions. Dawson wasn't sure he could give her any of the answers she sought. Come right down to it, he had plenty of questions himself.

He started with the most pressing.

"Are you sure?" he whispered.

She paused a moment, an eternity. When she finally nodded, he stood and helped her to her feet. They didn't speak a word as, hands clasped, he led her through the quiet house back upstairs to his bedroom.

CHAPTER ELEVEN

Eve woke to blaring rock music and a man's heavy arm draped possessively over her waist.

She smiled at the ceiling. Life was good.

The electric guitar was gearing up for its solo before Dawson finally stirred. He reached out a hand to swat off the alarm clock that sat on the bedside table. The only problem was that Eve was in the way. His eyes opened as he realized this. His gaze was bleary at first and then clouded with what she recognized as lust.

Oh, yeah. Life was good.

She stroked his scratchy face, reveling in its distinctive masculine feel. "Good morning."

"That remains to be seen."

"Oh?"

He rolled on top of her and murmured something into her hair that she couldn't quite decipher. Not that it really mattered. Words weren't necessary at that moment. Eve understood Dawson's meaning perfectly.

An hour later, they were both out of bed, showered

and dressed. Her clothes had dried. Her leather boots definitely were worse for the wear, but then she'd expected that. Thankfully, Dawson had found a new toothbrush for her in his linen closet, and Eve kept some makeup essentials in her purse. Without the taming effect of a flat iron, her hair had gone curly, but there was no help for that. She brushed it back as best she could and secured it in a ponytail. Satisfied that she looked presentable, Eve ambled downstairs.

It was Saturday, which meant Dawson's house-keeper had the day off. Eve was grateful for that. The last thing she wanted to do was run in to the older woman while wearing the same outfit she'd had on the evening before. She wasn't old-fashioned exactly, but neither was she one to advertise her private life.

She planned to just grab a cup of coffee and be on her way. It might be the weekend, but she had a busy day of shopping ahead of her. She found Dawson in the kitchen, looking every bit as sexy as he had when he'd smiled at her first thing that morning. With minimal effort and very few words, he talked her into staying for breakfast.

He stood in front of the six-burner gas cooktop like a captain standing at the helm of a ship. Glancing at the array of ingredients and utensils spread out on the counter around him, she asked baldly, "Can you actually cook?"

He looked insulted. "I went away to college. I lived in a fraternity house with nine guys."

"So we're having pizza and beer for breakfast?" she asked dryly.

"I can manage an omelet."

"Sorry. I don't know what I was thinking, questioning your culinary abilities. I mean, you did whip up that hot cocoa last night."

"Smart aleck." He motioned toward one of the stools on the opposite side of the granite-topped island. "Go sit down before I rescind the invitation."

"Right." After a two-fingered salute, she did as instructed.

Dawson was surprisingly efficient in the kitchen for a man who was used to having others wait on him. He mastered the eggs, though the toast wound up burned. The coffee was fine, excellent in fact. But Eve suspected that out of all of the appliances in his state-of-the-art kitchen that one was probably the one he operated on his own most frequently.

She ate the eggs, passed on the toast and asked for a second cup of the freshly ground French roast.

Sunshine streamed in through the tall window over the sink, making the room glisten. "I've got to tell you. This is a wonderful room, a chef's dream," she said. "My entire kitchen would fit in your sub-zero refrigerator."

"Can you cook?" he asked.

She couldn't help but laugh as he handed back her earlier insult.

"Yes. I can cook. I went away to college, too." Between student loans and scholarships, she'd managed four years at a state university. "And I get to practice on a regular basis. Unlike you, I can't quite afford to hire out the job during the week, although I do have a pretty close relationship with a Chinese restaurant a block up the street from my apartment. They're the first number programmed into my cell phone and I've got them on speed dial at home, too." She grinned.

"I think I'm insulted."

"Don't be. It goes without saying that after last night you've moved up considerably," she assured him, leaning over to peck his cheek.

Dawson cleared his throat. In the brief amount of time that took, his expression shuttered. Eve knew what he was about to say even before he began speaking. Her sudden clairvoyance, however, did little to blunt the impact.

"About last night, Eve. I hope that you…I mean, I hope that you understand I'm not…I'm not ready for something serious right now," he said. "I may never be."

"Define serious."

"You know what I mean."

"Apparently I don't." She pushed her plate aside and folded her arms over her chest. Beneath them, she swore her heart felt bruised. "Why don't you enlighten me?"

"Eve, I like you. I like you a lot. But I can't…I

can't…" He shoved a hand through his hair and expelled a frustrated breath.

"Actually, you can and you did. Very well, I might add. Twice last night and then again this morning."

She'd hoped for a smile, but he was dead serious when he replied, "I'm not talking about physically."

No. Of course he wasn't. "Which leaves emotionally," she said.

He nodded and she felt her heart start to break. For the first time since they'd made love, she wondered if she'd made a huge mistake. To think just an hour ago she'd awakened with a smile and thought her life grand.

Because far more than her pride was stinging at the moment, she told him, "I don't believe I mentioned expecting to march down a church aisle wearing white anytime soon."

"No. But I need to be sure that you understand where I'm coming from."

She swallowed, raised her chin. "I believe I do. You're saying that our relationship is only temporary."

"*Temporary* is not the word I would have chosen," he said quietly.

"Semantics aside, it's what you mean."

Dawson looked miserable. He looked remorseful. But he didn't contradict her.

Not good enough. The phrase echoed in her head, taunting her. It seemed to be the motto for her life, the tagline that summed it up. She hadn't been good enough for her ex-boyfriend's pedigreed family. And now she wasn't good enough to compete with Dawson's memories of his late wife and the previous life he'd enjoyed as a husband and father.

"I'm sorry, Eve."

Far from being appreciated, the apology only made matters worse for her. Around the lump in her throat she said, "Now I want to be sure that you understand something. I'm not the sort of woman who just hops into bed on a whim."

"I know that—"

"No." She slashed a hand through the air to silence him. "This obviously needs to be said. When I'm with a man, I'm not just marking time until something better comes along."

"I'm not marking time, Eve. I promise you that."

She nodded again. "Also, when I'm in a relationship I'm exclusive and I expect the same in return. Nothing about me is casual, Dawson, if you follow my meaning."

"I do."

"I stayed here with you last night because being with you *meant* something to me." When her eyes filled with tears, she hated herself for the weakness they represented, the futility, but she blinked them away and pressed on. She would have her say now. A good cry could wait until later. "I stayed here because *you* mean something to me."

He reached over and stroked her cheek with the

back of his hand. "God, I know that. I'd know that even if you hadn't said as much."

"I'm not expecting a marriage proposal." She'd learned her lesson about such expectations after her long-term relationship with Drew. "But I am expecting you to be honest with me and monogamous for as long…for as long as this lasts."

Her anger and outrage were spent. She wished them back, because insecurity began filling the void.

"You have both," he promised. Then, "And for the record, I'm not the casual sort, either."

She nodded and pushed back the stool so she could stand. Gathering up what remained of her pride, she forced a smile to her lips. "Well. Thank you for breakfast and dinner last night."

"You're leaving right now?"

"I need to be going." *Before I make a bigger fool of myself.*

"Eve." Dawson put a hand on her arm to stop her as she turned away. There really was no need, as his next words rooted her in place. "Since my wife died you're…you're the first woman I've been with. You're the first woman I've even wanted to be with."

She closed her eyes and tried to steel her heart. But how could she not tumble a little further into love with the man after such a soul-baring admission?

"Oh, Dawson." She framed his face in her hands, kissed him tenderly. "Thanks for telling me that."

"You're special to me," he whispered. "Please don't doubt that."

"Okay." Inside her head, a small voice whispered, *Am I special enough to make you let go of the past and start thinking about the future?* She ignored it, stepped back and straightened the hem of her sweater. "I really do need to be going."

"Work?" he inquired.

"Yes."

"It's Saturday."

"I know. There's a great sale at Macy's that started an hour ago. I try to save my clients money whenever I can, but at this point I've probably already missed out on most of the best deals."

Half his mouth lifted in a smile. "Then I suppose I should thank you for staying as long as you have."

She kissed him a second time and, despite the questions and doubts swirling in her head, Eve meant it when she said, "It was my pleasure."

The house seemed especially quiet after Eve left and empty in a way it hadn't felt as long as she'd been in it. Dawson felt empty, too. This emptiness was different than how he'd felt for the past three years and, oddly, less easy to accept. Perhaps because he didn't have to. He had a choice. He wasn't sure he wanted to have a choice.

Restless, he spent the next few hours wandering from room to room. Reminders of Sheila and Isabelle were everywhere in the house. Isabelle had taken her first steps in the great room. She'd earned her first major time-out in there too after she'd taken a crayon to the wallpaper.

Sheila had used their budding Picasso's artwork as justification for redoing the entire room. As he had throughout the house, Dawson had given his late wife free rein. So it was no surprise that everything reflected her appreciation for muted hues and soft fabrics. He'd never had a problem with the décor, but perhaps it was time for a change. He recalled the bold color choices in Eve's loft apartment. Maybe something along those lines.

Especially in the bedroom.

He stood at the side of the bed. Eve had straightened the covers. He picked up one of the pillows and brought it to his face. He swore he could smell her perfume. It haunted him. *She* haunted him. The woman was on his mind, under his skin. That was especially true now that he'd made love to her.

He sank down on the side of the bed with a groan, recalling how soft her skin had felt, how responsive she'd been to his touch, how smug her smile had been when she'd curled up against his side afterward.

Dawson had worried that he would regret making love to her. Not the actual act, but the fulfillment and sense of completion it brought. Surprisingly, he hadn't. He'd meant it when he'd told her that he'd been intimate with no one since the accident. Guilt had always managed to quell any arousal. But he hadn't felt guilty with Eve. In fact, even when he'd wakened with her beside him in the very bed he'd shared with his late wife, he hadn't felt guilty. He'd felt happy and optimistic and eager to not only start the day, but to end it…with Eve.

For the first time in three long years, Dawson had felt truly alive.

That was what had finally stoked his guilt.

Of course, he'd botched things horribly when he'd tried to keep Eve from reading too much into their lovemaking. *Temporary.* Was that really what he wanted it to be?

Even now he could see her happy expression cloud over, though she'd managed to rally admirably. She wasn't the sort to stay down for long. Or more likely she wasn't the sort to let someone see her down.

He'd hurt her. Of all his regrets, that was by far the biggest.

By midafternoon, he couldn't stand being alone in his house any longer. He considered going to his office at Burke Financial. He'd spent more than one Saturday tucked behind his desk browsing through spreadsheets and tracking market trends. But burying himself in work held no appeal today. Another option did. Before he could change his mind, he called for his driver.

"Where to?" Jonas asked as the limo idled in the drive.

"I'm not sure. Know a store where I can get a nice pair of women's boots?"

It was nearly six o'clock and Eve had just come in from shopping when the bell chimed. She expected to find a deliveryman at her door. She shopped online for hard-to-find items, so packages were arriving daily. When she opened the door, however, it was Dawson who stood on the other side. He looked tired and a little lost.

"Hi."

"Hi."

"I wasn't expecting you," she said.

"I know. Sorry. I probably should have called. I won't stay long. I just came to drop this off."

He held out the package that had been tucked under his arm. The rectangular box was wrapped in festive paper, though the print wasn't holiday-themed. The top sported a large and equally festive-looking bow, although at the moment it was slightly crushed.

"What is it?" she asked.

"You'll have to open it to find out."

"It's for me?" She blinked. For a moment she'd thought, hoped, that Dawson had decided to do a little of his Christmas shopping himself. The notion had pleased her, even if it would cut into her commission, but a gift for her? She wasn't sure how she felt about that given the perplexing nature of their relationship.

Dawson nodded. "Your name is on the tag. Unless

I've got the wrong Eve Hawley." He started to pull the package away.

"Oh, no. You've got the right one. And I happen to love surprises." She shook the package and then grinned because she couldn't stop the smile from curving her lips. "Come in," she invited, remembering her manners.

Though she was dying to open it right then and there, she set the gift aside to take Dawson's jacket and hang it up. Then she picked up the box and without another word shredded the paper. She recognized the logo and was laughing even before she lifted the top.

"You bought me boots."

"I said I would. I'm a man of my word," Dawson said.

"I can't believe you remembered the brand and style." She checked the side of the box then and chuckled in amazement. "And my size."

"You're not the only one who's good with details." But then Dawson cleared his throat and admitted, "Actually, I got lucky on the size."

"Well, thank you." She leaned over and kissed him on the cheek.

"You're welcome."

He didn't move, but Eve did. She set the boots aside and gave in to temptation. By the time this kiss ended she was backed up against the closed door with one leg hooked around his hips.

"Well…" he said.

"Uh-huh."

"I…"

"Me, too."

"We're not talking in full sentences," he said on a laugh.

"We are now. So, is Jonas downstairs?"

He glanced at his watch. "For another three minutes. I told him if I didn't return in fifteen he could leave and I'd call him when I needed him to come back."

"Hedging your bets?" she asked on a chuckle.

"I wasn't sure you'd be home or, for that matter, that you'd want to see me."

"So, if you leave right now, you'll still have a ride?"

He nodded. "Well, unless the elevator stops at every floor on the way down. Then Jonas might be gone by the time I reached the curb. Think I should chance it?"

"That elevator is notoriously slow. Just to be on the safe side, I think you should stay." When the corners of her mouth lifted in a smile, his followed suit.

By the time their second kiss ended, both of her legs were wrapped around his waist.

"Loft?" he asked on a labored breath.

"Couch. It's closer."

"Much," he agreed.

Neither one of them wasted time with words after that.

An hour later, as the lamp on the table clicked on thanks to an automatic timer, Eve roused beside him on the couch and stood, covering herself with a chenille throw. She looked uncertain. He knew how she felt.

"I wasn't planning that when I came here today," he said quietly.

"I know." The uncertainty vanished as she smiled. "That's what makes it special."

He smiled in return. "Yeah."

"I suppose I should play the hostess and ask if you'd like something to drink."

He felt chilled now that she wasn't beside him on the couch. "You wouldn't happen to have hot cocoa with little marshmallows? For some reason I have a real craving for that."

"No, sorry. No marshmallows." She huffed out a breath. "No milk for that matter. I haven't made it to the grocery store this week despite my good intentions."

He sat up and reached for his clothes, which were scattered about on the floor with hers. "You're a personal shopper, Eve."

She lifted her shoulders in a shrug. "And the cobbler's children have no shoes."

"Right." He laughed. "I won't ask how you're coming on your own Christmas shopping."

"Good, because I haven't started it. Luckily I don't have much to do."

Dressed, he followed her into the small kitchen, where she uncorked a bottle of wine and poured them each a glass.

"Will you be going back East to spend the holidays with family?" he asked.

"No."

Eve had no reason to make the trip. Her dad was on the road someplace. As for her extended family, even the relatives with whom she had lived as a child had never gone out of their way to make her feel welcomed back into their homes now that she was an adult. Since college she'd spent the holidays with friends or boyfriends. This year, with Carole leaving town to visit a sister in Seattle, Eve had neither.

"What about your father?"

"I got a postcard from him earlier this month. He's playing at a pub in Myrtle Beach through the New Year. He sent me a lovely Laura Ashley–print dress. The pattern is very similar to the wallpaper in your downstairs powder room."

"Floral? You?"

Dawson sounded so incredulous that it made her smile. "Yes. I'm not big on flower prints, but then my father doesn't know me well enough to have figured that out."

"So what will you do?" he asked.

"I could take it back. Whoever he talked into buying it included a gift receipt in the card. More likely, though, I'll donate it to charity." She shrugged. "It's a nice dress, even if it's not my style."

"That's not what I mean, Eve. Where will you go for Christmas?"

"Nowhere. I'll celebrate here. I'm going to put up a tree this week." She glanced toward the living room. "Nothing big, but I want it to be real. I haven't had a real tree in a while. Drew was allergic."

Dawson was frowning. "I guess I just assumed…"

"What? That you were the only one who would be spending Christmas alone?"

"Sorry."

"No, I am. Let's forget that." She raised her glass, inadvertently offering a tantalizing glimpse of flesh beneath the throw. "I saved this Chianti for a special occasion. This is special."

"I think so, too."

Their glasses clinked together before they sipped the wine. Then Dawson said, "Can I talk you into letting me take you out to dinner?"

"Gee, I have some moldy cheddar cheese, half a head of wilted lettuce and some leftover lasagna that could possibly walk out of the refrigerator on its own at this point. If you're offering to take me out to dinner, you won't find me playing hard to get," she assured him on a laugh.

"I'll call my driver. Tell him to give us half an hour."

"We don't need to bother Jonas," she said.

"It's no bother," Dawson objected. "It's what the man is paid to do."

Eve shrugged and reached for her cordless phone. Handing it to him, she said, "Give the poor man the night off then."

"How would I get home?"

"I can take you," she said.

"Oh?" He stepped closer.

"Or not," she added, letting the throw dip low on one shoulder. "I know how you like to make plans, Dawson, but how about we play that one by ear?"

He kissed her bare shoulder. "You know, I'm beginning to like spontaneity."

"I can tell." She sighed before backing up a step and pulling the wrap more securely around her. "I'm starved."

"That's not quite the spontaneity I had in mind."

"I know, but I need to eat. I skipped lunch today. There are a couple of really good restaurants just two blocks over. Or we could go to the market that's on the corner and bring home all of the ingredients for a meal." She smiled. "I could cook for you this time."

"Really?" His lips twitched. "Do you think you can outdo my breakfast, burned toast and all?"

"I'll give it my best shot. My specialty is a pasta dish made with chorizo sausage. It's very good," she promised.

"Sounds like I'll be asking for seconds," he murmured, sipping his wine. His gaze made it clear he wasn't talking about food.

"Asking?" She scoffed. "You'll be begging."

Dawson chuckled. "And what about dessert? Is that included in the meal?"

"Of course. I've got something decadent in mind. I'll

get dressed and we can go." With that she turned and started up the stairs, letting the throw fall as she went.

Dawson stayed the night with Eve and not just because he'd dismissed his driver and it seemed cruel to ask her to drive him home on such a cold night. No. He wanted to remain in her cozy home, in her company. It had nothing to do with sex—as incredible and satisfying as that was—and everything to do with the woman. Eve was like a crackling fire to cold hands, beckoning him to reach out and warm himself.

Parts of him were definitely starting to thaw. The prospect scared the hell out of him because he recognized the feelings that he had for Eve. He'd only felt them for one other woman in his life. And he'd married her.

CHAPTER TWELVE

WHEN Dawson awoke the next morning, the sound-track to *Les Misérables* was playing. He hunted around Eve's bedroom for his shirt, but he couldn't find it. Wearing only his pants, he padded down-stairs. He found her—and his shirt—in the small kitchen. She was wearing the button-down oxford and measuring grounds into the coffeemaker.

"This will be done in a minute," she said over her shoulder.

"No hurry. My shirt looks good on you." He came up behind her, settled his hands on her hips and nuzzled the side of her neck.

"Mmm." Eve issued a throaty sigh. "I live for caf-feine, but I could forgo my morning pot of coffee if I got to wake up to that every day."

He felt her stiffen after she said it and then she turned. "Sorry. I hope that didn't make you uncom-fortable."

"No." It hadn't.

But she was uncomfortable. That was clear when she added, "I don't want you to think we need to go through the whole this-is-temporary discussion again."

"I don't." And he meant it.

The soundtrack came to Fantine's heart-wrenching solo about the life she'd once dreamed of having and the man who'd used and discarded her. It wasn't the ideal song for lightening the mood, but Dawson decided to try to do that by saying, "How about a dance while we wait for our coffee? This time, I'll lead."

"Okay. Show me your moves, John Travolta." She laughed.

Dawson wiped the smile off her face by spinning her out and around.

"Nice," she said once she was back in his arms. "Have you got any others?"

"An entire repertoire."

"Really? Are they all as good as that last one?" She arched one brow.

"Better."

Her dark eyes glittered. "Well, then, by all means. Show me."

None of the moves would have won them any dance competitions, but they were a little fancier than the standard steps.

"Not bad," she said with a dismissive shrug when the song ended. "Maybe I'll let you lead the next time we dance out in public."

"Not bad? What do you think of this?" He levered her backward until her torso was nearly parallel to the kitchen floor. The drama of the move was mitigated by the fact that they'd both begun to laugh.

"I said show me, not show off and put both of our backs out in the process."

Oddly, his back felt perfectly fine. And his shoulders and neck, which were usually tight to the point of going into spasms, were pain-free and almost relaxed.

"Sorry. I couldn't resist doing that," Dawson said as he helped her straighten.

Eve stayed in his arms, her hands flat on his bare chest, her hips flush against his. "What else can't you resist?" she asked.

"I think you know."

"Tell me anyway," she whispered.

"You."

By the time they had both showered and dressed, the morning was spent and the coffeemaker, its pot still full, had shut off. Dawson found Eve sitting on the sofa with one foot perched on the coffee table in front of her. He groaned when he realized what she was doing: painting her toenails.

Red.

"I made a fresh pot of coffee. There's nothing worse than reheated java in my book. The mugs are in the cupboard next to the sink. Help yourself," she told him without sparing him a glance.

When he didn't move, she stopped what she was doing and looked up. "Everything okay?"

"Uh-uh. I've got this thing for red toenails."

Her lips twitched. "On women or is there something you want to tell me?"

"On women in general, but on *you* in particular," he clarified.

"Hmm. Sounds like a fetish."

"I guess you could call it that," he said as he took a seat on the chair opposite the couch.

She pointed the small brush from the polish bottle in his direction. "When we first met, I wouldn't have figured you for the fetish sort."

"Why not?" he asked.

She wrinkled her nose. "Are you kidding? You were much, much too controlling."

"Controlling people can't have fetishes?" he asked, intrigued by her logic.

"Pretty hard to give into your longings when you live by a rigid set of rules."

"You think I'm rigid?"

"No. Not anymore."

"What changed your mind?"

It was a good thing he was sitting down because her answer floored him. "I don't think my mind has changed as much as you've changed. You've loosened up a lot, Dawson."

If that was true, Eve was responsible. And so he told her, "I didn't loosen up, you loosened me. You've been good for me, Eve. A rare and truly unexpected gift."

It was the season for gifts—both getting and giving. But Dawson had long stopped caring about either. Or so he'd thought.

"That's…" Her eyes grew bright. It was a moment before she continued. "That's quite a compliment. I don't know that I deserve it, but thank you."

"You deserve it." He swallowed. "You deserve a hell of a lot more than that."

"So do you, Dawson."

He opened his mouth to disagree, but his standard arguments suddenly seemed worn-out, dated. On the stereo, the persecuted Jean Valjean sang out his name and prisoner number, determined to stop running from the intrepid and intractable Inspector Javert. Eve smiled at him—lovely and oh, so alive. Maybe it was time for Dawson to stop running from his past, too.

Eve drove him home later that afternoon. Halfway to his house, Dawson suddenly changed his mind about their final destination.

"Are you hungry?" he asked.

"Getting there. But I have leftovers from our meal back at my apartment."

"You can't eat that," he told her.

He sounded so resolute that she asked, "Why not?"

"You'll hurt the leftover lasagna's feelings if you do."

"Very funny."

He motioned with his hand. "Take the next exit."

"Where are we going?" she asked.

He compounded the mystery with his cryptic, "You'll see."

Eve followed his directions, turning right on this avenue and left on that one. They wound up in a high-end residential neighborhood where the houses were older and exuded elegance and charm. Almost all of them were decorated for the holidays. In the fading daylight, shimmering bulbs glowed along the eaves and followed the steep peaks of the rooflines.

Dawson told her to stop in front of the one that sported a full-sized manger and Nativity scene in the front yard. She had a good idea where they were even before he told her, "This is where I grew up."

She smiled, and though her throat had grown tight with emotions, she said, "Are you asking me to have Sunday dinner with your family?"

"Yes."

She glanced down at her clothes. "I wish you had said something earlier. For heaven's sake, I'm wearing blue jeans." She shifted in her seat to look in the rearview mirror. "And my hair."

"Is fine. Beautiful," he assured her, reaching out

for her hand when she started to fuss with the curls. "There's no dress code, Eve."

Yes, but outfitted in designer clothes, she would have more confidence. Her gaze cut to the lovely home. It was Tudor-style and even larger than Dawson's. Drew's family had lived in a similarly elegant house. The old vulnerability crept in. "I don't belong here," she whispered.

"Eve?"

She cleared her throat, tried again. "They're not expecting me, Dawson."

"It's a standing invitation," he said.

"For you."

"And for whomever I choose to bring as my guest." He swallowed. "Not that I've ever brought any guests."

And that was exactly why his invitation meant so much to her. Still, she asked, "Are you sure your mother won't mind me tagging along?"

"Not at all. You were at the charity ball. The more the merrier is her motto. Besides, there's always enough food on Sundays to feed a small army." He held out a hand. "So, what do you say, Eve?"

Banishing the last of her doubts, she nodded. "I'd love to."

Dawson's family didn't inspect Eve from a respectable distance this time. They quite literally mobbed her the moment she and Dawson entered the foyer, welcoming him home and welcoming her into their midst with hugs and handshakes, laughter and shouted greetings.

"Christmas came early," Tallulah said as the commotion died down. "I'm so glad you're here and that you brought Eve."

"I am, too," Dawson said. "I am, too."

CHAPTER THIRTEEN

CHRISTMAS Eve was the day after next, but Dawson had not begun to pack for his trip. Usually by this point he had at least worked up a list of summer clothes for Ingrid to wash and press if need be, but he hadn't even done that. He'd been too busy.

With Eve.

They'd spent nearly every evening together since having dinner with his parents. For that matter, they'd also spent nearly every night wrapped in each others arms, warm and worn-out from their lovemaking.

The dawn of a new year was just over a week away, and Dawson felt a sense of anticipation that had been lacking since the accident. And that remained so even with the anniversary of the crash looming like a thundercloud.

That night, he and Eve met Tony and Christine for dinner at the steak restaurant they'd mentioned being keen to try at the auction. The other couple had been surprised when he'd called them earlier in the week to see if they were free. He had the feeling they'd shuffled around their plans to accommodate him. He was glad, grateful.

The four of them chatted amiably through all of the courses. Dawson and Sheila had spent some wonderful evenings in their company. Tonight, the dynamic was different, as was so much of Dawson's life these days. They not only accepted Eve, he could tell they genuinely liked her.

"This was so much fun," Christine said after dinner. "Let's do it again."

"We will," Dawson assured her as he smiled at Eve. "We will."

Eve smiled in return.

Tony and Christine left right after dessert. They had some last-minute shopping to do for their children before heading home to relieve the babysitter. Dawson and Eve stayed for a second cup of coffee.

Eve wished they hadn't, given what happened next. While Dawson retrieved their checked coats, she waited to one side of the lobby. He was on his way to join her when he was stopped by a petite blond woman.

"Dawson!" The beautiful young woman threw her arms around him and then smiled up at him as if he'd hung the moon.

"Natasha, hello." He looked startled. Beyond that, Eve had a hard time gauging his expression.

"Mom and Dad are in the lounge having a drink. We're a little early for our reservation," the woman said.

"How—how are your parents?"

"All things considered, they're well." She sent him a sympathetic smile. "You know how it is. This time of year especially."

"Yes."

"How are you?" she asked.

"I'm fine."

"Dawson, no need for the stiff upper lip around me."

"I'm okay, Nat," he said, nodding. "Better."

She tilted her head to one side. "You've told me that before. But, you know, I almost believe you this time. You look good, happy...almost whole again."

His Adam's apple bobbed. "I'm getting there. And what about you?"

She shrugged, her bright smile wobbled. "I have good days and bad days. More good than bad now. So, I suppose that's progress."

He reached out to squeeze her hand. "I'm glad to hear that, Nat."

"It took a while," she admitted. "And I suppose I should warn you that Mom's not quite there yet."

He nodded solemnly. "I know."

"That's not your concern though, Daw. I know she said some things right after the accident and then at the funeral that made you feel differently, but it never was."

"I wish—"

"Don't," was all she said, giving her head a firm shake. Then her expression brightened. "So, who are you here with? Anyone I know?"

Dawson cleared his throat then and his gaze landed on Eve, who stood just beyond the young woman. He extended a hand to her, in that moment bridging the past and the present. "Eve Hawley, I'd like you to meet Natasha Derringer, Sheila's sister."

Eve had figured out the young woman's identity already. "Hello," she said, accepting Natasha's extended hand for a shake.

"Dawson's a wonderful man. The best." Natasha sent him a warm smile. "It's nice to see him out and looking happy again." The young woman's eyes were bright, her tone sincere.

Since Eve wasn't sure how to respond to such a heartfelt sentiment, she simply smiled.

That ended abruptly when an older couple joined them. While the man gave Dawson a jovial clap on the back, the woman said nothing. Her silence was damning.

"Hello, Clayton, Angela. How are you?" Dawson inquired, looking ill at ease.

"We're doing all right," Clayton bobbed his graying head. "You know how it is."

"Yes."

The older woman made a harrumphing noise and stared off in the opposite direction.

Dawson cleared his throat. "I would like you to

meet a friend of mine. This is Eve Hawley. Eve, this is Angela and Clayton Derringer."

Sheila's parents.

It was an awkward moment, to be sure. Everyone sensed it. Everyone seemed determined to make the best of it…except for Angela. While Clayton greeted Eve with a polite smile, the older woman glared at her with unmistakable contempt and snubbed her attempt to shake hands. Then she turned her venom on Dawson.

"How nice for you, Dawson, that you are able to go on with your life," she spat. "You're out with someone new, acting as if my daughter never existed. As if your own daughter never existed."

"Angela," the older man began at the same time Natasha said, "Mother, please."

"I can assure you, I haven't forgotten Sheila and Isabelle," Dawson said quietly.

He'd been holding Eve's hand. But as he said this, he released it. Connection broken, she thought. Part of her broke, too. Because she knew in that instant that Dawson had returned to the past.

After a round of apologies, none of which was offered by Angela, the Derringers left.

Eve and Dawson left, too. It came as no surprise to her that when they reached her apartment building, Dawson told Jonas to wait for him while he walked Eve to her door.

"You're not staying tonight." It was more statement than question.

He answered anyway as they stood in the elevator and waited for it to reach her floor. "No."

"Are we still on for dinner tomorrow evening?" she made herself ask.

She knew the answer even before he said, "Sorry, but I'm going to have to cancel."

The elevator doors slid open and they stepped out. "Did something come up?"

"I've got some loose ends I need to clear up before the holidays." They reached her apartment door and he cleared his throat. "I also have some packing to do."

"For Cabo?"

He took the key from her hand and slid it into the door's lock. "Yes."

"You're going."

"You knew that I was," he said defensively as they stepped into her apartment.

"I guess I'd hoped you had changed your mind and had decided to spend the holidays with loved ones."

"Christmas isn't a holiday for me, Eve. It's the anniversary of my wife and daughter's deaths. I have nothing to celebrate." The words came out forcefully, angrily.

And he wouldn't have anything to celebrate as long as that was his focus.

"I won't pretend to know how you feel, Dawson. My mother was thoughtful enough to die on a day that didn't hold any other special meaning for me. But I do know how your family feels. They didn't just lose Sheila and Isabelle on that Christmas Eve. For all intents and purposes, they lost you. Just as I lost my dad the day my mother overdosed."

"I'm sorry, Eve."

"I am, too. I'm sorry for my dad that in addition to missing out on so much of my life, he's missed out on so much of his own. He's not a happy man. Are you happy?"

"I don't—"

"Deserve to be happy? Stop playing the pity card. It's gotten old. They died. You lived. Deal with it!" she shouted. "Because in making yourself pay you're making everyone who loves you pay. I'm not just talking about your family now, Dawson."

"No, Eve." He closed his eyes. "You don't love me."

"That's not something you can control."

He stumbled back a step. It was sadly apropos that he was on one side of the threshold and she was on the other. "I'm going, Eve."

"Of course you are." She shook her head sadly. "I have something for you. Something I'd planned to give you on Christmas, but since it doesn't look like I'll be seeing you then, I'll give it to you now."

"You didn't have to buy me anything."

She shrugged. "I wanted to."

She turned to get it, heart all the heavier when Dawson remained in the hallway, ready to make his escape.

"It's not much," she said, handing him the small

package. Working up a smile, she added, "It's one of those it's-the-thought-that-counts type of gifts."

"Thank you."

When he started to peel back the paper, she stopped him. "Don't open it now."

"Okay." He tucked the present into the pocket of his overcoat with a nod. "Speaking of Christmas, my parents usually have dinner around three in the afternoon. I know you'd be welcome there."

The offer made her heart ache all the more. "Thanks, but I don't think so. I'd feel too awkward."

He frowned. "What will you do?"

"I'll celebrate here." And she would. It's what she'd planned before her relationship with Dawson had turned intimate. "I'm going to pick out a tree tomorrow. The apartment will smell like pine needles. I plan to string it with lights and garland and douse it in tinsel."

"And then what?" he asked.

"I'll go to the market and pick up all of the ingredients for a major feast. After eating, I'll put on my pajamas and watch *It's a Wonderful Life*."

"Eve, you don't have to spend Christmas alone," he began.

"Neither do you. We all have choices, Dawson." She stepped out into the hallway and kissed his cheek. "Merry Christmas."

He was still standing there frowning at her when she closed the door.

* * *

Dawson was in a nasty mood. Damn Eve. She was trying to make him feel guilty, he decided. Yes, that was it. She'd known he would be leaving town for the holidays. He'd never made her any promises.

Nor did she ask for any, his conscience reminded him. Even when they'd lain wrapped in one another's arms sharing their innermost thoughts, she hadn't asked Dawson about the future.

Temporary. That was the adjective she'd applied to their relationship at the very beginning. More accurately, it was what she assumed he intended. He'd let the assumption stand, even though as the days passed it began to feel far more permanent.

We all have choices, Dawson.

He didn't agree. Or at least he hadn't.

On Christmas Eve, he left the office just after one o'clock in the afternoon. The company party was later that day, but he wouldn't be there. He had a flight to catch at six o'clock. Mrs. Stern would see to it that the bonuses were distributed to the employees, just as she had seen to it that the gifts Eve had purchased for clients had been wrapped and delivered.

As for the gifts for his family, Jonas would take those over. Dawson called his mother from his cell phone on the drive home to give her the news. She was very disappointed he wouldn't be there in person, and let him know it. For the first ten minutes of the conversation he wasn't able to get a word in. But then she surprised him by saying, "Well, I hope you and Eve have a good time."

He cleared his throat. "Mom, Eve's not coming with me."

"You're going alone? But I thought… The way you look at her, Dawson. The way she looks at you. It's plain as can be that you're falling in l—"

"No!" He lowered his voice, moderated his tone. "I mean, we hardly know one another."

The excuse rang hollow even to him. The length of their acquaintance had nothing to do with it.

Sure enough, his mother pointed this out. "I fell in love with your father on our first date. He waited 'til we'd been seeing one another six months before he proposed, but he said he'd known I was the one for him the first time he laid eyes on me. That girl is special, Dawson."

"Sheila was special."

"Thinking Eve is too doesn't change that. Sheila was special. But she's gone, son. Don't stay so mired in the past that you let Eve get away."

Because his eyes had begun to sting, he closed them. "Things between the two of us probably aren't going to work out the way you're hoping, Mom."

Tallulah was quiet for a moment. Then she said, "Ask yourself this, Dawson—are they going to work out the way you were hoping?"

After the phone call, he stared out the window at the midafternoon traffic. When he shifted in his seat, something in his pocket bit into his side. He reached into his overcoat and pulled out the gift-wrapped box. Eve's gift. He'd forgotten all about it.

He decided to open it, peeling back the paper and then lifting the lid. She'd told him it was an it's-the-thought-that-counts type of gift. The thought left him staggered.

She'd given him—the man who had boycotted Christmas for the past three years, the man who had refused to acknowledge the past—a small glass ornament in the shape of two embracing angels. He pulled out the note that was tucked inside the box.

For your tree. Hang these angels on the highest branch and when you're feeling sad, take time to remember the love and laughter you shared and to celebrate their lives.

Dawson swallowed. He didn't have a tree. He hadn't put one up in three years. Apparently Eve had thought of that, too. It was being delivered even as the limo pulled up the driveway. Two men were holding the ten-foot-tall fir tree as Ingrid stood wringing her hands.

"I explained to them that you're going out of town and that you certainly would not have ordered a Christmas tree," his housekeeper said.

"It's all right. I'll handle this." And though Dawson was a man of action, a man used to making decisions, he stood rooted in place, staring at the tree for several minutes.

"You going to tell us where you want this, mister?" one of the deliverymen asked. "We've got another half-dozen deliveries to make yet today."

Take it back. That was what he intended to say. It made the most sense. He was leaving. But as his thumb stroked over the delicate angels cupped in the palm of his hand, the words that came out were, "It's time to let go."

To let go not of the memories, he realized, but of the guilt and the anger and all of the other negative emotions that had kept him from not only living but remembering Sheila and Isabelle as anything more than victims.

There was more to the life they had shared than the death that divided them. Eve had known that.

"You want us to let go of this thing?" The man looked incredulous.

"No. Take it in the house. Tell the housekeeper I said to set it up in the great room."

And with that, Dawson headed for the garage.

CHAPTER FOURTEEN

IT had been three years since Dawson had last driven a vehicle of any make or model. His car, a luxury sedan, had been totaled in the accident, but his insurance company had paid to replace it. Dawson had never been behind the new car's wheel. For the most part, it had sat in the garage, though his driver took it out regularly to see to its maintenance.

Parked on the other side of the car was the limousine he'd purchased when he'd hired his driver. It was still warm from his ride home. It was also longer and much larger than the sedan. Buckled in the center of the rear seat, he'd been able to beat back the worst of his fear by using the commute time to read the *Wall Street Journal* or make phone calls.

Now Dawson divided his gaze between the two vehicles. He could summon Jonas. The man probably hadn't yet shed his coat. He could be downstairs and ready to leave in a matter of minutes. But Dawson sucked in a breath and came to a decision.

He hung the angel ornament from the rearview mirror. His hands shook as he buckled his seat belt. It, an air bag and divine intervention had saved his life, or so he'd overheard one of the rescue workers at the scene of the accident say. Dawson prayed for that same intervention now as he shifted out of Park, released the brake and inched the car out of the garage.

He stayed to the side streets, driving slower than the posted speeds and testing the brakes often. The roads were clear, but he didn't want to take any chances. Forty minutes later, his confidence buoyed, he turned onto a busy four-lane, adjusting his speed to keep up with traffic. Finally, he decided to venture onto the highway. He bypassed the entrance ramp twice before he had the courage to turn down it. Thirty…forty…fifty… His heart rate accelerated along with the car. Then he was flipping on the blinker, merging into traffic, on his way to his future, assuming he wasn't too late. On the way, he would have to face his past first.

A mile up ahead was the spot where his life had changed, where Sheila and Isabelle's lives had ended. He hadn't traveled past it since then, even if that meant his driver had to go out of his way. How apropos that Dawson was the one behind the wheel for this trip.

He didn't stop, though he slowed down as he approached the overpass, forcing the cars behind him to brake and shift lanes. A couple of drivers went around him, one honking and gesturing his irritation. Dawson barely noticed. His attention was on the side of the road. He waited to be assailed by grief and guilt and memories. He worried that he wouldn't be able to continue driving and would have to call Jonas to come for him and have the car towed back home.

None of that happened.

What had been the scene of horrible carnage three years earlier, now looked innocuous and surprisingly nondescript. He felt sad as he drove past it, which was perfectly understandable under the circumstances. But that wasn't the only emotion he experienced. By confronting his fears he also felt free and, as he depressed the gas pedal, fully in control.

In his head he heard Tallulah asking if things between him and Eve were going to work out the way he had been hoping. This time he had an answer.

"If I have anything to say about it they will," he murmured.

One hour and two stops later, he arrived at Eve's apartment. Despite his earlier resolve, his knees felt a little shaky as he waited for her to answer his knock.

She opened the door wearing blue jeans and an oversized sweatshirt. Her hair was pulled back in a ponytail. She looked so lovely and so guarded that his heart took a tumble. What if he was too late? She'd been hurt before. What if she decided he wasn't worth a second chance?

"Dawson." She blinked in surprise, though beyond that he had a hard time gauging her reaction. Was she happy to see him? Angry?

"Can I come in?"

Christmas music was playing on her stereo and the scent of popcorn wafted out the door. It was a moment before she stepped back. "Sure."

A small tree was in the far corner of the room, completely dwarfed by the high ceiling. She'd already decorated it with multicolored lights and appeared to be in the process of stringing popcorn and cranberries for a garland.

"Looks like you could use the tree you had delivered to my house," he said.

She closed her eyes and let out a sigh. "I tried to cancel the delivery, but I called too late. Sorry. I placed the order when I thought…well, before."

When she'd thought he was ready to move on. "I also opened the gift you gave me."

She grimaced. "I shouldn't have given you that the other night. I nearly chased you down the hallway afterward and asked for it back. If I've offended you, I'm sorry. It wasn't my intent. I just wanted you to know—"

"That it's okay to be alive."

She nodded.

He walked to the couch and picked up the strand of popcorn and cranberries she'd been making. As he studied it, he said, "I'm never going to feel one hundred percent festive this time of year, Eve."

"No one who knows what you've been through would expect you to be," she said.

"I loved my wife."

"Of course you did. You always will."

"And my daughter." His voice hoarse, he added, "It's hard to imagine how deeply you can love another person until you have a child. All you want to do is protect them and keep them safe." His cheeks were wet.

Eve's heart ached for Dawson. She wanted to go to him and wrap her arms around him. But this was his journey. One he had to make alone.

"Not even the most devoted parent can do that. Some things are outside our control," she said.

He bowed his head and she watched his shoulders shudder with his sorrow, but when he spoke, his words gave her hope. "I've finally started to realize that."

"The accident wasn't your fault."

He exhaled heavily before looking up. "Part of me knows that."

She went to him, brushed away his tears. "The rest of you will accept it in time."

He was nodding as he reached for her hand and brought it to his lips for a kiss. Her heart hammered, but her voice was steady when she said, "I know Jonas is downstairs, but do you have time for a glass of wine before heading to the airport?"

He was still holding her hand, rubbing the palm in that erotic way of his. "Actually, I drove here myself."

"You d-did," she stammered. That was a big step for him, especially on this day of all days.

"It was time." He kissed her hand again.

What else is it time for? she wanted to ask, but she bit back the question. "Since you're driving maybe wine isn't a good idea. I can brew up some coffee. Got time for a cup?"

"Actually, I'm not in a hurry. I'm thinking of taking a later flight."

Something in the way he was watching her had Eve's heart bucking out an extra beat. "You are?"

"I am."

"How much later?" she asked.

"Depends."

Her throat was threatening to close, but she managed to ask, "On what?"

"On your answer to a question."

"A question?"

"More like a proposal," he clarified. At that, her heart sped up, beating so noisily that she wasn't sure she'd heard him correctly.

He was saying, "My travel agent says Cabo can be very romantic. Sandy beaches, gorgeous sunsets."

"Are you asking me to go with you?" Eve asked.

He nodded. "It's a great place to start a new life. A great place to spend a honeymoon."

From his pocket he pulled a small leather box. Her head felt light. "Oh, my God." When he'd said proposal, he'd meant Proposal. With a capital *P*. "You're asking me to marry you."

"I know we haven't known one another long, but I love you, Eve. I didn't think I could feel this way again. I didn't think I wanted to or deserved to."

"What do you think now?"

His cheeks were streaked with tears, but Dawson was smiling at her. He looked happy. He looked whole. He was every inch the authoritative business-man when he said, "I don't think, I know. You're my future, Eve."

Her own tears spilled over even as she kissed his away. She shared his conviction when she replied, "You're my future, too."

A BRAVO
CHRISTMAS REUNION

BY
CHRISTINE RIMMER

Christine Rimmer came to her profession the long way around. Before settling down to write about the magic of romance, she'd been everything, including an actress, a sales clerk and a waitress. Now Christine is grateful not only for the joy she finds in writing, but for what waits when the day's work is through: a man she loves, who loves her right back, and the privilege of watching their children grow and change day to day. She lives with her family in Oklahoma. Visit Christine at her new home on the web at www.christinerimmer.com.

For Betty Lowe, lifelong friend and loyal reader,
what endures is the laughter, the caring, the sharing.
In the end, there is always love.

Chapter One

Marcus Reid knew damn well that he should stay away from Hayley Bravo. Far, far away.

Since she dumped him and left Seattle, he'd worked harder than ever, rising before dawn to push his body to the limit in his personal gym, burning the midnight oil at the office, driving himself to exhaustion every day. Evenings when he didn't have to be at his corporate headquarters, he kept himself good and busy. He dated, making it a point to get out more—with gorgeous, attentive, appreciative women. Women more glamorous than Hayley, women more sophisticated than

Hayley. Agreeable women. Women who had sense enough not to ask the impossible of him.

Yeah. It had taken him months to get over Hayley. A lot longer, if you wanted the hard truth, than he'd expected. Getting over Hayley had turned out to be one hell of a job. Almost as hard as dealing with his ex-wife Adriana's final desertion.

But he'd managed it.

Or so he kept telling himself. *He was over Hayley*. Done. Finished.

So why was he standing on the doorstep of her Sacramento apartment on that cold evening in mid-December?

Since Marcus had no intention of answering that particular question, he banished it from his mind with a shake of his head.

The complex she lived in was perfectly ordinary, built around a central courtyard, the boxy units accessed from outside. Low to midrange in price, he would guess. She'd lived a lot better when she worked for him. He'd seen to it. Not only a fat salary, but a big expense account and a luxury car, compliments of his company, Kaffe Central. And then there were the gifts he'd showered on her....

Now she was on her own, she'd be watching her budget. That bothered him, the thought of her pinching pennies to get along. Though their relationship had ended, some part of him still wanted to take care of her.

Light glowed in the window to the left of her door. Through the partly open blinds, he could see she had put up a Christmas tree. And he could hear music, faintly. A Christmas song?

Hayley was into the Christmas crap big-time. Strings of lights twined on the railing of her second floor landing, where she'd made herself a sort of patio with a couple of wicker chairs and a wooden crate for a table. A miniature tree, tiny lights twinkling, topped the crate—and he was stalling, checking out her Christmas decorations instead of getting on with it.

Time to make a move. Ring the bell. Or get the hell out of there.

He sucked in a big breath, lifted his hand and gave her doorbell a punch.

After a few never-ending seconds, the door swung wide. The music from inside swelled louder: "White Christmas."

And there she was, the light from behind her haloing her red hair. Those eyes that managed to be blue and gray and green all at once went wide with surprise. And a bright smile died unborn on that mouth that he'd loved to kiss.

"Marcus!" Her expression was not encouraging. Far from it. She looked…pained. Slightly panicked, even. She brought her hand to her mouth and then lowered it—to her stomach.

He tracked the movement, watched as her palm

settled on the round shape of her belly, fingers curving gently. Protectively. He stared at her pale hand and the roundness beneath it, trying to accept what he saw.

It was…enormous, her stomach. It looked as if she had a beach ball tucked in there, beneath the tentlike red sweater she wore.

Too stunned to fake politeness, he shut his gaping mouth—and then opened it again to accuse roughly, "You're pregnant." He lifted his gaze and met her eyes again.

She was frowning, more worried now than panicked. "Marcus. Are you okay? You look—"

"I'm fine." Outright lie. His stomach churned, spurting acid. He needed to hit someone. Preferably whatever bastard had dared to put his hands on her, to do *that* to her.

God. Hayley with some other guy, having that other guy's baby…

It didn't seem possible. He couldn't believe it.

At the same time as he knew this couldn't be happening, some rational part of his mind saw clearly the ridiculousness of his disbelief. Why the hell *wouldn't* she be with some other guy? Some guy who made her happy. Some guy who loved her and cherished her and wanted to make a family with her….

"White Christmas" ended. Bells jingled as "Winter Wonderland" came next.

"Marcus…" She reached out a hesitant hand. "Please come in and—"

He cut her off by moving back just slightly, out of the way of her touch.

"Oh, Marcus…" She looked at him with what might have been pity.

He wanted to shout at her then, tell her loud and clear that she never, ever had to feel sorry for him. But he didn't shout. Far from it. Instead, he said what he'd planned to say. He doled out the stock phrases, just to show her that finding her big as a house with some other guy's kid didn't affect him in the least.

"I'm in town on business. Thought I'd stop by, see how you're doing…."

She wrapped her arms around herself, resting them on that impossible belly, and looked at him steadily. Now those eyes of hers looked sad. "I'm all right."

He parodied a smile. "Great. Did I catch you having dinner?"

She pressed her lips together and shook her head.

He craned to the side, hoping to see beyond her into the apartment. "Your, uh, husband home?"

She took forever to answer. Finally, so gently, she told him, "No, Marcus."

He waited, his gaze on her face, carefully *not* glancing down again at her bulging stomach.

Finally she heaved a big sigh. "Look. Are you coming in or not?"

"Yeah."

She stepped back. He crossed the threshold. She shut the door, closing the two of them in that apartment together.

The place was small. Straight ahead a hallway led into shadow. To the right was a narrow kitchen with a tiny two-seater table. On the left was the living room area. There, the brightly lighted tree already had a pile of festively wrapped presents beneath it. The TV cabinet dripped garland and fake red berries. She even had a Nativity scene on one of the side tables.

Leave it to Hayley to do Christmas full out. Last December, she'd…

But he wasn't going to think about last December. Last December was gone. Over. Done. He was only here to say hi and wish her and her baby—and the guy, too, damn him to hell, whoever he was—a nice life.

"Your coat," she suggested softly, reaching out.

He dodged her touch again. "It's all right. I'll keep it on."

She dropped her outstretched arm. "Okay." It was her turn to fake a smile. "Well. Have a seat." She indicated the blue couch in the living room. Obediently, he marched over there and sat down.

"A drink?" she offered, still hovering there on the square of tile that served as her entrance hall.

He realized a drink sounded pretty damn good. He *needed* a drink at a moment like this. Something to numb his senses, blur his vision. Something to make it so he didn't care that Hayley was having someone else's kid. "Great. Thanks."

"Pepsi?"

"No. A real drink. Anything but whiskey."

She blinked. She knew how he felt about booze, as a rule. "Well, sure. I think I've got some vodka around here. No tonic or anything, though..."

"Vodka. Some ice. Whatever."

She turned toward the kitchen. He watched her in there as she got down a glass. She disappeared for a moment. He heard ice cubes clinking. And then she was back in his line of vision, glass in one hand, a bottle in the other. She poured the clear liquor over the ice, put the lid back on the bottle and came to him, that belly of hers leading the way.

"Thanks," he said, when she handed it over. He knocked it back in one swallow and held out the glass again. "Another."

She opened her beautiful mouth to speak—but he glared at her and she said nothing. Silent but for a sigh, she took the glass and waddled back to the counter, where she poured him a second one. She approached again and held out the glass. He took it. And then he watched with bleak fascination as she moved to a chair across from him and carefully lowered herself into it.

The liquor, thankfully, had no smell. He considered knocking back the second glass. But he had a feeling if he did, it might just come right back up again. So he sipped the disgusting stuff slowly and told himself to be grateful that it had no more taste that it had smell, just a slight unpleasant oiliness on the tongue.

She asked, her chin tipped high, "How did you know where I live?"

"I kept track of you." Did he sound like some stalker? He qualified, "Just your address. Your phone number…" It was nothing obsessive, he'd told himself. But he did feel a certain…responsibility for her. He'd hired someone to get her address and phone number after she left him.

And about that phone number? More than once, when he was pretty sure she wouldn't be home, he'd dialed that number, just to hear her voice on her answering machine and know that if he needed to get in touch with her again, he could.

"I wanted to be sure," he said, "that you were doing okay."

"Well." She lifted both hands, as if to indicate everything around her—the cramped apartment, the blue couch he sat on, the tree in the window, the baby inside her. And the husband who wasn't home yet. "Doing fine."

He should have had the guy he hired find out more. He would have gotten some advance warning about that other man, about the baby coming. If he'd known, he wouldn't be here now, drinking vodka and looking like a fool.

"Your husband…" he said, and then didn't know how to go on.

She shook her head. "Marcus, I—"

"Stop." He tipped his glass at her. "On second thought, I really don't want to know." Another gulp and the second drink was finished. So was he. He set the glass down and stood. "I can see you're okay. That's good. You have a great life." He headed for the door.

"Marcus. Wait—"

But he wasn't listening. Four long strides and he reached the door.

As he yanked the door open, she called again, "Damn it, Marcus!" He shut the door behind him. Ignoring the sound of her calling after him, he made for the stairs, taking them two at a time, his throat tight and his chest aching.

In under a minute, he was across the central courtyard of her apartment complex, out the wrought-iron gate to the street and behind the wheel of his rented Lexus. He stuck the key in the ignition and turned it over. The engine purred.

But he didn't pull out into traffic. Instead, he flopped back in the seat and stared blindly at the

dark windshield, seeing not the night beyond, but
Hayley staring back at him through solemn eyes.
Hayley, coming toward him with that second drink
he'd demanded, her huge stomach leading the
way.

She hadn't been wearing a wedding ring.

He sat up straighter. She'd quit her job as his
assistant and left him in…May. Seven months
ago.

In his mind's eye, he saw her answering the
door again, her hand on her stomach. *Her beach-
ball-size stomach.*

Marcus was no expert on pregnancy. But
didn't she look further along than seven months?
Really, she looked to him to be almost ready to
have the kid…

His heart slammed into his breastbone and his
stomach rolled as the world seemed to tip on its
axis.

No ring on her ring finger. And the husband. He
wasn't there because…

There *was* no husband.

Marcus yanked the key from the ignition and
got out of the car. He raced across the sidewalk
and up the three stone steps to the gate.

Which was locked.

He swore, a harsh oath, though there was no
one but the night to hear him. Earlier, he'd lucked
out and slipped in behind a couple too busy

groping each other to notice they had company as they entered the complex. Not this time. He stood at the gate alone. Muttering another bad word, he punched the button that went with Hayley's apartment number.

She answered immediately, as if she'd been waiting by the receiver for him to finally add two and two and come up with four. "Marcus."

"Is it mine?"

By way of answer, she buzzed him in.

She was waiting in her open doorway when he reached the top of the stairs. Waiting in silence. No Christmas music now.

He asked, low, "Well?"

And she nodded. Slowly. Deliberately.

"And the husband?" he demanded. When she frowned as if puzzled, he clarified. "Is there a husband?"

Her head went back and forth. No husband.

He stared at her. He had absolutely zero idea what to do or say next.

She gestured for him to come in. Moving on autopilot, he reentered her apartment. She indicated the blue couch. So he went over there and lowered his strangely numb body onto the cushions again.

He watched as she reclaimed the blue chair, those ringless pale hands of hers gripping the chair arms. His gaze was hopelessly drawn to her belly.

He tried to get his mind around the bizarre reality that she had his baby in there.

His baby. His…

"Oh, Marcus," she said in a small voice at last. "I'm so—"

He cut her off by showing her the flat of his palm. "You *knew*, didn't you, when you left me? That's *why* you left me. Because of the baby."

She shook her head.

"What?" he demanded. "You're telling me you *didn't* know you were pregnant when you walked out on me?"

"I knew. All right? I knew." She pushed on the chair arms, as if she meant to rise. "Do we have to—?"

"Yeah. We do."

She sank back to the chair. "This is totally unnecessary. Really. I'm not expecting anything of you."

"Just answer me. Did you leave me because you got pregnant?"

"Sort of."

"Damn it. Either you did, or you didn't."

She shut those shining eyes and sucked in a slow breath. When she looked at him again, she spoke with deliberate care. "I left because you didn't love me and you didn't want to marry me and you'd already told me, when we started in together, you made it so *perfectly* clear, that you would never get married again and you would never have children. I felt guilty, okay? For messing up and getting pregnant. But still, *I* wanted this baby. And that meant I couldn't see it as anything but a losing proposition to hang around in Seattle waiting for you to feel responsible for me and this child I'm having, even though you didn't want me and you don't want a kid. It was lose-lose, as far as I could see. So I came home."

Her tone really grated on him. As if she was so noble, just walking away, telling him nothing. As if, somehow, he was the one in the wrong here. "You should have told me before you walked out on me. I had a damn right to know."

Spots of color stained her pale cheeks. She straightened her shoulders. "Of course I planned to tell you."

"When?"

She glanced away. "It's...arranged."

"Arranged." He repeated the word. It made no sense to him. "Telling me I'm going to be a father is something you needed to *arrange?*"

She let go of the chair arms just long enough to throw up both hands. Then she slapped them down again. Hard. "Look. I was stressed over it, all right? I admit I didn't want to face you. But I have it set up so you would have known."

"You have it...set up?"

"Isn't that what I just said?"

"Set up for when?"

"As soon as the baby's born. You were going to know then."

"You were planning to…call me from the hospital?"

She swallowed. "Uh. Not exactly."

"Damn it, Hayley." He glared at her.

She curved a hand under her belly and snapped to her feet. "Come with me."

He stayed where he was and demanded, "Come where?"

"Just come with me. Please."

"Hayley…"

But she was already moving—and with surprising agility for someone so hugely pregnant. She zipped over and grabbed her bag, flung open the entry area closet and dragged a red wool coat from a hanger in there. She turned to him as she shrugged into the coat. "Where's your car?"

"Out in front, but I don't—"

"Are you drunk?"

"Drunk? What the hell? Of course I'm not drunk."

"Okay." She flipped her hair out from under the coat's collar. "You can drive."

He muttered a string of swearwords as he rose and followed her into the cold, mist-shrouded night.

* * *

Ten minutes later, she directed him to turn into the driveway of a green-shuttered white brick house on a quiet street lined with oaks and maples.

He pulled in where she pointed, stopped the car and took the key from the ignition. "Who lives here?"

"Come on," she said, as if that were any kind of answer. A moment later, she was up and out and headed around the front of the vehicle.

Against his own better judgment, he got out, too, and followed her up the curving walk to a red front door. She rang the bell.

As chimes sounded inside, he heard a dog barking and a child yelling, "I got it!"

The lock turned and the door flew open to reveal a brown-haired little girl in pink tights and ballet shoes. The dog, an ancient-looking black mutt about the size of a German shepherd, pawed the hardwood floor beside the girl and barked in a gravelly tone, "Woof," and then "woof," again, each sound produced with great effort.

"Quiet, Candy," said the child and the dog dropped to its haunches with a sound that could only be called a relieved sigh. The child beamed at Hayley and then shouted over her shoulder, "It's Aunt Hayley!"

Aunt Hayley? Impossible. To be an aunt, you needed a brother or a sister. Hayley had neither.

A woman appeared behind the child, a woman with softly curling brown hair and blue eyes, a woman who resembled Hayley in an indefinable way—something in the shape of the eyes, in the mouth that wasn't full, but had a certain teasing tilt at the corners. "Hey," the woman said, wiping her hands on a towel. "Surprise, surprise." She cast a questioning glance in Marcus's direction.

And Hayley said, "This is Marcus."

"Ah," said the woman, as if some major question had been answered. "Well. Come on in."

The kid and the old dog backed out of the way and Hayley and Marcus entered the warm, bright house. The woman led them through an open doorway into a homey-looking living room. Just as at Hayley's place, a lighted Christmas tree stood in the window, a bright spill of gifts beneath.

"Can I take your coats?" the woman asked. When Hayley shook her head, she added, "Well, have a seat, then."

Marcus hoped someone would tell him soon what the hell he was doing there. He dropped to the nearest wing chair as the kid launched herself into a pirouette. A bad one. She stumbled a little as she came around front again. And then she grinned, a grin as infectious as her mother's—and Hayley's.

"I'm DeDe." She bowed.

"Homework," said the mother.

"Oh, Mom…"

The mother folded her arms and waited, her kitchen towel trailing beneath her elbow.

Finally, the kid gave it up. "Okay, okay. I'm going," she grumbled. She seemed a cheerful type of kid and couldn't sustain the sulky act. A second later, with a jaunty wave in Marcus's direction, she bounced from the room, the old dog limping along behind her.

Hayley, who'd taken the other wing chair, said, "Marcus, this is my sister, Kelly."

It occurred to him about then that the evening was taking on the aspect of some bizarre dream: Hayley having his baby. The kid in the pink tights. The decrepit dog. The sudden appearance of a sister where there wasn't supposed to be one.

"A sister," he said, sounding as dazed as he felt. "You've got a sister…"

Hayley had grown up in foster homes. Her mother, who was frail and often sick, had trouble keeping a job and had always claimed she wasn't up to taking care of her *only* daughter. So she'd dumped Hayley into the system.

"Oh, Marcus." Hayley made a small, unhappy sound in her throat. "I realize this is a big surprise. It was to me, too. Believe me. My mother always told me I was the only one. It never occurred to me that she was lying, that anyone would lie about something like that…."

"Ah," said Marcus, hoping that very soon the surprises were going to stop.

The sister, Kelly, fingered her towel and smiled hopefully. "We have a brother, too…."

Hayley piped up again. "I just found them back in June—or rather, we all found each other. When Mom died."

His throat did something strange. He coughed into his hand to clear it. "Your mother died…."

"Yeah. Not long after I moved back here. I met Kelly and our brother, Tanner, in Mom's hospital room, as a matter of fact."

"When she was dying, you mean?"

"Yes. When she was dying." Before he could decide what to ask next, Hayley turned to her sister. "Could you get the letter, please?"

Kelly frowned. "Are you sure? Maybe you ought to—"

"Just get it."

"Of course." Kelly left the room.

Marcus sat in silence, staring at the woman who was soon to have his child. He didn't speak. And neither did she.

It was probably better that way.

The sister returned with a white envelope. She handed it to Hayley, who held it up so that he could see his own address printed neatly on the front. "Tell him, Kelly."

Kelly sucked in a reluctant breath and turned

to Marcus. "I would have mailed it to you, as soon as the baby was born." She held up two balloon-shaped stickers, one pink, which said, It's A Girl and the other blue, with It's A Boy.

Hayley said weakly, "You know. Depending."

Marcus looked at the envelope, at the long-lost sister standing there holding the stickers, at Hayley sitting opposite him, eyes wide, her hand resting protectively on her pregnant stomach.

I'm going to wake up, he thought. *Any second now, I'm going to wake up.*

But he didn't.

Chapter Two

Hayley despised herself.

She'd blown this situation royally and she knew it. She stared at her baby's father in the chair across from hers and longed only to turn back time.

She should have told him. In hindsight, that much was achingly clear. She should have told him back in May, before she broke it off with him, before she quit her job as his assistant and slunk back to Sacramento to nurse her broken heart.

No matter his total rejection of her when she'd told him she loved him, he'd deserved to know. No matter that when she dared to suggest he might think again about them getting married, he'd given her a flat, unconditional no—and then, when she hinted they ought to break up, since they were clearly going nowhere, he'd agreed that was probably for the best.

No matter. None of it. She should have told him when she left him that he was going to be a dad. If she'd told him then, she wouldn't be looking across her sister's coffee table at him now, seeing the stunned bewilderment in his usually piercing green eyes, and totally hating herself.

She broke the grim silence that hovered like a gray cloud in her sister's living room. "Okay. I messed up. I know it." She glanced down at the envelope. "This is no way to find out you're a dad. I can't believe I was going to do this. I…" She dared to glance up at him. Not moving. Was he even breathing? She pleaded, "Oh, Marcus. I wish you could understand. After how it ended with us, I just didn't know how to break it to you. This was the only way I could make sure I wouldn't chicken out and *never* get around to telling you."

Marcus stood.

She gulped. "Um. Are we going?"

"Oh, yeah. We're going."

Hayley slid the envelope into her purse as he turned and headed for the door. Without a backward glance, he went through the arch to the entrance hallway. She pushed herself upright as she heard the front door open—and then shut, a way-too-final sound.

Kelly sent her a look. "Oh, boy. He's mad."

"Maybe he'll just leave without me…." She almost wished that he would.

"I don't like this. You sure you're going to be okay with him?"

She gave her sister a game smile. "I'll be fine. Really."

Kelly stepped close and caught her hand. "Call me. If you need me…"

"I will. I promise."

"I'm here. You know that."

"I do. I'm glad…."

With a final, reassuring squeeze, Kelly released her.

Outside, Marcus was waiting behind the wheel with the engine running. He stared straight ahead. Hayley got in, stretched the seat belt long to fit over her tummy and hooked it.

Without once glancing in her direction, he backed from the driveway and off they went.

The short ride back to her place was awful. She tried not to squirm in her seat as she wondered if he'd ever look at her again—let alone actually speak.

At her apartment complex, he followed her wordlessly through the iron gate, across the central courtyard and up the steps to her door. She stuck her key in the lock and pushed the door wide.

He took her arm as she moved to enter. "The letter," he said.

"I...what?"

"Give me my letter."

"But there's nothing in it you don't know now and I don't see why—"

"You don't want me to read it." It was an accusation.

"I didn't say—"

"The letter," he repeated. He was looking at her now. Straight at her. She knew that look from two years of working for him, of falling hopelessly and ever-more-totally in love with him. When Marcus got that look, it meant he wouldn't stop until he had what he wanted. She might as well give in now. Because in the end, he would get the damn letter.

"All right," she said, as if she'd actually made a choice. She took the letter from her purse and handed it over.

He let go of her arm, but then instantly threatened, "Don't even imagine you can run away again."

She felt the angry heat as it flooded her cheeks. "What are you talking about? I left—you, my job and Seattle. I didn't *run away*. And I certainly am not going anywhere now. This is my home. Especially now that I've found my family here."

"Just don't. Because I'll find you. You know I will."

She did know. But so what? She had zero intention of running off, so his point was totally moot. "I like it here," she insisted, hoping it might get through this time. "I'm going nowhere." She wrapped her arms around herself against the night chill and cast a longing glance toward the warmth and light beyond the threshold. "Are you coming in?"

"Not now," he replied, so imperious he set her teeth on edge. He spoke *at* her more than *to* her and he stared over her shoulder instead of meeting her eyes. She wondered as she'd wondered a thousand times, *why*, of all the men in all the world, had she gone and given her heart to Marcus Reid?

Probably her upbringing—or lack of one. Her mother had put her in the foster care system when she was a baby. And her father, the notorious kidnapper, murderer and serial husband, Blake Bravo? He'd been long gone by the time Hayley was born. Unavailable. That was the word for dear old dad. Unavailable in the most thorough sense of the word.

Which, she supposed, made it not the least surprising that she'd chosen an emotionally unavailable man to love.

"All right, then," she said. "Since you won't come in, good night." She started to turn toward the haven of her apartment.

But then he muttered distractedly, "I need to think. Then we'll talk."

She faced him once more. "That's fine with me." Though what, exactly, they would talk about was beyond her. What more was there to say? Not much. Not until after the baby was born, when they could discuss fun topics like custody and child support.

Oh, God. She dreaded all that. And she'd been avoiding facing what she dreaded.

Because she understood Marcus well enough to know that he'd never turn his back on his child. Even though he'd always insisted he didn't want children, now he was actually *having* one, everything would change. He was going to be *responsible* for a child. And Marcus Reid took his responsibilities with absolute seriousness.

He left at last. She went inside and shut the door and ordered her pulse to stop racing, her heart to stop bouncing around under her breastbone.

Marcus knew her secret now. Getting all worked up over the situation wasn't going to make him go away.

Chapter Three

Marcus,

I don't know where to start. So I guess I'll just put it right out there. If you're reading this it's because you're a father. I've just had your baby and this letter has been mailed to you because the baby is born and doing fine. The sticker on the envelope should tell you whether it's a boy or a girl.

I'm so sorry. I know you're furious with me about now. I don't blame you. I should have told you before I left Seattle, but... well, I just couldn't make myself do it.

So you're learning this way. In a letter.

Try not to hate me too much.

Try not to hate me too much....

Marcus read that sentence over twice. And then a third time.

After that, he loosened his tie. Then he dropped back across the hotel room bed and stared at the attractively coffered ceiling and thought how she was wrong: he didn't hate her. True, what he felt for Hayley right then wasn't pretty. It was fury and frustration and a certain wounded possessiveness all mixed up together.

But hate? Uh-uh. He wished he did hate her. It would make everything so much simpler.

He raised the letter and read the rest. She'd listed the address and phone number of the hospital she would be using. And also the infor- mation he already had—her own address and number.

She wrote at the bottom:

Try to understand. I realize this isn't what you wanted. I swear I was careful. I guess just not careful enough.
Hayley

That was it. All of it. It wasn't much more in- formation than he'd already had.

He balled up the letter, raised his arm and tossed the thing into the corner wastebasket. Slam dunk.

What the hell to do now?

He was due back in Seattle tomorrow, for a series of meetings, the first of which he had on his schedule for 11:00 a.m. His company was poised for a big move into the Central California market. They were high priority, those meetings.

But then again, so was the kid he'd just found out he was having.

And so was Hayley. She needed him now, whether her pride would let her admit that or not.

Still flat on his back across the bed, he grabbed his PDA off the nightstand and dialed—with his thumb, from memory. She answered on the second ring.

"'Lo?" Her voice was husky, reminding him of other nights, of the scent and the feel of her, all soft and drowsy, in his bed.

"You were already asleep." He didn't mean it to come out sounding like an accusation, but he supposed that it did.

"Marcus." She sighed. "What?"

"I'm flying out at 6:00 a.m. tomorrow. I've got meetings in Seattle I can't get out of."

"You've always got meetings you can't get out of. It's fine. I told you. I don't expect—"

"I'll clear my calendar in the next couple of days. Then I'll come back."

"You don't have to do that."

"Yeah. I do. We both know I do. I'll see you.

Thursday. Friday at the latest. If you need me before then, call me on my cell. You still have the number?"

A silence, then, "I have it."

"When's the baby due?"

"January eighth."

"You're not working, are you?" He heard rustling, pictured her sitting up in bed, all rumpled and droopy-eyed, her hair tangled from sleep. "Hayley?"

Reluctantly, she answered, "Yes. I'm still working."

"You shouldn't be. And now you've finally told me about the baby, you don't need to be. I'll make arrangements right away."

"Give me money, you mean." She sounded downright bleak. She'd damn well better not try refusing his money. "I'm managing just fine. I like working and I feel great and I'm going to stay on the job until—"

"Quit. Tomorrow."

"Uh. Excuse me. But this is *my* life you're suddenly running. Don't."

"I'm only saying—"

"Don't."

He had no idea where she worked, or what she did there. His own fault. He'd just *had* to play it noble seven months ago, which meant only allowing the detective to get the basic information.

So that now he was forced to ask, "Where do you work, anyway?"

"I'm an office manager. For a small catering company. There's the owner, the chef, the dishwasher and me. We're in a storefront off of K Street. Around the Corner Catering. We do a pretty brisk business, actually. We're hooked up with a staffing agency so we offer full service. Not only the food, but the staff, from setup to cleanup."

"A caterer. You work for a caterer."

"Yeah. Is that a problem for you?"

"It's high-stress work and you know it. Chefs are notorious for being temperamental. You're having a baby. You shouldn't be in a stressful work environment. You should—"

"Don't," she said for the third time.

He let it go. Later, when he got back, they could discuss this again. He'd get her to see this his way—the *right* way. "I'll be gone two days. Three at the most."

"You said that."

"No, I said I'd be back Thursday or Friday. On second thought, I should be able to make it sooner. Wednesday, I hope."

"All right. Wednesday, then. Is that all?"

He hated to hang up with all this…tension between them. He should say something tender, he supposed. But nothing tender occurred to him. "We'll work this out. You can count on me."

"I know that."

"Don't worry."

"I…won't," she said softly after a moment. Then, almost in a whisper, "Good night, Marcus." Then a click.

He put the device back on the night table and laced his hands behind his head. A kid. It still didn't seem possible. A child had never been part of his plans.

But plans changed. And sometimes allowances had to be made.

"His assistant called me at work an hour ago," Hayley told Kelly when the sisters met for lunch the next day. "Her name is Joyce. She sounds very…efficient."

"That's good, right?" Kelly forked up a bite of Caesar salad.

Hayley turned her glass of Perrier in a slow circle. "I mean, not young, you know?"

Kelly swallowed and frowned, puzzled. "Not young…like you?"

Hayley turned her glass some more. "It shouldn't matter, that he hired someone older to replace me."

"But you're glad he did."

Hayley tried to deny it—and couldn't. "I suppose I am. Even though, since I left, he's been going out with a bunch of beautiful women."

"Oh, really?"

"Oh, yeah."

"How do you know that?"

"I still get *Seattle* magazine. I saw a picture of him in a tux." She gazed wistfully down into her überpricey glass of bubbly French water. "He looks amazing in a tux. It was some opening of something. He had a drop-dead gorgeous blonde on his arm. He looked so…severe. And dangerous. And handsome—did I mention handsome?"

"Often."

"Practically broke my poor little heart all over again."

"Jerk."

"No. He's not a jerk. He's…just Marcus, that's all. He was true to me when we were together. As a matter of fact, he's not real big on the bachelor lifestyle. But then, when we broke up, well, he would have considered it a point of honor, to prove to himself that he was over me."

Kelly shook her head. "Did I already say the word *jerk?*"

"You did. And I said he's not. He's just…well, you'd have to know him."

Her sister wisely withheld comment. They ate in silence for a few minutes. Finally, Kelly spoke. "So the two of you got together…?"

"Six months after he hired me, when his divorce became final."

"He was married?"

"To his childhood sweetheart. But she dumped him and ran off with some European guy. I was just burning hot for him. And I was lying in wait for those final divorce papers to come in the mail. Then I seduced him. It's a plain, shameless fact."

Kelly chuckled, "My bad baby sister."

"Oh, yeah. I was so sure I could show him what real, true love could be." Hayley shook her head. "So much for that." She bit into her grilled chipotle chicken sandwich and chewed slowly. The last month or two, with the baby taking up so much space in there, eating fast meant heartburn later.

"So what did his new, *older* assistant have to say?" Kelly buttered a sourdough roll.

"She was just telling me a platinum card was on the way, wanting to know where I banked so she could arrange for a giant-sized wire transfer of funds."

"Money," Kelly said thoughtfully. "Well, it comes in handy, you gotta admit."

"It sure does. I suppose I should be more grateful, huh?"

Kelly chuckled. "Oh, hell no. *He* should be grateful, to have a beautiful, smart, capable, loving woman like you as the mother of his child."

"I'll tell him you said that."

"Do."

"He's just a little messed over, that's all. From the awful childhood he had, from his marriage that didn't last forever, after all. I should embroider myself a sampler and hang it on the wall...."

"Saying?"

"'There's no saving a messed-over guy, so you're better off not to even try.'" Hayley chuckled, a sound devoid of humor. "Hey. It rhymes."

"Pure poetry."

"Kelly?"

"Umm?"

"Do you think *I'm* messed over? You know, from the way I grew up?"

Kelly shrugged. "Maybe a little. But we all are, I'm sure. You, me, big brother Tanner—and all the other poor, lost souls who had crazy, bad Blake Bravo for a dad. Think about it." Blake had married a lot of women. *And* given them children. Each woman had thought she was the only one. And they all found out much later, after the notorious Blake finally died and it was all over the national news, that there were other wives. Several. Some no doubt were yet to be found— along with the children they'd borne him. "None of us ever knew our father," Kelly continued, "even the ones who saw him now and then. Because he wasn't the kind that anybody really knows. And then, we all had mothers with emotional issues. That's a given. Remember Mom."

"God. Mom. Yeah." Lia Wells Bravo had been frail both physically and emotionally, the perfect target for Blake Bravo's dangerous brand of charm. One by one, she put the children he gave her during his infrequent visits into foster homes. Lia told all three they had no siblings. And though she wouldn't take care of them herself, she refused to give them up for adoption.

"It's just a sad fact," Kelly said. "Anybody who'd fall in love with a man like Blake Bravo would have had to be at least a little bit out of her mind."

"You're not exactly reassuring me, you know." Hayley sipped her Perrier.

"Sorry…"

"It's so depressing, just thinking about Mom. I hate that I never understood her. And now she's gone, I probably never will." She looked down at her sandwich and knew she ought to eat more of it. "Did I mention that Marcus's childhood was terrible, too?"

"You did. Have you met his parents?"

"They're both long dead. His mother died when he was a kid, some kind of accident. Marcus was never really clear on what happened to her, exactly. His father was a drunk and Marcus despised him. He got millions when his dad died. Marcus put it all away, hasn't touched a penny of it. He has it set up so it funds a bunch of charities. The whole Kaffe Central thing? He built that himself. Starting from a corner coffee shop in Tacoma where he went to work as a manager straight out of college."

"Kaffe Central. You said it's like Starbucks, right?"

Hayley leaned across the table. "Never," she commanded darkly, "compare the Kaffe Central experience to Starbucks." And then she grinned. "But, yeah. Helpful, skilled baristas. Quality coffee. Lattes to die for, whipped up just the way you want them. Amazing ambience—special, but…comfortable. Selected bakery treats."

"Wi-Fi?"

"As a matter of course. Oh, and it's a progressive company, too. Good working conditions, good salaries, everybody gets stock options, good benefits including health insurance. And from what Marcus said, you'll have one in your neighborhood soon. They're opening several shops here in the Sacramento area."

"Can't wait—and he sounds…like a complex man."

"He is. And determined. Way determined. Now he knows about the baby, he's going to be pushing me to do things his way. And I mean *every*thing."

"Marriage?"

Hayley laughed. "Are you kidding? After what his ex, Adriana, did to him, Marcus has sworn he'll never get married again."

"But now that he's going to be a dad…"

"Not Marcus. No way, not even with a baby coming. He may push for full custody, though."

Kelly scoffed. "But I thought you said he didn't even *want* kids."

"He didn't. But now it's happening, it's all going to be about doing the right thing, whatever he decides the right thing may be. He can be… cold. Distant. There's an emotional disconnect there that can be way scary. But he does have an ingrained sense of fair play. So my guess is he'll probably be willing to share custody."

"Big of him."

"But he'll want me to move back to Seattle, you watch. And he's already been on me to quit work immediately."

"Don't let him scare you. We can sic Tanner on him." Their older brother was a private investigator. Strong. Silent. Smart. Possibly as determined as Marcus. And extremely protective of his sisters and his niece.

"Even Tanner isn't going to be able to keep Marcus Reid from doing it all *his* way."

"But *you* will," said Kelly. "You're tough and smart, Hayley Bravo. Nobody pushes you around. You survived our poor, screwed-up mom *and* the foster care system with a positive attitude and a heck of a lot of heart. You're going to be just fine—and your baby, too."

"Say that again."

"It'll work out. You'll see."

Hayley took another bite of her sandwich and fervently hoped that her sister was right.

She found Marcus sitting in one of the wicker chairs by her front door when she got home from work that night. He wore a pricey gray trench over a beautiful charcoal suit and he looked as if he'd just stepped off the cover of *GQ*.

She met those ice-green eyes and felt an unwilling thrill skate along the surface of her skin. In spite of everything—her stomach out to here, her wounded heart, and the threat he posed to the destiny of her child—the man could steal her breath away with just a look.

"It's after six," he muttered, those eyes of his looking dangerous and shadowed, the Christmas lights that twined the railing casting his sculpted cheekbones into rugged relief. "What kind of hours are you working, anyway?"

"Nice to see you, too." She unlocked the front door and pushed it inward, then stepped back to gesture him in ahead of her.

He rose with a certain manly, regal grace that made her want to do sexy things to his tall, lean body, things she *shouldn't* want to do to him after the way he'd turned her down months ago—things she probably *couldn't* do in her current condition.

"Are you all right?" He was scowling. "I don't

like it. You on your feet all day with the baby coming any minute now."

"I'm not due for almost a month. And I'm hardly working on my feet. I'm at a desk, thank you very much. Tonight, we had two events—a cocktail thing and a small dinner party—on the schedule, so I stayed a little late to give a hand with the last-minute details." As usual, there had been yelling on the part of the chef, Federico. Sofia, the owner, had yelled back. And it all came together beautifully in the end, just as it always did.

"Caterers," he grumbled. "I know how they are. Damn temperamental. Lots of shouting, every-thing a big drama." Okay, so he had Sofia—and Federico—nailed. No way she was copping to it. "It can't be good for the baby, for you to be in a stressful environment like that."

"You're repeating yourself."

"This issue bears repeating."

"It's not good for the baby if I get pneumonia, either." She pulled her coat a little closer against the evening chill. "But still, you seem determined to keep me standing out here all night."

He said something under his breath—some-thing unpleasant, she had no doubt—and then, at last, he acquiesced to enter her apartment. Close on his heels, she turned on the light and shut the door.

They faced each other across the cramped entry area.

"You're back early…." She forced a smile, feeling suddenly strange about all this: the two of them, the baby, all the ways he'd denied her seven months ago, the secret she'd kept that she had no right to keep, a secret as pointless as it was wrong.

Because, in the end, here he was again. Back in her life. Determined to look after her and the baby whether they needed looking after or not.

"I took a few days off," he said with a scowl.

"You never take days off."

"First time for everything."

"I thought you had…meetings."

"I did. I made them quick. I cleared my calendar. For tomorrow and the next day." His eyes held a flinty gleam and the determined set to that sensual slash of a mouth told her that he had plans. Plans concerning her and the baby and their future. Plans that he would implement within the next forty-eight hours—whether she liked them or not.

Hayley kept her smile in place. "Your coat?" He shrugged out of it. She hung it up, along with her own. "A drink?"

"No. Thanks."

Seeking a little good cheer—as well as an excuse to put some distance between them—she went to the tree. Dropping to an awkward crouch, she plugged it in. The Christmas lights came on, so happy and bright. Festive.

In all the years of her lonely childhood, there had always been a tree: in the group home, where she went between families. And in the various foster homes. And there was always at least one gift for her under each of those trees. So that she'd come to think of Christmas as something special, something magical and glowing in an otherwise drab life lived out in a series of other people's houses. Christmas was colorful, and optimistic, with joyous music that brought a fond tear to her eye.

Funny, but Kelly said she felt just the same way about the holidays....

"Come on." Marcus was there, standing above her. He held down a hand. She put hers in it, shocked at how good it felt—to touch his long, strong fingers again....

Oh, she would have to watch herself. She was just a big sucker when it came to this man.

He pulled her heavy body upward and she let him, leaning into him a little—but not too much. And as soon as she was upright, she stepped back, away from the delicious temptation to press herself and their baby against him, to find out if he would put those lean arms around her, if he'd cradle her close and put his lips to her hair.

She asked, "Have you eaten?"

"It's not necessary for you to—"

"Not the question. Did you have dinner?"

"No."

"I made spaghetti last night, before you… dropped in. There's plenty left. I'll just heat it up and do the salad. Have a seat. The remote's right there on the arm of the couch. Watch the news. It won't take long…."

He stared at her for several seconds. She wondered what he might be thinking. Finally, with a shrug, he went over to the couch and sat down.

A short time later, she called him to the kitchen. He turned off the news and came to join her at her tiny table. They ate mostly in silence. She found her small appetite had fled completely. Dread was taking up what little space there was in her stomach. Still, she forced herself to put the food in her mouth, to slowly chew, to grimly swallow. The baby needed dinner. And really, so did she.

When they were through, Marcus got up and cleared the table while she loaded the dishwasher and wiped the counters. Then they went to the living room. He took a chair and she sat on the couch.

Her pulse, she realized as she sank into the cushions, had sped into overdrive. Her palms had gone clammy. And her stomach was aching, all twisted with tension. The baby kicked. She winced and put her hand over the spot.

"Are you sick?" He frowned at her.

She shook her head. "Just…dreading this conversation."

"You're too pale."

"I'm a redhead. My skin is naturally pale."

"Paler than usual, I mean."

"Can we just get on with it? Please? Tell me what you want and we can…take it from there."

"I *don't* want to upset you."

She folded her hands over her stomach. "I'm fine." It was a lie. But a necessary one. "Just tell me what you have in mind. Just say it."

"Hayley, I think…" The words trailed off. He looked at her through brooding eyes.

"What? You think, what?" She fired the question at him twice—and as she did, somehow, impossibly, she *knew* what he was going to tell her, what he was going to want from her. It was the one thing she'd been beyond-a-doubt certain he *wouldn't* be pushing for.

But he was. He did. "I think we should get married. All things considered, now there's a kid involved, I think it's the best way to go here."

Married. The impossible word seemed to hover in the air between them.

Now that there was a baby, he wanted to marry her….

She unfolded her hands and lifted them off her stomach and then didn't know what to do with them. She looked down at them as if they belonged on someone else's body. "Married," she said back to him, still not quite believing.

"Yes." He gave a single nod. "Married."

She braced her hands on the sofa cushions and dared to remind him, "But you don't want to be married again. Ever. You know you don't. You *told* me you don't."

Did he wince? She could have sworn he did. "It's the best way," he said again, as if that made it totally acceptable—for him to do exactly what he'd promised he would never do.

Okay, now. The awful thing? The really pitiful thing?

Her heart leaped.

It did. It jumped in her chest and did the happy dance. Because marrying Marcus? That was her dearest, most fondly held dream.

From the moment she'd met him—that rainy Monday, two months out of Heald's Business College and brand-new to Seattle, when he interviewed her for the plum job of his executive assistant—she'd known she would love him. Known that he, with his piercing, watchful eyes and sexy mouth, his wary heart that was kinder than he wanted it to be, his dry sense of humor so rarely seen…

He was her love. He was the one she had been waiting for, dreaming of, through all her lonely years until that moment.

Marriage to Marcus. Oh, yeah. It was what

she'd longed for, what she'd hoped against hope might happen someday.

Because she loved him. She'd known from the first that she would. And within weeks of going to work for him, she was his. Completely, without reservation, though he refused to touch her for months.

She waited. She schemed.

And then his divorce became final. She went to his house wearing a yellow raincoat, high heels, a few wisps of lingerie and nothing else.

At last, they were lovers. No, he didn't love her. Oh, but she loved him.

God help her, she sometimes feared that she would *always* love him. And her love…it was like Christmas to her. It was magic. And bright colored lights. It was that one present with her name on it under a new foster mother's tree.

"Hayley?" His voice came to her. The voice of her beloved. Dreamed of. Yearned after—and yet, in the end, no more hers than all the foster families she'd grown up with.

She pressed her lips together, shook her head, stared bleakly past him, at the shining lights of her tree.

"Damn it, Hayley. What do you want from me? You want me to beg you? I'm willing. Anything. Just marry me and let me take care of you. And our baby. Let me—"

"Stop." The sound scraped itself free of her throat.

He swore. A word harsh and graphic. But at least after that, he fell silent.

She met his eyes. "What if there was no baby, if I wasn't pregnant…?"

"But you are."

"Work with me here. *If* I wasn't. Would you be asking me to marry me now?"

A muscle danced in his jaw. "I would, yes. I love you."

The lie was so huge, she almost smiled. And the knot that was her stomach had eased a little. She felt better now. She knew she could hold out against him, against her impossible dream that he would someday find his way to her, that at last he would see she was the only one for him.

But he hadn't found his way to her, not in his secret heart. And he never would.

"Marcus. Come on. You're lying."

"No. I'm not."

"Please. This is not going to work."

"The hell it won't. I came here to see you, didn't I, showed up at your door last night? And I had no damn clue about the baby then."

Okay. Point for him. But hardly a winning one.

She challenged, "You're telling me you came here because you realized you couldn't live without me?"

"That's right."

"You didn't want to go another day without me

at your side? You came here intending to ask me to marry you, after all, to beg me to give our love another chance and be your bride at last, to make you the happiest man on earth, make all your dreams come true?"

He looked at her steadily. It was not a pleasant look. "Damn you, Hayley. I want to marry you *now*. Why does it matter what I would have done if you hadn't been pregnant?"

"Is that a real question?"

"Excuse me?"

"Do you really want to know why it matters?"

"Yes. I do."

"All right. It matters because in all my life, except for the sister and brother I found in June at my mother's deathbed, I've never had anyone to really call my own. I've worn other people's hand-me-downs, lived in other people's houses, been the extra kid, the one who didn't really belong. The one who never had a home of her own."

"I'm offering you—"

"Wait. I'm not finished. What I'm trying to say is that I had no choice, about the way I grew up. But I do have a choice now. When I get married, I'm going to finally *belong* to someone. Completely. Lovingly. Openly. And the man I marry will belong to *me*."

"I *will* belong to you. I'll be true to you, I'll never betray you."

"Well, of course you wouldn't. You're not the kind to cheat. Except in your secret heart."

"That's not so."

"It is. You know it is. You'll never belong to me, Marcus. You belong to Adriana. You always have and you always will."

Chapter Four

Marcus regarded the pregnant woman on the blue couch. At least she had a little color in her cheeks now. Telling him all the nonsensical reasons she wouldn't have him as a husband had brought a warm flush to her velvety skin.

Terrific. She had pink cheeks and he wanted to…

Hell. He didn't know what he wanted to do, exactly. Something violent. Something loud. Something to snap her out of this silly resistance she was giving him and make it crystal clear to her that she was making no damn sense and she ought to smarten up and get with the program.

Adriana wasn't the issue here. She'd walked away, divorced him. That part of his life was over. For good.

Hayley loved him and needed him. He was willing, at last, to be what she needed.

He spoke, the soul of reason. "I'm here, now, today, and ready to do what you wanted. You left me because I wouldn't marry you. And now I *want* to marry you. I want to give you exactly what you were asking for all along. I don't understand why you have to be difficult about this. You're not behaving rationally. And one of your finest qualities has always been your ability to step back and assess a situation logically. I advise you to do that. Now."

"Marcus."

He hated when she said his name like that. So patiently. As if he were a not-very-bright oversize child. It was supremely annoying, the way she got to him, the way he *let* her get to him. He'd graduated from Stanford at the top of his class; he'd built a billion-dollar corporation from virtually nothing. He knew how to deal with people, how to get along and get what he wanted.

But with Hayley, somehow, since she'd decided she loved him and wanted to marry him, he hadn't known how to deal at all. First, she left him because he *wouldn't* marry her. And now that he said he *would* marry her, she was turning him down.

And she was talking again. All patience and gentleness, trying to make him understand. "No. You don't *want* to marry me. You want to take care of your child—and the mother of your child. You think marrying me is the best way to do that, to take care of us. I admire you for that. I truly do. You are a fine man and I'm proud to be having your baby. But that kind of marriage—marriage you want because it's the *right* thing? Uh-uh. That's just not what *I* want. And it's not what our baby needs, either. Our baby needs—no. Our baby *deserves* a loving home, a *happy* home. How can our baby have that if you're resentful because you felt you had to marry me?"

"Whoa." He waited, just to be sure she was going to stop talking and listen for a moment. When she stayed quiet, he said slowly and clearly, "Don't characterize me. Please. I'm not resentful. Not in the least. And you know me well enough by now to know that I never do anything because I have to. I never do anything I don't *want* to do."

She was shaking her head. "All right. Have it your way. You want to marry me. Because you feel that you *have* to."

He stood. "Hayley."

She gazed up at him, her expression angelic. "What?"

"I'm going to go now." *Before my head explodes.*

"Oh, Marcus…"

He went to the closet by the door and got his coat. "We can…work this out tomorrow." He'd regroup, come at this problem in a fresh, new way—true, at this point he hadn't a clue what that way might be. But something would come to him, some way to get through to her, to make her see reason.

"There's nothing to work out," she said brightly. "Not when it comes to marriage, any-way—and where are you staying?"

He named his hotel. "Tomorrow, then."

She was on her feet, her hands pressed together as if in prayer, her expression verging on tender, her eyes at that moment sea-blue. He wanted to cover the distance between them, sweep her into his arms and taste those lips he'd been missing for so many months.

But no. Later for kissing. After she realized he was right about this. After she agreed to marry him and come home with him where he could take care of her, where she—and their baby—belonged.

In his hotel suite, Marcus checked his messages. There were several, each representing a different potential disaster. He made a string of calls to his associates. They brainstormed and came up with the necessary steps to eradicate the issues before they became catastrophes. By the time he hung up from the final call of the night, he was reassured that things in Seattle were as under control as they were likely to get until he could handle this situation with Hayley and return to work.

Next, he checked his e-mail, one eye on CNN as he made his replies, keeping a couple of IM conversations going at the same time, taking two more calls and answering questions as he worked. At last, with the phone quiet and the replies made, he put on his gym clothes and went down to the guest gym to work out.

Aside from the night before, when he had learned about the baby, Marcus never touched liquor—or drugs of any kind. His father had been a hopeless and violent drunk and Marcus was determined, above all, not to follow in the old man's footsteps. But his high-stress lifestyle demanded he find some way to relax and blow off steam. So he worked out.

An hour and a half later, dripping sweat, his legs and arms rubbery from pushing every muscle to the limit, he returned to his rooms and hit the shower. It was after one when he went to bed. By then he'd decided on his next move with Hayley and his confidence had returned.

Tomorrow, she would see things his way and agree to be his wife. They could be married in Nevada ASAP. And then she could return to Seattle with him and take it easy until the baby was born. They would have a good life, a full life.

He'd long ago accepted that he would never be a father. But now that it was happening, he was realizing he really didn't mind at all.

At seven the next morning, when Hayley opened the blinds on the living room window, she saw Marcus sitting out there on her balcony next to the miniature tree. She was tempted, just for the sake of being contrary, to let him sit there.

But it was cold out. Even from the far side of the window, with him facing away from her toward the central courtyard, she could see the way his breath plumed in the air.

It just wouldn't be right, to let her baby's father freeze to death on her landing.

She went and opened the door. At the sound, he turned and looked at her. Once again, she was forced to ignore the shiver of pleasure that skittered through her, just from meeting those watchful green eyes.

"I thought you'd never get up."

She gathered her robe a little closer around her and spoke in a tone meant to show he didn't thrill her in the least. "How do you keep slipping through the security gate, that's what I'd like to know?"

His fine mouth hinted at a wry smile as he stood. "Nobody keeps me out when I'm determined to get in." His eyes said he was talking about more than a locked gate. Another shiver. She told herself it was the cold. "Make me some coffee?"

She couldn't help teasing him, "You know, there's a Starbucks just two blocks away on—"

"Very funny." He asked again—or rather demanded, "Coffee. I need coffee."

"Oh, all right."

He followed her in, put his coat in the closet, then sat at the table and got out his PDA as she ground the beans and got the pot started. He poked at the tiny keys a mile a minute while she heated the water for her own special pregnant-lady herbal tea blend.

"I'm having oatmeal," she told him. "Want some?"

He glanced up from the device in his hand. "Sounds good. Thanks." She got to work on the oatmeal as he finished on the BlackBerry and put it away. "Can I help?"

"Why not? Bowls are in there." She indicated a cabinet. "Mugs there." She pointed again. "Spoons in here." She pulled out a drawer.

He rose and washed his hands and then set the table. It was…nice, she thought. Peaceful and domestic, the two of them in her little apartment, putting the simple breakfast together.

Not that she was changing her mind about anything. She wasn't. Though she had no doubt he would be putting the pressure on again any minute now.

She was right.

She sat down to her bowl of oats and reached for the brown sugar. A ring waited behind it. A truly amazing ring. The enormous central diamond winking at her in the early-morning light.

The thing was gorgeous. The main stone had to be four carats, maybe five, Marquise cut—wasn't that what they called that near-oval shape that tapered to a point at either end? A matched pair of gorgeous round diamonds snuggled up close on either side. The setting? Platinum. Of course.

It was…*more*, that ring. More than she would have chosen. More than she had dared to imagine, more than she ever could have hoped for, back in the day when she allowed herself the luxury of fantasizing about such things as engagement rings.

It was showy and perfect and it probably cost more than her yearly salary at Around the Corner Catering. She just ached to grab it and try it on— and never take it off. Even with her finger puffy from pregnancy, she knew it would fit….

And Marcus was watching her. "I meant to give it to you last night. But you were so busy saying no, I never got the chance."

"It's absolutely beautiful."

"I'm glad you like it."

"But I can't accept it, and you know I can't."

He sipped his coffee. "I thought we could go to Las Vegas. We could be married this afternoon."

She repeated, gently, with honest regret, "I'm not going to marry you. I told you that."

He didn't say a word, only looked at her, eyes level. Zero emotion. It was one of those moments where you could have heard a feather stir the air as it drifted to the floor.

Finally, he set down his mug, took out a velvet box and put the ring inside. He snapped the box closed and slipped it into a pocket. "You through with that brown sugar?"

She spooned some on her cereal and passed it to him. Same with the milk. She took some; so did he.

He tried it. "Good."

She nodded, longing to insist that she really did love the ring. She did appreciate his effort—or his nice older-lady assistant's effort, which was probably more likely. No way he'd managed to clear his calendar and get back here in one day and *still* have time to choose a ring. Whatever. It didn't matter who chose the ring. She *was* touched and she did want him to know that.

But going on about how touched she was would only increase his confidence that he was making progress toward getting her to marry him. Uh-uh. Wedding bells were not going to be ringing for them and the sooner he accepted that, the better.

He asked, "What time are you due at work?"

"Nine."

"And you're there until six?"

"No. Unless something comes up unexpectedly, we have no parties scheduled for tonight. I should be done by two or three." She felt just bad enough about the ring to volunteer more details. "I'm training my replacement. My last day is a week from Friday, as a matter of fact."

His expression didn't change. "I'll drive you."

"Uh. To work?"

"Yes."

"Really. That's not—"

"Humor me, all right? I'll drive you there and pick you up when you're finished."

"But I don't…" She let the refusal fade off into nothing. She knew by his carved-in-stone expression that he wasn't backing down on this. Not without a fight. And right then, after getting a look at that beautiful ring she couldn't accept, she just didn't have the heart to hold the line that hard with him. "All right. A ride is great. Thanks."

Around the Corner Catering had space in a new-looking strip mall. A brick facade and lots of windows, with well-tended flower beds out front.

Not bad, Marcus thought. In an upscale commercial area. At least she wasn't working in a rough part of town.

Hayley asked him to drive around back, where she pointed at a steel door bearing a plaque that read Around the Corner. "That's it."

Marcus nosed the car into an empty space opposite the door.

She sent him an apprehensive glance. "I'm not sure exactly what time I'll be finished...."

"Call when you're ready. You have the number?"

"I do, thanks." She got out and started for the building. He waited until she disappeared through the door before he backed and drove away.

The morning had been pretty much a loss. He'd gotten nowhere with her. And given that he damn well wasn't leaving until she agreed to leave with him, he was stuck another day in Sacramento.

Hell. He'd been so certain the ring was going to do it. Women went nuts for a big, fat diamond.

Most women, anyway. Not Hayley, though. At least not nuts enough to stop being so damn stubborn and let him do right by her.

Maybe he hadn't been romantic enough. He wasn't much good at the romantic stuff, never had been. Adriana used to complain about that all the time—how he wouldn't know a romantic gesture if it hit him on the head.

Marcus accepted his limitations in that area. He'd always thought that Hayley did, too. When things were good between them, she'd sworn she loved him just the way he was.

"You're not the least romantic," she'd told him once. They were in bed. After an amazing hour of lovemaking. *"But you are sexy as hell, Marcus Reid. Never change...."*

He didn't intend to change. Still, hiding that big rock behind the brown sugar had been kind of cute. And the expression on her face when she saw it waiting there...

Priceless.

But he probably should have dropped to his knees the minute she spotted it and spouted something tender and poetic about how much she meant to him, about how he couldn't live another nanosecond without her at his side.

If he'd planned ahead better, he could have copped some flowery phrases off the Internet, been prepared to rattle them off at just the right moment.

Seeing him on his knees, spouting love poems. Now, that would have shocked her. Enough to get her to say yes?

He'd never know now. The opportunity was blown.

He headed for his hotel and a couple of hours on the phone, conferencing with his managers, getting them up to speed on how they would be handling things on their own for yet another twenty-four hours.

By noon, he felt he had everything on track—

or at least as on track as it was going to get until he could take the reins in person again. That left him a couple of hours to kill before he picked up Hayley.

He knew just how to make the best use of that time: the brother.

In a situation as sticky as this one was turning out to be, Marcus could use an ally. Someone to support his case with Hayley. He'd considered approaching the sister, trying to get her on his side. But having seen Kelly with Hayley Monday night, he didn't foresee much assistance coming from that angle. Whatever choice Hayley made, Kelly would back her up.

Even if it was the *wrong* choice. Kelly wouldn't presume to tell her sister what she ought to do unless Hayley asked for her advice.

A brother, on the other hand, might damn well presume. A brother might push for his sister to do what was right, even if he had to stick his nose in where it didn't strictly belong.

Tuesday, between meetings, Marcus had contacted that P.I. again—the one he'd hired months ago to find out where Hayley had gone. This time he'd asked for a full report.

Within hours, the P.I. got back to him with basic information about Kelly and Tanner Bravo. Things like addresses and phone numbers, where they worked and their marital status.

Neither was married. Or ever had been. Kelly was the director of a family shelter. And Tanner owned and operated his own P.I. firm, Dark Horse Investigations.

Marcus went to Tanner's office in Rancho Cordova without calling first—and got nowhere. The office, in an undistinguished two-story building, was locked. No one answered his knock.

So much for the advantage of the face-to-face approach. He called the number his own investigator had given him and left his name and cell number. Tanner returned his call within minutes.

Marcus said, "I'm the father of Hayley's baby. I'd like to meet with you. Now, if possible."

Tanner Bravo had one question—the right one. "Where?"

"My hotel." He gave the name and the address. "The bar off the lobby."

"Half an hour?"

"I'll be there."

Marcus was nursing a club soda at the bar, text messaging his assistant, when Tanner appeared. Dark-haired and dark-eyed, he bore only a faint resemblance to his sisters.

"You're Reid," he said. "My sister's former boss." It wasn't a question. And he didn't offer to shake hands.

Marcus grabbed his drink. "Let's get a table."

They moved to a deuce in a shadowed corner. A cocktail waitress approached.

Tanner put a ten on the table. "Water. Ice."

She trotted off and returned in under a minute. Marcus said, "That's all." And she left them.

Tanner glanced at his glass, but didn't bother to pick it up. He gave Marcus a dark look. "Welcome to Sacramento."

"Thanks. You should know I'm here to marry your sister."

The other man considered for a moment. In the end, he nodded. "Well. Good to know."

"She failed to mention the baby when she left me seven months ago. If she had, we'd be married now."

"And you wanted to meet with me because…?"

"I want to…get to know her family."

Tanner simply sat there. Marcus knew he was waiting for him to get to the point.

Might as well go for it. "She says she loves me. I've asked her several times in the past couple of days to marry me. But she refuses."

"Why?"

Marcus didn't want to go into how Hayley was so damn sure he didn't love her because of Adriana. So he gave the other man a partial answer. "Hayley thinks I'll resent her for *forcing* me into it."

"Will you?"

"Resent her? Hell, no. It's the best thing. I can take care of her and I want to take care of her."

"And you want my help with that, with getting her to say yes."

"That's right."

Tanner seemed to be thinking it over. In any case, he sat unmoving and silent for an extended period of time. At last, he said, "I don't want to butt in. I mean, you seem like an okay guy. But Hayley…she comes on all sweetness, with that big, bright smile. Underneath, though, she's pure steel. She had to be strong to keep going, the way she grew up. It's not a good idea to mess with her, you know what I'm saying?"

"I'm not asking you to mess with her."

For the first time, Tanner smiled. He looked more like Hayley when he smiled. "Whew. Had me scared for a minute there." And he was suddenly all seriousness again. "She trusts me, okay? But she doesn't open up to me like Kelly does. I got time and grade with Kelly." Tanner's level stare assessed him. "Hayley tell you anything about our mother?"

"That she was sick a lot and had trouble keeping a job. She put Hayley in foster care. And never told her she had a brother and a sister."

"Yeah." Tanner picked up his glass then, and drank until it was empty. "She did the same to me. But I had this vague memory of a baby sister." He set down the glass. "Kelly and I are four years apart and we went into the system at the same time, right after Kelly was born. Hayley came along later. I had no idea she existed until she showed up when our mother was dying. When I was twenty-one, I finally got our mother to tell me about Kelly, who was seventeen at the time. I got the court to rule that she could come and live with me. So Kelly and me, we're close…." His voice trailed off. Marcus wondered about Kelly's kid. Who was the little ballerina's dad? Was he in the picture?

He kept his questions to himself and stuck with the main point. "I can take good care of Hayley. And our baby. Plus, she does love me. She wants to be with me. She just refuses to believe that *I* want to be with her." He slid a business card across the table. "You're a P.I. Ask around about me."

Tanner took the card. "I'll do that."

"And maybe, if you're satisfied with what you learn, you'll put in a good word for me where it counts."

"No promises."

"Fine. Whatever you can do."

"How long will you be in town?"

"As long as it takes."

"Did Hayley mention the reunion in Vegas this weekend?"

Marcus frowned. "Reunion?"

Tanner grinned. "I'll take that as a no."

Marcus said nothing. He knew his silence spoke for him.

Tanner explained, "A couple of our half brothers run resort casinos there. Impresario and High Sierra. It'll be one hell of a weekend. Bravos from all over. A Christmas family reunion."

The Las Vegas aspect was interesting. A good place for a nice, quick wedding. But by the weekend, he intended to be back in Seattle—with his bride.

Marcus admitted, "No. She hasn't mentioned it. Yet."

Tanner was giving him that measuring look again. Then he said, "Tell you what. Consider yourself invited."

Federico was up to his old tricks in the kitchen, swearing in Spanish and throwing the pans around.

Sofia, the owner, put her hands over her ears and shouted toward the open doorway to Federico's domain, "Will you turn it down in there? I can't hear myself think!"

Federico only swore louder and banged another pot. The phone started ringing.

Hayley gave her boss a quick wave and headed for the back exit. Better to wait for Marcus outside, where he couldn't hear the yelling. She pushed the door wide—and found him there already, standing by the car, not ten feet from the door.

Behind her, Sofia shouted again and more pans went clanging. The door was automatic. It took forever to shut. Hayley leaned back against it and pushed until the latch clicked.

Then, wearing her most cheerful smile, she headed toward the tall man with the scowl on his face. "You got here quick."

He went around and opened the door for her. She got in and buckled up as he went around to his side.

He stuck his key in the ignition. "What was all that screaming in there?"

She granted him a superior glance. "The chef is…temperamental. But harmless. And you're exaggerating about the screaming."

"Sounded like screaming to me," he muttered as he started the engine. "Where to?"

"Just take me to my place." She turned on the radio to a soft rock station, hoping that might keep him quiet for a while. She needed a break from his constant griping about her job, a complaint that was bound to segue into yet another proposal of marriage. Her ploy worked. The music filled the car and he drove with his mouth shut and his eyes turned to the road.

At her place, she thanked him for the ride, thinking maybe he'd let her go for the day.

Not a chance. He was right behind her when she got to her front door.

She faced him. "Look. I'm just going to get my

car and go pick up a few things for the baby's room. Really boring stuff. You don't want to—"

"Why didn't you say so? Let's go."

Okay, it was sweet of him, really. To volunteer to drive her to the mall. And what else was he going to be doing in Sacramento that afternoon, anyway? "Maybe you have phone calls or something you have to make?"

"Handled."

It was the unrelenting pressure he put her under, to surrender and say yes, that was the problem. It was just so difficult to constantly say no when her poor heart kept screaming yes. She chewed on her lower lip.

And gave in. "All right. You can go with me."

"Well, of course, I'm going with you."

She raised a finger. "One condition."

"Damn it."

"Are you listening?"

"Is there a choice?"

She waited.

Finally, he grumbled, "Let me have it."

"For the rest of the day you will not mention marriage or my job."

He scowled. "What the hell?"

"Come on. It won't be so hard. Just let it be, for crying out loud. You might even enjoy yourself."

He made a scoffing sound. "I'm not here to enjoy myself."

"Hey. Go with the flow a little, why don't you, Marcus? You might be surprised."

"I don't want to be surprised."

"Fine. Have it your way. Don't be surprised. Don't enjoy yourself. Be as tense and controlling as you always are, just don't talk about my job or my marrying you. That's the deal. Take it or leave it."

"But I think that you should—"

She cut him off with an impatient sound. "Listen. Remember. No talk of marriage, no griping about my job. And you also won't tell me a single thing I *should* be doing. Agreed?"

"But if you would only…"

That time she stopped him with just a look. It was progress, of a sort. Wasn't it? She asked again, "Agreed?"

Judging by the determined set to that manly jaw of his, he wasn't the least bit pleased with her terms. Still, after several smoldering seconds, he gave her what she'd demanded.

"Agreed."

Hayley was the one who ended up being surprised. Because Marcus kept his word.

At the mall he was downright cheerful. And patient. He helped her choose a changing table, which the clerk promised would be delivered the next day. Hayley bought more receiving blankets and some onesies and rompers. He not only paid for all the baby things, he insisted on carrying the bags. And since she bought a few Christmas gifts, too, by the end of the afternoon, there were a whole bunch of bags.

They did have a little argument about who was going to buy the ballerina Barbie for DeDe and the sweater that was just perfect for Kelly. But in the end, he gave up on trying to pay for her Christmas presents and let her use her own money for those.

He was attentive, urging her to take frequent breaks to rest her tired feet. They would sit on the mall benches and talk about mundane things while the piped-in Christmas music filled the air.

Twice, his cell vibrated. He took it out and checked the display, but for once he didn't immediately start making calls or text messaging. He simply shrugged and put the phone away.

And never once did he mention her job or the *m* word.

It was…nice.

Nice. A strange word to think of in connection with Marcus Reid. Marcus was exciting. Focused. Sexy. Intense.

Nice, though?

Not hardly. Not in her experience—until that lovely, gray December day.

He bought her ice cream: mint chip in a waffle cone. They sat by the central fountain and she devoured the treat. "Good." She groaned in delight as she sucked the last of the sweet, minty coldness from the heart of the cone.

"You've got ice cream on your chin…." He dabbed at the sticky spot with the tip of his napkin—and she let him.

"Tired?" he asked when they rose and tossed their napkins in a trash bin.

She realized that she was totally exhausted. "Yeah. Ready to go home."

At her place, he carried all the bags up to her door and followed her inside. She led him to the baby's room. "Just put it all down in here for now. I'll sort it out later."

He set the pile of purchases on the floor. "A rainbow," he said as he rose. Though his back was to her, she knew he was smiling. She could hear it in his voice as he admired the mural on the wall opposite the door.

She'd had to get permission from the manager to do that mural, and to sign a paper that said she'd repaint the room a neutral color when she left—or sacrifice a substantial chunk of her deposit. "I painted it myself…." Along with the baseboard border of green grass and teddy bears.

He turned and saw her sagging against the door frame. "You're beat."

"Oh, a little. I get like this the past few weeks. All of a sudden, I can hardly keep my head up. An hour's nap. I'll be fine…."

He put his arm around her and it felt so good—to lean on him.

She let him lead her to the other bedroom. She drooped to the bed and he slipped off her shoes for her. With a grateful sigh, she sank back into the pillows, turning on her side, the position she found the most comfortable now she was so big. He waited, his head tipped to the side, looking a little puzzled, as she slid a pillow between her knees.

"Increases blood flow," she explained. "And enhances kidney function. Good things. Trust me."

He pulled up the blanket she kept folded at the foot of the bed and settled it over her.

"I had a nice time," she told him when he tucked it in around her.

His hand brushed her cheek. "Me, too." He said it as though he really meant it.

And she couldn't help thinking, *If only….*

Oh, yeah. If only….

"Rest now," he whispered, leaning closer. She looked in those green eyes and knew he would kiss her. In a vague, disconnected way she knew that she should tell him no.

But she didn't speak. She *wanted* him to kiss her.

And then it was too late for refusals, anyway. Slowly, so gently, those wonderful lips of his settled over hers.

Chapter Five

It wasn't a long kiss.

But oh, it was one of the sweetest she'd ever shared with him. A tender kiss. A brushing kiss. A kiss that was…enough in itself, somehow.

It was a kiss that made no demands, yet a kiss that conjured memories of the fine times they'd had together. Of the busy, exhilarating days and lovely, sexy nights.

When he pulled away, she almost reached out to hold him there. But she caught herself in time.

"We shouldn't have done that," she chided softly, speaking more to herself than to him.

"Shh. It was only a kiss."

Her eyes were drooping. She burrowed more deeply beneath the blanket and let them drift shut. Sleep claimed her instantly in its dark embrace.

Marcus left the bedroom quietly, shutting the door behind him.

He started down the hall, but found himself drawn to the baby's room. He stood in the open doorway and stared at the rainbow Hayley had painted on the far wall. It charmed him, that rainbow. It was…so like her, to paint a rainbow, a symbol of hope, on the wall of her baby's room.

She would be a good mother. Of that, he had zero doubt.

Would he—*could* he—be a good father? The question echoed uncomfortably inside his head. Until now, it had never occurred to him that he might someday be a dad. He'd thought that was for the best. The world didn't need more kids, not when so many children already grew up unwanted and unloved.

Finding Hayley pregnant, though…

Somehow, that changed everything for him, made him want exactly what he'd never expected to have, made him see at least the possibility of rainbows. Made him feel something resembling hope for the first time in a long while…

He felt a smile tug on the corners of his mouth.

Damn. He'd better be careful. A day away from work and an afternoon of mall-crawling and suddenly the world seemed a brighter place. If he didn't watch himself, he'd be humming "White Christmas," stringing popcorn, watching *It's a Wonderful Life* and actually enjoying it.

His phone vibrated. He should check the display, see if it was anything important.

But he didn't. Instead, for a while longer, he stood there in the doorway to his unborn baby's room, staring at that rainbow, feeling strangely light at heart.

Hayley woke as swiftly as she'd fallen asleep. Her eyes popped open. She blinked at the bedside clock. An hour and a half had passed since she dropped off. *Marcus…*

She freed a hand from the warm cocoon of the blanket and pressed her fingers to her lips. He'd kissed her, hadn't he? Just before she fell asleep. The sweetest, most tender kiss…

Really dumb. To have let him kiss her again.

Especially considering it only made her want to let him kiss her some more.

And what was that smell? Like…

Chinese food. Her stomach growled.

She sniffed the air. Oh, yeah. Definitely. Chinese. She kicked away the pillow between her knees and shoved the covers aside.

Out in the living room, she found Marcus watching *Hardball* and eating chow mein out of the carton.

He turned and their gazes locked. The familiar thrill skittered through her and the world was a golden place, bursting with promise. Right then, in the span of that shared glance, she reevaluated. Everything.

But all she said was, "What else you got in those cartons?"

"Come and see for yourself."

So she went and sat beside him and enjoyed a little popcorn shrimp and a couple of egg rolls. When they were done he put the leftovers in the fridge. She turned off the TV and waited for him to come back to the living room.

He sat down at her side. "Okay. I can hear your brain working. What are you thinking? What's going on?"

She took his hand. His eyes changed, went darker. He seemed surprised that she would make any kind of move toward him—even such a simple thing as to clasp his hand. She heard herself admit, "Maybe I was wrong."

He put his other hand on top of hers, enclosing it between his palms. It felt really good. Cherishing, somehow. Protective. And it brought to mind the feel of his arms close around her. Funny that she always felt so safe in his embrace.

For once, he had the sense not to speak, to let her say what she meant to say in her own time.

She told him, "I had such a great time this afternoon. Truly. And it's good to be with you. I…oh, I really have missed you, the past months. I've been waiting, to get over you. To *not* miss you quite so much. But what's in my heart for you, well, it's very strong. And now you're here and you seem to really want to make things work with me.…"

"I do." He said it firmly, like a vow.

And she couldn't help smiling as she gazed into those dear green eyes. "I'm thinking maybe, if we could have some time together, you and me, we might figure out if there's any chance we could make a go of it.…"

"We *can* make a go of it, Hayley. Just let me—"

"Wait."

"What?"

"The time. Do you think you could give me that?"

He squeezed her hand. "You know I can. Marry me. Tomorrow. Come back with me to Seattle. We'll—"

"No. Please. Not Seattle, not yet."

"But you just said—"

"I wasn't clear. What I meant was, will you take some time off, stay here with me in Sacramento for a while?"

His face fell. "Hayley…" He said her name with real regret. "I'm sorry. I can't."

It was the answer she'd expected. She knew how he felt about being away from his work. But she wasn't giving up yet. "Just think about it a little."

"There's nothing to think about."

"Sure, there is. Look. I know that you never take time off. You're a driven man and perfectly happy to be so. And I'm sure it's a bad time to take time off. Because it's always a bad time, really, isn't it?"

He didn't reply. There was no need. She'd just laid out his own arguments for him.

She went on, "Just…time. That's what I want from you. Stay here with me until after Christmas."

He let go of her hand. "Christmas is almost two weeks away. It's impossible. I can't—"

She interrupted, "Please. Before you start telling me all the reasons you can't, let's just talk it over. Let's explore the, er, possibilities."

"Which are?"

"There's a family reunion this weekend."

He grunted. "In Las Vegas."

She shook her head, but she was smiling. "How did you know that?"

He swore. But then he admitted, "I got hold of your brother. We had a talk. I asked him to put in a good word for me, with you. He told me about the reunion. Invited me, as a matter of fact."

"When was this?"

"Today, before I picked you up from the caterer's."

She grinned. "Working all the angles, huh?"

"Hell, yes."

She took his hand again in both of hers, turned it over, stroked his palm with her thumbs. "In the bedroom, when you kissed me…"

"Yeah?" The word was low and rough.

"I know I said we shouldn't have kissed, but what I *thought* was how much I'd missed your kisses. How I've longed for you. How I love you…."

"Then mar—"

"Don't." She touched his lips to stop the words. "Don't say it. Not now. Please. I don't want to talk about marriage. Yet. First, I want to have some time with you. I want us to be together without all the pressure and excitement and distraction of Kaffe Central. I want us to get to know each other in a whole new light. I want us to have time do nothing, except *be*."

He looked very worried. "Be. You want us to *be*."

"Tall order, huh?"

"You know how I am. I don't do *being*. I work. Hard. That's who I am."

"You let things just *be* this afternoon, didn't you? I think you did pretty well."

He reached out. She didn't duck away, but allowed him to run a finger down the curve of her cheek, to tuck a few strands of sleep-mussed hair behind her ear. To her, that touch was a pure miracle. It set off sparks along the surface of her skin, brought a tempting warmth down low in her belly.

She found she was glad. Joyous, even. That he had come to find her. That he wouldn't give up when she told him no.

His eyes had gone soft as some secret, green glen. He whispered, "Damn it, Hayley…"

Oh, yeah. Eight months pregnant and she still wanted him. Bad.

She caught his caressing hand, pressed it to her lips. And then, very gently, she let it go. "I want… honesty, with you, Marcus. And I also want us to be lovers again."

He blinked and slanted a swift glance at her huge belly. "Lovers…when?"

"Now." She laughed. "You should see your face. Too strange for you, to be the lover of a pregnant lady?"

And his eyes went all soft again. He looked almost innocent. Almost…young. "Can you?"

"Yes. If we're careful. And imaginative. If you don't mind taking it slow and easy. And if it doesn't turn you off, me being so enormous."

Again, he reached out. He touched her throat. When she shuddered and sighed, he slid his hand under her hair and caressed the back of her neck. "It doesn't turn me off. Not in the least. And I can be careful." The words were a rough caress. "And slow. And imaginative…"

"Oh, well. I really like all that in a man…"

He was looking at her mouth. "I want to kiss you."

"I want to kiss you, too…."

He picked up on her hesitation. "Okay. What's the catch?"

"Not a catch, really. But I do want honesty, between us. I think we have to start with that."

He took his hand away. "Are you saying I've lied to you?"

"Well, last night, you did say you loved me…."

He craned back from her and his eyes were watchful again—and wary.

She said, "You don't love me, do you?"

"Of course, I love—"

"Just the truth." She cut him off before he could lie again. "Please. We have to start from there."

An awful pause and then, at last, "No. I'm not in love with you. Whatever the hell that means. I'm not real crazy about the whole love thing, anyway. Love's brought me nothing but misery— and now you're mad at me, right?"

"No. Oh, no." She gulped to clear her clutching throat. "Okay. It hurts to hear you say it. But really, it's better. For you to tell me the truth."

His expression was doubtful. "If you say so."

"I just want to go into this with my eyes open, that's all. I know you're still in love with—"

"No." The word was sure and deep and final. "I'm not in love with anyone."

She didn't believe him. He *was* still in love with Adriana, even if he wouldn't let himself admit it. But she figured she'd pushed him far enough for one night. And in the end, he was an honorable man. No matter the secret yearnings in his heart, if they did get married, she knew she could trust him never to cheat on her.

And he certainly cared for her. He cared a great deal, as much as his wounded heart could bear. That much she didn't doubt. Surely, good marriages had been built on less.

"Can we move on?" he asked gruffly.

She nodded. "Let's. Where were we?"

"I was going to kiss you." He leaned in a little closer again. "Can we get back to that?"

"Oh. Kissing…."

"Objections?"

"Not a one."

"Excellent." He framed her face with gentle hands. She tipped up her lips to him, welcoming him. He smelled so good, all clean and manly, with a hint of that expensive aftershave he always wore. His mouth descended.

She felt his lips, again, on hers. At last. Nothing…nothing was as lovely as that. He brushed his mouth back and forth, teasing, tempting. And when she sighed, he took it as an invitation.

His tongue touched her lower lip. She gave a little moan and he was inside, stroking the edges of her teeth, sucking a little, making her sigh some more.

Too soon, he lifted his head. "You taste good," he said. "Better, even than I remembered…" He wrapped his hand around the nape of her neck again and he rubbed a little, massaging the bumps at the top of her spine. It felt just right, kind of eased out the tension—what was left of it, anyway, which wasn't a lot after that bone-melting kiss.

She guided his other hand to her belly. He whispered her name as he touched the high curve, his fingers spreading wide. "It feels so hard…."

"Like a watermelon, huh?"

"Is it all right if I…?"

She held his eyes. "Mmm-hmm."

He explored the shape of her, his palm curving out over the front of her, sliding inward again toward her lap.

The baby gave a nudge. "Oh!" She laughed and caught his wrist, guiding it to the side. "Wait…" She watched his face. "There. Feel that?"

His eyes held wonder. "A kick. I swear, he kicked me…"

She slanted him a teasing glance. "Could be a she, you know…"

"You didn't…find out?"

"Nope. A boy or a girl, I don't care either way. And sometimes, in life, a little mystery is good. I know he or she is healthy. So I can wait."

He kept his hand where she'd put it, waiting. "If she's a girl, she'll be pretty as her mother."

"Flattery. I like it. Tell me more."

"A little girl with red hair…"

"And green eyes," she added.

"There." His stern face seemed suddenly lit from within. "Another kick. She's athletic, no doubt about it."

She caught his hand, twined her fingers with his. "So. What do you say?"

"About what?"

"Marcus. Come *on*." Now she'd gone and proposed the impossible, she found she was eager to know if he would go for it. "Time. Over Christmas. You and me."

"Time?"

She groaned. "Stop teasing me."

He actually laughed, a rough sound. But so good to hear. And he said, "I'd have to fly back to Seattle first, get things in order there as much as possible…"

She felt warm all over, sparkly and bright. "I can't believe this. Are you telling me I can have a whole two weeks of you away from Kaffe Central?"

"Together."

"Of course. You make it sound like a warning."

"I'm just getting things good and clear about this. I would stay here, with you."

"That's what I was hoping for."

"Could have fooled me. Until tonight."

"I think it was that kiss in the bedroom that did it."

"Damn. One little kiss. How simple is that? I should have tried it sooner."

She realized she hadn't made herself totally clear. "It would still be…I mean, it still might not work out between us. We both have to keep that in mind."

"Sorry. No."

"But you have to—"

"Uh-uh. No way. I want to marry you. *That's* what I'll be keeping in mind."

"But for the two weeks, you'll let it alone."

He grunted. "I'm not supposed to ask you to marry me again, you mean?"

She nodded. "Yes. Please. You know how you are when you get focused on something. It's a little overwhelming. I don't want to be arguing about marriage all the time."

"Right. We're supposed to just *be*."

"That's it. Consider it a hiatus. A Christmas vacation."

"For two damn weeks."

"Well?"

"Kiss me again. Then we'll see."

Chapter Six

Marcus stole more kisses before he finally gave in and agreed to try her plan.

Taking two weeks away from Seattle…

He had to be stone cold out of his mind.

But there *was* Hayley. He would have Hayley. Round, ripe, soft, sweet-smelling Hayley. She would be fully available to him, not pushing him away, no longer denying him.

She was like a drug. A good drug. The kind that made dreary days bright.

Two years ago, after Adriana left him, he'd damn well never expected to get involved with another woman—not for a long while, anyway. After all, he'd loved Adriana from some distant time in childhood. He'd always known she was the one for him, the *only* one. His perfect match. She could be cruel and self-serving. But she understood him, she *knew* him in some deep and complete way that no one else ever had.

Or so he'd always believed.

Their marriage was supposed to have lasted them a lifetime. But Adriana was restless at heart. She resented the long hours he spent at work. She called him stuffy and distant. She wanted more from him—at the same time as she said he stifled her.

In the end, the union didn't hold. She ran off to a tiny middle-European principality with a guy named VonKruger. And she filed for divorce.

He had nothing then, but the company he'd built. His job kept him going.

Until Hayley.

She tempted him. She lured him. She offered him everything—her laughter, her sweetness, her pretty, sexy body. She was a sudden warm, healing light in a life that had spiraled down to a flat baseline of hard work and gray loneliness. Because of her, what might have been a slow slide into someplace really ugly became something else altogether. With Hayley, he was as close to happy as he'd ever been.

But then it ended. He couldn't give her the love that she wanted, so she left him.

Yet now, here he was. Sitting in her living room, agreeing to spend two weeks just *being,* whatever the hell that would entail. Funny, how a woman—the *right* woman—could make deserting the business he'd built from the ground up, the business that required his hand at the helm, seem like a perfectly reasonable idea.

But no. He knew what she'd say to that. *Not desertion, Marcus. A hiatus. A much-needed Christmas vacation....*

He kissed her some more. And he touched her. All over. It pleased him, aroused him, to feel the changes in her body. To explore the differences his baby had made.

As in the past, she held nothing back. Smiling, eyes shining, she let him undress her, let him reveal her new roundness. With no embarrassment, with only eagerness and soft sighs, she gave herself.

He was careful. It was no hardship, to be gentle, even cautious. She needed his care now and he was only too willing to give her what she needed.

Before, sex with her had been hot and satisfying—and fun, too. Hayley was always fun. And adventurous, as well. Him on top, her on top, whatever. She'd try any position; and she enjoyed variety. Whatever he suggested, she was up for it.

And she was always ready for a little fantasy, including dress up. She'd played his French maid. And a leather-clad temptress in dangerously high heels....

He grinned to himself, remembering the fine, sexy times they'd had.

And she demanded, "Okay, what's that grin about?"

They were in her bedroom by then. Naked, together. On her bed. He cradled her breast. Fuller than he remembered, the pale skin soft and pliant, traced now with delicate blue veins, the nipple darker than before. He lowered his head, touched his tongue to the dark red tip.

She didn't allow more, but put her hand under his chin and made him look at her again. "That grin?"

"Just...remembering. You and me. In bed. Before..."

She giggled like a little girl. "We had some fun, huh?"

He clasped her shoulder, loving the feel of her skin. Again. At last. "It was good, all right. *This* is good..."

"Oh, yeah..."

She put the pillows where she wanted them and then lay back, propped against them. He stretched out beside her and kissed her, letting his hands go roaming....

Over those swollen, tender breasts, down between them...

Again, he felt the baby move.

And then he went lower. He touched her where she was wet and waiting for him. She moaned and he deepened the kiss, as below, he stroked the soft, silky folds.

She shattered on a keening sigh. He smiled against her mouth.

"Good…" She stuck out her tongue and traced a wet trail over his lips.

He caught that tongue of hers, took it inside his mouth, and when he let go, he captured her lower lip between his teeth and bit down—gently. Until she gasped and whispered his name.

And then she found him, that soft hand of hers closing around him, tightening, holding firm, and then, oh-so-slowly sliding upward.

She caressed the tip. He moaned. She caught his mouth again and kissed him, deeply. Thoroughly. As that clever hand of hers drove him wild.

He caught her wrist just at the point where he was about to go over the edge and he trailed kisses over her cheek, giving her earlobe a tender nip before whispering what he wanted. "You. All around me. Is that safe?"

She turned her head enough to meet his lips again. "Lie down. On your back…" She breathed the words against his mouth.

And then she pushed him to his back, rising above

him, that red hair falling forward over her breasts, gleaming like pure silk in the light from the lamp.

She held his eyes with hers as she took him inside her—not all the way, but enough.

Enough. Oh, yeah. More than enough.

She rode him, a slow, easy, ride, one hand tucked under her heavy stomach, for support. He held himself in check, letting her be in control. It was pure torture, holding back, not lifting his hips to her, not taking all of her, resisting the burning urge to grab her close and push in so hard and tight…

And still, though his mind whispered warnings to go gently, to take care, he couldn't resist her body's call. He felt himself rising, reaching, finding the finish in spite of the way he reined in his desire….

He let out a low, strangled sound as it took him. Fisting his hands in the sheet to keep from grabbing her, he held on, still holding back at the same time as he lost himself completely.

She moved above him, making soft sounds of encouragement, as his climax rolled through him. The world flew away. There was only her softness, her wetness, her heat.

He went where she took him, up into midnight, over the moon….

Chapter Seven

Hayley felt the bed shift as Marcus got up.

For a few lazy seconds, she kept her eyes closed, kind of drifting, still half-asleep. But eventually, she peeked.

Marcus was getting dressed.

"Hey." She sat up, shoved her hair back from her face and squinted at the clock. "It's not even six yet...."

"Gotta get a move on." He dropped to the bedside chair to put on his shoes.

She flopped back to the pillows. "Ugh. The driven business tycoon returns. I knew last night was too good to last."

"Look who's talking. Who's still working when she doesn't need to be?"

"Marcus."

He winced. "When you say my name like that, I know there's a lecture to follow."

"I'm…in balance, when it comes to working. I have my job in perspective."

"See? What'd I tell you? Next you'll be shaking a finger at me."

"Me? Never. Just remember. Work fast. I want you back here in time to go to the reunion with me."

"I remember. Let the *being* begin."

"Oh, that is exactly right."

He frowned. "Is it safe for you to go to Las Vegas in your condition?"

She blew out a breath. "Oh, stop. Of course, it's safe. It's not like I'm having any problems, or even any signs of early labor."

"Are you allowed to fly?"

"Far as I know. I think it has to be a pressurized cabin, though. Pressure changes rob the baby of oxygen, or something like that. I can check with my doctor if you're worried."

"Do that. If you're good to go, we'll take a company jet. Faster. And more comfortable. Ask your sister and brother if they want to fly with us."

"I will. Thank you."

He hadn't stopped frowning. "As far as I know, they still allow smoking in Las Vegas casinos."

"Marcus. Stop. It's going to be fine. I've had no complications. This is a perfectly healthy pregnancy and the two casinos we'll be in are new, with those amazing, state-of-the-art air filtration systems. They suck that smoke right out of the air."

"I just don't think it's good for you."

She grabbed her robe from the foot of the bed and put it on while he sat there and watched her, looking grim. "Marcus…" She waddled on over to him and held out her hand. He took it, but he still looked a long way from happy. "Stop worrying." She gave a tug. Shaking his head, he rose. She cradled his beard-rough face in her hands and went on tiptoe to kiss his scowling mouth. "Be nice and I'll make you some coffee before you go…."

"I just want you to be safe."

"I will be. I promise."

At last, he gave in and put his arms around her. They shared a sweet, slow kiss, after which she took his hand again and led him to the kitchen where the coffeepot waited.

He was gone by seven, promising to return Friday afternoon to take her to Vegas and her family reunion. She ate breakfast and got ready for work, where they had three parties that night. Amazingly, Federico was working quietly in the kitchen when she arrived. Sofia told her that she'd had a long talk with the chef. Things would be a lot less noisy around there from now on.

Hayley's trainee looked relieved.

Hayley smiled while she supervised her replacement and hummed Christmas songs under her breath. The new girl was doing fine.

And she and Marcus would have two whole weeks, together.

Who knew when she left him all those months ago, that before their baby was born, they'd be together again—for the holidays, at least?

And maybe forever. Hey. Wilder things had happened.

But she wasn't going to get ahead of herself. Uh-uh. For now, the two weeks ahead were miracle enough.

Marcus met with his managers early that afternoon. Actually, things were going damn well. The company hadn't gone under in the few days he'd been away, after all.

He explained that he was taking a two-week hiatus. *Hiatus.* He hid his smile as he said it. It sounded more…elevated, somehow, than an ordinary vacation. He told them to get together with their people. Any issue that required his input should be on his desk by six that night.

They would meet again the next morning before he left for Sacramento to handle any immediate problems. He returned to his office feeling pretty good about things. He'd have his ring on Hayley's finger before the agreed-on two weeks were up. And next month, he'd be a dad.

The dad part was damn scary. But hey. One day at a time and all that.

He spent a half hour with Joyce, clearing his calendar. Once she left him, he got down to cleaning out his in-boxes. When his BlackBerry vibrated, he figured it was probably Hayley and answered without looking at the display.

"What?" He was smiling.

"Marcus?"

Adriana. His stomach hollowed out and his pulse went racing. Damn. His hands were sweating.

He knew he should disconnect the call. He had nothing to say to her.

And yet, for reasons he didn't care to examine, he stayed on the line.

"Oh, Marcus. Are you there? Tell me you're there…."

Somehow, he found his voice. "What do you want?"

"Oh, God. How are you?"

He realized he was absolutely furious. Coldly, for the second time, he demanded, "What do you want?"

"Oh, no. I can tell from your voice. You haven't forgiven me. I'm so sorry. It was terrible, what I did. I know it. Believe me. I know it too well…."

He had a sudden gut-twisting certainty that she had returned to Seattle. "Where the hell are you?"

"London. I've left Leo."

So she'd walked out on VonKruger, too. Why wasn't he surprised?

"Oh, Marcus. I know now. I see. I've made a horrible mistake. It was always you. Always. A nation of two, that's what we are. Nothing can change that. Our love is forever. You're alive because of me. And I can't live without you. I've been selfish and so wrong. I need to talk to you. In person. I need to *see* you."

"No."

A stunned silence, then, "You can't mean that. Tell me you'll—"

"Leave me alone, Adriana. Do not call me again."

"Oh, no. Please—"

He disconnected the call. Finally. And after that, he just sat there, holding the phone in a hand that wouldn't stop shaking, remembering....

Everything. Down all the years. In a series of knife-sharp flashing images.

You're alive because of me....

He saw himself at twelve. Skinny. Lonely. Scared. So sure that his father would kill him finally. Kill him in a drunken rage and still find some way to weasel out of facing the consequences. After all, his father was Darien Reid, heir to the Reid fortune. An important man. A man like Darien Reid didn't beat his only son to death....

It was a gray, rainy day. Like so many Seattle days. Marcus had stolen the housekeeper's stash of Darvocet and gone to school. He swallowed all the pills in the bottle, washed them down with a can of ginger ale and waited in the boys' restroom to die.

Adriana had found him.

He recalled that he came swimming up to a foggy half consciousness to find...

His head in her lap, her hair like a halo of pure gold around her beautiful face. She had screamed at him, hadn't she? That he'd better not die, that he *couldn't* die...

The device in his hand vibrated, yanking him back from the past.

He dropped the thing to the deskpad as if it had teeth. And he waited, until it finally stopped buzzing like a furious bee and sent the caller to voice mail. Then he picked the thing up, set it on the floor and ground it into the travertine tile with the heel of his shoe.

When the phone rang at eight that night Hayley knew it would be Marcus. Her caller ID said otherwise. "Hello?"

A low chuckle, then, "Tell me you quit your job today."

"Marcus. It *is* you."

"You thought it would be some other guy?"

"No. I thought it would be you. But the number on the display is different."

"New cell number. Got a pencil?"

"The number's in my phone. Why a new one?"

"Long, boring story. Use this number from now on."

"Okay—and no, of course I didn't quit my job."

"You said you were training someone."

"Well, I am, but—"

"How are we going to be together if you're working all the time?"

Together. It sounded so good when he said it. And, well, he did have a point. "Actually, my replacement is doing really well...."

"Quit. Tomorrow."

"I wasn't planning to quit. I'm taking a six-week leave."

"And if I tell you again to quit, that will be pushing, right? And I'm not supposed to push."

"See? You're learning."

"Start your *leave* tomorrow."

"Ever been called relentless before?"

"Frequently. Do it. Tomorrow."

All at once, she had the strangest sense that something wasn't right. Where did the feeling come from? She had no idea. He didn't sound any different, did he?

And there was nothing that he'd said….

"Hayley?"

"I'm right here."

"You all right?"

Funny he was asking *her* that question. "Fine. Truly."

"For a second there, I thought we'd lost the connection."

"Nope. And DeDe says to tell you she can't wait to ride in your jet."

"Will she be wearing her ballerina shoes?"

"Probably not. But only because Kelly won't let her."

"Your brother?"

"He'll fly with us, too. There's a big family dinner at Impresario tomorrow night to kick off the weekend. Think we can make it for that?"

"Sure. Things are in pretty good shape here. I should be there to pick you up by one tomorrow. If your sister and brother could meet us at Executive Airport around two, we can take off by two-thirty."

"I'll pass the word along."

"Did you talk to your doctor, about whether it's safe for you to be flying?"

"I talked to her nurse, will that do?"

"And her nurse said…"

"Just what I already told you. Really. I'm fine and it's perfectly safe for me to fly in a pressurized cabin—which the jet has, right?"

"Right."

"I have to tell you. I can't wait."

"You sound like a kid at Christmas."

She laughed. "Right season. And I *feel* like a kid—well, except for the big stomach and the swollen ankles, I mean."

"You're pretty amazing." He said it so tenderly. So…admiringly. "You don't let life get you down. You don't…expect to be taken care of. I always know I can count on you. *Trust* you…"

"Thank you—and is everything all right?"

He made a low sound. "What? You get suspicious when I tell you how terrific you are?"

"No, it's just…I don't know. Nothing, I guess. As long as you're sure you're all right…"

"I am. Very much all right."

"Well. Good."

They said good-night. As soon as she hung up, she copied his new number into her address book. And then she got busy packing for the weekend trip.

Strangely, the vague feeling that something was wrong didn't go away. It lingered in the back of her mind the rest of the evening and into the night, even kept her awake for a while.

When she finally did sleep, she dreamed of the father she'd never met, of herself as a little girl, Blake Bravo looming over her, more a shadow than anything real. She whimpered in her sleep as he bent down to reach for her.

* * *

Marcus lay in bed in his house in Madison Park. He'd moved when Adriana left him, but he'd kept the same home phone number.

Big mistake.

The phone rang, as he'd known that it would. He waited through the four endless rings, until the answering machine in his office finally picked up. Once he was sure Adriana had had enough time to leave her message and hang up, he took the phone off the hook.

Before he left for California the next day, he'd make arrangements to have the number changed.

Chapter Eight

"You're a half an hour late," Hayley said when she opened the door.

Marcus shrugged. "That final meeting…"

"I know the rest. It went long. Problems?"

"Nothing my managers can't handle. I hire good people. Time I gave them a chance to show their stuff."

She reached out and took his hand and pulled him inside with her, shoving the door shut as soon as he cleared the threshold. Then she threw herself into his arms.

"Oof," he said.

She slid her hands up to encircle his neck. "A hundred and sixty pounds of pregnant person. It's a lot to hug."

"Kiss me."

So she did. A long, wet one. He lifted his mouth from hers eventually, but only to slant his head the other way.

In the end, she was the one to pull back. "If we keep on like this, we'll never get to the airport."

"You started it."

"Yeah. Wild, huh? I don't understand it. I just couldn't help myself somehow."

He looked almost misty-eyed. "It's good. This. With us."

"It is." She beamed. "Who knew, huh?"

"A second chance…" He looked…bemused. It was so not an expression she'd ever expected to see on his face.

"Well, after all," she replied, "it's the season for miracles."

"Wow." DeDe giggled in delight. "It's like in the James Bond movies." The jet's cabin was furnished with easy chairs and tables, set up like a living area, where the Kaffe Central execs could work or relax en route. There were even bud vases mounted on the walls between the windows, each holding its own fresh-cut red rose. DeDe turned her bright eyes to her mother. "We could have martinis, shaken, not stirred."

"Only if you prove you're twenty-one first," muttered her uncle Tanner.

The grown-ups laughed and DeDe demanded to know if there would be movies.

"The screen is right there." Marcus pointed at the spot on the ceiling from which the forty-five-inch screen would descend before the movie began.

The attendant showed DeDe to a chair, gave her a set of headphones, handed her a remote and showed her how to scan the movie choices. They all took seats and buckled up for takeoff.

Once they were in the air, DeDe had a 7-Up and chose *The Santa Clause 3* in honor of the season. She put on her headphones and settled back as the big screen came down.

Her only complaint about the trip was that it was too short. The movie wasn't over when they landed. Marcus reminded her that she could watch the rest on the way home.

High Sierra and Impresario faced each other across the Las Vegas Strip. A glass breezeway crossed the Strip five stories up, connecting the two lavish resorts. Hayley had a suite in Impresario. Kelly and DeDe were next door and Tanner two doors down along the red-and-gold carpeted hallway.

One inside their suite, Hayley and Marcus

wandered together from the sitting room, with its gold-trimmed velvet sofa, to the bedroom where the enormous bed with its intricately carved headboard sat on a dais.

He said, "Kind of a French bordello effect, huh?"

"It's a Moulin Rouge theme, thank you very much."

"Oh. Well. I should have guessed."

She climbed up on the dais and perched on the bed, striking a playfully seductive pose by lacing her hands behind her head and fluttering her eyelashes. "What do you think?"

"Sexiest pregnant lady I ever saw."

She got up and went to have a look at the bathroom. In there, it was stark and simple, very modern, the walls and floor of some gray-and-gold stone, with an open shower. The long sweep of granite counter had double sinks. The tub was big enough to swim in. And through a door by the counter, there was also a big dressing area, complete with lots of closet space, a vanity with stage-style makeup lights and a four-foot-wide floor-to-ceiling mirror.

"All courtesy of the Bravo Group," she told him as she rejoined him in the bedroom. "Ever heard of the Bravo Billionaire?" She climbed the dais again and reclaimed her spot on the bed. "Turns out he's my second cousin."

Marcus was nodding. "That's right. The famous Jonas Bravo of the L.A. Bravos. Bad Blake Bravo was his uncle...."

"Yes, he was. Four or five years ago, Jonas got together with one of my half brothers, Aaron, who was already running High Sierra at the time. Jonas provided the funds to make High Sierra a Bravo enterprise. They brought Fletcher Bravo in when they decided to build Impresario. The way I heard it, Fletcher was running a casino in Atlantic City at the time. Had no idea at the time that he was one of us."

"Us? One of Blake Bravo's children, you mean?"

"Uh-huh."

"How many Bravos are coming for this thing?"

"Somewhere between fifty and a hundred, I think. Caitlin Bravo, one of my notorious father's many wives, put it together, with the help of her daughters-in-law. Aaron is one of Caitlin's three sons."

"Aaron. That's the one who..."

"Runs High Sierra." She laughed. "It's confusing, I know."

He mounted the dais and stood above her. "I hope someone's passing out name tags."

"Not a bad idea." She tipped her head back to look at him and a happy glow spread through her. "I'm glad. That you're here."

He sat beside her and put his arm around her. "Me, too."

She rested her head on his strong shoulder. "I started my leave from my job today."

He hugged her a little closer. "I was hoping. But you notice how I didn't ask?"

"You are becoming downright restrained."

"So glad you noticed."

Their room faced the mountains. Hayley stared out at the gray-and-purple peaks, shadowed now, as night came on, at the sprawling city that claimed the desert below. "Life has its moments, huh?"

He pressed his lips to her hair. "Yes, it does."

The dinner that night was wall-to-wall Bravos. There were speeches and toasts. And kids running everywhere. There was also a huge tree in the middle of the ballroom the family had claimed for the event. Under the tree? Presents for days.

There *were* name tags, as it turned out. A lucky thing, too.

With a new relative everywhere she turned, even Hayley had a hard time keeping them all straight—and in the months since she'd learned who her father really was, she'd made it her business to catch up on all the family relationships, to learn who Blake's wives were, who her half brothers had married and how many kids they had.

After dinner, they all pulled their chairs around

the tree for a serious game of Dirty Santa. When your name was called, you could take a gift from under the tree—or steal one that someone else had already opened and let them go to the tree again. The Bravos—kids included—showed no hesitation to snatch their relatives' presents.

Once every last package was opened, the party broke up for the evening. Some went to try their luck at the slots or the tables, some to put the kids to bed.

Tanner caught Hayley and Marcus as they were waiting for an elevator.

"We're putting together a card game in one of the private lounges over at High Sierra. Four or five tables. Texas Hold'em. You up for it, Marcus?" He sent a wry smile Hayley's way. "It's a man thing. Cigars will be smoked."

"No problem." Her back hurt, anyway, and she was beat. "I'm off to bed. Sleeping for two, you know." She brushed Marcus's shoulder. "You go ahead. Have fun."

He caught her hand, pulled her close enough to kiss the tip of her nose. "You sure you want me playing poker? Could be risky. I hear one of your brothers is a National Poker Champion."

"That would be Cade," Tanner said. "He's one of Caitlin's sons. He'll be there. But he promised to go easy on us."

Hayley grunted. "Oh, yeah. I'll just bet. Watch

your wallets, boys." She went on tiptoe to give Marcus one more quick kiss. "Hand over the loot." He gave her the rhinestone-studded Las Vegas T-shirt and the set of gold-rimmed shot glasses they'd ended up with from the Dirty Santa game. "Go. Try not to lose your shirt. And don't wake me up when you come in."

"Come on." Tanner was already turning to go back the way they'd come.

Marcus hesitated. "You're sure?"

Tanner groaned. "She's positive. Let's go."

She laughed. "Did you hear me? Go!"

He fell in step with Tanner as the elevator chimed and the doors slid wide.

In the suite, Hayley stood naked by the huge, deep tub. It had steps leading down into it and a nice, big handrail to hold on to, just in case. She turned on the taps and poured in some bath gel and sat on the rim as the froth of bubbles rose higher.

At last, with a long, luxurious sigh, she sank into the silky warm water, so glad to be having a baby in the twenty-first century. In the old days, or so she'd read in the tall stack of baby books at home, people believed that sitting in bathwater during the final weeks of pregnancy could cause infection.

Not anymore. Hooray for modern medicine.

And the bathtub was truly amazing, shaped just

right to relax and stretch out. There was even a fat, horseshoe-shaped pillow to cradle her neck and head. She leaned back with a sigh as one of those minor contractions—Braxton Hicks, they called them—tightened her abdomen. The cramp faded quickly. She'd been having them all day. Braxton Hicks were perfectly normal at this stage of the game. They were the mild, irregular contractions that often occurred in the final weeks before the baby was due.

Her back, though. It was really aching. She reached around and rubbed it for a while, but the pain didn't ease much. She'd pushed herself a little too hard that day and she knew it—up at six, a half day for her last day of work, the trip here, the long evening....

Tomorrow, she'd sleep late, take it nice and easy. If she had to miss one or two of the various get-togethers Caitlin and company had planned, so be it.

She sighed and closed her eyes—and moaned when another of those fake contractions struck.

The poker game was more about the Bravo men getting together than serious card playing. There were five tables, all filled with Bravos—along with a handful of guys who'd married Bravo women: Beau from Wyoming, Mack from Florida, Logan from California and Cole Yuma, a vet from the Texas Hill Country.

Marcus started at a table with Tanner, Aaron—the one who ran High Sierra—and Brand and Brett, who were full brothers, two of the four sons of Chastity Bravo, from a tiny Northern California town called New Bethlehem Flat.

There were good cigars and excellent whisky for anyone who wanted it. Word had gotten round that Marcus and Hayley weren't married. He took a lot of friendly ribbing about how he ought to get a ring on that girl's finger and make it quick, since she looked as if she'd be having that baby any minute now.

Marcus swore he was doing the best that he could. Then he went all in on the river and won that hand. And the next hand. And the hand after that.

The hours went by. As players went out, they consolidated the tables. Marcus managed to stay in the game longer than most. But in the end, he went all in with an ace and a jack and Tucker Bravo, from Tate's Junction, Texas, beat him with a pair of sixes.

Marcus was thinking he'd call it a night about then, head to the room and join Hayley in that big bed.

But Tanner said, "Come on, Marcus. Brett and Brand are waiting in the Forty-niner."

"That's a bar, right?"

"You bet."

Since he didn't drink, heading for a bar held little appeal. "Brett and Brand are waiting for what?"

"I told them that as soon as you had your clock cleaned at the tables, I'd drag you over there for one more round."

"I don't know. I've left your sister alone for hours now...."

Tanner grunted. "You're pretty damn attentive. I like that in a prospective brother-in-law."

"Thanks. I think."

Hayley's brother clapped him on the shoulder. "She's sleeping. She'll be fine."

Since he *was* going to marry Hayley as soon as he could finish breaking down her defenses, he figured it wouldn't be a bad idea to spend a little quality time with his future in-laws. Besides, Tanner was probably right. Hayley would be sound asleep by now. It wasn't as if she'd be up there missing him.

Tanner said, "Come on, you know you're just dyin' for one last club soda."

"Two's usually my limit, but hey. I'll go for a third just this one time."

Hayley woke with a cry.

She'd dreamed of her father again—or rather, Blake Bravo's scary shadow as he loomed over her.

Her back was aching. Bad. The pain had spread,

wrapping around her like strong fingers. Now it pressed hard at her abdomen, too.

She groaned as her mind surfaced through the layers of sleep—and groaned again, louder, as a hard contraction tightened her belly.

The wave of pain took over. She breathed in shallow pants as she'd learned in her labor classes. It passed at last.

And what the…?

She threw back the covers. The bed was soaking wet. She sniffed—sweet, it smelled sweet. And she was still leaking, the pale fluid sticky between her thighs.

No doubt about: her water had broken.

And she did know the signs, she'd studied up on them enough: the movement of the pain from her back around to the front; the longer, deeper, more painful contractions; the amniotic fluid streaked with pink, soaking the sheets…

She was in labor.

Chapter Nine

Marcus set down his club soda as his new PDA started vibrating. He tensed.

Adriana.

Why the hell couldn't she let it be, for God's sake?

But then again, no one had his new cell number except Hayley and Joyce, his assistant. Anyone in Seattle who needed to reach him had to go to Joyce, who would then contact him. Joyce Bowles was tough and smart. No one got by Joyce.

And that meant there was no way Adriana had charmed or cajoled his new cell number out of her.

He took out the phone and checked the display, smiling to himself when he saw it was Hayley. She must be missing him, after all.

He gave the men at the table the high sign and turned slightly away to answer. "I know it's late. I'm coming right now."

"Great. Because there's a little problem."

She sounded perfectly calm. Still, the air fled his lungs and his stomach jerked into a double knot. "Problem?"

"I think I'm having the baby."

His mind went blank as he struggled to process. The baby? She was having the baby? Was that possible? How could that be? "Uh. Now?"

"Yes, Marcus. Now."

He said a word he shouldn't have said and he said it really loud, simultaneously bolting upright, bumping the table in the process. Two of the four drinks went over, liquor and ice splashing across the mosaic of a gold pan and pick.

The other three men shoved back their chairs and jumped up to keep from getting wet.

"Hey…"

"Watch it."

"Marcus, what the hell?"

Brand headed for the bar, presumably to get something to mop up the spilled drinks just as someone won a big jackpot somewhere in the casino. Whistles blew and bells rang.

"Marcus?" Hayley asked. He could tell by her tone that now she was worried. For *him*. Incredible. *She* was worried about *him*. "Marcus, are you okay?"

"Hold on, sweetheart," he told her. "I'm just fine." He tipped the PDA away from his mouth and told the others, "Hayley..." He had to search for the impossible words. "She's having the baby."

She was talking again. He tried to focus on her voice. "Can you get a doctor?"

"Uh. Absolutely. No problem..."

Brand returned with a big towel and mopped up the spilled drinks as, for some unknown reason, Brett said, "Let's go have a look."

Marcus gaped at the other man. What the hell did Brett Bravo think he'd be looking at?

Brand said, "I'll get Angie. And your bag..."

"Go for it," said Brett. He spoke to Marcus. "Let me have a word with her. We'll see where we are here."

Marcus gaped some more. The man was making zero sense.

Hayley said, "Marcus? What's going on?"

Brand was talking to him, too. "I need a room number. Are you two here, at High Sierra?"

About then, Tanner got a load of Marcus's expression. He laughed. "Easy, Marcus. Brett's a doctor. His wife Angie's a nurse."

Marcus parroted, "Doctor. Nurse. I knew that. Didn't I?"

"I heard that," Hayley said in his ear. "That's good. Tell Brett to hurry…" And then she moaned.

"Hayley. My God. Hayley…"

She panted. And groaned. "Okay. It's okay…."

It didn't sound okay to Marcus. "I'm on my way. Brett, too…" The bells rang and the whistles kept blowing. His mind was mush. He glanced wildly around, seeking the exit. And from there, which direction to the escalators and the skyway back to Impresario? Damn it to hell. He'd known the way when he got here….

Tanner gave Brand the room number. "They're at Impresario," he said.

Brand took off as the bells and whistles finally stopped.

"Let's go," said Brett.

"Hold on," Marcus told the panting, moaning woman on the other end of the line. "We're coming." Brett and Tanner fell in on either side of him. He let them lead him, handing Brett the PDA when the other man held out his hand for it.

Thank God they seemed to know the way.

In the suite, Tanner waited in the sitting room.

Marcus and Brett went on into the bedroom. They found Hayley crouched on the dais, knees drawn up, wearing one of the red terry robes provided by the hotel. Moaning.

Marcus went to her, dropped down beside her and took her hand. She kept on moaning, a hard, keening sound, and wrapped her fingers tight around his, as if clutching a lifeline.

"Oh, my darling…" he muttered and didn't know what to do next.

For some unknown reason, Brett touched the sheet, and then sniffed his hand. "What's her due date?" Marcus was busy trying to soothe Hayley and the doctor had to prompt, "Marcus? Do you know her due date?"

"Ah…January eighth."

"Less than three weeks away. She's passed the thirty-six-week mark."

"And that means?"

"The baby should be fully developed, ready to survive outside the womb. Chances are this is a normal, though slightly early, birth."

"That's good?"

"Yes. Very good. I'll be right back." And he headed for the sitting room.

What the hell? The doctor was walking away? Marcus opened his mouth to shout at him to get back over here to Hayley where he belonged. But he shut it without making a sound. He didn't want to upset Hayley any more than necessary.

"Everything's okay," he told her, though he had

no idea if that was true, or not. "You heard what Brett said. A normal delivery, just a little bit early. It's all going to be fine, perfect, the baby's okay and so are you...."

He babbled on, hardly knowing what he was saying. She didn't seem to really hear him, but she clutched his hand as if letting go would be the end of her.

Seconds later, Brett returned from the sitting room. "Tanner's getting an ambulance."

"An ambulance? She needs an ambulance? I thought you said—"

"Just a precaution," Brett hurried to reassure. "Nothing to be alarmed about. If she's as far along as she seems to be, an ambulance is the best and safest way to get her to the hospital. The EMTs will be able to take care of her on the way."

"Okay," said Marcus. Total lie. At that moment, things were not okay. Not okay in a big, big way.

"Stay with her for a minute more," Brett instructed. As if he could leave her. As if he ever would. The doctor continued, "I'll scrub down as best I can. Then we'll see how far along she is."

"Yeah. Go." The doctor disappeared into the bathroom as Hayley let out a long, slow sigh.

"Marcus?" Her voice was soft, breathless.

"Right here." Her hair, sweat-soaked, clung to her clammy cheeks. He smoothed it back.

"It's...early," she said. "But not *that* early...

Please don't be scared. I think it's fine." She actually smiled at him. Incredible. In her state. Smiling at him.

Before he could figure out something suitably gentle and encouraging to say to her, the doctor returned with a stack of fat, white towels from the bathroom. "Let's get rid of those wet sheets and put these down...."

Hayley seemed calmer right then, so Marcus dared to pry his fingers free of her grip. He got busy stripping the bed. When the sheets and blankets were off, they spread the towels.

"Okay," Brett said. "Hayley, let's move you up on the bed—scoot close to the edge."

Marcus helped her up and Brett examined her. He asked her how far apart her contractions were, then rattled off a string of terms that Hayley seemed to understand.

"Damn it," Marcus cut in. Since Hayley winced as if he'd startled her, he forced himself to ask in a reasonable tone, "Is she okay? Is the baby all right?"

Brett granted him a very doctorly smile. "Everything looks normal. They're both doing well."

Just as he said that, Hayley started moaning again. She slid off the bed and back onto the dais.

"Wait...no..." Marcus tried to stop her.

Brett said, "It's okay. Let her do whatever she's comfortable with. She's fine. Her body knows what it needs."

Hayley crouched on the dais, knees wide, groaning.

Brett said, "Pant. Easy. Don't push. Remember. Easy. Not yet…"

About then, a pretty, dark-haired woman wearing jeans and a zip-up green hoodie appeared from the sitting room. She said a soft, "Hello," as she set down a black bag and went into the bathroom.

Marcus put it together: *Angie. Brett's wife. The nurse…*

He heard the water running in the bathroom—until Hayley's loud groan blocked out the sound.

The nurse reappeared. Her husband stepped back as she approached Hayley on the other side.

"Angie…" Hayley managed somehow to get the word out between groans. "Thanks…for coming…"

"Glad to help."

Hayley reached for her hand and Angie gave it. Now Hayley had Marcus's fingers clasped with one hand and the nurse's with the other. Angie urged her to breathe in shallow pants—and not to push yet….

The doctor disappeared into the sitting room again.

Marcus watched him go, scowling.

Angie said, "He'll check on the ambulance."

Time slowed in the strangest way. There were moments when Hayley was calm, almost dreamy. And then she would moan again and the pain would take her.

Brett's wife stayed right with them. She said soothing things, including that Hayley was doing great.

Marcus was inordinately thankful to hear that—at the same time as he wanted to shout that this wasn't great in the least. Hayley was suffering. He hated every damn minute of her agony. He wanted to help her.

And yet he was powerless. Good only to be there, to hold her hand....

Though he'd always believed he'd never have kids, in the past week or so, Hayley had almost succeeded in convincing him that having a kid was a good thing.

Now, seeing her agony, he was sure all over again that having a kid was the worst idea nature ever dreamed up.

He didn't say that, though. It was too late to back out now. Now, he just stood by helplessly as Hayley sweated and moaned, trying to bring their baby into the world.

After forever, two guys in jumpsuits with a stretcher and more medical gear appeared. They checked Hayley over and consulted with Brett, who'd reappeared in the bedroom when Marcus wasn't looking. At last, they helped Hayley to lie on her side on the stretcher, covered her with a blanket and started to carry her out.

Marcus followed.

One of the guys in jumpsuits said, "It'll be crowded in the van."

"Too damn bad." If all he could do was be there, he wasn't letting anyone keep him from it. "I'm going with her."

"Please," said Hayley. "Let him come...."

The paramedic stopped arguing and Brett said, "You'll need her purse—identification, insurance information...."

"Table. Sitting room," Hayley panted.

"We'll follow you," Brett promised.

Marcus grabbed her purse on the way out the door.

The paramedic had been right. They were packed in that van like sardines in a can. Marcus pressed himself against the back of the driver's seat, trying his damnedest to stay out of the way during the short, uncomfortable ride.

At the hospital, the registration process fell to Marcus. They took Hayley off to "prep" her, whatever the hell that meant. He tried to argue that he wasn't letting her go without him, but she reassured him that it would only be a few minutes and then they'd bring him back to her.

He filled out all the papers and then he waited. For endless, torturous minutes. The others— Tanner, Brett and Angie—arrived. They sat with him. Or rather, they sat and he paced.

He thought he'd lived through hell in his life. How wrong he'd been. There was no hell like the hell of waiting to be led to Hayley's side, praying she was doing all right, sure something terrible would happen while he was out here and she was in there, without him, when she needed him the most....

At last, they came and got him, gave him a hospital gown and showed him where to wash with antibacterial soap.

And then, finally, they took him to her. She reached for his hand.

The rest went by like some kind of dream—or maybe a nightmare.

Nurses and a doctor went in and out. Hayley suffered. He stayed with her, provided what comfort and encouragement he could.

Finally, the doctor said she could push.

Things happened pretty fast after that. Hayley groaned and sweated and, in agonizing increments, the miracle happened.

The doctor said, "The head has crowned. There we go. Very good. Push. Push."

The nurse said, "Here come the shoulders...."

The rest was so swift. Instantaneous, really.

He heard a baby's cry.

It was 5:17 on Saturday morning the sixteenth of December, and the doctor said, "It's a girl."

Chapter Ten

They named her Jenny, after Marcus's mother. She had a clump of dark hair on the crown of her head. Hayley said she just knew that her eyes would be green once they changed from newborn blue.

The nurses offered Marcus a rollaway bed so he could stay in the room with Hayley and the new baby. All day Saturday, they rested. Visitors were limited in order to give the new mother and her baby a chance to rest and recuperate from the birth.

Saturday afternoon, Kelly and Tanner visited

briefly. They brought Marcus and Hayley their things from the suite at Impresario—along with a brand-new car seat and a diaper bag packed with all the essentials.

"The car seat's from me, so my niece will be safely buckled up when they let you out of here," Kelly said. "The diaper bag and everything in it is from Tanner."

"Don't let her kid you," muttered Tanner. "I paid for that stuff, but Kelly's the one who went out and got it all."

"However you two worked it out," Hayley said. "Thank you. You did good."

Kelly held the baby and Tanner said that everyone at the reunion sent them congratulations—and a whole bunch of baby gifts, which Caitlin was having mailed directly to Hayley's place in Sacramento.

"When I get home, I'll send thank-you notes," Hayley said. "But for now, will you tell them how much I appreciate their thoughtfulness—how much I appreciate *them?*"

"Will do," Tanner promised.

"They're calling this little darling the Reunion Baby," Kelly said. "There have been lots of new Bravos born in the past few years. It's appropriate, I think, that there should be a new baby born at the family reunion."

After she and Tanner left, Hayley said again

how glad she was to have a big family at last. "I always wanted siblings. A lot of family, that was my dream. Now I've got a big brother—and half brothers all over the country. And a sister who's also my best friend…"

Marcus couldn't resist ribbing her. "They can be dangerous, those Bravos."

"No way."

"Oh, yeah. You have to watch them at the poker table. No end to their tricks."

Hayley wasn't buying. "I know you. You held your own just fine in that card game."

"Naw. They cleaned me out."

In the hospital bassinette beside Hayley's bed, Jenny started fussing. Hayley picked her up and put her to her breast. Jenny latched right on.

Marcus watched them, the mother and the child…

His child.

He was a father now. It hardly seemed possible.

And yet, now fatherhood had happened to him, it seemed so right, somehow. As if he'd waited his whole life.

To know this one special woman.

To father this beautiful, perfect child.

When she was through nursing, Hayley passed him the baby. He cradled her with care. She hardly weighed a thing in his arms. "She's so little…."

"Not for long. Kelly says they grow up way too fast. We'll be fighting off the boyfriends before you know it."

He glanced up and their gazes met. The smile she gave him made his chest feel tight. He put on a threatening scowl. "Boyfriends? No way. Never. Not my little girl."

"I do believe all fathers with daughters say that at one time or another—at least the loving fathers do…." Her eyes held a sudden sadness. She was thinking of the father she'd never known.

"I'll be here," he vowed. "No matter what, Hayley, I'll be the best father I can be, for her. And when you're ready, if you say yes, I'll be a true husband to you…."

She didn't say anything, only smiled a glowing, tender smile. It was enough. For now.

He turned his gaze to the baby again. "Beautiful," he said. "She is just beautiful…."

Hayley laughed. "Marcus. She's a newborn. She looks like Winston Churchill."

He spoke to the angel in his arms. "Don't you listen to her, Jenny Reid. You're gorgeous. Incredible. Completely amazing."

"Incredible and amazing. No argument there," Hayley said fondly.

Jenny puckered up her tiny mouth and then yawned. He couldn't get enough of just holding her, of looking down at her scrunched-up little face. "I wanted brothers and sisters, too," he said softly. "My mother was pregnant, when she died."

"You never told me that." Hayley's voice was so gentle. Warm. And accepting.

He looked up at her again. Her red hair, always silky, vibrant as fire, drooped in limp tendrils on her shoulders. Dark smudges of fatigue stained the skin beneath her eyes.

And yet, she was so beautiful. As beautiful as Jenny.

He said, "My father got drunk and pushed her down the stairs. It was a wide, curving staircase. And a long way down. I had snuck out of my room when I heard him yelling at her and I was crouched in the shadows at the opposite end of the landing when it happened. Neither of them knew I was there.

"My mother was…I don't know. At least six or seven months pregnant at the time. I remember she would put my hand on her big stomach and tell me how my baby brother or sister was in there."

"How unbelievably horrible for you."

"Hey. I lived. Imagine how my mother felt about it. And what about that innocent baby who never had the chance to be born? I remember my father shoving her. And she screamed when she flew backward. She hit the wall of the stairwell, bounced off. She landed on the stairs and went rolling. And rolling. All the way to the bottom where she lay so very still. I was six years old. I put my hand hard against my mouth to keep from screaming. Because I knew, if *he* knew I'd seen, he'd kill me, too.

"Later, I told my nanny. She told me that nothing of the kind had happened, that it was only a bad, bad dream I'd had because I missed my mother. I wanted to believe her. So I pretended, at least for a while, that I did believe her. That it was only a nightmare I'd had." He shut his eyes, muttered a low oath. In his mind's eye, he could still see his father's face, puffy from drinking, the whites of his eyes yellowed, traced with broken red veins. "When I got older, ten or so, I confronted him with what he'd done. He beat me. Bad. And then he said I'd better never tell a lie like that again if I wanted to keep on breathing."

"Oh, Marcus...I'm so sorry."

"My old man was monster."

"I do understand. Since mine was, too."

"I know," he said. "And I don't believe I just told you that."

"I'm glad. That you did. That you trust me that much."

He sat beside her on the edge of the bed, their daughter in his arms. "I'd do anything for you, Hayley." He glanced down at the baby. "And for Jenny..."

"Marcus." She reached out, laid her hand on the

side of his face. "I believe you would." She spoke so softly, those changeable eyes a light hazel now, brilliant as stars.

He bent near to her, the baby in his arms stirring and sighing, but not waking. "Anything…"

Hayley offered her sweet mouth and he took it. So gently. With care. He brushed his lips back and forth across hers. She sighed.

When he pulled away, she rested against the pillows and closed her eyes. He remained there beside her, holding their child, watching her face as sleep claimed her.

Guilt crept through him, stealthy. Insistent. He did have her trust now. She believed again. In him. In what they—the two of them and Jenny—could share. She believed in his honesty, that he had kept his word to her to give her only the truth.

But he hadn't been honest. Not about everything. Not about Adriana.

He should tell Hayley that Adriana had contacted him.

That she'd left the man she'd left *him* for. That she'd said she wanted to come back to him, that she thought she could reclaim what she'd tossed so carelessly away. That she believed the two of them were bound together. Forever.

He should explain that what Adriana wanted, what Adriana believed, didn't matter to him in the least.

That he was over her and the cruel kind of loving she offered, that there was no room left in his life—or his heart—for the woman who had once been his world.

He had a new world now. A better world. He wouldn't trade what he had now, with Hayley and Jenny, for anything....

Hayley stirred, sighing. And the baby in his arms, as if connected by some invisible link to her mother, stirred, as well. She made a soft, mewling sound, wrinkled up her tiny nose—and then was still, seeming to settle into a deeper sleep than before. Hayley slept on, as well.

With care, he rose and lowered the baby into her bassinet. Then he slid off his shoes and stretched out on the rollaway, shut his eyes and told his guilt and doubts to go away.

They didn't, not really. But he was just beat enough that within moments, he slept, too.

He woke when Jenny started fussing again. Hayley nursed her, though as Hayley had explained it, the first few days, the mother had no milk. The baby, she said, needed to nurse anyway, and received some special fluid that provided protection from disease and helped clean out the baby's digestive system and prepare it for real food.

It all sounded way complicated to Marcus. But if it was good for Jenny, he was all for it.

A nurse came in to perform routine examinations of Hayley and the baby. Marcus went down to the cafeteria to get some coffee. While he was out of the room, he considered turning on his PDA, seeing if he had any messages that needed dealing with immediately.

He took the device from his pocket—and then he put it back without powering it up. Today—and tomorrow—were for Hayley and Jenny. Kaffe Central could get along without him till Monday.

And if Joyce had messages from Adriana to pass on to him, he'd just as soon skip hearing about them, for now, anyway.

When the kitchen people brought up Hayley's dinner, they provided a tray for him, as well. After the meal, he and Hayley fell asleep watching TV. A couple hours later, Jenny cried and the feeding and changing process started all over again.

In the morning after breakfast, they had a visit from the doctor, who examined mother and child and said they were ready to go home that day.

"Home is Sacramento," she reminded him. "Is it all right for us to fly?"

Marcus explained that they would travel in comfort in his company's jet.

"Well, then," said the doctor. "A short flight

with minimal stress. That should be perfectly safe."

Once he left them, Hayley said she was ready for a shower.

Marcus rubbed at the stubble on his jaw. "That makes two of us."

She ran a hand down her limp hair. "We're pretty scruffy, that's for sure."

"You want to go first?"

"Please."

She allowed him to carry her overnight bag in for her, but when he came back to help her, she insisted on getting there under her own steam. "Ugh." She reached the door frame and sagged against it. "I'm a wreck."

"Another day or two, you'll be good as new."

"Spoken like a man."

"Sure you don't need some help? I could scrub your back for you."

"I'll manage. Thanks." She took a step into the green-tiled room—and whipped her head around to catch him eyeing her backside, which was temptingly revealed between the ties of her hospital gown. "Don't even go there, mister."

"Hey. A man can dream."

"True. And you'll need your dreams. Because I'm never having sex again."

He laughed.

And then, slowly and stiffly, she turned around

and came back toward him. When she reached him, she put her hands on his chest. "It's good to hear you laugh like that."

"Like what?"

"Like you're a happy man."

"I *am* a happy man." Damned if it wasn't true.

"I like you happy."

"You *make* me happy—and you look like you need a kiss."

"Hmm. What do you know? I believe that I do."

"But wait. I thought you just swore off sex."

"I could be convinced to rethink my position. In time…with the right kind of encouragement."

He lowered his head enough to brush his lips across hers. "Like this?"

"Umm. Perfect. More."

He wrapped his arms around her—not too tight—just enough that it could be considered an embrace. And then he kissed her again, a kiss that was still chaste, though it lasted a little longer than the one before it.

When he lifted his head, she said, "Now, see? That's what I'm talkin' about."

"The right kind of encouragement?"

"That's it. What I need. Again, please." She tipped up her mouth, offering it to him.

He kissed her again. A kiss of promise. Tender. Sweet—and just a little spicy.

When he lifted his head, she said, "Oh, yeah. Exactly what I'm looking for."

"Anything. For you."

Her smile grew wistful. "Here we are. With a baby. So much for our two weeks of just you and me…"

"Can't have everything. And Jenny's worth it."

"It's only the second day with her. It's all new and different. And we're here in our own private little world, just the three of us. With nurses and hospital staff to take care of us. Things will get challenging, believe me. Babies bring stress and change. And sleep deprivation."

"I'm willing to help. However I can."

"That could be difficult, with you in Seattle and Jenny and me in California…."

He dared to suggest, "Maybe you'll try Seattle again. Just to see how it goes."

"Maybe I will."

He took her by the shoulders. "You're serious."

"I am, yes. But even if I try moving back to Seattle, we both know how you are. You'll get buried in work the way you always do. In the end, you'll have no time for changing diapers and rocking the baby at two in the morning."

"I'll make time, just watch me."

She looked at him sideways. "I'm not blaming you for working so hard. It's what you do best, what you love to do."

"Yeah, it is. But it's about damn time I learned how to delegate. My people are up for taking more responsibility. They've proved that in the past week."

"Marcus. You're almost convincing me that you actually want to be a hands-on kind of dad."

"That's because I do."

"You're making me think you'll try to be patient, with Jenny. With me."

Because I will."

"Then I have a question...."

"Hit me with it."

"Will you marry me?"

Chapter Eleven

At first, he was certain he hadn't heard her right. He gaped. "Uh. Huh?"

She shut her eyes and groaned. "Ohmigod. You've changed your mind, right? You've realized you don't want to marry me, after all. And you're going to say no again, just like you did in May…."

He gazed down at her scrunched-up face. She looked just like their daughter right then. "Hayley."

She kept her eyes squeezed shut and hunched up her shoulders. "Oh, God. What?"

"Look at me."

"No. I don't think so…."

He brushed a finger under her chin. "Come on. Don't be scared. Open your eyes."

"It's a bad idea. I can't take the rejection."

"Hayley…"

Finally, she opened one eye to a slit. "What?"

"Come on."

"Oh, fine. Sure. You want me looking at you while you turn me down." She opened both eyes at last. "Well?"

"Yes. Of course, I'll marry you."

She gasped. Then she frowned. "Say that again. Just the yes-word, that will do it."

"Yes."

"Oh, Marcus!" She laughed and threw her arms around his neck, wincing a little when her battered body resisted. "Now, you kiss me."

So he did. A very long kiss that time. And a deep one.

When he lifted his head, he asked, "How about here in Vegas? Today?"

She blinked. "Today? But…we're flying back to Sacramento today."

"Yeah. So?"

"It's a lot to do, all in one day. I mean, especially after having a baby yesterday."

"The jet is on call. It'll be there when we're ready for it. If we're not ready to go until nighttime, it won't be a problem. And don't worry. I'm not asking you to stand up before a justice of the peace."

"Good news. I'm seriously not up for putting on street clothes and actual shoes."

"How about this? We'll go back to Impresario. I'll get us a nice, big suite for the rest of the day. I'll arrange for a preacher or a justice of the peace—and a license. All of it. You have to know Caitlin and the others will help me get whatever we need. You can marry me in bed."

A smile broke wide across her face. "Now you're talkin'."

"With Jenny in your arms. A reunion wedding to go with the reunion baby."

"Okay. I admit it. I'm liking this."

"Hold on a minute…"

"What?"

"Don't move. Stay right there…"

"Marcus?"

He left her just long enough to go to his suitcase and take a certain small velvet box from a hidden compartment.

"You brought the ring with you, here, to Las Vegas?"

He returned to her. "What'd I say a few minutes ago? A man can dream. Give me your hand." She laid her fingers in his and he slipped the engagement ring into place.

She admired the sparkling stone. "I love it. Thank you."

"We're engaged," he said, grinning. Engaged to Hayley. The thought pleased him immensely.

She said, "It will be the world's shortest engagement, lasting…oh, maybe six hours?"

"Or less."

Hayley was still turning her hand this way and that, watching the way the enormous stone caught and reflected the light. "Did I say I love it?"

"You did—and don't worry. I've got the wedding ring, too. All ready for when you say 'I do' this afternoon."

"Talk about your whirlwind courtship."

He kissed her again. Then he took her by the shoulders and turned her toward the open bathroom door. "Now take your shower and let's get a move on."

Obediently, she trotted in there and shut the door. A moment later, he heard the water running.

He sank to the edge of the bed, hardly daring to believe that he was getting what he wanted: Hayley for a lifetime. His beautiful daughter to raise…

Adriana.

Her name came creeping, silent as a shadow, into his mind.

He should have told Hayley about the thing with Adriana. Before he said yes to her proposal.

Hayley wanted honesty. And he knew damn well she'd only proposed again because she believed she was getting just that from him: the whole truth.

He should tell her....

But then she'd worry. Maybe she'd doubt him, wonder if he really wanted to be with his ex.

The shadow of Adriana looming between them could tip the scales in the wrong direction. Hayley might decide she wanted to slow things down a little. She'd start thinking how they didn't *need* to get married today. She'd want him to explain to her why he hadn't mentioned Adriana's call earlier.

And damn it, why the hell hadn't he? It should have been a simple enough thing to say, "Adriana called me. She said she wants to try again with me. I told her no."

Simple. Direct. Clear.

But something had held him back.

And, now he really thought it over, was keeping his mouth shut about it such a bad thing?

What was the damn point in going into all that old garbage? Why couldn't they just let the past go?

He had found happiness, with Hayley and their baby. Adriana, who very well might have changed her mind again by now and returned to VonKruger, couldn't be allowed to get in the way.

* * *

Hayley could hardly believe how quickly it all was arranged.

They were married at three that afternoon.

In bed, as Marcus had promised. At Impresario, in the same suite they'd had before. Hayley wore white satin pajamas that Celia, Aaron's wife, had found for her in one of High Sierra's most exclusive boutiques. Jenny, in Hayley's arms, was wrapped in a satin-edged pink blanket with a pink, ribbon-threaded hat on her head.

Jilly, the wife of Will Bravo, who was Aaron and Cade's third brother, had scoured the bridal shops until she found a Renaissance-style circlet of greenery with white roses at the front for Hayley to wear in place of a veil. Her red hair, clean and shining now, fell loose on her shoulders. Jilly had done her makeup, too. All Hayley had to do was sit there, while Will's wife worked her magic with blusher and concealer, eyeliner and mascara.

For a woman who'd been in labor not thirty-six hours before, Hayley thought she'd cleaned up pretty damn good.

Marcus wore a tux. He wasn't actually *in* the bed, like Hayley and the baby. Rather, he sat on the edge, at Hayley's side, holding her hand. The minister stood at the foot of the bed, below the dais.

And the rest of the large, luxurious red-and-gold bedroom? It was wall-to-wall Bravos. They all came, even the kids and the babies, so many that they spilled through the arch into the sitting area.

The ceremony was brief. A quick, sentimental speech from the minister. The all-important exchange of vows.

Hayley looked in Marcus's wonderful green eyes as she said, firmly and clearly, with all the love in her overflowing heart, "I do."

Marcus slipped on the ring. It snuggled right up to the gorgeous engagement diamond. He repeated after the minister. "With this ring, I thee wed."

Then the minister said he could kiss the bride. Marcus bent close. His warm lips covered hers in a kiss so sweet and tender, it broke her heart and mended it, all in the space of a few shining seconds.

The minister said, "I now pronounce you husband and wife. Ladies and gentlemen, Hayley and Marcus Reid."

And two rooms full of Bravos erupted into applause, whistles, catcalls and cheers. Several babies, startled by the sudden shouting and clapping, began wailing.

Jenny's eyes popped open in surprise. But then she only yawned hugely and went right back to sleep.

There was champagne. And a whole bunch of toasting. Since everyone seemed to be talking at once, those giving the toasts had a little trouble being heard.

But not Caitlin. In her trademark tight jeans and sequined red shirt, she stepped up on the dais at the foot of the bed and let out a whistle so loud it had the babies wailing all over again. "Do I have your attention?"

"Go for it, Ma!" shouted Cade from the back of the room.

"You bet I will. I'm so glad you could all make it. I had one hell of a time and hope the rest of you did, too." A murmur of agreement went up. Caitlin raised her champagne high. "Here's to the bride and groom. To love and marriage. To happiness and new life. And most of all, to family." She drank.

And so did the rest of them, even the kids caught on and lifted their champagne flutes full of sparkling fruit juice.

It was a great moment, Hayley thought. And she was downright teary-eyed, to have so much family, to be married to the man she loved, with all of them there to witness their vows.

Marcus leaned close. "You look happy."

"Oh, Marcus. I am."

After Caitlin's toast, things wound down swiftly. People had planes to catch, or faced a long drive home. Many took a moment to personally congratulate the newlyweds. And then, within an hour of the "I do's," the two rooms emptied out.

Kelly and DeDe left to get their suitcases.

"Half an hour?" Marcus asked Tanner. "I'll have a van waiting downstairs to take us to the plane."

"We'll be ready." Tanner left them.

Marcus shut the wide doors to the other room and came to sit on the bed again, next to Hayley. "How are you holding up?"

"Pretty well, all things considered."

He leaned close and kissed her forehead, right below the crown of flowers. She freed a hand from cradling their daughter and hooked her fingers around his neck, pulling him closer, lifting her mouth. He kissed her lips.

"Umm." She stroked the hair at his temple. "I'm looking forward to a lifetime of kisses."

He smiled against her mouth. "Care for a quickie before we go?"

She stuck out her tongue and licked the seam where his lips met, just to let him know that while she might not be up for a quickie, she wasn't dead, either. "Hmm. Rain check? Ask me again in about six weeks?"

He caught several strands of her hair between his fingers and rubbed them, as if the feel of them pleased him. "That long? You're killin' me here."

"Oh, I think you'll survive."

"Maybe. Barely."

"Plus, there's how good I am with my lips and my hands."

He groaned. "Don't remind me. It's cruel."

"I can't help myself. You know how I am, a postpartum sex goddess."

"Okay. Now you're scaring me." He brushed another kiss across her lips and then, reluctantly, he pulled away. "I'll change. Then I'll help you wherever you need me."

She cast a glance at the wheelchair Marcus had rented from the hospital. "I gave you a hard time when you brought that thing with us. But now I'm so glad you did. I don't think I could make it anywhere on my own steam right now."

"We could stay another day…."

"No. Really. I can manage. I'll be on wheels the whole way to the plane. And once we board, I'll go right to sleep."

He disappeared into the dressing area. Hayley watched him go, feeling all mushy and sentimental. She was totally exhausted. But really, her world had never been so right.

Jenny stirred, fussing. Hayley readjusted her pajama top and put her to her breast. Jenny latched on. Hayley winced. It hurt. Though the pain did ease after a moment. The books she'd studied explained that her nipples would toughen up over time—though the pain would likely get worse before it got better.

Babies. First they turned you into a walking beach ball. Then they split you open being born. And then came nursing, which could be lovely and fulfilling, the books said—*after* the nipples stopped hurting like hell.

She rubbed a gentle finger along the beautiful curve of her baby's cheek. "All worth it," she whispered. "I wouldn't change a thing…."

With a long sigh, Hayley let her head droop back against the pillows. The corona of roses Jilly had bought for her slid down her forehead until it almost covered her eyes.

Not that she cared. Her eyes were closed anyway. She felt so very peaceful….

Marcus emerged from the dressing area five minutes later to find Hayley conked out, her crown of flowers drooping over her eyes and Jenny starting to fuss.

Hayley stirred but didn't wake when he took the crying bundle from her arms. He changed Jenny and put her in her car seat, where she waved her little hands and made soft cooing noises.

He turned to look at his new wife again. Dead to the world.

If they were going, he really did have to wake her….

He took a step toward the bed—and then changed his mind and detoured through the other room. Bracing the door with the security arm, he went out into the hallway. He knocked on Kelly's door. When she answered, he told her that Hayley was too beat to travel. "I'm just going to send you three on to Sacramento as planned. Hayley and Jenny and I will go tomorrow."

DeDe, lurking behind her mother, piped up, "Oh, Mommy, can we stay? We could go to Circus Circus. Puleeeassse!"

Kelly shushed her. "DeDe *is* out of school for the holidays and I could use an extra day off, anyway. I think we'll stay on with you and Hayley."

Marcus went down the hall and checked with Tanner, who said he was fine with staying. "Just so happens a few of my half brothers are hanging around, too. We're talking about organizing another card game for tonight. You in?"

"I'd love to, but…"

Tanner clapped him on the shoulder. "No need to explain. Go back to your bride and my new niece."

When Marcus returned to the suite, Hayley was still fast asleep. By then, the crown of flowers had drooped halfway down her nose. He took it off and set it on the night table. She didn't so much as sigh.

Jenny gurgled at him from her car seat, so he

picked her up, seat and all, and carried her into the sitting room, stopping to pull the double doors shut behind him. He made some calls from the phone in there and scored a crib courtesy of Cleo Bravo, who lived on-site right there at Impresario with her husband, Fletcher, and their kids. Cleo also ran the top-quality day care the twin resorts provided for employees; she had access not only to cribs but to a whole boatload of baby stuff: blankets and sleepers and little baby T-shirts. The crib arrived, packed with baby gear, within thirty minutes of his conversation with Cleo. Marcus snapped Jenny into one of the sleepers and got her settled into her borrowed bed.

Then he stretched out on the couch and channel surfed and resisted the temptation to turn on his PDA. He was still avoiding learning if Adriana had been harassing his assistant in a continued effort to contact him.

But eventually, it was just too much free time being wasted. He could check e-mail, see how things were going at Kaffe Central while he was lying here doing nothing. He turned on his BlackBerry and checked what he dreaded most first: voice mail.

"You have one new message...."

He punched Play, and got Joyce's no-nonsense voice with a late-Friday-afternoon update. She ran down what was happening in the various departments. All good there. Everything under control. A couple of the managers had requested conference calls next week.

"But nothing urgent," Joyce said. "Strictly routine. When you get back to me, we'll set them up.

"And lastly—" Her voice changed, grew tighter, almost prim "—you received two calls today from London. Your ex-wife, she said. An Adriana Von-Kruger? Apparently, she's having trouble reaching you. I followed your instructions and declined to give her any of your numbers, though by the second call, she became…quite insistent. She wishes you to call her immediately." Joyce read off the number. "And that's it." Suddenly, she was laying on the brisk good cheer. "Have a good weekend, Marcus, and give me a call Monday, if you will, to set up those phone conferences for next week."

A click. And a recorded voice read the time and date stamp.

"Couldn't resist, huh?" He jerked around to see Hayley, in her white satin wedding pj's, standing in the doorway to the bedroom, eyes still drooping a little from her nap. She chuckled in a lazy, half-awake way. "You should see your face. Guilt-ee." And then she grew more serious. "Something wrong?" She spiked her fingers through that silky red hair, raking it back off her forehead.

He held up the BlackBerry and played it sheepish. "I confess. I just checked messages."

She padded over on bare feet and sat down next

to him—carefully, but a little less stiffly than before. Already, she seemed to be getting her strength back. He put an arm around her and she cuddled right into his side.

"It's okay," she teased, and kissed the side of his neck. "I forgive you. Checking messages and e-mail is definitely all right…." She gasped and jerked upright. "My God. What time is it? Don't we have to get to the plane?"

He touched her shining, sleep-messed hair. "Not happening."

"Huh?"

"We all decided to go tomorrow, instead."

"We did?"

"Yeah. Your sister and niece are heading over to Circus Circus, I believe. And Tanner and some of your half brothers are playing cards tonight." He guided her hair behind her ear, not because it needed to go there, but as an excuse to touch her. He loved touching her. It made him feel…happy. Grounded. *Right.* Who knew that he, Marcus Reid, would ever have a life that was grounded and happy?

It didn't seem possible.

But somehow, it had happened.

And nothing—and no one—was going to screw it up.

"Marcus." Her smooth brows were drawn together.

"Um?"

"You look…angry. Is something going on?"

"Not a thing."

"But you look—"

"Seriously. There's nothing. Come back here." He pulled her close again. She came to him with a sigh. He stroked her hair and ran a lazy finger down the side of her arm.

"How long was I asleep?"

"Oh, couple of hours…"

"We're staying over because of me, right?"

"Yeah. So what? Give yourself a break, woman. You had a baby yesterday."

She didn't argue, just sighed softly again and said, "Jenny's in a crib. How did that happen?"

"I called Fletcher's wife. She sent it up, along with a bunch of other baby stuff."

"I adore my family."

"They're pretty terrific, all right."

"Life's just so strange sometimes, you know? I mean, there's this crazy, bad guy named Blake Bravo. He does any number of awful, unforgivable things in his life—among them, marrying lonely women all over America and getting them pregnant, only to vanish from their lives, leaving them to do the best they can to raise his children. You'd think every one of those kids would turn out messed up and hopeless. But instead, somehow, they find love and they get married. And they have babies of their own."

He kissed the crown of her head. "Some of them have babies first and *then* get married."

"Oh, well." She snuggled in closer. "That, too. And they…find each other, you know? They find out that they have brothers. And sisters. They have a huge family, after all. When for so long they thought they were the only ones." She touched his chin and he looked down into her upturned face. "I'm so glad," she said, "to have them. And to be married to you, to have our daughter…."

"Me, too." He bent and kissed her soft lips.

In her crib, Jenny stirred. She made a fussy little noise. And then another.

Hayley groaned. "Babies. Just when you're thinking how wonderful they are, they're ready to eat again."

Later, they ordered room service and watched a movie. By nine, they were in bed.

Hayley dropped right off to sleep.

Marcus lay beside her, listening to the even sound of her breathing, knowing he needed to tell her about Adriana. They were married now. He didn't need to hold off for fear she would stall out the wedding.

He should wake her up, tell her now, get it over with.

But no. Not now. She needed her sleep.

Hayley wanted the truth from him. She

deserved the truth and nothing less. He needed to tell her.

And he would.

Very soon.

Chapter Twelve

They landed at Sacramento Executive Airport at eleven the next morning and were back in Hayley's apartment before noon.

They got Jenny settled into her new room and ate some sandwiches. Then Hayley went back to the main bedroom to unpack and Marcus called Joyce.

He told her he'd been married over the weekend. And that his new wife had given him a daughter.

"Well," said Joyce, brisk and cheerful as ever. "Congratulations. I'm sure you'll be very happy."

"Thank you," he said. Joyce did have the basic background information. Before he left for the two-week hiatus, he'd told Joyce that there was a special woman—the one he'd had her set up accounts for—that she was pregnant and he was hoping to convince her to be his wife.

They settled on Wednesday morning for the conference calls.

Joyce asked, "You'll be staying on there for the full two weeks, then?"

He realized he wanted those two weeks now—just Hayley and Jenny and him. Away from all the pressures of his work.

And away from Adriana, should she make good on her threat to return to Seattle.

"Yes," he said. "We're just married, with a new baby. A little time away seems like a good idea."

Joyce read off his messages and he took down the phone numbers—or told her what to say when she called them back.

He waited, a sinking feeling in his gut, for her to tell him that Adriana had been calling again.

But instead, she said, "I'll speak with you Wednesday, then?"

And he realized the call was over. He said goodbye, turned off the BlackBerry, and just sat there, staring at the Christmas tree, which Hayley had plugged in the minute they walked in the door.

If Adriana had called the office again, Joyce

would have told him. She was an excellent assistant. She would have made a note of it and passed it along with the rest of the messages, no matter how uncomfortable it made her to speak of the odd behavior of his ex.

So great. Terrific. He wouldn't get his hopes up or anything, but it was just possible that Adriana had finally gotten the message. Or that she'd returned to VonKruger.

Whatever. This could be the end of it. She'd never call again.

Hayley came in from the bedroom. She went straight to the tree and adjusted a wooden nutcracker ornament, anchoring it more firmly on the branch. Then she came and sat beside him.

"So? How's everything at Kaffe Central?"

He faked a look of shock. "You won't believe what's happened."

"What? Is it bad? Tell me..."

He let his mouth hang open a second more, before confessing, "They seem to be getting along just fine without me."

She rolled her eyes. "Unbelievable."

"And yet...true."

"So. Are you saying that even though we're married and everything's settled, I still get you alone here for the rest of our two weeks?"

"Would you like that?"

"Oh, yes."

"Then, okay. You got it."

She clapped her hands like a kid. "Christmas, here. Oh, I was hoping. DeDe's got a dance recital this coming Friday."

"Can't miss that."

"And Kelly's throwing a Christmas party Saturday. I was supposed to bring the cream-cheese roll-ups."

"Wouldn't be a party without them."

She grabbed him by the shoulders. "I'm so *glad*."

"Good."

"And now I have this burning urge to play a bunch of Burl Ives Christmas songs."

"Please. Anything but that." He reeled her in and kissed her.

Then she grabbed his hand. "Come on, lazy. Since we're staying, we need to get unpacked."

The next day? Doctor visits. Marcus took Hayley and Jenny to the gynecologist and the pediatrician. He went into the examining room both times and held the baby when Hayley was busy with the doctor.

That night, Hayley's milk came in. Her breasts were swollen and sore and she cried when Jenny nursed.

Marcus wanted to call the damn doctor and see if there was something that could be done about it—and Hayley laughed through her tears.

"Oh, Marcus. It's fine, really. It's exactly the way it's supposed to be."

It didn't seem fine to him. But he let it go. He felt vaguely foolish and altogether powerless. Running a corporation was nothing compared to learning how to be a husband and father.

Wednesday Hayley went to see the caterer and tell her that she wouldn't be coming back to work there, after all. Gifts started arriving from various Bravos, and Hayley got busy on thank-you letters.

That afternoon, Joyce gave him his messages after he took his conference calls. Nothing from his ex-wife. And nothing Thursday, either. Or Friday.

By then, he was glad he'd never mentioned the thing with Adriana to Hayley. It was starting to look as though there would be no need to upset her, after all.

Friday night was DeDe's dance recital. They sat in the back of the auditorium, so that Hayley could duck out if Jenny fussed. But the baby slept right through the performance in which DeDe played minor parts in three of the dance numbers. She was a mushroom and a frog and one of Santa's elves—and what she lacked in talent, she made up for in attitude. She performed each of her tiny roles with a beaming smile and a whole lot of enthusiasm.

"She's really a terrible dancer, isn't she?"

Hayley said after they got home to her apartment and put Jenny in her crib. They were on the sofa. She'd kicked off her shoes and stretched out, with her head in his lap.

"I'll say this. That kid's got a whole lot of heart."

"Yes, and heart counts. More than anything, I do believe."

He ran a finger down the side of her neck. "So what's the deal with her father? He never comes around?"

"He's long gone. His name was Michael Valutik—or Vakulic? Or something. He was Kelly's first love. They met in high school. All they had was each other, the way Kelly tells it. When they broke up, she didn't know she was pregnant."

"So then, when she found out about DeDe, did she go and tell him then?"

"She tried. She called. The line was disconnected. And then she went to the trailer where he'd lived with his mom. Strangers were living there. The trailer park manager said that his mother had died and that Michael had gone, left no forwarding address. Tanner is still looking for him. No luck, though. I think they believe he must have died or something, for him to have dropped off the face of the earth like that...."

"Maybe Tanner's not looking all that hard."

She sat up. "Marcus. Of course, he's looking hard. And he's a P.I. It's what he does for a living."

"Well, and that's my point. He would have a lot of avenues to check. There should have been *something,* some lead as to where the guy went or what happened to him."

"Well. There's not." By then, she'd retreated to the other end of the couch. "If there were, Tanner would have come up with something."

"I'm just saying, DeDe's father has a damn right to know about her."

"And I'm saying, I agree with you." She stared straight ahead—in the direction of the tree, though he knew she wasn't really looking at it. A moment later, she asked, "Is this about Jenny?" Her voice had gentled. She turned to meet his eyes again. "Because even if you'd never come to find me, you *would* have known. It was a lousy way to tell you, I realize that. But you would have gotten that letter. You would have gotten the news."

He reached for her hand. She allowed that. After a moment, she even scooted close again.

He said, low, "It's not about the letter. I'm over that."

She smiled, the sun coming out from behind gray clouds. "Whew."

"It's just…"

"Tell me."

"First love, that's all. It's a bitch. When you're

young and you don't know anything and love is all that you've got…you get desperate. You make all the wrong decisions. You'll do the most crazy, self-defeating things to try and keep the one you love with you."

"Is that what happened…with you and Adriana?"

Had he actually brought up this subject? It appeared so. "I guess."

She leaned her head on his shoulder. But she didn't say anything more, didn't press him to dig up all the crap and lay it on her.

And because she didn't pressure him, he realized he *wanted* to tell her. He wanted her to understand.

How it had been. The mistakes he'd made— and maybe why he'd made them. He wanted her to have the truth of the past. It seemed important, that he should give her that.

And it came to him that he trusted her enough now to know she wouldn't misread him. Hayley wouldn't make assumptions, wouldn't insist on in-jecting herself into the middle of it. She wouldn't insist on making it all about her, the way Adriana would have done.

He squeezed Hayley's hand and he said, "Adriana was…the blond-haired little girl who lived in the house down the hill and around the corner when I was small, before my mother died.

She was the only daughter of my mother's best friend.

"Much later, once we became lovers and were inseparable, I told her that I'd always loved her, from the first time I saw her. I think I even had myself convinced by then that it was true. But now, looking back, I remember it differently. Adriana always had to be the center of everything. She was her mother's only girl, her father's little darling. I remember once, when we were maybe five, she hit me with one of my own toy trucks. Because I told her to leave me alone. It took six stitches to patch me up. When we were little, she hated that I didn't want anything to do with her. The more I tried to get away from her, the more she insisted on following me everywhere.

"Then my mother died. My world changed. It was me and the nannies, a series of them, and my father, who was drunk most of the time. I hardly saw Adriana after that, for three or four years, at least. Except from a distance. Now and then. We went to different private schools and her parents didn't want their precious darling mixing it up with the son of the man they suspected of murder. Twice during those years, she came to our house on her own. She knocked on the door and she demanded to see me. Both times the housekeeper called her mother, who came and took her home.

"Then, in eighth grade, her parents moved her

to my school, for some reason I'm still unclear about. She fell in step with me in the hallway that first day. 'Hello, Marcus,' she said. 'Here. You can carry my books for me.' I walked faster, I pretended she wasn't there. I had this sense that once I gave her what she wanted, she would *own* me somehow. I…resisted. For weeks, I ignored her, but she wouldn't allow that. Everywhere I went, it seemed like she was always there, watching. Waiting for me to acknowledge her, to carry her books, to follow *her* around the way she was following me.

"I avoided her. Until the day I tried to commit suicide with some prescription painkillers I'd stolen from my father's housekeeper."

Hayley spoke then. "Oh, Marcus…" She squeezed his hand, but she kept her head on his shoulder and she said nothing more.

He went on. "At the time, it seemed like a good choice, to take those pills, to fall asleep and never wake up again. I thought my dad was going to kill me, anyway. I figured I'd beat him to it. Hey. I was twelve. It seemed to me that dying was the only way to escape my miserable life. I took the pills at school, in the boy's restroom. Don't ask me why I decided to off myself there."

She softly suggested, "Maybe so someone would find you. *Help* you?"

"Maybe. I must have passed out. And *she* found me. Adriana. She…saved me. And after that, well,

I guess I surrendered to her, somehow. I gave her my love, such as it was. She was everything to me.

"Sometimes she was kind and mostly she wasn't. She liked the power she had over me. And she got off on…resistance, I guess. Her parents tried for the next ten years to break us up. That only made her love me more. We had what I guess you would call a stormy relationship. Always fighting and making up. It was…what I knew. *All* I knew, really. I didn't imagine there could be anything better. I didn't imagine…this."

Hayley lifted her head from the cradle of his shoulder. She didn't speak, only looked at him. A look that was so tender. And accepting. And then she laid her head back down again.

He said, "Adriana told me she was never having kids. She didn't want them. When she was eighteen, she had her tubes tied. She laughed about that, said it was a good thing, because she'd make a really bad mother, anyway."

Hayley made a low sound in her throat. "So you decided you didn't want kids, either…."

"That's right. And I believed I didn't. I was so sure about it. Even after she ran off with VonKruger and divorced me, I was firm on that score. No children. Ever."

She raised her head again to look at him. "And you were also certain you would never marry again."

"I thought I was…dead inside. That there was nothing left to live for, with Adriana gone. But then you showed up. I couldn't resist you, which seemed really wrong, not to mention impossible. Adriana was supposed to be the only one. My life was supposed to be empty without her. But there you were, as determined as she'd been, but in a whole different way."

She looked at him steadily. "Oh, Marcus…."

He lifted her hand and kissed it. "What?"

"You're a good man. A fine man. I'm proud to be your wife. Jenny's so lucky to have you for her dad. And as for Adriana, well, she's gone off with someone else. You're free of her now."

It was his chance. The exact right moment. To tell her about the phone calls, to let her know that his ex had been…back in touch. Not because he expected to hear from Adriana again.

But because it was the right thing, the honest thing, to tell his wife.

The seconds ticked by.

"Marcus?"

"Hmm?"

"You look so…sad, suddenly."

Instead of the truth she deserved, he gave her another lie. "No. I'm not. Not sad in the least…"

"You know I'm going to hate it when you leave for Seattle," Kelly said.

"I know." Hayley spread the Christmas cloth across the table. "I'll miss you, too. A lot."

"Here we just found you—and you're leaving again. And taking my niece with you, which I find seriously annoying."

It was just the two of them in Kelly's dining room. Jenny was fast asleep in the spare room. They were setting things up for the party that night. Marcus had dropped Hayley and the baby off a half an hour before, and DeDe was at the YMCA pool with some friends.

Hayley smoothed the gold-trimmed green cloth. "I didn't expect this, I have to admit. I was all set *not* to get married."

Kelly put the empty serving dishes down. "But you're happy…."

"Yeah…"

"Okay. I'm picking up mixed signals here."

"Something's bothering him. He won't say what."

Kelly took the centerpiece of boughs and berries from the pass-through to the kitchen and placed it in the middle of the tablecloth. "Something… serious?"

"Can't tell, since he won't say what it is."

Kelly took her hand and led her into the kitchen. They sat at the table in there. "I want to give you some really helpful advice. Unfortunately, I'm totally out of my depth here. I've never had a husband. I don't even have a boyfriend. I had sex once, though...."

Hayley laughed. "Well, I kind of figured. I mean, there's DeDe."

"No. I mean I had sex with someone other than Michael."

"Shocking."

"Yeah, right. I met this guy at a Parents Without Partners discussion group. He was an anesthesiologist. I thought, hey. Michael's been gone for six years. I need to find someone else. And this guy, he's getting out, mixing it up a little, not letting his divorce get him down. And he's got a steady job. What's not to like? We went out. An actual date. His kids were with his ex that night, so we went to his place. It was just that one time."

"You...didn't like him?"

"He was fine. It just wasn't meant to be, you know?"

"And since then?"

"Can you spell *nada*? That's it. The full extent of my expertise with relationships. My high school boyfriend, who broke my heart, gave me DeDe—and disappeared never to be heard from again. And the one-night stand with the guy from the PWP discussion group."

Hayley slanted her sister a wary look. "Are you trying to tell me something in particular?"

"Only that I'm here. I want to be helpful. But

do I have any hands-on experience with the subject in question? No."

"I'm just glad. *That* you're here."

The two of them shared a look. Fond. Sisterly. It remained a wonder to Hayley, to *have* a sister—especially a truly terrific one like Kelly.

Kelly said, "Okay, I'll take a crack at it—how 'bout this? Do you love him?"

"Passionately. Totally. Tenderly."

"Are you glad you married him?"

"Every day, every hour. With every single beat of my heart."

"Is this a deal-killer for you, this…whatever's bothering him?"

"No. Not at all."

"Have you made it clear that you're ready to listen when he's ready to start talking?"

"I think so—wait. Scratch that. I *have* made it clear. I'm sure I have."

"Is he good to you—well, I mean, so far?"

"He's amazing. He's…different than before. More attentive. Kinder. He's happy. He even said so. And if you knew him before, well, *happy* is not a word I ever would have called him in my wildest dreams."

"Are you sure you're okay with moving back to Seattle?"

"Huh? What's that got to do with something bothering *him?*"

"Never hurts to examine your own motivations a little, see if the problem might actually be yours."

"You know, for someone who claims to know zip about relationships, you're doing really well here."

"Well, there *was* that Marriage and the Family class I took when I was earning my degree."

"You must have aced it."

"As a matter of fact, I did." Kelly smiled sweetly. "Now answer the question."

"Um. Yes. I'm fine with moving back to Seattle. I like it there. I'll miss you and DeDe. And Tanner. But we'll get together. It's not *that* far away."

"Do you feel that Marcus is…opening up to you, that he's telling you what's going on inside him?"

"Funny you should ask that one. I do feel he's opening up. More and more so, every day."

"Maybe it's just a matter of time, then. Maybe you just need to be patient, let him tell you what's on his mind when *he's* ready to talk about it."

"Kelly. I am not kidding. You're really good at this."

"Thanks. But the fact remains. I haven't had sex since the anesthesiologist from the PWP discussion group. Except with myself, but that doesn't really count, now does it?"

* * *

The party that night consisted mostly of Kelly's neighbors and the people she worked with. There were also several couples whose kids went to school with DeDe.

Tanner came solo. In the kitchen, where Kelly and Hayley were taking various hot hors d'oeuvres from the oven and arranging them on serving platters, he appeared looking for a beer and then hung around to sample the crostini.

Kelly nudged him with her elbow when he reached for a roast pepper and mozzarella treat she'd just put on a plate. "If you must, would you mind eating the ones on the rack?"

He shrugged. "Fine with me." He grabbed another one and popped it into his mouth.

"And I thought you said you were bringing a date," Kelly groused.

He grunted. "Look who's talkin'."

Marcus came in and wrapped his arms around Hayley. "Jenny's sound asleep." They'd put her to bed in Kelly's room, since the spare room was the coatroom tonight.

Hayley turned her head to share a kiss with him and then went back to refilling the serving platter.

Kelly said, "You two look disgustingly happy. You almost make me want to join another discussion group."

When Hayley laughed, Tanner grunted again. "Huh? That was funny?"

"Little private joke." Kelly turned and handed him the full platter. "Here. Put this on the dining room table—and don't eat them all. Leave some for the guests."

Tanner frowned. "*I'm* a guest."

She turned him by the shoulders and gave him a push. "Go. Please." She picked up the platter that Hayley had just finished filling and followed him.

Hayley turned in the circle of her husband's arms. "Hear that?" She sang along to the CD on the stereo…. "One of my favorites."

"They're *all* your favorites." He bent his head and kissed her. A nice, long, slow one.

When they came up for air, she said, "And we're not even under the mistletoe…."

The next day was Christmas Eve. They spent it at the apartment, in their pajamas, watching holiday programming on television.

They went to bed early—and then were up again at a little after eleven, when Jenny got hungry. Once the baby was fed and changed and back in her crib, Hayley led Marcus into the living room.

She plugged in the tree and she put on a slow Christmas song and they danced in their pj's and slippers.

"It's midnight," she said, when the song was over and the stereo fell silent and it was just the two of them, standing in the middle of her living room, swaying together in the quiet. "Merry Christmas."

"Merry Christmas, my darling," he whispered.

She left him, but only long enough to play that song again.

The next morning they went to Kelly's to open presents. Then Kelly made French toast for their Christmas breakfast. They had a big turkey dinner at three that afternoon.

It was a great Christmas, Hayley thought. The best she'd ever had. Her first Christmas with her family and it was everything she'd ever dreamed it might be.

Tuesday, the twenty-sixth, she told him at breakfast that she was going to start packing. But Marcus was having a moving company handle moving all her things.

He told her she didn't have to lift a finger.

So she took him at his word. They hung around the apartment in the morning, went out and bought groceries in the afternoon. Marcus carried Jenny and walked along beside the cart as Hayley picked up what they needed to get by for the next few days. They rented movies and sat on the couch watching them, their arms around each other.

The rest of the week went more or less the same way. They joked that they were turning into a couple of couch potatoes. Before long, they'd start calling each other Spud.

Friday came and their two weeks in Sacramento were up. But Marcus suggested they could just stay until after New Year's. It was only three more days and nothing much was going on at Kaffe Central over the big holiday weekend anyway.

As it turned out, Kelly had a party to attend at a friend's house on New Year's Eve. Tanner had a date.

So Hayley and Marcus and the baby spent the big night with DeDe at her house. They watched a Disney double feature and DeDe tried to keep her eyes open till midnight.

She didn't succeed. At eleven-thirty, she was crashed out in her nest of blankets in the family room.

On New Year's Day, they took down the tree, put away all the decorations and packed their suitcases. Hayley felt wistful. The holidays were winding down. Tomorrow they'd be heading for Seattle.

The next day, they were in the air by eight in the morning. And at five to eleven, Marcus eased his Jaguar in next to the Hummer in the garage of the house in Madison Park.

The two-story place was just as she remembered it: Ultramodern. Gorgeous. Sleek and just a little bit sterile. So clean it squeaked because of his housekeeper who came in twice a week.

For the time being, they put Jenny's soft-sided porta-crib in the sitting area of the master suite. Hayley started unpacking and Marcus went down to his office to check his phone messages.

He was back in no time, standing in the doorway to the combination closet/dressing room. "Three messages. One from a guy selling siding, one from the Democratic National Committee and one from the March of Dimes. I should change my number more often."

She glanced over her shoulder as she put a stack of sweaters in a drawer. "You changed the house number, too?"

"Yes, I did." He offered no explanation.

And it seemed kind of silly to ask for one. But it did strike her as odd. It wasn't as if he'd moved or anything.

He said, "I hate to leave you all alone, but I think it's probably time I checked in at work."

She went to him and slid her arms around his lean waist. "Jenny and I will be just fine."

He kissed her nose and then took one of her hands from behind his back and put a card in it. "The current alarm code and the new number here. Also, there's my number at Kaffe Central in case you've forgotten it. And if you need to go any-where, the keys to the Hummer are—"

"The secret kitchen compartment?" There was a section of cabinet in the kitchen that held a hidden door.

He nodded. "I should be back by six."

"I doubt that."

"I'll try."

"I know you will." She kissed him goodbye and finished unpacking.

It didn't take long. There wasn't a whole lot to unpack. Most of her clothes would be coming up with the movers next week.

She had the usual mountain of baby necessities for Jenny. She put the baby stuff in one of the empty drawers in the master suite's giant closet/-dressing room for now, so everything would be in easy reach.

They'd left a gray day in Sacramento. Seattle was the same, but colder, the streets and sidewalks dotted with thick patches of snow from a recent storm. Hayley sat on the end of the bed, which was bigger than king-size, had a block of brushed steel for a headboard and a quilted bedspread the color of a cloud. She stared out the big window at the gray sky and the gleaming surface of Lake Wash-ington beneath it.

Already, she missed her tiny apartment and her old, comfortable furniture. No, none of that stuff would fit in here. Except for a few pieces she just couldn't bear to part with, the rest was already slated to be picked up in Sacramento next Tuesday by Goodwill.

She lay back with a sigh and imagined the changes she was going to make to the house. Brighter colors would do the place a world of good. And soon she'd be unpacking her personal treasures, setting them around.

When she lived here before, the place had never really felt like home. This time, it would. Hayley planned to make sure of that.

"That's it, then?" asked Marcus.

Joyce rose from the chair on the other side of his desk. "You're all caught up. I'll set up the meetings for tomorrow, as we discussed."

Again, there'd been no mention that Adriana had called. "Thanks, Joyce."

She left him.

It was now more than two weeks since his ex last tried to contact him. Adriana must have finally accepted the hard fact that he never wanted to see or hear from her again.

He was glad he'd kept his mouth shut about the issue with Hayley. He'd gambled she didn't need to know. And he'd won.

Marcus sat back in his chair, feeling good. He was meeting with the head of the Central California expansion project for updates in half an hour. And he had a couple of high-priority calls he had to make. What remained of the day after that, he'd spend checking in with his people in person, getting anything that had strayed off the rails firmly back on track.

Hell. Maybe he'd surprise Hayley and get home by six, after all.

The doorbell chimed at a little after four, just as Hayley finished changing Jenny's diaper. She snapped the baby back into her sleeper, wrapped her in a fluffy blanket and carried her downstairs with her to the entry hall.

The bell chimed again, an impatient sound, as Hayley pulled open the wide door. The woman standing on the gray flagstone steps wore skinny black pants and high platform heels and a short, bell-shaped cashmere jacket.

She ran a slim hand back through her gorgeous mane of tawny-colored hair. "Hayley." Bored. Dismissive. Her amber-colored gaze made a slow pass over Hayley's clean-scrubbed face, her too-big sweater, her baggy cords and comfortable clogs. "Hello."

Hayley cradled her baby closer. Even if she hadn't seen pictures, she would know this woman. There was something about her: an air of privilege, the scent of money, an absolute assurance that anything she wanted would automatically be hers.

It all snapped into place for Hayley in that instant. Her instincts had been right. Something *was* bothering Marcus.

Now she knew what.

Chapter Thirteen

"And you must be Adriana," Hayley said coolly. "Marcus has told me so much about you." She found a lovely, petty satisfaction in the look of wary surprise that crept over the blonde's perfect face. "And I'm sorry, but he isn't here right now. Try him at his office." She swung the door shut.

Adriana stuck her designer shoe in it before it closed all the way. "I came here to talk to *you*."

Hayley considered the concept of letting her in, of hearing what she had to say. But no. That would bring nothing but Trouble. Capital *T*. "Look. I'm just not comfortable inviting you in. I don't know you—I mean, beyond what Marcus has said about you. It wasn't all that good, frankly. And he said nothing about your…stopping by today. Because I'm sure he had no idea that you were coming."

Adriana tossed her shining hair again. Even in the gray light of the winter afternoon, that hair shone with glints of pure gold. "A baby," she muttered. "I knew it, but I couldn't believe it. Marcus doesn't even *want* children. But he is so very honorable, isn't he? So he's married you. He would have felt that he *had* to. So…archaic. But that's part of his charm. Oh, what a fool that man can be."

"Please take your foot out of the door."

She kept it right where it was. "I'm back in Seattle now. And I'm not going away. He's going to have to deal with me. I'd advise you to tell him that."

Hayley resisted the powerful urge to say something really rude. Self-control mattered in a situation like this. "Your foot. Move it. Now." Her heart was suddenly thudding in a sick, swift way and Jenny, picking up on her distress, was starting to fuss.

"You won't keep him. He's mine. And he knows it, too."

Hayley rocked the baby and pressed her lips to the velvet skin at her temple. She whispered soothingly, "Shh…"

And Marcus's ex still had her foot in the door. "I just think you should know where you stand."

Hayley patted Jenny's back and stroked her head—and spoke with a calm confidence that surprised even her. "I have nothing to say to you. And I've asked you to leave, repeatedly. This is a gated community. I have no idea why the guy in the gatehouse let you in, but you're not welcome here. Do I have to call security to get you to go?"

"Oh, please. You wouldn't dare."

"See, that's the problem, isn't it? You might have hired a detective to find out all about me. But that doesn't mean you know me. You don't have a clue what I might do."

There was a stare-down.

It surprised Hayley no end when Adriana blinked first.

She pulled her foot out of the way. "Tell Marcus he's being childish. I need to see him. And I will."

Hayley didn't waste time replying. She pushed the door shut and turned the dead bolt.

Then, since her knees felt absurdly weak, she leaned back against the sturdy hardwood and tried to breathe normally.

Jenny let out a wail.

Hayley rubbed her tiny back and rocked her gently from side to side. "It's okay, honey. Okay. All right…"

But it was not all right.

As soon as Jenny settled down, Hayley put her

in her crib. Then she picked up the phone, started to dial Marcus's cell—and hung up before she hit the final digit. This wasn't an issue to be dealt with on the phone.

She stared out the window at the gray day and wondered what she ought to do next.

Kelly…

She'd never wanted her sister as much as she did at that moment. Kelly would be at work now. But maybe Hayley would luck out and get her at a quiet moment. She reached for the phone again, half dialed her sister's cell—and stopped.

Wait. Calm down, her wiser self advised.

Really, what was she so afraid of? Marcus's ex was hardly going to break into the house and attack her. The woman had done what damage she could for the day.

And that damage was plenty.

He's going to have to deal with me. Please tell him that…he's being childish. I need to see him.

So Marcus had been refusing to see her. For how long?

Hayley knew the answer instantly: from that first night she'd sensed that something was wrong. On the phone. When she was in Sacramento and he'd come back here to Seattle to set things up for their two weeks together.

God. That was before the reunion. Almost three weeks ago.

* * *

Marcus called at seven-thirty. "I'm scum. I'm late and I know it. But I'm on my way home now."

"Great."

"Hungry? How about Italian? I can—"

"There's food here. Jenny and I went shopping." Actually, it had been therapeutic. By the time she put the groceries away, she'd started to get a little perspective on the creepy visit from Adriana.

The situation wasn't good. But it didn't have to be the end of the world unless she let it.

"I believe you are my ideal woman," he teased.

"It's only lasagna and salad."

"See? You're a mind reader. Italian. Just what I wanted. Half an hour."

"We'll be here."

He found her upstairs. She'd just fed and changed Jenny and was putting her to bed.

He came up behind her and wrapped his arms around her. "Mmm. You smell good..." He nuzzled her neck and she sighed and thought about how maybe she should wait to tell him about his ex until after he'd eaten, at least.

But really. Honesty was the deal here. To put it off any longer, to sit down to the table with him, share a meal, hear him talk about his day, to give herself time to think about how much she loved him, how she wished this problem would just go away, to possibly allow herself to put it off till later still….

That would be a lie.

And the whole point was *no lies*.

She turned in his arms.

One look in her eyes and he knew that something wasn't right. He cradled her face between his palms. "What?"

She stepped clear of his touch. "Let's go downstairs."

They sat on a beige sofa in the living room. Like the master suite above, it faced the lake, though on the ground floor, the view was framed by the winter-bare shapes of nearby trees, trees that were illuminated now by strategically placed in-ground lanterns. Here and there, in the distance, boats lit up at bow and stern bobbed on the gleaming dark water. The sky was overcast, hiding the stars.

"What?" he asked again, those straight sable brows drawn together over worried eyes.

She laid it right out there. "Adriana was here today."

He winced as if she'd struck him. And then he swore, a single, raw word.

Hayley went on, "She just showed up at the front door, out of nowhere. A…surprise visit."

His frown deepened. "How the hell did she get past the gatehouse?"

"You'll have to ask her that. She knew my name. And she knew about Jenny. She said she's moved back to Seattle now. I told her you weren't at home and she claimed that she'd come to see *me*. Then she started giving me messages to pass on to you—stuff like how you would have to deal with her. That you were being 'childish,' that she needed to see you and she wanted you to call her."

He swore again. "I damn well don't believe this."

"Yeah. Well. I hear you. I have to tell you, it freaked me out. That's one scary, determined woman. I get a bad feeling she'll go a long way to make you realize that you belong with her."

"God. Hayley. I'm so sorry. She won't bother you again. I'll make sure of it." He tried to take her hand.

She didn't allow that. "She's already been in touch with you, right?"

"Hayley—"

"Please. Just answer the question. Just tell me the truth. You know that's what I wanted. Always. The main thing, between us. Honesty. Had she already contacted you before today?"

It took him a moment. But then he finally said, "Yeah. She called me on my cell while I was back here, getting things cleared up for our two weeks together. I told her it was over, that I didn't want to get back with her. I told her never to call me again. She started calling the house."

"So you had the number changed. And your cell number, too. Because of her."

"I thought, if she couldn't reach me, she'd give it up."

"Marcus."

"Could you just not…look at me like that?"

"How can you have believed that that woman would just go away?"

"I hoped, okay? Is that such a bad thing?"

"It's unrealistic. She's…obsessed with you. I don't even know her and I wouldn't have expected her to give up. Not after what you told me about her. You said yourself she…how did you put it? She…*gets off on resistance?*"

"You don't understand."

"No. Actually, I think I do."

"What the hell is that supposed to mean?"

"You're not over her."

"Damn it. That's not true."

"Maybe you *want* to be over her, maybe you even believe that you are over her. But if you were, you would have dealt with this situation openly, you would have told me what was going on."

"I told her never to call me again. I changed my phone numbers. She's made no attempt to contact me since the Friday we went to Vegas when she called the office—twice, according to Joyce. After that, until today, nothing. I thought she'd gotten the message. I figured she'd gone back to her second husband or…moved on. Hell. I don't know. I just thought she wouldn't be bothering me anymore."

Hayley scooted farther away from him.

"Damn it, Hayley. Please…"

She put up a hand. "The question I can't get past, the thing that sticks in my brain, is why didn't you tell me? You've been lying to me for almost three weeks now."

"The hell I have."

"Marcus. You have. You know you have."

He made a low, frustrated sound. "All right. Yes. By omission."

"A lie is a lie, no matter how you try to pretty it up."

"Look. I see now I should have told you. But I really thought that there was no need for you to know."

"But there *was* a need. Between two people who are building a life together, there's *always* a need. For trust. And for truth. I don't want a life built on knowing only what you think I *need* to know. I deserve better. We both do."

Anger flared in his eyes. "There is nothing going on between Adriana and me."

"I never said there was."

"Then why are you so damn mad at me?"

"I think you know why. I've said why. More than once. And not only is there the lie you've been telling me, there's the fact that you left me swinging in the wind today."

"Hayley—"

"Uh-uh. I was not prepared to open the door and find your ex-wife standing there. I was not prepared because you didn't tell me what was going on."

"I thought it was finished."

"Adriana would say differently—and she did. This afternoon."

"Damn it, Hayley…" He let the muttered words trail off. Then he rose, went to the window and stared out over the lake. She watched as he lifted a lean arm and rubbed the back of his neck. There was something so…sad in the gesture. So infinitely weary.

God. How she loved him. So much that she'd learned to bear his not belonging to her completely. She'd learned to live—and happily—without hearing the words *I love you* from his lips.

But this…this lying. This holding back the truth from her and then trying to convince her it had been for her own good. She just couldn't live with that.

At last, he faced her again. "You act like I've been having an affair with her or something."

"No. That's not true. I know you haven't been having an affair with her. I know you would never do such a thing. The issue is that you lied to me when you knew that honesty was what I wanted above all."

"Damn it. I didn't tell you because I knew it would upset you. Apparently, I was right."

She shook her head. "Oh, no. Uh-uh. That's not going to work on me. You don't get to hold back important information so as not to *upset* me. I'm not some wilting little flower you have to protect from real life. My father was a murdering, kidnapping, double-dealing polygamist. My mother was a basket case who wouldn't take care of me—but wouldn't let me go, either. I know a whole bunch about real life. I know how to take the hardest kind of truth."

"I said I was wrong. I *know* I was wrong. I don't know what else I can tell you. Except that I swear to you, I want nothing to do with Adriana. Since she divorced me, I've *had* nothing to do with Adriana. I spoke with her on the phone *once*, almost three weeks ago. I told her to get lost and I hung up. That's the extent of my connection with her."

"Oh, Marcus. You're not only lying to me. You're lying to yourself."

"What the—?"

"You *are* still connected to her."

"No."

"Yes. You're still not sure, what, exactly you feel about her. You're *running* from her, Marcus. You're afraid to face her."

"That's bullsh—"

"No. Please. Think. If you had no…fears about your connection with that woman, if you were completely over her, you would have told me that she'd called you. You would have been secure in the knowledge that she was no threat to you, to me or to our marriage."

"Oh, come on. You've met her now. She's bound to make trouble, we can both see that now. She *is* a threat. Who the hell knows what she'll pull next?"

Hayley rose—because she found she couldn't sit still. "You're determined not to admit your part in this."

His face looked carved in stone—except for the furious fire that burned in his eyes. "What the hell do you want me to tell you? I've said it a thousand times. I'll say it again. I know where I stand in this. I know my part in this. I'm with you. I want to be with you. That bitch is nothing to me anymore."

She longed to believe him. But she simply didn't. "When she's nothing to you, you won't have to lie to me about her."

He swore some more. "When will you listen? When will you hear me? I feel like I'm talking to a damn brick wall." He took a step toward her.

She put out a hand. "Don't. I mean it. Just don't."

He veered the other way, headed for the back of the house.

Silent moments ticked past. She didn't hear the utility room door to the garage open and close, but she knew he was gone.

Slowly she sank to the couch again. She sat there for a long time, staring out through the naked branches of the trees, at the lake, at the lights of the boats bobbing in the darkness.

Chapter Fourteen

The days went by.

Wednesday. Thursday. Friday.

Marcus went to work early and came home late. He said nothing more about Adriana. Hayley had no idea whether or not he'd contacted the woman. She didn't ask. And he didn't tell.

The silence between them was deep and wide as an ocean, impenetrable as stone. She knew she should find a way to bridge that silence, to break through it. She knew that she'd hurt him, bad. By calling him a liar, by accusing him of still having feelings for the woman who'd left him flat for another man.

She knew that he really thought he'd been protecting her by keeping the truth from her, that he honestly believed he'd behaved honorably. She knew he would never betray her. Such behavior just wasn't in him. He was loyal to the core.

But something still bound him to Adriana. And until he admitted that was so, he would never understand the bedrock reason he'd kept the truth from her, Hayley. He would keep on lying about his own motives—to her and to himself.

She felt numb at the core, but she made herself go through the motions of living her new life as Marcus's bride. She went to the paint store and chose brighter colors for most of the rooms, made arrangements for the painters to come the following week. Once Jenny's room was painted, she planned to do a mural on one wall and a border along the baseboards, as she had at the apartment. Something cheerful and childlike—what, exactly, she hadn't decided. She sketched a number of possibilities, but she hadn't made her mind up yet which idea she'd go with.

Not a rainbow, though. Not unless she and Marcus worked out this big problem they were having first. Every time she thought of rainbows, she remembered the first time Marcus saw the rainbow in Jenny's room in Sacramento—that musing, hopeful look on his usually guarded face.

No. She couldn't do a rainbow now.

Friday night, when he finally got home from work, she lay in bed beside him, yet miles and miles away. She ached to scoot over close to him, to wrap her arms around him, to whisper, *I'm sorry. Can we please just get past this? Can we please just let it be like it was before?*

Yet somehow, she couldn't. Somehow she just wouldn't make herself apologize to him when he was the one who'd done the damage here.

And it was never going to be the way it was before. It could be better. Or worse and worse. But never the same. Those happy, magical beginning days of their marriage were gone. They'd had their first fight.

And it had been a doozy.

Yes, she did know that all relationships required compromise. A marriage that lasted necessitated give and take. At some point, one of them was going to have to make the first move, reach out a hand, try and bridge the gap.

But he hadn't done it yet. He was too angry.

And she hadn't done it—she was too hurt.

Very late, she finally drifted into a restless sleep, only to wake an hour later when Jenny started fussing in her temporary crib in the sitting room.

"I'll get her," he mumbled from way over there on the far side of the giant bed.

"No. It's all right. She's hungry. I'll do it."

* * *

In the morning, when Hayley woke, Marcus was already gone. Off to work on Saturday—which was nothing new, really. He worked long hours and she'd known that when she married him. It only seemed crappy now because of the trouble they were having.

Fussy, whiny sounds came from the sitting room. Jenny was ready to eat again.

Hayley fed and changed the baby. Then she carried her downstairs and put her in the kitchen playpen. She got the water going for tea, put the bread in the toaster and cracked a couple of eggs into a pan. The phone rang.

Her stomach clenched and her heart beat faster. Maybe it would be Marcus, making the first move toward her at last. Or it might just be Adriana, mounting another surprise attack….

The display showed it was neither. Smiling, she put the phone to her ear. "Kelly. Hey!"

Her sister teased. "What is it with you? You never call, you never write…."

Because she knew if she called Kelly, she'd only cry on her shoulder. And Kelly would worry, and she didn't want that. "Sorry. It's been a zoo around here."

"I kind of figured. I thought I'd give you a few days to get settled in before I got in touch. I knew I'd only get all teary-eyed because I miss you so dang much. And guess what?" She made a soft little sniffling sound.

"Don't say it. I feel exactly the same way." Hayley turned off the fire under the eggs and whipped a paper towel off the roll to dab at her suddenly misty eyes. "I miss you, too. Even worse than I thought I would, and that's a whole lot."

"Hold on. I have to blow my nose." There was a loud honking sound.

Hayley laughed. "Better?"

"A little—and honestly. I didn't only call to cry over how much I miss you...."

"What's up?"

"Let me say this first. Tanner told me not to bug you. I said forget that noise. You'd want to know—and don't get all freaked on me. It's nothing that awful. Well, I mean. It's not good. But—"

"Kell."

"Yeah?"

"What is it?"

"Tanner got broadsided by a one of those humongous four-wheel-drive pickups last night."

"Omigod." Hayley pulled out a chair and sank into it. "Is he—?"

"He'll be okay. In time. Broken arm, broken leg. A couple of cracked ribs. And a concussion. The guy who hit him was totally hammered. And wouldn't you know that fool walked away without a scratch?"

"Where's Tanner now?"

"Sutter General. Under duress. You know how he is. Always on the move. Well, he won't be moving a lot for the next few weeks. And he's completely freaked because if he can't move, he can't work. He hates to miss a job and he'll miss a few with this, believe me. I keep trying to remind him that he can damn well afford this. The guy who hit him is going to be paying big-time. And besides, Tanner has insurance and money in the bank. But you know, it's not the money. It's the lack of control. Our big brother could never stand to be *not* in control."

"But he's…okay? Right?"

"Well, yeah. He'll be fine. In time."

"What about right now?"

"He hurts everywhere. He can barely move. He's one big bandage with swollen slits for eyes."

"Oh, no. That's horrible."

"And did I mention, he's really, really mad?"

Hayley stood up. "You know what? I'm not letting you guys deal with this on your own. I'll be there. I'll call you back as soon as I know when my flight gets in."

"Huh? You've got a three-week-old baby. And a brand-new husband. There's no need for you to leave your new home. Hey, it's not like he's dying. He's going to be fine. I just wanted you to know."

"Well, of course you did. I'm coming."

"Hayley, don't. There's no need for you to—"

"You already said that. I'm coming. So stop telling me not to."

She called Marcus, something she hadn't done since the big blowup Tuesday night. He surprised her by answering the phone.

"Yeah?" Cautious. And completely noncommittal.

"I, um, Kelly just called. Tanner's been in an accident."

That got a reaction. "My God. Is he okay?"

"He will be. But he's in the hospital and he's pretty messed up. I'm going to go ahead and go down there…."

A silence. A heavy one. Then, "Of course. I'll arrange for the jet."

"Oh. Really. That's not necessary."

"As far as I'm concerned, it is. You don't want to take Jenny on a commercial flight when you don't have to."

"Marcus. She'll be fine."

"No. I'll have a car sent to get you."

"But I—"

"Two hours. Is that enough time?"

"But I said—"

"If you're taking my daughter to Sacramento, by God you'll do it in my private plane."

Well. That pretty much settled it. "All right. Two hours. I'll be ready."

"Give Tanner my best. Tell him if he needs anything, to let me know."

"I will. Yes. Absolutely."

"Have a safe trip."

"Thank you."

He hung up.

She hadn't said when she was coming home—and he hadn't asked.

"What the hell are you doing here?" Tanner growled when Hayley entered his room.

"Good to see you, too—well, except you look like holy hell." He was trussed up like a mummy, hooked up to an IV—among other things. What she could see of him didn't look good. All swollen up, battered, black-and-blue.

"Where's the baby?"

"Kelly's got her, out in the waiting room. Oh, God, Tanner…" She moved up right next to him and lightly laid her hand on his gauze-covered shoulder. "I'm so sorry. I know it must really hurt."

He made a soft snorting sort of noise. "You drag Marcus down here, too?"

"No. He stayed in Seattle."

"Well, at least one of you has some sense."

"He sent his…condolences. Said if you need anything, you should let him know."

"I need to get out of this bed and get on with my life. I've got work I need to be doing."

"Sorry. Don't think he can help you with that."

Tanner swore. "You shouldn't have come. I'll be fine. You didn't *need* to come."

"There was no way anyone could stop me."

"Well." He cleared his throat and gruffly confessed, "It's good to see you…."

She bent close enough to brush her lips on the bandage that covered his head. "Good to see you, too. You really look awful."

He chuckled—and then he moaned. "No kidding. And don't make me laugh, okay? It hurts too damn much."

Marcus sat on the neatly made bed in the master suite. It was after midnight. He'd stayed at the office as long as he could.

But eventually, he'd had to come home to this empty house.

He ran his hand over the smooth fabric of the gray quilt. Sleeping alone, without Hayley. It would be bad.

But really, how much worse could it get? The past few nights had been grim enough. In bed together, with both of them wishing they weren't.

She could have called. Just to say she'd gotten to Sacramento all right.

Though he knew that she had. She'd flown

there in his plane, after all. And he'd given orders that he was to be informed when they landed. He'd even had a car waiting, to take her to Kelly's, since Kelly had the keys to the apartment.

He stared out the window at the lights on the lake, not really seeing them, thinking that Hayley's lease wasn't up till June. Kelly was supposed to make arrangements for a sublet, and Tanner was handling selling Hayley's five-year-old compact car. The movers hadn't even picked up her things yet. And her furniture was still there, wasn't it?

She could walk right back into her old life without missing a beat. If that was her plan.

Had she left him? Was that what was really going on here?

He shut his eyes, blocking out the sight of the lake, closing his mind off from the idea that she wasn't coming back, that he could have lost her, that their future consisted of a divorce and a custody agreement.

Give it time, he thought. *We both just need a little damn time*.

Hayley made herself call Marcus the next morning at eight.

"Hey," she said after his hello.

"Hey. So. You got in all right."

"Perfect. Thanks for arranging for the car."

"No problem. How's Tanner?"

"He's a mess. And he's mad. He'll be flat on his back for a while."

"But he'll be okay, in the end?"

"Yeah. He'll pull through fine. The doctors say everything should heal up good as new."

"Tell him to take it easy."

"It's not like he has a choice—but yeah. I will."

"How's Jenny?"

"Fine."

"Good."

"I'm…well, I think I'll stay on here. Stick by Tanner, until he gets through the worst of this…." Tomorrow she would call Goodwill and the movers, let them know she was putting off clearing out the apartment. And she would also call the painters up in Seattle, tell them she was canceling the job for now. She added, "It's just for a while…."

"A while," he repeated. But he didn't ask how long a while might be. The silence stretched. And then he said, "All right, then. Goodbye."

And the line went dead.

Hayley clutched the phone against her chest. She should call him again. Right now. Tell him she'd changed her mind, she was coming home tomorrow. She should say that she hated what was happening between them and she longed only to work things out, make it better, make the silence and the distance go away.

But then Jenny cried.

Hayley set down the phone and went to get her. And somehow, later, Hayley couldn't quite bring herself to make that second call.

Two weeks went by before Kelly started asking questions. Tanner was out of the hospital by then, getting around on crutches with great difficulty, since he also had that broken arm, constantly complaining but also swiftly improving.

It was Saturday. The sisters sat at the round table in Kelly's kitchen. Jenny cooed in her bouncy seat and DeDe was down the street at a girlfriend's. Candy, DeDe's ancient dog, lay curled on the rug in the corner.

Chocolate chip cookies cooled on a rack on the counter and a plate of them, still warm, sat on the table within easy reach.

"Okay," said Kelly. "I keep trying to figure out a smooth way to say this…." Hayley knew what was coming. It was. "What's going on? Is there a problem between you and Marcus?"

Hayley stared into her mug of decaf. "Long story."

Kelly waited for her to continue. But she didn't. "What? You don't want to talk about it."

Slowly, Hayley shook her head. Then she made herself meet her sister's eyes. "Thanks. No."

"God, Hayley. I don't like this. I worry, you know?" Kelly's hand rested on the table.

Hayley put her own hand over it. "Don't. It'll all work out."

Would it? It didn't really look that way.

Everything was all wrong, yet Hayley did nothing. She took care of her baby and spent time with her family.

She was waiting. But for what?

She had absolutely no idea.

Two weeks and two days after Hayley took Jenny and went back to Sacramento, Adriana started calling Marcus again. On his new cell number.

It wasn't a surprise. Whatever detective she'd hired would have found his new numbers for her.

He lucked out the first time she called. He was in a meeting, so she got bumped to voice mail.

Later, when he checked messages, hers was waiting.

"I know that she's left you, Marcus, that she took that baby you didn't even want and went back to California. I know everything. And I've been waiting. For your call. But I can see you've decided to continue being stubborn. To make me pay. Because of Leo. Fine. I'm a patient woman. Within reason. But eventually you will have to come to me. And when you do—"

He stopped the damn thing there and erased it. He didn't need to hear the rest. He knew it already.

It was pretty much the same message she'd been sending since he was four years old.

After that, he checked the display before he picked up any ringing phones. She left a lot of messages. He never played a single one of them back, just hit Delete and got on with his life.

Such as it was.

Sunday, the twenty-eighth of January, Jenny was six weeks old. Kelly offered Sunday dinner and Hayley was happy to accept.

After the meal, Hayley used the spare room to feed Jenny. The baby was through eating and Hayley was changing her on the bed when there was a tap on the door.

"Come on in."

It was Tanner. Leaning on his crutches, he stuck his head in. "Got a minute?"

She pressed the tabs on Jenny's diaper. "Sure."

He hobbled in, braced both crutches against the wall and shut the door behind him. His arm had healed quickly, but he still wasn't comfortable putting much weight on his broken leg. He leaned against the door frame for support. "Hayley…" He looked down at the floor, or maybe at the removable cast.

"All right." She snapped Jenny into a sleeper. "What's the matter?"

He cleared his throat and lifted his dark head

with some reluctance. "Kelly and me, we're worried about you. And Marcus."

She picked up the baby and put her on her shoulder. Gently, she rubbed her little back. Jenny yawned and put her head down with a contented sigh. In a minute, she'd be sound asleep, ready for a long nap in the playpen Kelly kept in the corner for Jenny's use when they visited.

It took so little to make a baby happy: food, a clean diaper, a pair of loving arms....

"Please don't worry," Hayley said. "Yes, we're having problems, Marcus and me. But there's nothing you or Kelly can do about it."

"Kelly says you won't talk about it."

"That's right. I...well, talking won't solve anything. I've got nothing to say, really."

Tanner frowned. "I don't believe that. I mean, don't women need that, to talk? I never met a woman who didn't have a whole hell of a lot to say about whatever was bothering her."

"Tanner." She shook her head. "You get the feeling you're out of your depth here?"

He actually chuckled. "Oh, well. Yeah. Guess I am—but I just wanted you to know..."

"What?"

"Well, I could call the guy. Have a talk with him, if you think maybe that will help."

"And say...what?"

"Hell. Whatever you want me to say."

"It's good——" she gave him a smile "——to have a big brother."

He grunted. "Glad you feel that way. And you didn't answer my question. Want me to have a talk with him?"

"No. But I do appreciate that you care. That you want to help. Right now, though, there's nothing you can do."

"I can break his face in. How 'bout that?"

She chuckled. "Not an especially constructive approach."

"Damn it. I hate to see you hurting."

"Thanks. But it's my problem."

"Gotta tell ya. You don't seem like you're doing a whole lot to work it out."

"Tanner. My problem."

He muttered a swearword. "You're damn stubborn, you know that?"

"Maybe."

"Uh-uh. No maybe about it. When you finally get ready to, will you talk to Kelly?"

"I will. I promise."

He jumped on his good foot as he levered his crutches under his arms. "Well. Guess there's nothing else to say…."

"I mean it. Thank you. For trying. For…caring."

"Work this out," he commanded gruffly.

She only smiled at him fondly and turned to put Jenny in the playpen.

* * *

The next day, Hayley went to see her gyne-cologist for her postpartum checkup.

She got a clean bill of health and a prescription for progestin-only birth control pills, which were safe for nursing mothers. The doctor told her to begin taking the pills right away. She'd be fully protected against pregnancy within a month. And the doctor also gave Hayley a complimentary box of condoms to use until the pills took effect.

Great. She was ready for anything, free to have all-the-way, unrestricted, wild and wonderful sex at last. Too bad there was no one to have sex with—unrestricted or otherwise.

It was just so pathetic. At home, Hayley put Jenny down for a nap and then sat on her bed and cried.

The waterworks didn't help in the least. Finally, after sobbing for an hour, she called Kelly, who came over during her lunch break.

Hayley told all.

Kelly handed her yet another tissue and declared, "Sorry. I don't believe that husband of yours is, was, or ever will be cheating on you."

Hayley blew her nose for the hundredth time that day. "I know he hasn't cheated. That's not the point."

"O-kay. Then the point is…?"

"Kelly. He lied to me. It's the one thing I wanted from him, the one thing I asked for. Honesty. But still. He lied."

"That's right. He lied. He tried to protect you from his psycho ex-wife. And then, when he thought he was rid of her, he decided to just let the whole thing go rather than worry you. Is that so terrible?"

"God. You sound just like him."

"Well, I'm only saying, look at it from his point of view."

Hayley rubbed her red eyes. "There's more to it than that. He loved that woman. He gave her everything. He believed that she would always be the only one for him. I think, deep down, maybe he still believes it."

"EEEuuu. You think he wants to get back with her? Please. He couldn't be that self-destructive."

"It's…complicated. Remember I told you the guy had one of those hell-on-earth childhoods?"

"And we didn't?"

"His was worse."

"Than ours? Not possible."

"But true. And to answer your question, no. I don't think he wants to get back with her."

"Well, good. You kind of had me scared there for a minute. I mean, no way you should think that. It's so painfully clear that the guy's crazy in love with you."

Hayley felt the tears rising all over again. "Oh, don't I wish." She grabbed another tissue and blotted her eyes.

Her sister said, "You've got to go back to him, work this out. Time goes by, you know? You stay here, he stays there. You're only going to drift farther and farther apart...."

"I know. You're right. I know..."

Yet somehow, another week went by and Hayley did nothing to reach out to her husband. By then, they'd been apart for a month.

She was mindful of Kelly's warnings. And she did long to go to him.

But stronger than her yearning was her fear of what she might find when she got there.

Even a workaholic can't work late *every* night.

For the first time since Hayley left him, Marcus got home at six. He changed into jeans and a sweater and he heated up the meal his house-keeper had left for him.

He ate. He was just putting the plate in the dish-washer when the doorbell chimed.

His heart turned over. *Hayley.*

But no. She had a key. No need to ring the bell...

His pulse settled back into its regular dull rhythm.

The bell chimed again when he reached the front of the house. He knew by then who it would be.

He realized it was time. He was ready at last. He pulled the door open.

On the other side, Adriana looked at him melt-ingly. Behind her, beyond the porch, snow swirled in the icy dark.

"Oh, Marcus. At last." She wore a leather trench coat and impossibly high heels and her hair sparkled, dusted with snow. She looked like something out of some old Hollywood movie. Something…unreal.

He looked into those wide, whiskey-colored eyes and felt absolutely nothing. He might as well have been looking at a picture of a model in some fashion magazine. Objectively, he saw how stunning she was, a portrait of feminine perfection.

But what did she have to do with him? Not a thing. It seemed so strange to him, that he'd once been married to her.

The truth came clear to him, in that instant.

Adriana Carlson had never had any power over him that he hadn't given her, hadn't handed over, like an offering. Like a sacrifice.

He stepped back. She entered the foyer. He shut the door.

"Oh, at last, at last…" She reached for him.

He took a second step backward, free of her grasping touch.

"Oh!" The huge brown eyes filled with tragic tears. She pressed the back of her slim hand to her mouth. "Oh, what do I have to do? How can I show you I know I was wrong? We need to stop this. You know that we do. We need to heal this horrible breach between us, so we can be together again."

"Adriana. Cut the crap, okay?"

She gasped. It was very dramatic. "What? I don't know what you—"

"Yeah. You do. You know exactly what I mean. You've got some wild idea that I still have feelings for you. You're wrong. I don't. I love my wife." *I love my wife*.

Had he really said those words?

Oh, yeah. He had.

And they were true.

Damn. What a hopeless, witless idiot he'd been.

Hayley. He loved Hayley. For months now, he'd loved her.

Since well before she left him that first time, back in May.

How many times was he going to let her leave him? How many times did he have to lose her, before he finally got a clue and admitted that she was the one for him? That he loved her, would always love her.

That this thing with Adriana was truly over.

There was no room for that old, tortured love in his heart now. How could there be? His heart was filled.

With light. With hope. With goodness.

With Hayley.

Adriana gasped again. Strangely, that second time, her gasp almost sounded real. "You're serious...." It came out in a stunned whisper.

He reached for the door again and pulled it open. "Please don't bother me, or Hayley, anymore. There's no point. She has my heart. I belong to her. Do you see that now?"

"I..." She put her hand to her mouth again, and then let it fall. And then, at last, she said it. She admitted it. "Yes. All right. I see." She turned and stepped out into the snowy darkness.

He shut the door behind her.

There were bells ringing.

Hayley groaned and rolled over.

The bells rang some more.

She opened one eye. It was pitch-dark in her bedroom, except for the glow of the digital clock, which said it was five minutes of midnight.

Five minutes of midnight.

And some fool was ringing her doorbell.

The fool rang it again. Any second now, Jenny would start crying.

Hayley turned on the light, threw back the covers, shoved her feet into her waiting slippers, grabbed her old robe from the end of the bed and raced to the front door. She couldn't wait to yank it wide and give the idiot on the other side a large piece of her mind.

Hayley glared through the peephole before turning the lock. What she saw made her throat clutch and her knees tremble.

Marcus.

Chapter Fifteen

Hayley's hand shook as she turned the dead bolt. She flung the door wide.

He was wearing old jeans, a tan sweater and a heavy leather jacket. He looked…amazing.

She wanted to throw herself at him, wrap her arms tight around him, kiss him and kiss him. Hold him forever. Tell him how very much she'd missed him, promise him her love and her undying devotion. Swear to him that now he'd come to get her at last, she would never, ever let him go.

But *had* he come to work things out?

Or to tell her it was over?

Oh, Lord. Why didn't he say something?

Why didn't *she* say something?

A terrible shyness had overtaken her. So many of those passionate things she yearned to tell him. But somehow, her throat had locked up tight and her lips had got to trembling—*all* of her was trembling. She could only wrap her arms around herself, only swallow and shiver and stare.

They stood there in the near-freezing middle of the night, in the open doorway, just looking at each other.

He was the one who finally spoke. "I know it's late. I guess I should have called and warned you I was coming, but…" The sentence wandered off. He showed no inclination to finish it. "You're shaking…" He reached for her.

She lifted on tiptoe and swayed longingly toward him.

But the contact didn't quite happen. His hand dropped to his side at the same time as she caught herself and drew back, settling onto her heels again with a sad little sigh.

They stared at each other. She felt absolutely miserable. Judging by his bleak expression, he did, too.

He asked, "Are you all right?"

Somehow, she managed to croak, "Yes… No… Oh, God. I don't know…."

"Is it okay if I come in?"

She swallowed again, and bobbed her head. "Yes. How silly. Of course you should come in." Somehow she made her shaking legs move, stepping back enough to clear the doorway.

He entered.

She shut the door, turned the lock. "Your jacket…"

He handed it over. She hung it in the closet.

And another unbearable silence ensued, a silence thick with all the things neither of them seemed to know how to say.

She had the strangest sense that they were making a kind of progress toward something monumental, and they were doing this in tiny steps, by slow, agonized degrees.

"Uh, how's Tanner?" he asked.

"Better every day. Still on crutches, and griping about it constantly. But he should be good as new within the next few weeks…."

"Your sister? And DeDe?"

"Fine. Both of them. Just…fine."

"Well. Good. That's real good."

Another silence. More staring.

"Coffee," she said finally, sounding downright desperate. "Would you—?"

"I'd love some." He looked relieved. "Yes."

She turned toward the kitchen area—and then stopped herself. "Wait."

"What?" Dark brows drew together.

"Jenny. You'll want to see Jenny…."

"I do. Very much. But isn't she sleeping?"

"God. I hope so."

Did he almost smile? It seemed he did. And then he suggested, "Maybe if we went in quietly…"

"Yes. Quietly. Good idea."

"I'll take off my shoes, why don't I?"

"Please."

He sat in the straight chair by the door, and removed his handmade Italian boots, setting them neatly out of the way. When he rose again, he waited for her to lead him down the hall.

In Jenny's darkened room, Hayley stood back by the rocker as he stepped up to the crib. Through the shadows, she watched him. He grasped the crib rail lightly. His head was tipped slightly down.

Jenny made a sound in her sleep, as if she were dreaming. And then she sighed.

It seemed to Hayley that Marcus smiled, but it was hard to tell for sure in the wedge of light that bled in through the half-open door to the hallway.

Finally, he turned to her. He lifted a hand and gestured toward the door. She followed him out, quietly pulling the door shut behind her.

They didn't speak until they reached the kitchen.

"She's bigger." He seemed surprised.

She shrugged. "Babies grow fast. And it's been weeks."

"Four weeks," he said.

She glanced at the clock. It was five past midnight. "And three days," she added. "As of five minutes ago."

"Too long," he said. His eyes were the deepest green right then. There was no mistaking the meaning of that look.

Relief, warm and sweet, went flooding through her.

He hadn't come to end it.

This was *not* goodbye.

But still, as swiftly as relief came over her, it fled. Could she have misread that look, after all?

She loved him so. And she wanted it to work out between them. That made her prone to read more into a tender expression than might actually be there.

It was altogether possible that he only meant he missed his daughter, that he hadn't been referring to her, to Hayley, at all.

Coffee. She'd offered him coffee. He lingered at the end of the counter as she got down the coffee beans and measured them into the grinder. The grinding sounded impossibly loud, and the silence when she finished, profound.

She poured the fresh grounds into the brew basket, filled the water reservoir, set the carafe in place and pushed the button, achingly aware as she performed each familiar movement, that he watched her.

Staring at the red brew light as the machine began to sputter, she cleared her tight throat and suggested, "We could sit. Until it's ready."

Neither of them moved.

She slanted him a glance. Yep. Watching.

He spoke at last. "You look good."

A short burst of laughter escaped her. "Oh, yeah. Fresh out of bed in my old robe and fuzzy slippers with my hair all over the place."

"That's right. You look beautiful." His voice was low, with a certain roughness in it now.

A tempting roughness.

He took a step toward her along the counter. Her body tightened. She made herself turn to face him fully, lifting her chin, letting the light of challenge gleam in her eyes. Her breath snagged in her throat as he stole another silent step.

Oh, yes. She was really starting to believe now.

This was *not* a man who'd come to say goodbye.

And oh, it had been forever. A lifetime, since she'd felt his hands, hungry and seeking, on her eager flesh.

They had so much to say to each other.

And yet, in that moment, she didn't give a damn for the words. She wanted the contact. Needed it. Craved it.

She wanted *him,* wanted Marcus. Touch to touch. Skin on skin.

Silent and sure on stocking feet, he approached.

It was only a matter of two more steps and he was there, right in front of her.

The scent of him, so tempting and so well remembered, taunted her. He lifted a hand and touched her hair.

"God," he said. "Hayley…" Those green eyes scanned her face, hungry. Seeking.

"Yes," she whispered. "Oh, Marcus. Yes…"

"Sometimes I wondered if I'd ever touch you again…."

All she could manage was another yearning, breathless "Yes!"

He eased his fingers under her hair, curving them around her nape, brushing the tiny hairs there, sending hot shivers shimmering upward, over her scalp.

It was too much, the feel of his hand on her, at last. Too much—and never enough.

She surged up, pressed her mouth to his, parting her lips so she could taste him, lick him. He opened on a groan. She speared her tongue inside, tasting the sweetness, the heat, the wonder.

Feeding the fire.

His fingers slid boldly down the front of her, skimming her right breast, teasing the nipple to hardness. But only in passing.

His goal was the sash of her robe. He found it, grasped it and tugged. The sash came undone. She felt the front of the robe fall open.

She moaned as he followed her tongue back into her mouth. He sucked, sweet little tugs that beckoned, that teased, that set her aflame. He caught her top lip and drew on it, tongue sliding along the inner surface, thrilling her with its wet, rough glide. He guided her lower lip into position, and then he sucked it, too.

He pushed the robe off her shoulders. It fell to the floor with a tender little plopping sound. Under it, she had on her favorite old button-front nightshirt. And under that...

Nothing.

Except for his warm, big hand which immediately curved around the front of her right thigh, high up, beneath her frayed flannelette hem. His fingers dug in, so that she moaned and let her head drop back, losing the glorious wonder of his kiss.

"Closer," he muttered. "Closer to me..."

His free arm snaked around her and he pulled her body up against him, lifting her toes right off the floor. Her slippers slid off, one and then the other.

Bending her back, he nipped tender kisses, from the hollow of her throat, up along her neck and over her chin. Then, at last, he took her mouth again, while the hand that cupped her thigh moved higher.

And higher still....

He curled those clever fingers around to the

back, up high and tight, his index finger just brushing the moist curls that covered her sex.

She quivered in longing and anticipation, couldn't wait to drag him into the bedroom, whip out the protection her doctor had so thoughtfully provided, and take him deep inside her.

She clasped his shoulders, wiggling until he let her back down on her feet again, then trying to guide him backward, making hungry little moaning sounds, urging him to move.

He caught her lower lip between his teeth again. She whimpered some more.

He muttered, his voice rough velvet, "Uh-uh. Going nowhere. Not yet…"

He explored her, caressing fingers trailing upward, over the curve of her hip. She moaned into his mouth. He gave a low growl in response and clasped her waist, only to slip his hand fully between them and lay it, palm flat, on her belly, where she had held their child.

Below, she was melting, yearning, *dying* for more. For him never, ever to stop holding her, touching her, kissing her in that thorough, deep, overwhelming way.

She lifted her hips, ground them against him, felt the hard ridge that said how much he wanted her.

It was far too tempting, that ridge. She slipped her hand between them and eased it under his sweater. Grabbing his belt, she unhooked it in quick, eager moves. She had that buckle undone in no time and she slithered the belt off and away. The clasp made a sharp clinking sound as it hit the tile floor.

She undid the button at the top of his jeans. He helped her then, taking one side of the placket as she grabbed the other.

Together, they yanked that zipper wide. He groaned and worked his hips against her, wrapping his strong fingers around her wrist, guiding her hand where he wanted it, flat on his hard belly and then under the elastic of his boxers.

She found him, at last, so hot and hard and ready.

She wrapped her fingers around him and stroked him and he muttered her name against her parted lips, pleading in ragged whispers, "Yeah, like that. Hayley, oh, yeah…"

But then he stopped her, grabbing her wrist again, tighter than before, groaning low in his throat, pleading with her wordlessly.

She gave in and followed his lead. She knew him so well, after all. She understood that he wasn't ready yet, to let her have that much control over him, to let her take him all the way before he'd done as much for her.

She smiled a knowing smile against his mouth. "Too proud…"

"Uh-uh. Too eager. To touch you. To feel you come…" He covered her mouth in a searing kiss.

And his hand was up under her nightshirt again, touching her, petting her, those knowing fingers easing between her wet folds. Sensations—hot, melting, streaked with light, spun out from where he touched her. They claimed her whole body.

She cried out and her knees gave way. He supported her, kept her upright with his arm wrapped tight around her.

And he played her, fingers stroking her, in a rhythm that stole her breath and sent her mind reeling. Until she shattered, moaning, spangles of light behind her eyes, shimmers of wonder bursting at the center of her, sending glittery trails of purest pleasure singing along every nerve.

"I think I just died," she whispered, once the pleasure had crested and faded to a lovely, warm glow. She clutched his big shoulders. "Please don't let go of me. I'll melt into a puddle right here on the kitchen floor."

He made a low sound of satisfaction and nuzzled her neck. "Never," he vowed. "I'm never letting you go…."

The coffeepot gave a final sputter. "Just in time," she told him with a breathless laugh. "Your coffee's ready."

He already had one hand at her back. He slipped the other under her knees and lifted her high. "It can wait." He turned and carried her out of the kitchen, across the living room and down the hall.

In her room, he set her gently on the bed.

He tugged on the hem of her sleep shirt. "I want you naked. Get this off...."

She lifted her arms and he whipped it away.

"Beautiful," he said, standing back a little, so he could see what he had revealed.

"Thank you." She gave him a tender smile. "You always say that, you know?"

"Because it's always true."

"Did I sound like I was complaining? I wasn't. I like it, when you call me beautiful."

"Good." The fly of his jeans still gaped wide. He shoved them down, his boxers with them, skimming off both socks, as well.

"The sweater," she commanded, leaning back on her hands.

"You can be damn bossy, you know that?"

She didn't even try to deny it. "Just take off that sweater, just do what I say."

He took the sweater, pulled it up over his head, and tossed it somewhere behind him.

They regarded each other. She thought of how she loved this moment: the two of them, together. Naked.

It didn't get better than this.

But then he frowned. "Damn. I'm guessing it won't hurt you now, for us to be doing this."

"It's safe. I had my checkup last week."

"But what about protection? I don't have anything. And I have a feeling you don't really want to get pregnant tonight."

She already had the bedside drawer open and she held up the box of condoms. "Say thank you, Dr. Wright."

He wasn't frowning anymore. "A wonderful woman, that doctor of yours."

"Yes. Skilled. And thorough. Kind to her patients." She took out one of the pouches and set the box next to the bedside clock. "Not to mention, generous with the free samples." She reached out her arms for him.

He came down to her. She removed the condom from the pouch and slowly rolled it over him.

They stretched out, facing each other. He touched her, his palm skimming the swell of her hip.

"Too long, since we've been like this…" He said it softly, almost reverently.

She caressed his shoulder, loving the feel of his smooth flesh, the hard muscle beneath. His body never failed to amaze her. He was beautifully formed. Even the thin, white scars that crisscrossed his strong back were dear to her. A mute testimony to his father's abuse, they showed what he'd endured.

"Much too long," she whispered. "Tell me this isn't a dream."

He trailed the back of his index finger downward,

into the curve of her waist. "No dream. Real." He pulled her close.

They kissed. Endlessly.

And then, at last, the moment came. He rose above her. She took him inside, wrapping her legs around him. He braced himself on his fists, sparing her his full weight as he levered his hips more tightly to hers, so she felt him even more deeply than the moment before.

Stretched in the most luxurious way, filled with him, she looked up into his eyes. Amazing. Nothing like it, to be joined with him. To be one with him in this intimate way.

She reached up, touched his face, traced the smooth, tempting softness of his warm lips. He kissed her fingers, sucked her thumb into his mouth.

Tears welled and escaped, twin trails along her temples.

Still, she hardly dared believe this was happening—the two of them, here, in her bed.

So often she'd dreamed of this moment. She *had* doubted, had wondered if they would ever share this bright magic again.

He bent close, whispered her name, kissed away the tear tracks, on one side of her face and then the other.

She smiled, nodded, so he would know she was okay. So he could rise above her again, and press in so tight and dear.

He moved within her. She picked up his rhythms and gave them back to him, lifting her hips to him, meeting each thrust.

He came down upon her, his hard chest crushing her breasts. But only to wrap her close and roll, giving her the top position.

She took control. Getting her knees under her, bracketing his lean hips with her soft thighs, she rode him. Her hands on his chest, her head thrown back, she took him deep. They stilled, pressed tight together. Until, slowly, she rose up, letting him out to the tip—and then taking him in all the way again.

He grasped her hips in his hands and he helped her—to rise until she almost lost him, to sink down upon him once more…and again.

And again, after that.

The rhythm claimed them. They gave themselves over to it. Her body was his and his body, hers.

She felt the end approaching, curling up like a high wave. And then rolling down, roaring like thunder as it came crashing through her. He surged up into her, holding her so tight against him.

Silence. A glowing stillness.

"Yes," she whispered, "Oh, yes…" The wave engulfed her, swallowed her. She went under gleefully, groaning his name.

Chapter Sixteen

From Jenny's room, they could hear the first fussy, questioning cries.

Hayley groaned and rubbed her cheek against the crisp dark hair on Marcus's chest. "Oh, no…"

He chuckled and the sound echoed pleasantly beneath her ear. He had his arms wrapped around her, secure and tight. "Hey. Her timing could have been worse."

The cries got louder.

Hayley blew out a breath. "Okay, okay…I'm coming…"

"I'll go with you."

She sat up and raked her hair back off her face. "I can do it." She slid away from him and rose to her feet beside the bed. "Go get your coffee." The door to the small master bath was only a few steps away. She went in there and shut the door.

A minute later, when she emerged, he was still stretched out on the bed, gloriously naked, those gorgeous muscular arms of his laced behind his head—and Jenny was still crying. "I *want* to go with you."

"Well, all right, then. Come on." She darted a glance around the room. "Where's my robe—and my slippers?"

"The kitchen, I believe."

She scooped up her nightshirt and pulled it on as Marcus got up, grabbed his jeans and took a quick turn in the bathroom. She went ahead to Jenny's room.

"Okay, okay. I'm here. Settle down."

Marcus appeared in the doorway. "That girl has a set of lungs on her."

"She's hungry." Hayley scooped up the squalling baby and started unbuttoning as she sat in the rocker. She put Jenny to her breast. Blessed silence descended. Hayley grinned up at Marcus, who stood by the crib. "Nothing so sweet as the sound of a baby *not* crying."

"I don't mind the crying."

"You've always been more patient than I am."

His eyes were moss-green right then. He approached. She tipped her face up to him as he touched her hair. "No. I don't think so. There's no one as patient as you."

The words seemed weighted with special meaning. She turned her face into his touch, so she could press her lips into the center of his palm.

He smiled at the kiss and then brushed the backs of his knuckles across her cheek. "I've missed you. Missed you so damn much." He curved his hand, so lightly, on Jenny's mostly bald head. "And her."

Hayley's throat clutched. She gulped to relax it. "I missed you, too."

"I should have come for you sooner, worked out all my old garbage sooner. I know it."

Her baby drew on her breast, the sensation, once so painful, brought only a glow of contentment now. "I was waiting," she said. "But I really didn't know what for. Somehow, I didn't expect you to come…."

"God. I hope you're glad that I did."

She nodded. "I am, Marcus. So very glad."

He was quiet. He seemed not to know what to say next.

She could relate to that. And it was okay with her. Sometimes it was hard to find the right words….

"I think I'll go get that coffee," he said.

"Good idea."

He left her.

Jenny finished at one breast and Hayley settled her at the other. Marcus came back. He stood over by the bureau, sipping from the red mug he'd claimed as his own back at Christmastime. When Jenny was through eating, Hayley rocked her until she needed changing.

"Let me…" Marcus set his mug on the bureau.

So Hayley handed Jenny over and left him to do diaper duty. She returned to her bedroom and sat on the edge of the bed.

Eventually, he came in and sat beside her. "She's asleep. Looking like an angel…"

Hayley nodded. "Yeah. No doubt about it. They're adorable when they're sleeping." She sent him a smile.

But he didn't see it. He was looking straight ahead, at the open door to the hallway. "I keep thinking I'm going to figure out how to say this…."

She didn't know what to tell him, how to encourage him. Since no words came, she put her hand on his knee and gave a reassuring squeeze.

He put his hand over hers. It felt so good. Cherishing. Right. He said, "I was furious, when you accused me of lying to you."

"Oh, yeah. I remember."

"You hit a nerve. Because I did lie. In more ways than just by not telling you that Adriana was after me again."

Hayley gulped and silently reminded herself,

yet again, that she had to let him say this in his own way and in his own time. The urge was so powerful, to cut in, to start protesting that she didn't need to hear it, that it was all right. That he was here and she was glad he'd come for her and that was enough.

But it wasn't enough. She *did* need to hear it. Whatever it was. However much it hurt. She needed to hear—and he had to say it.

The truth was important. The truth, or rather, the lack of it, was the reason they'd just spent all these weeks apart. They'd come so far. No way could she let herself deny the truth now.

He said, "About two weeks ago, she started calling me again. I refused to take her calls. I erased her messages without even listening to them. Except for the first one, the one where she said that she knew you had left me and she couldn't wait for me to come to my senses so that she and I could pick up where we'd left off…."

Hayley had been staring at the door to the hallway. When his voice trailed off, she turned her head and met his waiting eyes.

"You okay?" He gave her hand a squeeze.

She blew out a breath. "I keep telling myself not to hate her. But I do. She betrayed you, left you flat, broke your heart so bad. Walked away without so much as a backward glance. She divorced you because she wanted to marry someone else…and now she waltzes back on the scene and can't understand what's wrong with you that you aren't waiting for her with open arms."

His mouth kicked up at one corner. "Yeah. Well. It never occurs to Adriana that things won't go her way. She wants what she wants when she wants it. And if she doesn't get what she wants, as a rule, there's hell to pay."

"Sheesh. Tell me about it."

"I'm trying to."

They both laughed then.

Hayley said, "Sorry. Continue. Please."

After a moment's thought, he did. "Last night, she came to the house. I took one look at her and I knew. I understood."

Hayley's heart started thumping as if it would beat its way out of her chest. She sucked in a slow breath. She waited for the worst.

He said, "I realized the truth. At last."

"Oh, God," she heard herself whisper on an indrawn breath.

And then he said, "I realized that I love *you*, Hayley. I've loved you for a damn long time. Since before you walked away from me last spring."

Her heart had stopped, just froze in midbeat. There was a rushing in her ears and her cheeks burned like hell's own fury. "I'm sorry. What did you say?"

He lifted her hand and he kissed it. "Damn it.

I love you. *Have* loved you. You came into my life and you were—you *are*—like sunshine. Something bright and clean and sweet and good."

She swayed toward him. "Marcus?"

"Yeah?"

"Why didn't you tell me? Why didn't you just say so?"

He let go of her hand—but only to wrap his arm around her shoulder and draw her close against his side. "I thought I just explained that." Their lips were inches apart. She felt his breath, warm, scented of coffee, saw that shining rim of blue around the green of his eyes.

"I know you did," she whispered. "Tell me again."

"Because I'm too damn proud. Because I couldn't let myself admit how wrong I'd been, to think that what I'd had with Adriana was love. I didn't know squat about love. Didn't know what the real thing could be. Until you."

She rested a hand on his warm chest, felt the strong, even beat of his heart beneath her palm. "Oh, see. Now, I am really liking the sound of this."

He stole a quick, sweet kiss. "I had a feeling you might."

"So…as soon as you saw Adriana again, *that's* when you knew that you loved me?"

"That's right."

"Life is so strange sometimes."

"It damn sure is."

"You probably should have agreed to see her sooner. It would have saved us both a whole lot of misery."

"Yeah. If I'd only known."

"Oh, Marcus. I love you, too."

He curled a finger under her chin. "I know you do. And I love to hear you say it."

"I'll never stop saying it."

"Good. It's a fine thing for a man to hear— when the right woman says it."

"I love you, love you, love you, love you." She clasped his shoulder and brought her mouth right up to his. "Now's the moment you should kiss me."

"My pleasure."

He claimed her lips. She sighed and opened. It was a perfect kiss. Slow and deep and wet, full of heat and tenderness. A kiss that promised a lifetime of joy. And truth. And mutual trust.

When he lifted his mouth from hers, she let out a happy sigh. They dropped back across the bed in unison, and turned their heads to grin at each other.

He said, "So I'm hoping this means you'll come home with me now."

"Oh, yes. Absolutely. We love each other. And we're a family, you and Jenny and me. Of course I'll come home with you. Now I know you're mine, that you're with me and you've got no doubts, I can handle anything. Even that ex of yours, if I have to."

"I don't think Adriana will be bothering us anymore."

"Well, we can hope," she teased.

"Seriously. After last night, I don't think she'll be coming around. I think she finally got the message—and yeah, I know. With her, you can never be absolutely sure. But I know she heard me loud and clear when I told her that I love you. I asked her not to bother us anymore."

"And...?"

"She said she would leave us alone."

"Wow."

They grinned at each other, both of them more than satisfied.

She scooted closer. "I don't think I've ever been happier."

"Good."

"Also, my feet are freezing."

"Then let's get under the covers."

He took off his jeans and she got rid of her nightshirt and they snuggled up under the blankets together. He gathered her close. She tucked herself against him, her hand curled near his heart, her head beneath his chin.

She closed her eyes. She had it all. Everything she'd ever wished for, during all the Christmases of her lonely childhood. She had a family—a sister and a brother, a sweet little niece and a whole bunch of Bravo relatives all over the country.

She had Marcus and Jenny. She belonged to them and they belonged to her.

"Dreams do come true," she whispered drowsily.

He made a low noise of agreement and she felt his lips brush the crown of her head.

Home in her husband's loving arms at last, Hayley sighed in contentment and drifted off into a deep and peaceful sleep.

* * * * *

MARRY-ME
CHRISTMAS

BY
SHIRLEY JUMP

New York Times bestselling author **Shirley Jump** didn't have the will-power to diet, nor the talent to master under-eye concealer, so she bowed out of a career in television and opted instead for a career where she could be paid to eat at her desk—writing. At first, seeking revenge on her children for their grocery store tantrums, she sold embarrassing essays about them to anthologies. However, it wasn't enough to feed her growing addiction to writing funny. So she turned to the world of romance novels, where messes are (usually) cleaned up before The End. In the worlds Shirley gets to create and control, the children listen to their parents, the husbands always remember holidays, and the housework is magically done by elves. Though she's thrilled to see her books in stores around the world, Shirley mostly writes because it gives her an excuse to avoid cleaning the toilets and helps feed her shoe habit. To learn more, visit her website at www.shirleyjump.com.

CHAPTER ONE

FLYNN MACGREGOR hated Riverbend, Indiana, from the second his Lexus stalled at the single stop light in the quaint town center, right beneath the gaily decorated Christmas swags of pine needles and red bows. The entire snow-dusted town seemed like something out of a movie.

There were people walking to and fro with wrapped gifts, stores bedecked with holiday decorations, and even snowflakes, falling at a slow and steady pace, as if some set decorator was standing in the clouds with a giant shaker.

Okay, so *hated* might be a strong word. Detested, perhaps. Loathed. Either way, he didn't want to be here, especially when he'd been forced into the decision.

His editor at *Food Lovers* magazine had assigned him this story in Riverbend, knowing Flynn, of everyone on staff, could get the job done. Write an incisive, unique piece on the little bakery—a bakery rumored to have cookies that inspired people to fall in love, his editor had said. So here he was, spending the Christmas holiday holed up in the middle of nowhere penning one more of the stories that had made him famous.

Flynn scowled. He couldn't complain. Those stories had been his bread and butter forever, a very lucrative butter at that. And after that little fiasco in June, he needed to get his edge back, reestablish his position at the top of the writer pack. To do that, he'd do what he always did—suck it up, feign great joy at the festive spirit surrounding him and get to work.

Then he could get back to Boston, back to Mimi, and back to civilization. This town, with its Norman Rockwell looks, had to be as far from civilization as Mars was from Earth. Not that he had anything against quaint, but he lived in a world of iPods, e-mail and high-speed Internet connections. Riverbend looked like the kind of place that thought Bluetooth was a dental disease.

So, here he was, at the Joyful Creations Bakery.

Oh, joy.

He pushed his car to the side of the road, then grabbed his notebook and headed across the street. The crowd in front of the Joyful Creations Bakery blocked most of the plateglass window, but Flynn could see that storefront, too, had not been spared by the town's festive elves. A trio of lighted wreaths hung in the window, one of them even forming the *O* in the business's name.

"Nauseatingly cute," Flynn muttered under his breath.

He circumvented the line that stretched out the door, around the bakery and all the way to the corner of Larch Street. Ignoring the snow falling from the sky, couples stood together—most of the men looking none too keen on the idea of being dragged off to a bakery purported to be a food love source, while groups of women chatted excitedly about the "romance cookies."

It took sheer willpower for Flynn not to roll his eyes. The airline magazine that had first broken the story had clearly created an epidemic. By the time this piece hit *Food Lovers*' Valentine's Day issue, the shop would be overrun with the lovelorn. He hoped the owner was prepared for the onslaught. Flynn knew, from personal experience, how a too-fast rocket to success could be as destructive as a too-quick drop to the bottom.

Regardless, he was here to do a job, not offer a business consultation.

He brushed by a woman holding a toddler and entered Joyful Creations. A blast of warm air and holiday music greeted him like he'd jumped into a Christmas bath. The scent of fresh-baked bread, coupled with vanilla, cinnamon and a hint of raspberry, assaulted his senses. The waiting patrons were surely impressed, but Flynn had seen all this and smelled all this before.

"Hey, no cutting," the woman said.

"I'm not buying anything," he replied, and kept going. Get in, get the story, get out. Get back to Boston. Hopefully before Mimi even noticed he was gone. *If* Mimi even noticed he was gone.

"Why would you battle this crowd if you weren't going to buy anything?" the woman asked, shuffling the kid to the other hip.

"For…" Flynn turned toward the counter where two women were busy filling orders as quickly as they were being shouted over the din. One, gray-haired and petite, the other, tall and blond, curvy, with the kind of hips that said she didn't spend her days obsessing over having two pieces of celery or one.

Wow. The airline magazine hadn't run a photo of Samantha Barnett with their story, just one of the cookies. But clearly, she was the owner that the writer had described as "energetic, friendly, youthful."

"Her," Flynn said.

"Sam? Good luck with that." The woman laughed, then turned back to her kid, playing with his nose. Pretending the thing was a button or something. Flynn had no experience with other people's children and had no intention of starting now, so he moved away.

It took the navigational skills of a fleet admiral to wade

through the crowd inside the shop, but a few minutes later, Flynn had managed to reach the glass counter. He stood to the far right, away from the line of paying customers, most of them looking like they'd come straight from placing a personal ad. "Are you Samantha Barnett?"

The blonde looked up. Little tendrils of her hair were beginning to escape her ponytail, as if the first few strands were thinking of making a break for the border. She wore little makeup, just a dash of red lip gloss and a dusting of mascara. He suspected the slight hint of crimson in her cheeks was natural, a flush from the frantic pace of the warm bakery. A long white apron with the words *Joyful Creations* scrolled across the middle in a curled red script hugged her frame, covering dark denim jeans and a soft green V-neck sweater. "I'm sorry, sir, you'll have to get into the line."

"I'm not here to buy anything."

That made her pause. Stop putting reindeer-shaped cookies into a white box. "Do you have a delivery or some mail for me?"

He shook his head. Vowed to buy a new dress coat, if he looked like a mailman in this one. "I just want to talk to you."

"Now is not a good time." She let out a little laugh. "I'm kind of busy."

"Yeah, well, I'm on a deadline." He fished a business card out of his pocket and slid it across the glass case. "Flynn MacGregor with *Food Lovers* magazine. Maybe you've heard of it?"

Her face lit up, as so many others before hers had. Everyone had heard of *Food Lovers*. It was *the* magazine about the food industry, carried in every grocery store and bookstore, read by thirty million people nationwide. A print mention in its pages was the equivalent of starring in a movie.

Even if *Food Lovers* magazine's focus had shifted, ever since Tony Reynolds had taken over as editor a year ago. His insistence on finding the story behind the story, the dish on every chef, restaurant and food business, had given the magazine more of a tabloid feel, but also tripled readership in a matter of months.

At first, Flynn hadn't minded doing what Tony wanted. But as each story became more and more invasive of people's personal lives, Flynn's job had begun to grate on him. More than once he had thought about quitting. But Flynn MacGregor hadn't gotten to where he was by turning tail just because he butted heads with an editor or ran into a roadblock ot two.

"Wow," Samantha said, clearly not bothered by *Food Lovers'* reputation. "You want to talk to me? What about?"

"Your bakery. Why you got into this business. What makes Joyful Creations special…" As he ran through his usual pre-interview spiel, Flynn bit back his impatience. Reminded himself this was his four hundredth interview, but probably her first or second. Flynn could recite the questions without even needing to write them down ahead of time. Heck, he could practically write her answers for her. She got into baking because she loved people, loved food. The best part about being in business in a small town was the customers. Yada-yada-yada.

As for the cookies that made people fall in love, Flynn put no stock in things like that. He'd seen soups that supposedly made women go into labor, cakes that were rumored to jump-start diets, appetizers bandied about as the next best aphrodi-siac. None of which had proven to be true, but still, the magazine had run a charming piece in its pages, appealing to its vast readership.

While he was here, he'd track down a few of the couples who owed their happiness to the sugar-and-flour concoctions, then put some kind of cutesy spin on the story. The art depart-ment would fancy up the headline with dancing gingerbread men or something, and they'd all walk away thinking Joyful

Creations was the best thing to come along since Cupid and his trademark bow.

"That's pretty much how it works, Miss Barnett," Flynn finished, wrapping up his sugarcoated version of the article process.

The bakery owner nodded. "Sounds great. Relatively painless."

"Sam? I hate to interrupt," another woman cut in, just as Flynn was getting ready to ask his first question, "but I really need to pick up my order. I have a preschool waiting. And you know preschoolers. They want their sugar."

Samantha Barnett snapped to attention, back to her customer. "Oh, sure, Rachel. Sorry about that. Two dozen, right?"

The other woman, a petite brunette, grinned. "And one extra, for the teacher."

"Of course." Samantha smiled, finished putting the reindeer into the box, then tied it with a thin red ribbon and handed the white container across the counter. "Here you go."

"Will you put it on my tab?"

Samantha waved off the words. "Consider it a Christmas gift to the Bumblebees."

Not a smart way to run a business, giving away profits like that, but Flynn kept that to himself. He wasn't her financial consultant. "The interview, Miss Barnett?"

Behind them, the line groaned. Samantha brushed her bangs off her forehead. "Can I meet with you later today? Maybe after the shop closes? I'm swamped right now."

She had help, didn't she? On top of that, he had somewhere else he wanted to go before beginning that long drive back to Boston, not endless amounts of time to wait around for pre-schoolers to get their sugar rush. "And I'm on deadline."

The next person had slipped into the space vacated by Miss Bumblebee, a tall senior citizen in a flap-eared flannel cap and a Carhartt jacket. He ambled up to the counter, leaned one arm on the glass case and made himself at home, like he was planning on spending an hour or two there. "Hiya, Samantha. Heard about the article in that airline magazine. Congratulations! You really put our town on the map, not that you weren't a destination from the start, what with those cookies and all." He leaned forward, cupping a beefy hand around his mouth. "Though I'm not so sure I want all these tourists to stay. They're causing quite the traffic jam."

Samantha chuckled. "Thanks, Earl. And sorry I can't do anything about the traffic. Except fill the orders as fast as I can." She slid a glance Flynn's way.

"You give me my interview, Miss Barnett, and I'll be out of your hair."

"Give me a few hours, Mr. MacGregor, and I'll give you whatever you want."

He knew there was no innuendo in her words, but the male part of him heard one all the same. He cleared his throat and took a step back. "I have to get back on the road. Today. So why don't you just cooperate with me and we can both be happy?"

"I have customers to wait on, and it looks like now you're going to have a long wait either way." She gestured toward the windows with her chin as her hands worked beneath the counter, shoveling muffins into a bag. "You might as well make yourself comfortable."

Flynn turned and looked through the glass. And saw yet another reason to hate Riverbend.

A blizzard.

By noon, Sam was already so exhausted, she was sure she'd collapse face-first into the double-layer cinnamon streusel. But she pasted a smile on her face, kept handing out cookies and pastries, all while dispensing directions to her staff. She'd called in her seasonal part-timers, and everyone else she could think of, right down to Mary, who did the weekend cleaning, to help keep up with the sudden influx of tourists. It seemed every person in a three-state area had read the article and turned out to see if Joyful Creations would live up to its reputation of bringing love to people who tried Grandma Joy's Secret Recipe Cherry Chocolate Chunk Cookies.

Sam had long heard the rumors about her grandmother's cookies—after all, they were the very treats Grandma Joy had served to Grandpa Neil when they had first met—but had never quite believed all the people who credited the tiny desserts for their happy unions. Then a reporter from *Travelers* magazine had tried them on a trip through town and immediately fallen in love with one of the local women. The two of them had run off to Jamaica and gotten married the very next weekend. Afterward, the reporter had raved about the cookies and his happy ending in the airline publication, launching Sam's shop to national fame, and turning a rumor into a fact.

Ever since, things hadn't slowed down. Sam had worked a lot of hours before—but this was ridiculous. Nearly every spare moment was spent at the bakery, working, restocking and filling orders. But it was all for a larger goal, so she kept pushing, knowing the bigger reward was on the horizon.

"I can't decide." The platinum-blond woman, dressed head to toe in couture, put a leather-gloved finger to her lips. "How many calories did you say were in the peanut butter kiss cookies?"

The smile was beginning to hurt Sam's face. "About one hundred and ten per cookie."

"And those special cherry chocolate chunk ones?"

"About a hundred and fifty."

"Do those cookies really work? Those love ones?"

"That's what people say, ma'am."

"Well, it would really have to be worth the calories. That's a lot to work off in the gym, you know, if I don't meet Mr. Right. And if I meet Mr. Wrong—" the woman threw up her hands "—well that's even more time on the treadmill."

Sam bit her lip, then pushed the smile up further.

"Do you happen to know the fat grams? I'm on a very strict diet. My doctor doesn't want me to have more than twenty-two grams of fat per day."

From what Sam could see, the woman didn't have twenty-two grams of fat in her entire body, but she kept that to herself. "I don't know the grams of fat offhand, ma'am, but I assure you, none of these cookies have that many per serving."

The gloved finger to the lips again. She tipped her head to the right, then the left, her pageboy swinging with the indecision. Behind her, the entire line shifted and groaned in annoyance. "I still don't know."

"Why don't you buy one of each?" Sam said. "Have one today and one tomorrow."

"That's a wonderful idea." The woman beamed, as if Sam were Einstein. She handed her money across the glass case to Ginny while Sam wrapped the cookies in wax paper and slid them into a bright white Joyful Creations box, then tied a thin red ribbon around the box. "But…"

"But what?"

"How can I decide which one to have today?"

Sam just smiled, told the woman to have a merry Christmas, and moved on to the next customer. Four hundred of Grandma Joy's secret recipe cherry chocolate chunk cookies later, the line had finally thinned. Sam bent over, taking a moment to straighten the trays, whisk away a few crumbs and bring order back to the display.

Then, through the glass she glimpsed a pair of designer men's shoes, their glossy finish marred by road salt, dots of dried snow. Her gaze traveled upward. Pressed trousers, a dark gray cashmere dress coat. White shirt. Crimson tie.

He was back. Flynn MacGregor.

Blue eyes, so deep, so dark, they were the color of the sky when a thunderstorm came rolling through. Black, wavy hair that had been tamed with a close cut. And a face set in rigid stone. "I have waited. For hours. Watched dozens of customers come through here, thinking you have the answer to love, marriage and apparently the beginnings of the earth." He let out a breath of displeasure. "I had no idea you could get such bonuses with your coffee cake."

His droll manner told her it wasn't a joke, nor a compliment. "I don't purport to offer anything other than baked goods, Mr. MacGregor."

"That's not what the people in that line thought. That very *long* line, I might add. One that took nearly three hours to clear out. And now—" he flicked out a wrist and glanced at his watch "—I'm never going to get to where I needed to go today if I don't get this interview done. Now."

"I don't think you're going to be able to make it farther than a few miles. I doubt the roads are clear. The weather is still pretty bad."

"My editor is from the mailman school of thought. Neither blizzard nor earthquake shall stop a deadline."

She eyed him. "And I take it you agree with his philosophy?"

"I didn't get to where I am in my career by letting a little snow stop me." He leaned forward. "So, do you have time *now*, Miss Barnett?"

Clearly, Sam's best bet was to fit in with his plans. Business had slowed enough for her to give the reporter some time anyway. "Sure. And it'd be great to sit down for a minute."

Sam turned toward her great-aunt. "Aunt Ginny, could you handle the counter for a little while?"

The older woman gave her a grin. "Absolutely."

Sam pivoted back to Flynn. The man was handsome enough, even if he was about as warm and fuzzy as a hedgehog. But, he had come all the way from Boston, and Lord knew she could use the publicity. The airline magazine story had been a great boon, but Sam was a smart enough business person to know that kind of PR wouldn't last long. "Can I get you some coffee? A Danish? Muffin? Cookies?"

"I'd like a sampling of the house specialties. And some coffee would be nice."

He had good looks, but he had all the friendliness of a brick wall. His words came out clear, direct, to the point. No wasted syllables, no wide smiles.

Nevertheless, he offered the one gift Sam had been dreaming about for years. A positive profile of the bakery in the widely popular *Food Lovers* magazine would be just the kickoff she needed to launch the new locations she'd been hoping to open this year. Heck, the exposure she'd hoped and prayed for ever since she'd taken over the bakery. Coupled with the boost in business the airline magazine's story had given her, Joyful Creations was on its way to nationwide prominence.

And she was on her way out of Riverbend.

Finally.

Not to mention, she'd also have the financial security she needed to fund her grandmother's long-term care needs. It was all right here.

In Flynn MacGregor. If that didn't prove Santa existed, Sam wasn't sure what did.

She hummed snippets of Christmas carols as she filled a holly-decorated plate with a variety of the bakery's best treats.

Gingerbread cookies, pecan bars, cranberry orange muffins, white mocha fudge, peppermint chocolate bark, frosted sugar Santa cookies—she piled them all on until the plate threatened to spill.

"Don't forget some of these," Ginny said, handing Sam a couple cherry chocolate chunk cookies.

"Aunt Ginny, I don't think he needs—"

"He came here for the story about the special cookies, didn't he?" Her great-aunt gave her a wide smile. "And if the stories are true, you never know what might happen if he takes a bite."

"You don't seriously believe—"

"I do, and you should, too." Ginny wagged a finger. "Why, your grandmother and grandfather never would have fallen in love if not for this recipe. I wouldn't have married your Uncle Larry if it hadn't been for these cookies. Why, look at all the proof around you in this town. You just don't believe in them because you've never tried them."

"That's because I'm too busy baking to eat." Sam sighed, accepted the two cookies and added them to the plate. What was the harm, really? There was nothing to that legend. Regardless of what Aunt Ginny thought.

Balancing the plate, Sam crossed the room and placed the treats and a steaming mug of coffee before the reporter. "Here you are, Mr.—"

And she lost the next word. Completely forgot his name.

He had taken off his coat and was sitting at one of the small round café tables in the corner, by the plate-glass windows that faced the town square. He had that air about him of wealth, all in the telltale signs of expensive fabric, perfectly fitting clothing, the way he carried himself. His sleeves were rolled up, exposing defined, muscled hands and forearms, fingers long enough to play piano, touch a woman and—

Whoa. She was staring.

"Mr. MacGregor," she finished. Fast. "Enjoy." Sam took a couple steps back. "Uh, enjoy."

He turned to her and a grin flashed across his face so quickly, she could have almost sworn she'd imagined it. But no, it had been there. A thank-you, perhaps. Or maybe amusement at her discomfit?

Either way, his smile changed his entire face. Softened his features. Made Sam's pulse race in a way it hadn't in a long time.

"You already said that," he said.

Okay, it had been amusement. Now she was embarrassed.

"Did I? Sorry. You, ah, make me nervous." No way would she admit public humiliation.

"I do? Why?"

"I haven't had a real reporter in the shop before. Well, except for Joey from the *Riverbend Times*, but that doesn't count. He's nineteen and still in college, and he's usually just here to get a cup of decaf because regular coffee makes him so hyper he can hardly write." She was babbling. What was wrong with her? Samantha Barnett never babbled. Never got unnerved.

Way to make a first impression, Sam.

"I should get back in the kitchen," Sam said, thumbing in that direction.

"I need to interview you. Remember? And I'd prefer not to shout my questions."

Now she'd annoyed him. "All right. Let me grab a cup of coffee. Unlike Joey, I *do* need the caffeine."

He let out a laugh. Okay, so it had been about a half a syllable long, but still, Sam took that as a good sign. A beginning. If he liked her and liked the food, maybe this Flynn guy would write a kick-butt review, and all her Christmas wishes would be granted.

But as she walked away, he started drumming his fingers on the table, tapping out his impatience one digit at a time.

Ginny tapped her on the shoulder when she reached the coffeepot. "Sam, I forget to mention something earlier."

"If it's about getting me to share Grandma's special recipe cookies with a man again—"

"No, no, it's about that magazine he's with. He said *Food Lovers*, didn't he?"

Sam poured some coffee into a mug. "Yes. It's huge. Everybody reads it, well, except for me. I never get time to read anything."

Ginny made a face. "Well, I read it, or at least I used to. Years ago, *Food Lovers* used to just be about food, you know, recipes and things like that, but lately, it's become more…"

"More what?" Sam prompted.

Her aunt paused a moment longer, then let out a breath. "Like those newspapers you see in the checkout stand. A lot of the stories are about the personal lives of the people who own the restaurants and the bakeries, not the food they serve. It's kind of…intrusive."

"What's wrong with writing stories about the people who own the businesses?"

Ginny shrugged. "Just be careful," she said, laying a hand on Sam's. "I know how you guard your privacy, and your grandmother's. I might not agree with your decision, but you're my niece, so I support you no matter what."

Sam drew Aunt Ginny into a hug. "Thank you."

"Anything for you, Sam," she said, then drew back. She glanced over the counter at Flynn MacGregor. "There's one other thing you need to be careful of, too."

"What's that?"

Ginny grinned. "He's awfully cute. That could be the kind of trouble you've been needing, dear niece, for a long time."

Sam grabbed her coffee mug. "Adding a relationship into my life, as busy as it is?" She shook her head. "That would be like adding way too much yeast to a batter. In the end, you get nothing but a mess."

CHAPTER TWO

SAM RETURNED with her coffee, Aunt Ginny's words of wisdom still ringing in her head, and slipped into the opposite seat from Flynn MacGregor. He had a pad of paper open beside him, turned to a blank page, with a ready pen. He'd sampled the coffee, but none of the baked goods. Not so much as a crumb of Santa's beard on the frosted sugar cookies. Nary a bite from Grandma's special cookies—the ones he'd presumably come all this way to write about.

Sam's spirits fell, but she didn't let it show. Maybe he wanted to talk to her first. Or maybe he was, as Aunt Ginny had cautioned, here solely for the story behind the bakery.

Her story.

"Are you ready *now?*" he asked.

"Completely."

"Good. Tell me the history of the bakery."

Sam folded her hands on the table. "Joyful Creations was opened in 1948 by my grandmother Joy and grandfather Neil Barnett. My grandmother was an amazing cook. She made the most incredible cookies for our family every holiday. I remember one time I went over to her house, and she had 'invent a cookie' day. She just opened her cabinets, and she and I—"

"The bakery, Miss Barnett. Can we stick to that topic?"

"Oh, yes. Of course." Sam wanted to kick herself. Babbling again. "My grandfather thought my grandmother was so good, she should share those talents with Riverbend. So they opened the bakery."

He jotted down the information as she talked, his pen skimming across the page in an indecipherable scrawl.

Sam leaned forward. "Are you going to be able to read that later?"

He looked up. "This? It's my own kind of shorthand. No vowels, abbreviations only I know for certain words."

She chuckled. "It's like my recipes. Some of them have been handed down for generations. My grandmother never really kept precise records and some of them just say 'pecs' or 'CC.' They're like a puzzle."

He arched a brow. "Pecs? CC?"

"Pecans. And CC was shorthand for chocolate chips." Sam smiled. "It took me weeks to figure out some of them, after I took over the bakery. I should have paid more attention when I was little."

His brows knitted in confusion. "I read it was a third-generation business. What happened to the second generation?"

"My parents died in a car accident when I was in middle school. I went to live with my grandparents. Grandpa Neil died ten years ago." Sam splayed her palms on the table and bit her lip. Flynn MacGregor didn't need to know more than that.

"And your grandmother? Is she still alive?"

Sam hated lying. It wasn't in her nature to do so. But now she was in a position where telling the truth opened a bucket of worms that could get out of hand. "She is, but no longer working in the bakery."

He wrote that down. "I'd like to interview her, too."

"You can't."

Flynn looked up. "Why?"

"She's…ill." That was all he needed to know. Joy's privacy was her own. This reporter could keep the story focused on the present.

Nevertheless, he made a note, a little note of mmm-hmm under his breath. Sam shifted in her chair. "Don't you want to try a cranberry orange muffin?"

"In a minute."

"But—"

"I'm writing an article, Miss Barnett, not a review."

She shifted some more. Maybe her unease stemmed from his presence. The airline magazine had done the interview part over the phone. The reporter had come in and bought some cookies, then found his happy ending, unbeknownst to Sam, at a different time. Talking to someone she couldn't see, and answering a few quick questions, had been easy. This face-to-face thing was much more difficult.

More distracting. Because this reporter had a deep blue, piercing gaze.

The bell over the door jingled and a whoosh of cold air burst into the room. "Sam!"

"Mrs. Meyers, how can I help you?"

"I need more cookies. My dog ate the box I brought home. I didn't even get a chance to feed the batch I bought to my Carl and that man is in the grumpiest of moods." Eileen Meyers swung her gaze heavenward. "He's hanging the Christmas lights."

"In this weather?"

"You know my husband. The man is as stubborn as a tick on a hunting dog, Sam. There are days I wonder why I'm even buying those cookies."

"Because they're your husband's favorites," Sam reminded her. Eileen had been in the day before, plunked down her money, her love for her husband still clear, even in a marriage that had celebrated its silver anniversary, and was edging its way toward gold.

Eileen harrumphed, but a smile played at the edge of her lips. "Will you get me another dozen?"

"Ginny can help you, Mrs. Meyers."

Eileen laid a hand on Sam's arm, her brown eyes filled with entreaty. "I love your Aunt Ginny, Sam, I do, but you know my Carl better than I do some days. He says you're the only one who can pick out the cookies he likes best."

Across from her, Flynn MacGregor's pen tapped once against his notepad. A reminder of where her attention should be.

"Please, Sam?" Eileen's hand held tight to Sam's arm. "It'll mean the world to Carl."

"This will just take a minute," she told Flynn. "Is that all right?"

"Of course." A smile as fake as the spray-paint snow on the windows whipped across his face. "I've already waited for that massive line of customers to go down. Dealt with my car breaking down, and a blizzard blowing through town, which has undoubtedly delayed my leaving, too. What's one more box of cookies?"

Sam filled Eileen's order as quickly as she could, trying to head off Eileen's attempts at conversation. And failing miserably. Eileen was one of those people who couldn't buy a newspaper without engaging in a rundown of her life story. By the time she had paid for her cookies, she'd told Sam—again—all about how she and Mr. Meyers had met, what he'd done to sweep her off her feet and how he'd lost his romantic touch long ago.

"Are you done playing advice columnist?" Flynn asked when Eileen finally left.

"I'm sorry. Things have been especially crazy here since word got out about those cookies." Sam gestured toward the plate, where the trio of Grandma's special recipe still sat, untouched.

"The ones that are purported to make people fall in love?"

She shrugged. "That's what people say."

"I take it you don't believe the rumors?"

She laughed. "I don't know. Maybe it's true. If two people find a happy ending because they eat my grandmother's cookies, then I think it's wonderful. For them, and for business."

Flynn arched a brow. "Happy endings? Over cookies?"

"Not much of a romantic, are you?"

"No. I'm a practical man. I do my job, and I don't dabble in all this—" he waved his hand "—fanciful stuff."

"Me, too." Sam laughed, the chuckle escaping her with a nervous clatter. "Well, not the man part."

"Of course." He nodded.

What was with this guy? He was as serious as a wreath without any decorations. Sam laced her fingers together and tried to get comfortable in the chair, but more, under his scrutiny. The sooner this interview was over, the better. "What else did you need to know?"

"How long have you been working here?"

"All my life. Basically, ever since I could walk. But I took over full-time when I was nineteen."

Surprise dropped his jaw. "Nineteen? Isn't that awfully young? What kind of business person could you be at that age?"

"You do what have to, Mr. MacGregor." She sipped at her coffee, avoiding his piercing gaze. He had a way of looking at a woman like he could see right through her. Like Superman's X-ray vision, only he wasn't looking at the color of her underwear, but at the secrets of her soul.

She pushed the plate closer to him. "I think you'd really like the sugar frosted cookies. They're a Joyful Creations specialty."

Again, he bypassed the plate in front of him, in favor of his notes. "Did you go to culinary school?"

She shook her head. "I couldn't. I was working here. Full-time."

"Having no life, you mean."

She bristled. "I enjoy my job."

"I'm sure you do." He flipped a page on his notepad, bringing him to a clean sheet of paper.

"What's that supposed to mean?"

"I'm not here to tell you how to run your business."

"And yet, you're judging me and you hardly know me."

Flynn folded his hands over his pad. "Miss Barnett, I've been covering this industry for a long time. Talked to hundreds of bakers and chefs. This is the kind of business that consumes you." He let out a laugh, another short, nearly bitter sound that barely became a full chuckle. "Pun intended."

"My business doesn't consume me." But as the words left her mouth, she knew Joyful Creations had, indeed, done that very thing, particularly in the last few weeks. The business had taken away her weekends. Vacations. Eaten up friendships, nights out, dates. Left her with this empty feeling, as if she'd missed a half of herself.

The half that had watched her friends grow up. Get married. Start families. While she had toiled in the bakery, telling herself there'd be time down the road. As one year passed, then two, then five, and Sam hit twenty-five, and tried not to tell herself she'd missed too much already. She had plenty of time—down the road.

There was a reason she worked so hard. A very important reason. And once she'd reached her goals, she'd take time off.

She would.

"I watched you earlier. And I've watched you as you've talked about this business. I can see the stars in your eyes," he went on. "The *Travelers'* magazine article has probably put the lofty idea in your head that you can become the next McDonald's or Mrs. Fields Cookies."

"It hasn't," Sam leapt to say, then checked her defensive tone. "Well, maybe a little. Did you see those lines? It's been that way nonstop for two weeks. I'm sure you've seen many businesses that became mega-successes after something like that. Don't you think it's possible for me to hit the big time?"

"I have seen it happen," he conceded. "And let me be the first to warn you to be careful what you wish for."

She leaned back in her chair and stared at him, incredulous. Ever since she'd met him, he'd been nothing but grouchy, and now here he was, trying to tell her how to run her own company. "Who put coal in your stocking this morning?"

"I'm just being honest. I believe in calling the shots I see."

"So do I, Mr. MacGregor," Sam said, rising. If she didn't leave this table in the next five seconds, she'd be saying things to this man that she didn't want to see in print. "And while we're on the subject of our respective industries, I think yours has made you as jaded and as bitter as a bushel of lemons." She gestured toward his still-full plate, and frustration surged inside her. With the busy day, with him, and especially with his refusal to try the very baked goods he was writing about yet already judging. "Maybe you should have started with the cookies first. A little sugar goes a long way toward making people happy. And you, sir, could use a lot of that."

CHAPTER THREE

"Well, I was wrong."

Flynn bit back the urge to curse. "What do you mean, wrong?"

"I replaced the air filter. And it turned out, that wasn't it. That means, I was wrong." Earl Klein shrugged. "It happens." He put out his hands, as if that explained why Flynn's car was sitting inside Earl's Tire and Repair on a lift six feet off the ground, a jumble of parts scattered below.

"Did you fix it?" Flynn asked. Of all the people to end up with, Earl would have been Flynn's last choice. He had asked around once he left the bakery, and it turned out the hunting cap guy he'd seen earlier owned the closest garage to Flynn's broken-down car. Although, given how circular a conversation with Earl was turning out to be, Flynn was beginning to regret his choice.

Earl stared at Flynn like he had all the intelligence of a duck. "Does your car *look* fixed?"

"Well, no, but I was hoping—"

"Your fuel filter needs to be replaced. I usually have one for your model on hand, but used my last one yesterday. Damnedest thing, too. Paulie Lennox comes in here, his car was running fine, then all of a sudden—"

"I don't care about Paulie Lennox. I don't even know him."

"Oh, you'd know him if you see him. He's six foot seven. Tallest man in Riverbend. Sings in the church choir. Voice of an angel. Ain't that weird for a guy that big? Must have organ pipes in his chest."

Flynn gritted his teeth. "How long?"

"How long are his vocal cords? Damned if I know. I'm no doctor."

"No, I meant how long until my car is fixed?"

"Oh, that." Earl turned around and looked at the Lexus as if it might tell him. "Day. Maybe two. Gotta wait for the part. You know, 'cept for Paulie, we don't get many of those fancy-dancy cars in here. If you'da come in here with a Ford, or Chevy pickup, I'd have you fixed up a couple minutes. But this, well, this requires what we call special treatment."

Flynn hoped like hell this guy would give the Lexus special treatment, considering what the car cost. "Did you order the part? Or can you go get it?"

"I ordered it. Can't go get it."

Flynn wanted to bang his head into a brick wall. He'd probably get further in the conversation if he did. This was like playing Ping-Pong by himself. "Why can't you go get the part?"

Earl leaned in closer to Flynn. "Have you looked outside, son? It's *snowing*. Blizzard's on its way into town, hell, it's already here. Only an idiot would drive in this. And I'm no idiot."

Flynn would beg to differ. "It's four days before Christmas."

"That don't change the icy roads. Old Man Winter, he doesn't have the same calendar as you and me."

Flynn dug deep for more patience. "Is there another garage in town?"

Earl's face frowned in offense. "Now, I'm going to pretend you didn't even ask that, because you're from out of town. My garage is the best one for miles, and the only one."

Of course. Flynn groaned. "I have some place I need to go. As soon as possible."

That was if he even decided to make that stop in southern Indiana. On the drive out here from Boston, it had seemed like a good idea, but the closer Flynn got to the Midwest, the more he began to second-guess his impromptu decision. That was why he had yet to make any promises he couldn't keep. Better not to say a word. That way, no one was disappointed. Again.

"Well, that ain't happenin', is it?" Earl grinned. "You best get down to Betsy's Bed and Breakfast. She'll put you up and feed you, too." He patted his stomach. "That woman can cook. And she's real pretty, too. But she's spoken for. So don't go thinking you can ask her out. Me and Betsy, we have an understanding." Earl wiggled a shaggy gray brow. "Thanks to those cookies of Sam's, which helped us out a lot. Brought me and Betsy together, they did."

Flynn put up his hands, hoping to ward off the mental picture that brought up. "I don't want to know about it. Just point me in the general direction."

Thirty seconds later, Flynn was back outside, battling an increasingly more powerful wind. The snow had multiplied and six more inches of the thick wet stuff now coated the sidewalks. The earlier tourist crowds had apparently gotten the hint and left for their hotels or real cities. Traffic, what there was left in Riverbend, had slowed to a crawl. Within minutes, the damp snow had seeped through Flynn's shoes and he was slogging through slush, ruining five-hundred-dollar dress shoes. Damn it. What he wouldn't do for a sled dog team right now.

"Do you need a ride?"

He turned to see Samantha Barnett at the wheel of an older model Jeep Cherokee. Or what he thought was Samantha Barnett. She was bundled in a blue parka-type jacket that obscured most of her delicate features, the hood covering all of her blond hair. But the smile—that 100-watt smile he'd seen earlier in the bakery—that he could see.

Only a fool would say no to that. And to the dry, warm vehicle.

"Sure." He opened the door and climbed inside. Holiday music pumped from the stereo, filling the interior of the Jeep like stuffing in a turkey. Again, Flynn got that Norman Rockwell feeling. "Is this town for real?" he asked as Sam put the Jeep in gear and they passed yet another decorated window display—this one complete with a moving Santa's workshop.

"What do you mean?"

"It's a bit too jolly, don't you think? I mean, it's almost nauseating."

"Nauseating? It's Christmas. People are feeling…festive."

"Festive? In this?" He gestured out the window. "My feet are soaked, nearly frostbitten, I'm sure. My car is being worked on by the village idiot, I'm on a deadline that I can't miss and I'm being held hostage in a town that thinks Christmas is the be-all and end-all."

"Well, isn't it?"

"There are three hundred and sixty-four other days in the year, you know."

Sam stared at him. Never before had she met anyone with as little Christmas spirit as Flynn MacGregor. "Don't you celebrate Christmas? Put up a tree? Drink a little eggnog?"

Flynn didn't answer. Instead he glanced out the window. "Do you know a place called Betsy's Bed and Breakfast?"

"Of course I do. It's a small town. Everyone knows everyone else, and everything. You burn your toast in the morning and Mrs. Beedleman over on Oak Street is on your doorstep, lending you her toaster before lunch." Sam smiled. "I'm on my way to make a couple of deliveries, so I have time. Besides, driving you to Betsy's is the least I can do to say I'm sorry for being so short with you earlier." She took a left, using caution as she made the turn and navigated through the downtown intersection. "I guess I'm just a little protective when it comes to the bakery."

"Most business owners are." He kept watching out the window. "Is that a *live* reindeer I see in the park? This town is Christmas gone overboard."

She turned to him. "You're kind of grumpy, aren't you? This whole anti-Christmas thing, the way you jumped on me about my business… Grumpy."

He sat back. "No. Just…honest."

She shrugged. "I call it grumpy."

"Honest. Direct. To the point."

She flashed another glance his way. "You know who else was grumpy? Ebenezer Scrooge. Remember him? He got a pretty bad preview of his future."

Flynn rolled his eyes. "That was fiction. I'm talking real life."

"Uh-huh. Let me know when the ghost of Christmas Future comes knocking on your door."

"When he does, I'll know it's time to put away the scotch."

Samantha laughed. Her laughter had a light, musical sound to it. Like the holiday carols coming from the stereo. Flynn tried hard not to like the sound, but…

He did.

"Listen, you had a rough day," Sam said, "so you're excused for any and all grumpiness. And don't worry, you're in good hands with Earl."

Flynn let out a short gust of disbelief. "I'd be in better hands with a troop of baboons."

"Oh, Earl's not so bad. He's really easygoing. You just gotta get used to him. And, indulge him by listening to his stories once in a while. Nothing makes him happier than that. You might even get a discount on your service if you suffer through his account of the blizzard of '78 and how he baked a turkey, even though the power was out for four days." She shot him a grin.

"I don't have time for other people's stories."

"You're a reporter, isn't your whole mission to get the story?"

"Just the ones they pay me for." That pay had been lucrative, ever since he turned in his first article. Flynn had risen to the top of his field, becoming well-known in the magazine industry for being the go-to guy for getting the job done—on time, and right on the word count.

Then he'd hit a road bump, a big one, with the celebrity chef back in June. His editor had lost faith in Flynn, but worse—Flynn had temporarily lost faith in himself.

He refused to get sucked into that emotional vortex again. He'd gotten to the top by staying out of the story, and he'd do that again here. Get in and out, as fast as possible.

And then make one stop, one very important stop, before heading back to Boston.

But he couldn't do either if he didn't shake off that silly whisper of conscience, write the story his editor wanted and get it in on time, no matter what it took.

The interior of the Jeep had reached a comfortable temperature and Sam pulled off one glove, then the other. Her hands, he noticed, were slim and delicate, the nails short and no-nonsense, not polished. She tugged on the zipper of the parka, but it stuck. "Oh, this coat," she muttered, still tugging with one hand while she drove with the other.

"Let me." He reached over, intending only to help her, but his hand brushed against hers, and instant heat exploded in that touch. Flynn's hand jerked upward. He hadn't reacted with such instantaneous attraction to a woman—a woman he'd just met—in a long time. Granted, Samantha Barnett was beautiful, but there was something about her. Something indefinable. A brightness to her smile, to her personality, that seemed to draw him in, make him forget his reporter's objectivity.

Not smart. If there was one thing Flynn prided himself on being, it was smart.

Controlled. He didn't let things get out of hand, get crazy. By keeping tight reins on his life, on himself, he was able to manage everything. The one time he had lost control, he'd nearly lost his career.

He cleared his throat. He clasped the tiny silver zipper and pulled. After a slight catch, the fastener gave way, parting the front of the coat with a low-pitched hum as it slid down.

Beneath the coat, she wore a soft green sweater that dipped in a slight *V* at the neck and skimmed over her curves. From the second he'd met Samantha Barnett, Flynn had noticed the way the green of the sweater enhanced the green in her eyes, offset the golden tones in her hair. But now, without the cover of the apron, he noticed twice as much.

And noticed even more about her.

The scent of her perfume…cinnamon, vanilla, honey—or was it simply the leftover scents of the bakery?—wafted up to tease at his senses. Would her skin taste the same? Taste as good as the baked delights in the cases of the shop?

Flynn drew back. Shook himself.

Get back on track, back in work mode.

Getting distracted by a woman was not part of the plan. It *never* was. He did not get emotionally involved. Did not let himself care, about the people in the story, about people in general. That was how he stayed in control of his life.

No way was he deviating from the road he had laid for himself. Even Mimi, with her need for no real tie, no commitment, fit into what he needed. A woman like Samantha Barnett, who had small-town, commitment values written all over her, would not. "Your, ah, zipper is all fixed."

"Thanks." She flashed that smile his way again.

That was when Flynn MacGregor realized he had a problem. He'd been distracted from the minute he'd walked into that bakery.

Betsy's Bed and Breakfast was located less than six blocks from Earl's repair shop, but with Flynn MacGregor so close, the ride seemed to take ten hours instead of ten minutes. Sam was aware of his every breath, his every movement. She kept her eyes on the road, not just because visibility had become nearly zero, but because it seemed as if the only thing she saw in her peripheral vision was Flynn.

She hadn't been out on a date in—

Well, a long time. Too much work, too little personal life. That must be why her every thought seemed to revolve around him. Why she'd become hyperaware of the woodsy notes of his cologne. Why her gaze kept straying to his hands, his broad shoulders, the cleft in his jaw.

This ride was a prime opportunity to impress him. To tell him more about the bakery. Not flirt. Not that him jumping in to help with her zipper was flirting…except she had held her breath when he'd gotten so close. Noted the fit of his jacket. The flecks of gold in his eyes. The way the last rays of sun glinted in his hair.

Business, Sam. Business.

"Have you interviewed many bakery owners?" she asked. Then wanted to kick herself. She hadn't exactly hit the witty jackpot with that one.

"A few. Mostly, I cover high-end restaurants. Or, I did." He gave her a wry grin, one that made her wonder about the use of the past tense. "All those chefs courting heart attacks, trying to maintain their five-star ratings."

Sam stopped the Jeep, the four-wheel drive working hard

to grip the icy roads, and let a mother and her three children cross the street. Sam recognized Linda Powell, and waved to her through the front window. The littlest Powell waved back, a small red mittened hand bringing a smile to Sam's face. "Is the restaurant business really that competitive?"

He snorted. "Are you kidding? In some cities, these places campaign all year to garner those ratings. They agonize over their menus, stress over the tiniest ingredients, sometimes shipping in a certain fish from one pocket of the world because the chef insists absolutely nothing else will do. Every detail is obsessed over, nitpicked at like it's life and death. They'll accept nothing less than the unqualified best. A bad review can close a place, a good review can skyrocket it to the top."

"But…that's ridiculous." She halted at a stop sign, waiting to make the right onto Maple Street. The Jeep's wipers clicked back and forth, wiping snow off the frosty glass. "A review is simply one person's opinion."

"Ah, but people like me are paid to be the experts." Flynn put a hand on his chest, affecting a dramatic posture. "They live or die by our words."

They had reached Betsy's Bed and Breakfast, where a small hand-painted sign out front announced the converted Victorian's vacancies. Sam stopped in front of the quaint home and parked alongside the front walk. Betsy, a complete Christmas fanatic, had decked the entire porch in holiday flare, with a moving Santa, twinkling lights and even a lighted sleigh and reindeer on the roof.

"And what about me?" Sam asked, turning to Flynn before he exited the Jeep. "What do you think will be my fate? Do you think I'll skyrocket to the top?"

Flynn studied her for a long time, his gaze unreadable in the darkening day, a storm in his blue eyes rivaling the one in the sky. "That, Miss Barnett, is still to be determined."

CHAPTER FOUR

BETSY WILLIAMS, the owner of the bed and breakfast, greeted Flynn with bells on. Literally.

The buxom, wide woman hurried across the foyer and put out her arms, the bells on her house slippers jingling and jangling as she moved, like a one-person reindeer symphony. "Welcome! It's so nice to have another guest! At Betsy's Bed and Breakfast, there's always room for one more!"

Flynn would have turned and run, except Samantha Barnett was standing behind him, blocking the sole exit. "I'm only here until my car is fixed."

And hopefully not a single second longer.

"As long as you want, my heart and home are open to you." She beamed, bright red lips spreading across her face and revealing even, white teeth. Her hand shot out, and she pumped his in greeting, extracting his name and reason for coming to Riverbend in quick succession. "Oh, that's just so exciting!" Betsy said. "Now, tell me what you want for breakfast. Waffles, French toast or eggs?"

Flynn forced a smile to his face. "Surprise me."

Betsy squealed. "I'll delight you, is what I'll do. And I'll have plenty of baked goods to choose from, too, won't I, Sam?"

"You're my first delivery of the day, Betsy. Not to mention, my best customer."

Betsy hustled around and took Flynn's arm, practically hauling him toward the front parlor. "I was her *only* customer, don't you know, back when she first took over. So many people didn't think a girl, still practically a teenager, could run a shop like that. And she did have her mishaps, didn't you, Sam? A few burned things and well, that one teeny-weeny explosion, but you moved past those little setbacks." Betsy beamed. "You're a regular baker now, even if you had no formal training."

Flynn glanced over at Samantha. Her smile seemed held on by strings.

"And those romance cookies, why they worked for me and my Earl. Oh, he's such a cutie, isn't he?" Betsy barreled on, saving Flynn from having to offer an opinion. "Those cookies have fixed up many a person who has come through my door. I serve them every morning on the buffet table." Betsy wagged a finger at him. "If you're looking for love, Mr. MacGregor, you be sure to try those cookies."

"I'm fine, thank you."

She assessed him like a Christmas ham. "I don't see a ring. That means you need the cookies." Betsy nodded. "And our Sam, here, she's available."

"Betsy, Mr. MacGregor needs a room," Sam interjected.

"Oh, my goodness, I almost forgot! And here I am, the hostess and everything." Betsy tsk-tsked herself. "And you need to get back to work, missy, right?"

"I do," Sam replied. "Business is booming lately."

"Well, why wouldn't it? Where else are people going to go to get their cookies? You're the only bakery for miles and miles!" Betsy grinned, as if she'd just paid Samantha a huge compliment. Flynn supposed, in her own way, Betsy thought she had, but he could see the sting in Samantha's eyes. The implication that her success was due solely to a lack of competition, not hard work and expertise. Maybe Betsy still saw Sam as that young kid who burned the muffins.

For a second, his chest constricted with sympathy, then he yanked the emotion back. The first rule in reporting was not to get involved with the story, stay above the fray.

He'd used that as a yardstick to measure every personal decision he'd ever made. After years of sticking to that mantra like tape to a present, Flynn wasn't about to start caring now. To start putting his heart into the mix. He did not cross those boundaries.

Ever.

He didn't care if Riverbend had issues with Sam Barnett or vice versa. Didn't care if her business was going gangbusters or going bust. He'd made a very good living without ever putting his heart into a story, because Flynn MacGregor had learned a long time ago that doing so meant putting his emotions through a meat grinder. He'd rather write about kitchen implements than experience them.

"I'd like to get settled, Miss Williams," Flynn said. "And find out how to log onto your network."

"Network?" She frowned, then propped a fist on her ample hip. "I'll have you know Betsy's Bed and Breakfast is not a chain."

"*Internet* network," Flynn said. "I wanted to check my e-mail."

"Oh, that." She crossed to a side table, to straighten the green-feathered hat on a stuffed cat in an elf costume, then walked back to Flynn. "I don't have one of those either."

"Well, then your dial-up connection. That'll do."

"Dial-up to what? Anytime we need to talk to somebody, we either walk on down to their house or call 'em on the phone." Betsy wagged a finger at him. "By the way, local calls are free at Betsy's Bed and Breakfast, but there is an extra charge for any long distance. The parlor phone is the one set aside for guest usage."

Flynn pivoted back toward Samantha. "There *is* an Internet connection in this town, isn't there?"

"Well, yes, but…" Samantha gave him a smile. "It's not very reliable, so most people here don't bother with it."

He truly had landed in the middle of nowhere. Flynn bit back his impatience, but it surged forward all the same. "What *exactly* does that mean?"

"Meaning when there's a storm, like there is now, the Internet is the first to go."

"What about cable? Satellite?"

"Not here, not yet. Companies look for demand before they start investing the dollars in technology and, well, Riverbend has never been big on embracing that kind of thing." Samantha shrugged.

"How the hell do you do business out here?"

"Most people still do things the old-fashioned way, I suppose. Face-to-face, with a smile and handshake."

A headache began to pound in Flynn's temples. He rubbed at his forehead. He couldn't miss his deadline. Absolutely could not. It wasn't just that *Food Lovers* was holding the Valentine's Day issue especially for this article, and being late would risk raising Tony's ire. Flynn had already earned a slot on the ire list.

There was more than his career to consider. In the last few months since that interview that had blown up in his face, Flynn had found himself searching for—

A connection. To a past he thought he'd shut off, closed like a closet door full of memories no one wanted to look at. He'd done everything he could to take care of that past, to assuage his guilt. But suddenly throwing money at it wasn't enough. He needed to go in person, even if he wasn't so sure his shoes on that doorstep would be very welcome. Either way, one glance out the window at the storm that had become a frenzy of white, told him the chances of leaving today—even if his car was fixed—were nil.

Until the storm eased, he'd work. Write up this thing about magic elves baking love cookies, or whatever the secret was, turn it over to his editor, and then he could get back to the meat that fed his paycheck and his constant hunger to find the scoop—scathing restaurant reviews exposing the true underbelly of the food industry.

"How am I supposed to work without an Internet connection?" he said.

"We have electricity," Betsy said, her voice high and helpful. "You can plug in a computer. That's good enough, isn't it?" Upstairs, someone called Betsy's name, mentioning an emergency. She sighed. "Oh, Lord, not again." She toodled a wave, then headed up the stairs, while her slippers sang their jarring song.

Flynn turned back to Samantha. "If Scrooge's ghosts do come visit me, they better bring a connection to civilization. And if they can't, just put me out of my misery. Because this place is Jingle Hell."

"He's awful, Aunt Ginny." Sam shuddered. "He hates this town, hates me, I think, and even hates Christmas."

"But he's easy on the eyes. That kind of evens things out, doesn't it?" Ginny Weatherby, who had worked at Joyful Creations for nearly twelve years, smiled at her niece. The two of them were in the back of the bakery, cleaning up and putting it to rights after the busy day. The front half of Joyful Creations was dark, silent, the sign in the window turned to Closed, leaving them in relative peace and quiet. "Your grandmother would have agreed."

"Grandma liked everyone who came through this door." Sam groaned. "I think he purposely sets out to frustrate me. How am I supposed to give him a good interview? I'm afraid I'll say something I'll regret."

"Oh, you're smart enough not to do that, Sam. I'm sure you'll do fine."

"I don't want him to find out about Grandma," Sam said.

Ginny's gaze softened. "Would it be so bad for people to know?"

Sam toyed with the handle on the sprayer. "I just want people to remember her the way she was, Aunt Ginny."

"They will, Sam." She put a hand on her niece's shoulder. "You need to trust that people of this town are your friends, that they love and care about you, and your grandmother."

"I'll think about it," Sam said. Though she had thought about the same question a hundred times over the past five years, and come back to the same answer. She didn't want people's pity. And most of all, she didn't want them to be hurt when they found out the Joy Barnett they knew and loved was no longer there. "For now, I'm more worried about that Flynn guy. He gets on my last nerve, I swear."

Ginny loaded the dishwasher and pushed a few buttons. "Give him cookies. That'll sweeten him up."

"I did. He wouldn't eat them." Sam sprayed disinfectant on the countertops and wiped them down, using the opportunity to work out some of her frustrations.

Aunt Ginny made a face. "Well, then I don't trust him. Any man who won't eat a plate of cookies, there's something wrong. Unless he's diabetic, then he has an excuse. Did you check for a medical ID bracelet?"

"No. Maybe I should have looked for a jerk bracelet."

"Have some patience, dear." She patted her niece's hand. "This guy could give the shop lots of great publicity."

"I'm trying to be patient."

"And you never know, he could be the one."

Sam rolled her eyes. "Stop trying to fix me up with every man who walks through that door."

Aunt Ginny took off her apron and hung it on a hook by the door, then crossed to her niece. The gentle twinkle of love shone in her light green eyes. "Your mother wouldn't want to see you living your life alone, dear, and neither would your grandmother."

"I'm not alone. I have you."

Sam would forever be grateful to her Aunt Ginny, who had moved to Riverbend from Florida a few months after Sam took over the bakery. Not much of a baker, she hadn't exactly stepped into her sister Joy's shoes, instead becoming the friend and helper Sam needed most. Though making cookies had never been her favorite thing to do, she'd been an enthusiastic supporter of the business, and especially of Sam.

Ginny pursed her lips. "Not the same thing and you know it."

"It's good enough for now. You know why I have to pour everything into the business." Sam went back to wiping, concentrating on creating concentric circles of shine, instead of the thoughts weighing on her. The ones that crept up when she least expected them—reminding her that she had stayed in this shop instead of going to college, getting married, having a family. The part that every so often wondered what if…she didn't have these responsibilities, these expectations?

But she did, so she kept on wiping, and cleaning.

Ginny's hand on her shoulder was a soft reminder that they had visited this topic dozens of times. "You don't have to pour everything into here, dear. Leave some room for you."

"I will," Sam promised, though she didn't mean it. Ginny didn't understand—and never really had—the all-consuming pressure Sam felt to increase business, and revenues.

Grandma Joy deserved the best care—and the only way to pay for that was by bringing in more money. Not think about possibilities that couldn't happen.

"And as far as this reporter goes," Ginny said, grabbing her coat as she waited for Sam to finish putting away the cleaning products, "I think it's time you tried the cranberry orange bread. The frosted loaf, not the plain one. I haven't met a person yet that didn't rave about it."

Sam let out a breath, relieved Ginny hadn't suggested sweetening him up with a date, or something else Sam definitely didn't have time or room in her life for. "Okay. I'll bring some over to Betsy's in the morning. Try to sweeten him up."

"And wear your hair up. Put in your hoop earrings, and for God's sake," Aunt Ginny added, wagging a finger, "wear some lipstick."

"Ginny, this isn't a beauty contest, it's an interview."

Ginny grinned. "I didn't get to this age without learning a thing or two about men. And if there's one thing I know, it's to use your assets, Sam," she said, shutting off the lights and closing the shop but not the subject, "every last one."

Flynn woke up in a bad mood.

He flipped open his cell phone, prayed for at least one signal bar, and got none. Moved around the frilly room, over to the lace-curtained window, still nothing. Pushing aside a trio of chubby Santas on the sill, Flynn opened the window, stuck the phone outside as far as his arm would reach and still had zero signal. Where was he? Mars? Soon as he got back to Boston, he was switching wireless carriers. Apparently this one's promise of service "anywhere" didn't include small Indiana towns in the middle of nowhere.

Flynn gave up on his cell phone, got dressed and went downstairs. The scent of freshly brewed coffee drew him like a dog to a bone, pulling him along, straight to the dining room. Several guests sat at one long table, chatting among themselves. Swags of pine ran down the center, punctuated by fat pinecones, puffy stuffed snowmen with goofy grins, unlit red pillar candles. A platoon of Santa plates had been joined by an army of snowman coffee mugs and a cavalry of snowflake-handled silverware. The Christmas invasion had flooded the table, leaving no survivors of ordinary life.

He'd walked into the North Pole. Any minute, he expected dancing elves to serve the muffins.

"Good morning, good morning!" Betsy came jingle-jangling out of the kitchen, her arms wide again. Did the woman have some kind of congenital disease that kept her limbs from hanging at her sides?

"Coffee?" he asked. Pleaded, really.

"On the sideboard. Fresh and hot! Do you want me to get you a cup?"

"I'll help myself. Thanks." He walked over to the poinsettia-ringed carafe, filled a Mrs. Claus mug, then sipped deeply. It took a few minutes for the caffeine to hit his brain.

"I don't know what your travel plans are, but the plows are just now getting to work, and the Indianapolis airport is closed for a couple more hours. They're predicting more snow. I'm so excited. It'll be a white Christmas, for sure!" Betsy applauded the joyful news.

"Thank you for the update." A little snow wouldn't stop him from getting the story out of Samantha Barnett. It might delay his trip down to southern Indiana, but the job—

Nothing delayed the job.

"No problem. It's just one of the many services I provide for my customers. No tip necessary." She beamed. "Oh, and Mr. MacGregor, we'll be singing Christmas carols in the parlor after breakfast, if you'd like to join us."

He'd rather do *anything* but that. "Uh, no. I—"

The front door opened. Flynn turned. Samantha Barnett, her arms loaded with boxes, entered the house. Excellent timing. Flynn hurried forward, taking the top few from her.

"Thanks. I thought I might lose those." She flashed him a smile that slammed into Flynn with more force than the caffeine's punch.

He told himself it didn't matter, that it hadn't affected him at all. Instead, he put on the friendly face that had won over many an interview subject. "It's not often that I get to come to the rescue of baked goods. Or that they come to mine."

"My goodness, Mr. MacGregor. Did you just make a joke? Because I didn't think you had it in you." Samantha paused in laying the boxes on a small table in the dining room. "Sorry. Sometimes my mouth gets ahead of my brain."

Betsy handed Samantha a set of serving platters, but didn't linger to chat, because one of the guests called her over to ask her a question about local events.

"It's this town," Flynn said after Betsy was gone, keeping his voice low, lest she overhear and come back to argue. "It's like bad lighting on an actress. It brings out the worst in me."

Samantha bristled. "Riverbend? It's not perfect, but I can't imagine why anyone would hate it. You really should give this place a chance before you condemn it. You never know, it might grow on you."

"So do skin rashes."

"You *are* Scrooge," she whispered. "Don't let Betsy hear you say that. People around here are proud of their town."

"I know. She's been trying to recruit me for the caroling crew all morning."

Samantha gave him a nonchalant shrug. "It might do you some good. Infuse you with some Christmas cheer."

Flynn let that subject drop. Infusing wasn't on his menu.

He didn't settle in, didn't get to know the locals. Of course, once he came in and ripped apart the local steakhouse in the pages of *Food Lovers*, he wasn't exactly invited back for tea anyway. "You know, there's a big world out there that offers a lot of great things like *civilization*, Internet connections, cellular towers, reliable public transportation. All without paying the price of Christmas carols in the parlor."

Samantha placed the last of the baked goods on the platters and let out a long sigh. "All my life I've dreamed of seeing that world, but…"

"This bakery is as binding as a straightjacket." He'd written that story a hundred times. Shop owners complaining about how small-business life drained them, yet they stayed in the field.

But he understood them. He might not be braising roasts or reducing sauces, but he knew the spirit that drove entrepreneurs. That hunger to climb your own way to the top. To be the only one who fueled success. It didn't matter what it took—long hours, financial worries, constant demands—to make it from the bottom to the top of the food chain.

Because he had done it himself, and his climb had paid off handsomely. Flynn had become known as the top writer for the food industry and his ambition had created a career that allowed him to call his own shots. Because he was the one that got the story, no matter what it took. No matter how many hours, how many weekends, how many holidays.

He remained unencumbered, without so much as a mortgage, a wife, kids. And though he may have lost his footing this summer—that was a temporary setback. He'd be back on top, after this piece.

"It's not just that the bakery keeps me tied down," Samantha said. "I have other reasons for staying here."

Her tone, almost melancholy, drew him. He could hear the

scoop underlying the words, note them like a bloodhound on the trail of a robber. "Like what?"

She quickly pulled herself together. "You're interviewing me about Joyful Creations, Mr. MacGregor, not my personal life." A smile crossed her face, but it was one that had a clear No Trespassing sign. "Let's stick to that, okay?"

"Certainly. Business only, that's the way I like things, too."

Except…she'd intrigued him with the way she'd shut that door so firmly. Most people Flynn interviewed spilled their guts as easily as a two-year-old with an overfilled cup of milk. Samantha Barnett clearly wouldn't be letting a single drop spill.

And he wouldn't let a drop of sympathy spill, either. He refused to fall for whatever had brought that wisp of emotion to her eyes. To let her move past his reporter curiosity.

Except…a part of him did wonder about the story behind the story. He had to be crazy. Clearly made delusional by all this Christmas spirit surrounding him. That was it.

Except, Flynn wasn't a Christmas spirit kind of guy.

"How's the weather out there?" Flynn asked, even though he already knew the answer. His comment was simply meant to retreat to neutral ground. He'd circle around to the article in a while, once he got his head back in the game.

"The storm has eased a bit, but they're expecting another front to move in, later this morning."

"If Earl's got the part for my car, that gives me just enough time to get out of town, if you have time for us to finish our interview before I have to go."

Samantha laughed. "Go and do what? The road travel will be awful again in a couple of hours, not that it's all that great right now to begin with. You might as well stay. In fact, I don't think you'll have a choice."

"There's always a choice, Miss Barnett."

"Well, unless you convince the National Guard to convoy you out, Mr. MacGregor, I think your only choice is to stay put." She closed the last of the boxes and stacked them into a pile. "I have to get back to the shop, but if you want to finish your interview, I'll be free at lunch for twenty minutes or so."

He'd be here all day, from the sounds of it. Have hours and hours of time to kill. He could, most likely, get what he needed from Samantha Barnett in twenty minutes. But the idea of rushing the questions, scribbling down the answers over a corned beef on rye—

Simply didn't appeal like it normally did. He must be in need of a vacation. Why else would he not be in a rush to meet his deadline? To move on to the next headline?

"No," he said.

"No?" One eyebrow perked up.

"I want more than that."

"More?" Now the other eyebrow arched.

"Dinner." The noise from the other bed-and-breakfast guests had risen, so Flynn took a step closer, and caught the scent of vanilla in her hair. Had he just said that word? Offered a dinner date?

Yes, he had, and now, he found himself lowering his voice, not for intimacy he told himself, but for privacy. Yet, everything about their closeness, the words, spelled otherwise. "A long, lingering dinner. No rushing out to fill boxes with cranberry muffins or to bring frosted reindeer to screaming three-year-olds."

"Just you and me…"

"And my pen and notepad. This is an interview, not a date, Miss Barnett," Flynn added, clarifying as much for himself as for her.

"Of course." Her gaze lingered on his, direct and clear. "But either way, would you do me one favor?"

"What?"

"Stop calling me Miss Barnett. I feel like a schoolteacher, or worse, the lone spinster in town, when you do that. My name is Samantha, but my friends call me Sam. Let's start with that."

He nodded. "Sam it is." Her name slipped off his tongue as easily as a whisper.

"And one more thing." She picked up a cookie from one of the platters and held it out to him. "I'm not leaving here until I know you've tasted my wares."

His grin quirked up on one side. "That could be taken in many ways, Sam."

She brought the cookie to his lips. "The only way I'm meaning is the white chocolate chip kind, Mr. MacGregor."

"Call me Flynn, and I'll do whatever you ask." Was he *flirting*? He never did that. Ever. Maybe Betsy had spiked the coffee.

"Flynn," she said, so softly, he was sure he'd never heard his name spoken like that before, "please take a bite."

"These aren't those special romance cookies, are they?"

"No," Sam said. "Although my Great-Aunt Ginny thinks I should give one to every eligible male that crosses my path."

Her face colored, and he knew she regretted sharing that tidbit. So. Samantha Barnett's life was a bit lonelier than she wanted to admit.

"You've never tried them?" he asked. Then wondered why he cared.

"No. But I assure you, Flynn, that my white chocolate macadamia nut cookies are just as delicious." A smile crossed her lips. "And even better, there's absolutely no danger of falling in love if you eat one."

Before he could tell himself that it was far smarter to resist, to ignore whatever silly, impractical feelings Sam had awakened in him, Flynn found his lips parting and his mouth accepting the sweet morsel.

The minute the cookie hit his palate, Flynn knew this interview would be unlike any other.

And that would be a problem indeed.

CHAPTER FIVE

SAM CHANGED into a dress. Out of a dress. Into jeans. Out of jeans. Into a skirt. Out of the skirt and back into the jeans. Finally, she settled on a deep green sweater with pearl beading around the collar and black slacks, with pointy-toed dress boots. Nothing too sexy, or that screamed trying to impress the guy.

Even if she was.

Though she couldn't say why. Flynn MacGregor had been incredibly disagreeable, and not at all her kind of man. Even if he did have nice hands. Deep blue eyes. Broad shoulders. And a way of entering a room that commanded attention.

All that changing and fussing over her appearance made her ten minutes late. She entered Hall's Steaks and Ribs, brushing the snow from her hair and shoulders, half expecting Flynn to make a note in his notebook about the Joyful Creations' owner's lack of punctuality. Instead, he simply gave her a nod, not so much as a smile, and rose to pull out her chair. "Is it still snowing?"

Okay, so she was a little disappointed that he hadn't said she looked pretty. Hadn't acknowledged her one iota as a woman.

She was here for an interview, not a date. To grow her business. "It's a light snow now. The weatherman said we'll only get another inch or two tonight."

"Good. Hopefully Earl has my car fixed and I can get back on the road in the morning." Flynn took the opposite seat, then handed one of the menus to Sam.

She put it to the side. "Thank you. But I already know what I want."

"Eat here often?"

"When there's only one restaurant in town, this is pretty much *the* date hot spot." Sam felt her face heat. Why had she mentioned dates?

"Are you here often? On dates?" He glanced around the dark cranberry-and-gold room, decorated in a passably good imitation of Italianate style, considering the building was a modern A-frame. The restaurant was crowded, the hum of conversation providing a steady buzz beneath the instrumental Christmas carols playing on the sound system.

"Me?" Sam laughed. "Yeah, in all my spare time. Like those five minutes I had back in 2005."

He let out a chuff. "Probably the same five I had."

A waitress came by their table—a willowy blonde on the Riverbend High School pep squad whose name temporarily eluded Sam's memory—and dropped off two glasses of water, but didn't pause long enough to take their orders.

"You must travel a lot for your job," Sam said.

Flynn took a sip and nodded. "About half the year I'm on the road. The other half I'm behind a computer."

"So I'm not the only workaholic in the room?"

"My job demands long hours."

Sam arched a brow. "Oh, I get it. You're a special case. Whereas I'm…" She trailed off, leaving him to fill in the blank.

"Ambitious, too." He tipped his glass toward her, in a touché gesture.

"Exactly. Then you can understand why I want to expand the shop."

"I do. I just think you should understand what you're getting yourself into when you start pursuing fame, fortune, the American dream."

"I do." The way he'd said the words, though, made Sam feel as if what she wanted was wrong. That she was being self-serving. Had she expressed her dream wrong? No, she hadn't. He'd simply misinterpreted her.

Besides, Flynn MacGregor didn't know the whole story, nor did he need to. She *had* to get out of Riverbend. Away, not just from this town, but from things she couldn't change, things she'd given up on a long time ago. The life she'd wished she could have had, and had put on hold for so long, it had slipped through her fingers. Maybe then—

Maybe then she'd find peace.

Flynn picked up his menu and studied the two pages of offerings. "And where do you fit into that equation?"

"What's that supposed to mean?"

"Exactly what I said." His voice was slightly muffled by the vinyl-bound menu.

"You mean, free time for me?"

Flynn put the menu down. "From what I've heard around town, you're not exactly…the social butterfly. You work. And you work. And you *work*. You're like a squirrel providing for a never-ending winter."

"You write for this industry. Of everyone, you should know how demanding a bakery can be."

"That's what the classified ads are for. To hire people to bake."

"People around here," Sam began, then lowered her voice, realizing how many of those very people were situated right beside her, "expect the baked goods to be made by a family member. Third generation, and all that."

He scoffed. "Oh come on. In this age of automation, you

don't actually think that everyone believes you're truly popping on every last gumdrop button?"

She stared at him, as if he was insane. "But I do."

"Who is going to know if you do it, or a monkey from the zoo does?" Flynn asked.

"Well…I will, for one."

"And the harm in that is…?" He put out his hands. "You might actually have some free time to see a movie? Go out on a date? Have a life?"

She shifted in her chair. His words sprung like tiny darts, hitting at the very issues Sam did her best to avoid. "I have a life."

Flynn arched a brow. "You want me to write the story for you? Young, ambitious restaurateur, or in your case—" he waved a hand in her direction "—baker, goes into the business thinking she'll be *different*." He put special emphasis on the last word, tainting it with disgust.

"My circumstances were different."

But Flynn went on, as if he hadn't even heard her. "She thinks she'll find a way to balance having an outside life with work. That she'll be the one to learn from her peers, to balance the business with reality. That she, and only she, can find the secret to rocketing to the top while still holding on to some semblance of normality." He leaned forward, crossing his arms on the table. "Am I close?"

"No." The lie whistled through her lips.

"Listen, I admire your dedication, I really do. But let me save you the peek at the ending. You won't end up any different than anyone else. You'll look back five, ten, twenty years from now, and think 'where the hell did my life go?'"

"Who made you judge and jury over me?" Sam's grip curled around her water glass, the temptation to throw the beverage in his face growing by the second. "I'm doing what I have to do."

"Do you?"

"What?"

"Have to?"

His piercing gaze seemed to ask the very questions she never did. The ones that plagued her late at night when she was alone in the house her grandmother used to own, pacing the floors, wondering…

What if.

Before she had to come up with an answer, the waitress returned, introduced herself as Holli with an i and took out a notepad. "What can I get you?"

"Lasagna with extra sauce on the side," Sam said, grateful for the change in subject.

"I'll have the same." Flynn handed his menu to Holli, who gave each of them a perky smile before heading to the kitchen. "Enough of me giving you the ugly truth about your future. I'm not here to play psychic."

"And I'm not asking for your advice."

"True." A grin quirked up one side of his mouth. "I get the feeling you're not the kind of person who would take my advice, even if I gave it."

His smile was contagious, and she found herself answering with one of her own. He had charm, she had to give him that. Grudgingly. "I might. Depending on what you had to say."

"Admit it. You're stubborn."

"I am not." She paused. "Too stubborn."

He laughed then, surprising her, and by the look on his face, probably even himself. "Now there's a line I should quote." He dug out his pen and paper.

Disappointment curdled in Sam's stomach. "Are you always after the story?"

He glanced up. "That's my job."

"Yeah, but…just like you were saying to me, don't you ever take a moment for you?"

His blue gaze met hers, direct and powerful. "You mean treat this as a date, instead of an interview?"

"Well—" Sam shifted again "—not *that* exactly."

The grin returned, wider this time. "How long *has* it been?"

"Has it been for what?"

"Since you've been out on a date?"

Sam took such a deep sip of water, she nearly drowned. "I could ask you the same thing."

"My answer's easy. A week."

"Oh." She put the glass down. "I thought you said you didn't have that much free time."

"I was exaggerating. I'm a writer." That grin again. "Given to hyperbole and all that."

Was he…flirting with her? Holy cow. Was that why everything within her seemed touched with fever? Why her gut couldn't stop flip-flopping? Why she alternately wanted to run—and to stay?

It was simply because he was right. She hadn't been out on a date in forever. She wasn't used to this kind of head-on attention from a man. Especially a man as good at the head-on thing as he was.

"So which would you rather?" Flynn asked. "A date? Or an interview?"

The interview, her mind urged. Say interview. The business. The bakery needed the increase in revenue. Her personal life could wait, just as it always had. The business came first.

"A date."

Had she really just said that? Out loud? To the man who held the future of Joyful Creations in his pen? Sam's face heated, and her feet scrambled back, ready to make a fast exit.

But instead of making a note on his ubiquitous notepad, Flynn leaned back in his chair and smiled. "You surprise me,

Samantha Barnett. Just when I think you're all work and no fun, you opt for a little fun."

"Maybe I'm not the cardboard character you think."

"Maybe you're not." His voice had dropped into a range that tickled at her gut, sent her thoughts down a whole other path that drifted away from fun and into man-and-woman-alone territory. He pushed the notepad to the side, then leaned forward, his gaze connecting with hers. When he did that, it seemed as if the entire room, heck, the entire world, dropped away. "Well, if this *was* a date, and we were back in Boston, instead of the pits of Christmastown here, do you want to know what we'd be doing?"

"Yes," Sam replied, curiosity pricking at her like a pin. "Why not?"

He thought a second, considering her. "Well, since you haven't been out on a date in a while, our first date should be something extraordinary."

"Extraordinary?" she echoed.

"A limo, for starters. Door-to-door service."

"A limo?" She arched a brow. "On a reporter's salary?"

"I've done very well in my field. And they tend to reward that handsomely."

Quite handsomely if the expensive suit, cashmere coat and Italian leather shoes were any indication. "What next, after the limo?"

"Dinner, maybe at Top of the Hub, a restaurant at the top of the Prudential building in Boston. Lobster, perhaps? With champagne, of course."

"Of course," she said, grinning, caught in the web of the fantasy, already imagining herself whisked away in the long black car, up the elevator to the restaurant, sipping the golden bubbly drink. "And after dinner?"

"Dancing. At this little jazz club I know where the lights

are dimmed, music is low and sexy and there's only enough room for me to hold you close. Very, very close."

Sam swallowed. Her heart raced, the sound thundering in her head. "That sounds like quite the place."

"A world away from this one."

A world away. The world she had dreamed of once, back when she'd thought she was going to college, going places—

Going somewhere other than Riverbend and the bakery.

For just a second, Sam allowed her mind to wander, to picture a different future. One without the bakery to worry about, without the future of several potential additional locations to fret over. Without other people to worry about, to care for.

What if she were free of all that and could pursue a love life, a marriage, a family? A man who looked at her with desire like Flynn did—

And she had time to react, to date him? To live her life like other women did?

Guilt smacked her hard. She didn't have time to dally with those thoughts. Too many people were depending on her. Later, Sam reminded herself with an inward sigh.

Later, it would be her turn.

Sam looked away, breaking eye contact with Flynn MacGregor. With the temptation he offered, as easily as a coin in his palm. She toyed with her silverware, willing her heart to slow, her breath to return to normal, and most of all, her head to come down from the clouds. "Well, that would be nice. If I lived somewhere else besides here."

"If you did. Which you don't." Flynn cleared his throat, as if he, too, wanted to get back to business, to put some distance between them. "So, tell me. Why the lasagna?"

Of all the questions he could have asked, that one had to be the last one Sam would have expected. "I like lasagna, and the way they make it here is even better than my grandmother did—does," she corrected herself. Darn. She had to be more careful. Sam brushed her hair off her face and opted for another topic, trying to stay on safe, middle ground. "Don't you meet many women who like lasagna?"

That made him laugh. Flynn MacGregor's laugh was deep and rich, like good chocolate. "No. Definitely not. Most of the women I know spend their entire day obsessing about how to whittle their waists down to the next single digit."

Sam patted her hips. "Well, as you can see, that's definitely not me. My waist has never been considered whittled. Though maybe if I did cut back on the—"

"Don't." Flynn's steady gaze met hers. "Enjoy the lasagna. Your waist is perfect just the way it is."

Heat pooled in Sam's gut. Other men had looked at her with desire of course. She'd had boyfriends who had made her feel wanted, even pretty, but never before had a single sentence set off a blast of fireworks in her veins. And here was this big-city playboy, seeing her as a sexy woman.

"You don't have to butter me up," she said. "I already agreed to the interview."

He leaned forward in his seat, his blue eyes assessing her intently. "I'm not buttering you up for anything at all. You look beautiful tonight, Sam."

A trill of joy ran through Sam, skating down her spine. "Well then, thank you." She felt a blush fill her face, and she cursed under her breath. Time to get the focus off herself. Every time he looked at her like that, she got distracted from what was important. "I've told you plenty about me. It's your turn."

He paused. "I'm from Boston. I write for a magazine. I live alone, have no pets."

She laughed. "You're not a man who shares a lot about himself, are you?"

"Just the facts, ma'am." He smiled.

But behind that smile, an invisible wall had been erected. Curiosity rose in Sam. What made Flynn MacGregor tick? What made him smile? Until tonight, he'd rarely done so. When his mouth did curve into a grin, the gesture transformed his face, his eyes, and seemed to make him into an entirely different person. The kind of person she would—under other circumstances—want to get to know.

Not today. Despite their agreement to put the interview on hold, she reminded herself to watch her words. Aunt Ginny's warning about *Food Lovers'* tendency to want the story behind the story came back to Sam. She'd have to be on guard tonight. Flynn MacGregor could be doing all this simply to get her to open up.

And not because he wanted her.

She should be happy. For one, she had no time for a relationship. She had a business to run, a business that was on the cusp of taking off and becoming something so much bigger than this little town, that corner location. She had people depending on her to take Joyful Creations to the next level—and getting sidetracked by dating was just not part of the recipe.

But what if it could be?

The lasagna arrived, and Flynn immediately took a bite of the steaming Italian food. "It pays to follow the locals when ordering food. This is delicious."

"I know. It may say steaks and ribs on the sign out front, but the owner is a full-blooded Italian, so that's his specialty, which also explains the décor. I think he just has the other things on the menu, because that's what tourists expect when they come to Indiana. Not that we get many in Riverbend, at least until the last few weeks."

"Because of the airline magazine's mention of the shop."

Sam buttered two pieces of bread, and handed one slice to Flynn, who thanked her. "That article, and the boost in business, was a blessing and a half, but one that has kept us hopping from sunup to sundown. In fact, after I leave here, I'm going back to the shop to get a start on tomorrow's baking."

"Tonight? But you already put in a long day, didn't you?"

"That's the life of a baker. No free time."

"And yet, you want more."

"I'm not a sugar addict, Flynn. I'm a success addict." She shot him a smile.

Flynn pulled his notepad over and jotted down those words. If anything reminded her this wasn't a date, that did. A flicker of disappointment ran through her, but Sam brushed it off.

For a minute, he'd given her the gift of a normal life. Let her feel again like a normal woman, a beautiful woman. That would be enough. For a while.

A really long while.

"Why?" he asked.

"Why does anyone want success?" Sam bent her head and took a bite of food, chewed and swallowed. "To prove you did well with your business."

"That's all? No other reason?"

No other reason she wanted in print. "That's all." She signaled to Holli to box up her dinner and pushed her plate to the side, her appetite gone. But that wasn't what had her wanting to get out of the restaurant so bad. It was the way Flynn kept studying her, as if he could see behind every answer she'd given him, as if he knew she was holding something back. "Is that all you need? Because I really have to get back to the shop."

"Sure. Thank you for your time, Miss—" He paused. "Sam."

She reached into her purse to pull out some money for dinner but Flynn stopped her with a touch of his hand on hers. A surge of electricity ran up her arm.

"My treat," he said.

"I thought you said this wasn't a date."

"It's not. I have an expense account."

Once again, disappointment whistled through her as brisk and fast as winter's winds. "Oh. Well, in that case, thank you." Sam rose and grabbed her coat off the back of her chair. "If you have any other questions, call me at the shop. That's pretty much where I live." She turned to go.

"Wait."

Sam pivoted back, part of her still hoping—some insane part—that all this really had been a date, and not an interview. "Yes?"

"You mentioned something about having dial-up Internet access at Joyful Creations. Do you think I could come by tonight, if you're going to be there anyway, and access my e-mail?" A grin flashed on Flynn's face. "I'm having acute withdrawal symptoms. Fever, aches, pains, the whole nine yards."

She'd been wrong.

He wanted her—but for her Internet connection only. That was for the best. Even if it didn't feel that way.

"Certainly," Sam said. "Like I said, that shop is my life."

CHAPTER SIX

FLYNN STARED at the picture for a long time. The edges had yellowed, the image cracked over the years, but the memories were as fresh as yesterday. Two boys smiling, their hair tousled by the wind whisking up the Atlantic and onto Savin Hill Beach, their grins as wide as the Frisbees they held in their hands. One day, out of thousands, but that one day—

Had been a good one.

Flynn put the picture back in his wallet, flipped open his cell phone and scrolled through his contact list until he got to the name Liam.

Flynn shut the phone without dialing. He didn't have a signal anyway. Not that he would have called if he had. He hadn't dialed that number in over a year.

Liam hadn't answered his calls in two.

He'd driven all this way, with a crazy idea that maybe Liam would see him if Flynn called. If he said he was a few towns away, and asked if Liam wanted to see him? Or maybe if he just showed up on Liam's doorstep and surprised him, saying "hey, it's Christmas, why don't we just put all this behind us?"

Flynn shook his head. Maybe too much time had passed to heal old wounds.

Flynn rose and put his wallet into his back pocket. He swallowed back the memories, the whiff of nostalgia—had it been nostalgia or something else?—that had hit him for a brief second, then grabbed his laptop and headed out of the bed and breakfast and over to Sam's shop.

From outside the window, he could see her inside, softly lit by a single overhead light, the golden glow spreading over her features. If he hadn't known better, he'd have thought she was an image from a Christmas card—the painted kind famous for their lighting and muted colors.

Flynn shook off the thought. What was with him today? He was going soft, that was for sure. First, the picture, followed by the quick detour down Memory Lane, then the temptation to call Liam, and finally the comparison of this woman to an artist's impression, for Pete's sake. He was not the emotional type. Clearly, he needed to get out of this odd little town and back to the city. He entered the shop, his presence announced by a set of jingle bells above the entrance.

Jingle bells. He scoffed. Of course.

"I'm in the kitchen," Sam called to him.

He headed through the darkened shop, pulled as much by her voice as by the scent of baked goods. The quiet notes of vanilla, mixed with the more pungent song of nutmeg, all muted by the melody of fruits and nuts. The scents triggered a memory but it was gone before he could grasp it. "Smells good in here."

She looked up and brushed a tendril of blond hair off her forehead with the back of her hand. "Thanks. I'm usually too busy to notice anything other than how low the flour supply is getting."

He slipped onto a stainless steel stool in the corner and laid his laptop on the small desk beside him. "Don't you take breaks to taste the cookies? Dip into the muffins?"

"Me? No. I rarely have time."

"Didn't we already have this discussion about all work and no play…?" He let the old axiom trail off, tossing her a grin.

She gestured toward his computer. "Hey, speak for yourself, Mr. Nose to the Grindstone."

Right. Get back to work. Flynn had no intentions of missing this deadline, because doing so meant putting his road trip on hold, and even though he wasn't so sure of the reception he'd receive, he knew it was time to see Liam. That meant he needed to check in with the office and get a head start on writing his article. Procrastinating wasn't going to restore his reputation at the magazine, nor was it going to get him any closer to seeing Liam. "Speaking of which…Can I use your Internet connection?"

"If you get lucky." Sam colored. "I, ah, didn't mean that the way it came out. I meant—"

"If the lines are working."

"Yes." She nearly breathed her relief.

"I wouldn't have thought anything else."

But hadn't he, for just a second? Samantha Barnett was an attractive woman. Curvaceous, friendly and she was surrounded by the perfume of cookies. Any man with a pulse would be enticed by her, as he had been—very much so—at dinner a little while ago. Mimi had never seemed so far away.

Not that he and Mimi had what anyone would really call a relationship. They were more…convenience daters. When either of them needed someone to attend a function or to see a movie with, they picked up the phone. Days could go by before they talked to each other, the strings as loose as untied shoelaces. Mimi liked it that way, and so did Flynn.

Samantha Barnett, who wore her small-town roots like a coat, was definitely not a convenience dater. He'd do best to keep his heart out of that particular cookie jar.

Flynn cleared his throat, turned to his bag and unpacked his laptop, plugging the machine into the outlet on the wall and the telephone line into his modem. Sam gave him a phone number to dial and connect to her provider. He typed in all the information, then waited for the magic to happen.

Nothing. No familiar musical tones of dialing. No screeching of the modem. No hiss of a telephone line. Just an error message.

He tried again. A third time. Powered down the computer, powered it back up and tried connecting a fourth time.

"No luck?" Sam asked.

"Are you sure we're not on Mars?"

Sam laughed. "Pretty sure. Though there are days…" She tossed him a smile, while her hands kept busy dropping balls of chocolate chip cookie dough onto a baking sheet. "That remoteness, that disconnect from city life, is all part of the charm of Riverbend, though. And what draws those droves of tourists."

Flynn shot her a look of disdain. "All five of them? Not counting your temporary flood, of course."

"Actually, it's pretty busy here in the summer. And you saw the lines outside the shop today. People from big cities really like the rural location, and the fact that we have lots of lakes nearby for boating and camping."

"The cityfolk roughing it, huh?"

"Yep. Except we have running water here." Again, another grin. He noticed that when she smiled, her green eyes sparkled with gold flecks. They were the color of the forest just after a storm, when the sun was beginning to peek through the clouds.

Or maybe that was just the reflection from the overhead lights. Yeah, that was it.

Flynn gave up on his computer and shut the laptop's cover. He rose and crossed to Sam. Was it the light? Or was it her eyes? "Why do you live here?"

She paused in making cookies, as if surprised by the question. The scent of vanilla wafted up from the dough. "I grew up here."

He took another step closer. Only because he still couldn't decide what caused the gold flecks in her eyes. Mother Nature or sixty watts. He'd been intrigued all night, first in the restaurant and now, wondering, pondering…thinking almost nonstop about her. A bad sign in too many ways to count, but he told himself if he could just solve this mystery of her eyes, the thoughts would stop. "Okay, then why did you stay? You didn't have to keep the business open. You could have closed it and moved on."

She opened her mouth, then shut it again, as if she had never considered this question before. "Joyful Creations has been in my family for three generations. My family was depending on me to keep it open."

Another step. Flynn inhaled, and he swore he could almost taste the air around Sam. It tasted like…

Sugar cookies.

"What did you say?" Sam said.

Had he said that out loud? Damn. What the hell was wrong with him? He did *not* get emotionally involved with his interview subjects.

He did *not* lose his focus.

He did *not* forget the story. He went after it, whatever the cost.

Flynn backed up three steps, returned to his laptop and flipped up the top. It took a few seconds for the hibernating screen to come back to life. Several long, agonizing seconds of silence that Flynn didn't bother to fill. "If it's all the same to you, I'd like to work here for a little while. That way, if I have any questions while I'm writing, I can just ask them." Meaning, he intended to probe deeper into the clues she'd dropped at dinner, but he didn't say that. "And, I can try to connect to the Internet again."

"Sure." Her voice had a slight, confused lilt at the end. She put the sheet of cookies into the oven, then started filling another one.

Keeping his back to her, Flynn sought the familiarity of his word processing program. He tugged his notepad out of his bag and began typing. The words did what they always did—provided a cold, objective distance. It was as if the bright white of the screen and the stark blackness of the letters erased all emotion, scrubbed away any sense of Flynn's personality. He became an outside observer, reporting facts.

And nothing else.

He wrote for ten minutes, his fingers moving so fast, the words swam before his eyes. Usually, when he wrote a story, pulling the paragraphs out of his brain was like using camels to drag a mule through the mud. He'd never been a fast writer, more a deliberate one.

But this time, it seemed as if his brain couldn't keep up with his hands. He wrote until his fingers began to hurt from the furious movement across the keyboard. When he sat back and looked at the page count, he was stunned to see he had five solid pages in the file already.

Flynn scrolled up to the opening paragraph, expecting his usual "Established in blah-blah year, this business" opening, followed by the punch of personal information, the tabloid zing he was known for. Nearly all his stories had that straightforward, get-to-the-facts approach that led to the one nugget everyone else had missed. It was what his editor liked about him. He delivered the information, with a minimal peppering of adjectives.

"Can I read it?" Sam asked.

He hadn't even realized she had moved up behind him. But now he was aware, very aware. He jerked back to the real world, to the scent of fresh-baked cookies, and to Samantha Barnett, standing right behind him.

"Uh, sure. Keep in mind it's a first draft," he said. "And it's just the facts, none of the fluff kind of thing the airline magazine…" His voice trailed off as his eyes connected with the first few paragraphs on the screen.

"Visions of sugar plums dance in the air. The sweet perfume of chocolate hangs like a cloud. And standing amidst the magic of this Christmas joy, like the star atop a tree, is the owner of Joyful Creations, Samantha Barnett.

"She knows every customer by name, and has a smile for everyone who walks through the door of her shop, no matter how many muffins she's baked or how many cookies she's boxed that day. She's as sweet as the treats in her cases…."

Flynn slammed the top of the laptop shut. What the *hell* was that?

"Wow." A slow smile spread across Sam's face. "And here I thought you were going to write one of those scathing exposés, the kind I've heard the magazine is famous for. I mean, you barely tasted any of the food here and…"

"And what?" he asked, scowling. He did *not* write that kind of drivel. He was known as a bulldog, the writer that went for the jugular, got the story at all costs. Not this sweet-penning novelist wanna-be.

"And well…it didn't seem like you liked me."

He didn't know how to answer that. *Did* he like her? And what did it matter if he did or didn't? He'd be leaving this town the second his car was fixed and the roads were clear. After that, Samantha Barnett would simply be one more file among the dozens in his cabinet. "I don't like this town. It's a little too remote for me." That didn't answer the question of whether he liked her, he realized.

Either way, his editor was expecting a Flynn MacGregor story. The kind free of emotion, but steeped in details no other publication had been able to find. Flynn dug and discovered, doing whatever it took to get the real story. That chase was what had thrilled him from his first days as a cub reporter at a newspaper, and it was what had made him a legend at the magazine.

Getting the story was a game—a game he played damn well.

Sam crossed her arms over her chest and stared at him. "Ever since you arrived here, I've been trying to figure you out. Aunt Ginny would tell me that if I had any common sense at all, I'd keep my mouth shut, but I've never been very good at that."

He had turned toward her, and when they'd both been reading the story on his computer, the distance between them had closed. Now Flynn found himself watching that mouth. A sassy mouth, indeed. "And I suppose you're about to tell me exactly what you think of me? Point out all my faults?"

"You do have a few." She inhaled, and the *V* of her sweater peeked open just enough to peak his desire.

She had more than a sassy mouth, that was for sure. He reached out and tipped her chin upward. "What if I do the same for you?"

She swallowed, but held his gaze. Desire burned in his veins, pounding an insistent call in his brain. Everything within him wanted to kiss her, take her in his arms, end this torturous curiosity about what she'd feel like. Taste like.

And yet, at the same time, the reporter side of him tried to shush that desire, told him to take advantage of the moment, to use it to exploit the vulnerable moment.

"I'm not the one going around with a chip the size of Ohio on my shoulder," she said.

"Maybe I have a good reason for that chip."

"At Christmas? No one has a good reason to be grumpy at Christmas."

He released her jaw. "Some people do."

The clock above them ticked, one second, two. Three. Then Sam's voice, as quiet as snow falling. "Why?"

The clock got in another four ticks before Flynn answered. "Let's just say I never stayed in one place long enough for Santa to find me."

"Why?"

A one-word question. One that, in normal conversation, might have prompted a heartfelt discussion. Some big sharing moment over a couple cups of coffee and a slice of streusel. But Flynn wasn't a coffee-and-streusel kind of guy. He hadn't done show-and-tell in first grade, and he wasn't going to do it now.

The oven timer buzzed, announcing another batch of cookies was done. And so was this conversation. Somehow it had gotten turned around, and Flynn was off his game, off his center of gravity. He needed to retreat and regroup.

"The story is about you, not me," Flynn said. "When you get a job as a reporter, then you get to ask the questions."

Without bothering to pack it in the bag, he picked up his laptop, yanked the cord out of the outlet and headed out of the warm and cozy shop. And into a biting cold, the kind he knew as well as his own name.

This was the world where Flynn found comfort, not the one he'd just left.

Today her grandmother thought she was the maid.

Sam told herself not to be disappointed. Every time she drove over to Heritage Nursing Home, she steeled herself for that light of confusion in Joy Barnett's eyes, that "Do I know you?" greeting instead of the hugs and love Sam craved like oxygen.

And every time disappointment hit her like a snowplow.

"Have you cleaned the bathroom?" Joy asked. "I'm afraid I made a mess of the sink when I washed my face. I'm sorry."

Sam worked up a smile. "Yes, I cleaned it."

It took all Sam had not to release the sigh in her throat. How she wanted things to change, to turn back the clock. There used to be days when her grandmother had recognized her, before the Alzheimer's had robbed her grandmother of the very joy that she had been named for. The smiles of recognition, the friendships, the family members, and most of all the memories. It was as if she'd become a disconnected boat, floating alone in a vast ocean with no recognizable land, no horizon.

So Sam had, with reluctance, finally put Grandma Joy into Heritage Nursing Home. The care there was good, but Sam had visited another, much more expensive facility several miles away from Riverbend. The bakery simply didn't make enough money, at least with a single location, to pay for Grandma Joy's care at the other facility, one that boasted a special Alzheimer's treatment center with a nostalgic setting, an aromatherapy program and several hands-on patient involvement programs designed to help stimulate memory and brain activity. It might not bring her grandmother back to who she used to be, but Sam hoped the other facility would give her grandmother a better quality of life than Heritage Nursing Home, which was nice, but offered none of those specialized care options.

After all Grandma Joy had done for Sam, from taking her in as a child to raising her with the kind of love that could only be called a gift, Sam would do anything to make the rest of Joy's years happy, stress-free and as wonderful as possible. There might not be any way to bring back the grandmother she remembered, but if this other center could help ease the fearful world of unfamiliarity that Joy endured, then Sam would sacrifice anything to bring that to the woman she considered almost a mother.

Including living her own life. For a while longer.

Grandma Joy looked at Sam expectantly, as if she thought

Sam might whip out a broom and start sweeping the floor. Sam held out a box. "Here, I brought you something."

Joy took the white container and beamed. "Oh, aren't you sweet." She flipped open the lid and peeked inside. "How did you know these were my favorite?"

Sam's smile faltered. Her throat burned. "Your granddaughter told me."

Grandma Joy looked up, a coconut macaroon in her hand. "My granddaughter? I have a granddaughter?"

Sam nodded. Tears blurred her vision. "Her name is Samantha."

Joy repeated the name softly, then thought for a moment. "Samantha, of course. But Sam's just a baby. She can't hardly talk, so she can't tell you about my favorite cookies, silly. She is the cutest thing, though. Everyone who meets her just loves her. She comes to the bakery with me every day." She leaned forward. "Did I tell you I own a bakery?"

"Yes, you did."

"My husband and I started it when we first got married. So much work, but oh, we've had a lot of fun. Sam loves being there, she really does. She's my little helper. Someday, Sam and I are going to run it together." Joy sat back in the rose-patterned armchair. As her thoughts drifted, her gaze drifted out the window, to the snow-covered grounds. The white flakes glistened like crystals, hung in long strings of diamonds from the trees. She sighed. "That will be a wonderful day."

"Yes," Sam said, closing her eyes, because it was too painful to look at the same view as her grandmother, "it will."

Sam Barnett was leaving something out of her personal recipe. Flynn had rewritten the article into one more closely resembling the kind he normally wrote—where that poetic thing had come from last night, he had no idea—and realized not all the whys had been answered. There was still something, he wasn't sure what, that he needed to know. But the bulldog in him knew he'd yet to find that missing piece.

He had to dig deeper. Keep pawing at her, until he got her to expose those personal bits that would give his article the meat it needed. The kind of tidbits *Food Lovers'* readers ate like candy.

It was, after all, what he was known for. What would put him right back on top. Then why had he hesitated? Normally, he did his interviews, in and out in a day, two at most. He never lingered. Never let a subject rattle him like she had last night.

Damn it, get a hold of yourself. Get the story, and get out of town.

Flynn rose, stretching the kinks out of his back he'd picked up from sitting in the uncomfortable wooden chair at the tiny desk in his room. He crossed to the window and parted the lacy curtains. Outside, snow had started to fall.

Again.

Where the hell was he? Nome, Alaska? For Pete's sake, all it did was snow here.

He pulled on his coat, and hurried downstairs. Betsy, who was sitting behind the piano in the front parlor, tried to talk him into joining the out-of-tune sing-along with the other guests, but Flynn waved a goodbye and headed out of the bed and breakfast, turning up his collar against the blast of cold and ice. By the time he made it to Earl's garage, his shoes and socks were soaked through, and his toes had become ten Popsicles.

"Well, howdy-ho," Earl said when Flynn entered the concrete-and-brick structure. He had on his plaid earflap hat and a thick Carhartt jacket. "What are you doing here?"

"Picking up my car."

"Now why would you want to do that?"

"So I can go back to Boston." First making a side trip, but he didn't share that information with Earl.

"Tomorrow is Christmas Eve," Earl said. "You got family in Boston?"

Flynn bit back his impatience at the change in subject. By now, he'd learned the only way to get a straight answer out of the auto mechanic was to take the Crazy Eights route. "All I have back there is an apartment and a doorman."

"A doorman?" Earl thought about that for a second. "Can't say I've ever heard of anyone having their doorman over for Christmas mornin'. He must be really good at opening your door."

Flynn sighed. This was going nowhere. "My car?"

"Oh, that. The part's on order."

"It hasn't arrived yet?"

"Oh, it arrived." Earl scratched under one earflap.

"And?"

"And I sent it back."

Flynn sighed again, this time longer and louder. "Why would you do that?"

"Because I'm getting old. Forgot my glasses on Tuesday."

Flynn resisted the urge to scream in frustration. "And what would that have to do with my car?"

"Made me order the wrong part. I got my two's all mixed up with my seven's. But don't you worry," Earl said, patting his breast pocket, "I brought my glasses today. So you'll be all set to leave by Friday at the latest."

"Can't you fix it now?"

"Nope. Gotta go work the tree lot at the Methodist church." Earl patted his hat down farther on the top of his head, then strode out of the shop, waving at Flynn to follow. "The ladies' bingo group is coming by at three to get their trees, and they're counting on my muscles to help them out. I can't be late."

Earl strode off, leaving Flynn stuck. He should have been

mad. Should have pitched a fit, threatened to sue or have his car towed to another garage. He could have done any of the above.

But he didn't. For some reason, he wasn't as stressed about the missing part as he should have been. He chalked it up to still needing more information from Sam.

As his path carried him toward the bakery again, something pretty damned close to anticipation rose in his chest. If there was one thing Flynn needed from Santa this year, it was a renewed dose of his reporter's objectivity.

CHAPTER SEVEN

A PAY PHONE.

Who'd have thought those things still existed?

Flynn's hand rested on the receiver. Stumbling upon the phone on his way to the bakery had taken him by surprise. In his opposite hand, he jingled several coins, and debated. Finally, he picked up the phone, dropped in several quarters and began to dial. He made it through nine of the ten digits that would connect him to Liam's dorm room before he hung up.

It had to be this town that had him feeling so sentimental. Especially considering he was surrounded by so much Christmas spirit, it was like being in the company of a woman wearing too much perfume. Even the pay phone was wrapped in garland, a little red bow hanging from the handle. That must be what had him thinking of mending fences so broken down, it would take a fleet of cement trucks to build them up again.

Would Liam see him when he arrived in town this week? Assuming, that was, that his car ever got fixed. Or would Liam slam the door in his face? Maybe it was better not to know.

The change dropped to the bottom of the phone. Flynn dug it out of the slot and redeposited the coins, then added some more change to reach his editor at *Food Lovers* magazine.

But while he waited for the four dollars in quarters to

connect him, he realized the money would have been better spent on a lifetime supply of candy canes. At least then he could have used them to sweeten Tony Reynolds up—

Because at this point he could use every tool in Santa's arsenal to assuage the inevitable storm that was about to come.

"Where the hell is that bakery piece?" Tony Reynolds barked into the phone. "We held the damned issue to get this piece in there because you promised to get it to me, remember? Or did you lose your brain back in June, too?"

Flynn winced. Even now, he couldn't tell Tony why he had walked out in the middle of the interview of the year, ticking off a celebrity chef. It was intended to be the cover story for the magazine, one they had advertised for the last three months, a coup that Tony had worked his butt off to finesse, promising the celebrity chef everything from a lifetime subscription to the magazine to a limo ride to the interview.

Flynn hadn't just dropped the ball at that interview—he'd hurled it through the window. He'd been working day and night to get back to the top ever since.

He hadn't expected to walk into that room, meet "Mondo," the chef to the stars, and see one of the first foster fathers he'd ever had. A man he and Liam had lived with for a total of six months before the man had decided the two boys were too much for the man and his wife, who were busy making a go of their restaurant, and he'd asked the department of children's services to find them another home.

The recognition had hit Flynn so hard, he'd never even made it into the room. Never said a word to the man. He'd made up some excuse to Tony about a bout of food poisoning, but the damage had been done. Mondo had stalked out of the building, furious about being stood up, and refused to reschedule.

Flynn had worked too damned hard building his reputation

to let that one mistake ruin everything, which explained why he was the one out on assignment at Christmas while all the other writers were at home, toasting marshmallows or whatever people did with their families the day before Christmas Eve.

"I'll have the story," Flynn said. "You know I will."

"Yeah, I do. We're all allowed one mistake, huh?" Tony chuckled, calmer now that he'd blown off some steam. "You're the only guy who'll work on Christmas, too. Hell, you *never* take a day off. What is it, Flynn? You got some extra ambition gene the rest of us missed?"

"Maybe so." That drive to succeed had fueled him for so many years, had been a constantly burning fire, unquenchable by hundreds of cover stories, thousands of scoops. Then he'd faltered, and he'd been working himself to the bone to recover ever since. There'd be no messing up again. "I'll have the story, Tony," he repeated. "You can count on me."

"That's what makes you my personal Santa, Flynn." Tony laughed, then disconnected.

Flynn hung up the receiver. For a moment there, he'd let himself get sidetracked by Samantha Barnett. Hell, last night he'd even talked about *dating* her, got caught up in a whole champagne-and-lobster fantasy. No more.

He needed to eviscerate the emotion from this job. Get back to business. Then he could get out of this town, and get back to his priorities.

Sam hadn't spent this much time outside the bakery in…well, forever. She could thank Aunt Ginny's matchmaking, though she didn't want to be matched with anyone at all, but she was grateful for the break from work. The minute Flynn MacGregor had entered Joyful Creations and said he needed to talk to her, Ginny had practically shoved Sam out the door and told the two of them to go ice skating.

"Do you know how to do this?" she asked Flynn.

He paused in lacing up the black skates. "Not really. Do you?"

"You can't grow up in rural Indiana without learning to ice skate. There's practically a pond in every backyard." She rose, balancing on her rented skates, then waited for Flynn to finish. Several dozen children and their parents were already skating on a small pond down the street from the park that was set up every winter as a makeshift rink.

He stood, teetering on the thin blades, reaching for the arms of the bench. "This isn't as easy as it looks."

She laughed. "Is anything ever as easy as it looks?"

"I suppose not." He rose again, then let go, taking his time until he was balanced. "Okay, I'm ready to go."

"If you've ever Rollerbladed before—" She cut off her words when she saw his dubious look. "Okay, so you're not the Rollerblading type."

"Limos, champagne and lobster, remember?"

Oh, yeah. She remembered. Very well. In fact, she hadn't been thinking of much but that since their date—no, it hadn't been a date, had it?—last night.

They made their way through the compacted snow on the bank and down to the ice. Sam stepped onto the rink first, then put out her hand. Flynn hesitated for a second, then took her hand and joined her, with a lot of wobbling. Even through two pairs of gloves—his and hers—a surge of electricity ran up Sam's arm when Flynn touched her. This was *so* not in the plan for the day.

"Okay, so where do we start?" he asked. "Hopefully, it's not a position that lands me on my butt."

She laughed. "I can't promise that."

"Then I can't promise to be nice in my article."

She couldn't tell if he was joking or not. She hoped he was. But just in case, she held on to him, even as part of her told her to let go, because every touch awakened a stirring of feelings she hadn't expected. "First, pretend you're on a scooter. Take a step, glide, take a step, glide. Put your arms in front of you to balance."

He let go of her and did as she said, while Sam skated backward, a few feet before him. He wobbled back and forth, scowling at first, frustrated with the whole process. "I give up."

She laughed. "So soon?"

He swayed like a palm tree in a hurricane. "You said you wouldn't let me—"

She caught him just before he fell, the two of them colliding together in that close—very, very close—position of the dancing he had mentioned last night. Hyperawareness pulsed through her, and she tried to pull back, but Flynn's balance still depended on her, and she found her body fitting into the crook of his, as naturally as a missing puzzle piece.

"Fall," he finished, his voice low and husky.

"I didn't," she answered, nearly in a whisper.

He bent down to look at her, his mouth inches from hers, and Sam held her breath, desire coursing through her, the heat overriding the cold air. "Thank you."

"You're…you're welcome."

A crowd of teenagers whipped past them, laughing and chattering, their loud voices jerking Sam back to reality. She inserted some distance between them, locking her arms to keep herself from closing that space again.

"Let's try this again," Flynn said. He started moving forward, one scoot at a time, while Sam slid backward, her gaze first on their feet, and the milky white surface holding them up, then, as Flynn began to master the movement, she allowed her gaze to travel up, connecting with him.

He was intoxicating. Tempting. Her skate skipped across a dent in the ice, and she tripped. Flynn's grip tightened on hers. "Careful," he said.

"I'm trying," Sam said. Trying her best.

"Do you do this often?"

They swished around the rink, going in a wide circle, circumventing the other skaters with an easy shift of hips. "Not often enough. I love to skate. Love the outdoors."

"You? An outdoorsy girl?"

She laughed. "I didn't say I was Outdoorsy Girl, but I do like to do things outside. Garden, skate, swim."

"Swim?" Heat rose in his gaze, the kind that told her he was picturing her in a swimsuit, imagining her body in the water. Another wave of desire coursed through Sam.

"You must have gone swimming a lot, growing up near an ocean."

A shadow dropped over his face. "I used to. But then I…moved."

"Oh." Flynn didn't seem to want to continue that line of questions, so Sam moved on. "What made you get into writing about restaurants?" She grinned. "Do you just like food?"

"I do," he acknowledged. Flynn began to glide forward, his steps becoming a little surer, even as his conversation stayed at a near standstill. "As to the restaurant business, I have some personal acquaintance with it."

Something cold and distant had entered Flynn's gaze, like a wall sliding between them. Not that he'd ever been that open to begin with, but Sam had begun to feel like they were sort of making headway, and now—

He had gone back to being as impersonal as that first day. Was it because the issue wasn't with her…

But with him?

"What happened in your life?" she asked, emotionally and

physically invading his space by sliding her body a little closer, not letting him back down this time, or back away. She sensed a chink in his armor, a slight open window, something that told her there was more to Flynn MacGregor than a man who didn't want to sing "Jingle Bells."

"Nothing."

"I don't believe you. And I don't believe all that hooey about seeing one too many restaurateurs give up their lives to their restaurants. This all seems so personal to you, Flynn. Why?"

Sam was sure, given the choice, he would have moved away, but he was stuck on the ice, stuck holding on to her. He paused a long time, so long she wasn't sure he was going to answer. "I know someone who chose their business over their family."

"Over…you?"

Flynn swung his body to the side, breaking eye contact. He had clear natural athletic ability, which had allowed him to pick up the ice skating quickly, and he let go of one of her hands. "I'm not in Riverbend to talk about me."

"Does every second of our time together have to be about the article?"

"No." But he didn't elaborate. Another group of teenagers whooshed past them, their raucous noise a stark contrast to the tight tension between Flynn and Sam.

She sighed. He was as closemouthed as a snapping turtle. Why? Perhaps she had treaded too close to very personal waters. Could she really blame him for pushing her off? If he had started asking about her grandmother, she would have likely done the same. "I guess it's not too fun to be on the other end of the interview, huh?"

A slight grin quirked up one side of his mouth. "It's not a position I like being in, no."

"Join the club. I know it's good for business and all, but…" She toed at the ice, stopping one skate so that she swung around to skate beside him instead of in front of him, figuring then he'd let go of her hand, but he didn't. "But it's uncomfortable all the same."

"Why?"

"I'm afraid I'll say something I'll regret. And you—" She cut the words off.

"And I'll what?"

Sam cursed the slip of tongue. Now she had to answer. "You'll write one of those tabloid type stories."

"The ones the magazine, and I, am known for."

She watched the ice pass beneath her, solid and hard, cold. "Yes."

"You don't trust me?"

She glanced at him. "Should I?"

The same group of teenagers hurried past them, one brushing past Flynn, causing him to wobble. "Let's take a break for a little while."

"Sure." They made their way off the ice and over to the park bench where they had stored their shoes. The bench sat beneath two trees, long bared by winter's cold. Before them, the skaters continued in repeating circles.

As soon as they sat down on the small bench, the tiny seat making for tight quarters, the tension between them ratcheted up another couple of notches. Sam wished for someone else to come along and defuse the situation. For the teens to rush by, for Aunt Ginny to pop out of the woods, for Earl to amble by, heck, anyone.

"Listen, ah, I didn't mean to pry," she said, diverting back to the earlier topic. It would be best not to make an enemy of this man. "Your personal life is your own."

"And I didn't mean to bite your head off. I'm just not used to women who take such an interest in me personally."

"I'm not, I mean…" She felt her face heat again. Damn.

Why did he have to look at her so directly, with those blue X-ray eyes? "What are they interested in?"

"Let me put it this way. They're not looking for deep, meaningful relationships when they date me."

"And neither are you?"

He chuckled. "No. That's not me, at all."

"Oh." Disappointment settled in her stomach. She couldn't have said why. For one, he was here as a reporter, not as a potential boyfriend. For another, Flynn MacGregor was leaving town in a day, maybe two, and he wasn't the kind who believed in permanence, settling down.

Besides, when did she have time to do either? She couldn't have a relationship, even if she wanted to. Guilt pricked at her conscience, for even thinking she could. She had priorities. Priorities that did not include a man.

Yet, he was tempting, very much so, especially when he was this close. She could see why women would be attracted to him. He had a curious mix of mystery and charm, of aloofness, yet a hint of vulnerability, as if there was something there, something wounded, that he was trying to cover.

"I'm just not the settling down kind," Flynn said. "And most of the women I date understand that." He draped one arm over the back of the bench, then leaned a little closer to Sam. "But I bet you aren't like that at all, are you? The kind that would understand a guy like me."

"We may be more alike than you think," she said quietly.

"You think so?"

She could only nod in response. The noise of the skaters on the pond seemed to disappear, the world becoming just the two of them.

"Maybe you're right." His voice was deep, the timbre seeming to reach crevices in Sam's heart that hadn't been touched in a long time. And all he'd said was three words.

Geez. She really needed to get out more.

Flynn closed the gap between them. For the first time, Sam noticed how the light blue of his dress shirt seemed to make the blue of his eyes richer, deeper. Her pulse began to race, thudding through her veins. "There's only one way to find out."

Sam swallowed hard, her heart beating so loud, she was sure Flynn could hear the pounding. "Find out what?"

"If you would be interested in me."

He caught a tendril of her hair between his gloved fingers, letting it slip through the leather. "We've been dancing around the subject all week."

"Have we?" she asked, the slight catch of laughter in her voice, a clear giveaway of her nerves. "Or is this…"

"What?" he prompted.

"Nothing," she said, not wanting to voice her greatest fear, not wanting to break the sweet, yet dangerous tension.

The silence between them stretched one second. Two. Three. Heat filled the few inches separating them, building like a fever. Sam gazed up at Flynn, her breath caught somewhere in her throat, as if her lungs had forgotten their job. He released her hair, then pulled off his glove and cupped her jaw, using the same hand that had slid down her zipper. A hundred times over the last couple of days she had stolen glimpses of his hands, fascinated by the definition of his fingers, the implied power in his grip, and now, now, he was touching her, just as she'd pictured, and she leaned into the touch, into his thumb tracing along her bottom lip, the desire building and building.

Flynn leaned forward. Slow. Tentative. Taking his time. Because he was unsure? Waiting for her response? His gaze never left hers. Then his fingers slipped down to her neck, dancing along the sensitive skin of her throat—

And he kissed her.

CHAPTER EIGHT

FLYNN HADN'T INTENDED to kiss Samantha Barnett—he could honestly say in all the years he had covered the restaurant business that he had never kissed anyone that he had interviewed. But something had come over him, and the temptation to taste those lips—to see if his theory about neither of them being interested in the other would hold up—had overwhelmed him.

He knew it wasn't her grandmother's cookies; he hadn't even eaten any of those. And either way, truth be told, he'd wanted to kiss Sam pretty much from minute one. Okay, maybe minute two. And now that he finally had—

The experience had lived up to his every expectation. And then some. Kissing Samantha Barnett was like coming home, only Flynn had never really experienced a home, just dreamed of one. She was soft, and welcoming, warm and giving, and yet, she inspired a passion in him, a craving, for more.

But that would be unwise. He was a bulldog, the one who got the article at all costs, not the puppy cowed by a sweet treat.

So Flynn pulled back. "That, ah, won't be part of the article."

"Good." Sam let out a little laugh. "I definitely don't need Bakery Owner Kisses Reporter in Exchange for Good PR as part of the headline." She traced a line along the edge of the painted green bench. "Then what was that? Research?"

He chuckled. When was the last time he'd laughed, really laughed? Hell, if he couldn't remember, then it had definitely been too long. Sam was intoxicating, in more ways than one, and that was dangerous ground to tread. "No, not part of the research. Though, if there is a line of work that lets me kiss you as part of my job—"

"Sorry, no. I'm not part of anyone's resume."

"Pity. And here I was all ready to fill out a job application, too."

What was he saying? He needed to grab hold of his objectivity, and not let go.

A smile slid across her lips, and something that approached joy ballooned in Flynn's chest. The feeling was foreign, new. "You're turning into a joke a minute, Flynn MacGregor. Before you know it, you'll be appearing on a late night comedy special."

"Oh, yeah, that's me. Flynn the comic." He chuckled. Again. Twice in the space of one minute. That had to be an all-time personal record.

He watched her join him in laughter, and the temptation to kiss her again rose inside him, fast and furious. Flynn jerked his attention away and began to unlace his skates. "I should probably get back to work."

"All work and no play?"

He looked up at her. "I could say the same for you."

"Oh, I play. Sometimes."

"When?" He moved closer to her, ignoring the warning bells in his head reminding him he should be working, not flirting. "Is there a nonbusiness side to Samantha Barnett?"

It was a pure research question. The kind he could use to delve deeper, expose a vulnerable vein. He'd done it a hundred times—

Except this time he found his attention not on how he would write up her answer, or what his next question would be, but on whether her answer would be something that would interest him, too. Something they could do together.

She brushed her bangs out of her face, revealing more of her heart-shaped countenance. "Well, Christmas, for sure. I love this time of year."

"I think it's a prerequisite for living in this town."

"You might learn to love the holiday, too," she said. "In fact, if you're looking for something to cultivate your feelings for Christmas, you could go to the Riverbend Winterfest."

"Winterfest?"

Sam nodded, her eyes shining with excitement, a fever Flynn could almost imagine catching. "The town recently started holding this really big Christmas celebration. C. J. Hamilton does it up big, bringing in all kinds of decorations and moving props. He dresses up as Santa, and his wife is Mrs. Claus. Even Earl gets into the spirit. This year, I hear he's dressing up as an elf and handing out candy canes to all the kids who come to Santa's workshop. That alone should be worth the price of admission, which is free anyway. It's a really fun time."

What it sounded like was another date. Another temptation. Another opportunity to be alone with Samantha Barnett.

And a bad idea.

"It's, ah, not really my cup of tea. Besides, I should probably be working on my article." He slipped off his skates and put his shoes back on, as a visual and physical reminder of getting out of here.

"The Winterfest starts at night. You have plenty of time to do your article and anything else you might want to accomplish today." She took off her own skates, then met his gaze. He found himself watching her mouth move, fantasizing about kissing her again. And again. "You should reconsider. You'll be missing something really cool. Trust me, Winterfest is fun for more than just kids. I love going."

"I'm not much of a Christmas person."

"Oh. Well, it was just an idea."

"I didn't mean to offend you."

"You didn't." She tied her skates together, then slid her feet into her boots.

"It's just…" He paused. "Where I grew up, Christmas wasn't a big deal."

Sam smiled. "When I was a kid, Christmas was the biggest day of the year. My family was total Christmas-holics, and after my parents died, my grandmother did Christmas up even bigger, as if to make up for losing my mother and father." Her smile died on her lips, and her gaze drifted to the skaters rounding the rink. "I miss those days."

"What happened?"

"My grandmother isn't there like she used to be."

Flynn opened his mouth, as if he intended to ask her what she meant by that, then closed it again. Sam regretted saying anything at all. She had done her best to keep her grandmother's condition private, from everyone in town. Not just to protect Grandma Joy, but to prevent the inevitable questions. The visitors who would stop by to see Joy, and be hurt that she didn't know them. The pity parties, the people who wanted to help lift the burden from Sam's shoulders.

No one understood this burden couldn't be lifted. Her grandmother didn't remember her. Didn't know her. No amount of sympathy would ever change that.

So Sam kept the details to herself, told people Joy was happily living a life at a retirement home, and buried herself in her work. Carrying on her family's legacy, living up to generations of expectations—not from her grandmother, but from this town. There'd been a Barnett behind the stove at Joyful Creations since it had opened, and that's what customers expected when they walked in the door.

Even if a part of Sam wanted to walk out that door one day and keep on walking. To pretend that she didn't have those responsibilities waiting for her every morning. To imagine a different life, one that was more—

Complete.

"This Winterfest thing is probably the social event of the year, huh?" Flynn said, drawing Sam out of her thoughts.

"It is. People look forward to it. Myself included." She laughed. "I spend days baking like crazy before it, to supply the festival's stand, while a few people work the downtown shop. We get a lot of out-of-towners for Winterfest, so it's a busy day for all the stores around here." Sam rose and put a fist on her hip. "It's a big deal, for those who dare to go. So, do you?"

One corner of Flynn's mouth curved up. "Are you challenging me?" He took a few steps closer, the distance between them shrinking from feet to inches in an instant. He flipped at the laces on her skates, dangling from her fingers, hanging near her hips. Sam inhaled and her breath caught in her throat, held, waiting, for—

What? For Flynn to make a move? For him to kiss her again?

Oh, how she wished he would, even as another part of her wished he wouldn't.

He distracted her, awakened her to the possibilities she had laid aside for so long. He had this way of forcing her to open her eyes, to confront issues she'd much rather leave at the door.

"I am," she said, the two words nearly a breath.

"I should…" Flynn began, his body so close she could feel the heat emanating from his skin, and the answering heat rising inside her. Then the grin widened, and before Sam could second-guess her challenge, it was too late. "Suddenly I can't think of anything else I should do, but go with you."

CHAPTER NINE

FLYNN SHOULD HAVE put the pieces together sooner. He used to be really good at that. Figuring out what parts of the story people held back. And why.

But this time, his objectivity had been compromised. By his attraction to Sam? By the town? By that one assignment going so horribly awry? Whatever it was, Flynn had lost his tight hold on his life, and that had caused him to stop paying attention to the details.

Until now.

Until he'd returned to the bed and breakfast after ice skating, and Betsy Williams had started chatting up a storm, first pointing out a photo on the wall of Sam and her grandmother, then telling tales about the two of them working together, then finally segueing into rumors about the cookies.

"You wouldn't believe how fast people are eating those cookies up," Betsy was saying as Flynn helped her carry the dishes out to the dining room table and set up for dinner.

Betsy had pronounced Flynn a "sweet boy" for volunteering, having no idea of his ulterior motive. How many times had he employed a similar tactic? Using a nice gesture as a way to get more information out of someone? Never before had it bothered him. He was doing his job, just as he should.

But today, every dish he carried, every fork he laid on the table, while Betsy chattered on, seemed to nag at him, like stones on his back.

"I feel like I'm running *The Dating Game* right in my little B and B," Betsy went on. "Maybe I should open a wedding chapel next door." She laughed. "Oh, wouldn't Sam's grandmother get such a kick out of this, if she could see what was happening with that bakery."

"Where is Sam's grandmother, by the way?"

Betsy shut the door of the dining room hutch and turned back to Flynn, a silver bread platter in her hands. "She didn't tell you?"

Flynn shrugged, feigning nonchalance. "We didn't talk much about her."

"Oh, well, that's because Sam hardly ever talks about Joy. No one in this town does, either, though they like to speculate, being a small town and all."

"Why?"

"Well…" Betsy looked around, as if she expected Sam to appear in the dining room at any second. "I don't know the whole story, but I heard from Estelle, who heard from Carolyn, who heard from Louise, that Joy isn't really living at a retirement home and playing golf every day."

A tide rose in Flynn's chest. This was the missing piece, the nugget he searched for in every story, the one that made headlines, the one that earned his reputation on every article. He could feel it, with an instinct bred from years on the job. "Really? Where is she?"

"No one's really sure because we never see Joy anymore, and if you ask Sam or Ginny, they just put on a brave face and keep on sticking to that retirement home story. But you know…" Again, Betsy looked around, then returned her attention to Flynn. "Before she 'retired,' Joy was getting real forgetful. Doing things like wandering around town in her night-gown, showing up to work at the bakery in the middle of the night, telling Earl, a man she's known all her life, that she didn't know him. We just thought she was overworked, you know? That bakery, it's a handful, I'm sure. I know, because I have this bed and breakfast. It's a lot for one woman."

The pieces of the story assembled in Flynn's head, and he could nearly write the article already, see the bold letters of the headline leaping from the pages. His editor would be crowing with joy when this came across the transom. "You think Joy went to a home for people with Alzheimer's?"

"Maybe. I mean, where else could she be? And that leaves poor Sam with hardly no family, except for her Aunt Ginny." Betsy pressed a hand to her heart. She sighed, then looked back at the photo on the wall, taken outside of Joyful Creations. "Well, she does have that shop. That place has been her real family, for a long time. And you know, I think that's the saddest part of all."

A couple burst through the bed and breakfast's doors just then, giggling and feeding each other bites of the special cherry chocolate chunk cookies. The reporter in Flynn knew his job was to pursue that couple—they personified the kind of happily-ever-after that would be perfect for his article—but another part of him was still tuned to Betsy's words, even as she said something about getting pies in the oven and hurried off to the kitchen.

Flynn pulled his notepad out of his back pocket, and took two steps toward the couple. Then he paused, stopping by the black-and-white photograph of Sam and her grandmother, one photo among the several dozen crowding Betsy's wall. Even back then, Sam was smiling, beaming, really, with pride, standing beneath the curved banner of the store's name. And the woman beside her, an older version of Sam, reflected the same joy and pride.

Flynn's notepad weighed heavy in his palm. He knew where the rest of his story lay. The problem?

Deciding whether it would be worth the price he'd pay to go after it.

"We fell in love, just like that." The couple beamed and leaned into each other, looking so happy, they could have been an ad for a jewelry store.

Flynn had spent his afternoon tracking down couples who attributed their romances to the legendary cherry chocolate chunk cookies from Joyful Creations. The process had been easy. After talking to the duo at the bed and breakfast, he'd simply asked Betsy for recommendations. One chat led to another and to another. In a small town, just about everyone had a neighbor, a sister, a friend who believed the treats were the reason for their marital bliss.

Every single one of them thanked the legendary Joy Barnett for their bliss. They extolled the virtues of Sam, for carrying on Joy's legacy, during Joy's retirement.

Retirement.

There was no retirement, of that Flynn was sure. Every reporter's instinct he had told him so. Sam was trying to keep the truth the secret.

The question was why.

Finding that out would make for an interesting story. A very interesting story, indeed.

"Did you know the cookies were supposed to make people fall in love?" he asked.

"Well, it wasn't a *known* fact," the woman said, "not until the magazine story came out. But now everyone in Riverbend knows. And, all over the country, too."

"So this was just kind of a coincidence?"

"Not at all. We went out on a date, we had cookies and we fell in love."

Flynn kept himself from saying anything about the possibility that a sugar high might have led to a hasty infatuation. He just jotted down the quote, thanked the couple for their time and left their small Cape house. The snow had frozen enough to keep from soaking his pants and shoes as he walked through the streets of Riverbend and back to the bakery to meet Sam. He had everything he needed for his article—

Except the story of Sam's grandmother.

He could, of course, write the article without it. Just turn around, go back to the bed and breakfast, plug in what he had and leave it at that. But it wouldn't be the article his editor was expecting, nor would it be the kind of article he was known for.

Flynn MacGregor didn't quit until he got to the real story. He made a lot of enemies that way, but he also made a lot of reader fans, and a hell of a lot of money.

The magazine was called *Food Lovers* because its readers loved to know the real story behind the food. They didn't just want recipes and tips on choosing a knife; they wanted to know what kind of childhood their favorite chef had, or whether that restaurant failed because the hostess divorced the owner.

And that meant Flynn would find out what happened to Sam's grandmother. He'd want to know—because his readers would eat it up. Pun intended.

Since Sam had agreed to meet Flynn downtown, he stopped by the pay phone again. His cell still wasn't having any luck finding a signal, and calling from Betsy's meant using the public phone in the front parlor—with the carolers hanging on his every word.

So he deposited his change into the public phone, and dialed Mimi's number. On the other end, three rings, then a distracted, "Hello?"

"Mimi? It's Flynn."

The sounds of music, laughing and bubbly conversation carried over the line, nearly drowning out Mimi's response. "Flynn MacGregor, I can't believe you didn't show up at my Christmas party. Didn't even RSVP. That's so totally rude."

"I told you, I had to go out of town on assignment."

Mimi let out a gust. "Again? You know I can never keep track of your schedule."

"I don't expect you to." But a part of him was disappointed that once again, Mimi hadn't paid attention. Hadn't even cared.

Sam wouldn't do that to someone. Sam would have noticed. Sam would have baked him a box of cookies to take along for the ride, for Pete's sake.

Where did that come from? He didn't need a woman like Sam. He liked his life unencumbered. He could come and go as he pleased. No one waiting for him, no one expecting him to make a home, settle down.

"Listen, Flynn, I can't talk right now. I have, like, fifty people here." Then Mimi was gone, the congestion of people silenced with a click.

"Everything okay back in Boston?"

Flynn turned. Sam stood behind him, bundled as always in her thick, marshmallowlike jacket. Mimi, who followed every fashion tip espoused by the editors of *Vogue*, would never have worn anything even close. She preferred sleek, impractical coats in a rainbow of colors that accented her attire like diamonds on a necklace. "It's the same as always," he said.

"Ready to go to the Winterfest?"

Flynn would have rather taken a dip in Boston Harbor than

spend his evening at the town's homage to all things Christmas. But what else did he have to do? Spending a little more time with Samantha Barnett could only help him fill in those few more details he wanted. Maybe get her to open up, tell him about her grandmother without him having to probe.

Hell, who was he kidding?

The details Flynn was interested in had less to do with his article and more to do with the way she filled out her sweater, the way her smile curved across her face, and the way her laughter seemed to draw him in and make him wonder if maybe he'd been missing out on something for the last thirty years of his life.

Even as he told himself not to get emotionally involved, to hold himself back.

Not to make the same mistake twice.

They headed down the sidewalk, past several shops that were so decorated for Christmas, they could have been advertisements for the holiday. A toy store, a deli, a church. On every light pole hung a red banner advertising the Riverbend Winterfest, while white lights sparkled in the branches of tiny saplings that lined the street. People hurried by them, chattering about Christmas, while children stopped to peer into the windows of the shops, their hands cupped over their eyes to see deeper inside.

Flynn took Sam's hand. It seemed a natural thing to do, something dozens of other couples were doing. She glanced over at him, a slight look of surprise on her face, but didn't pull away. His larger palm engulfed hers, yet a tingle of warm electricity sizzled up his arm at her touch.

"This way." She tugged him down a side street.

When he turned, he saw the park where he'd seen the live reindeer earlier. Only now it had been transformed into a mega-winter wonderland with the atmosphere of a carnival, taken to the nth degree. The grassy area was filled with people, and looked like something straight out of a movie. Hundreds of lighted Christmas displays, featuring every image associated with the holiday that a human being could imagine and hook up to ten gazillion watts, ringed the central gazebo, while little stands from local vendors sold everything from Riverbend T-shirts to hot pretzels.

Sam stopped walking and let out a sigh. "Isn't it perfect? It's like every child's dream of the perfect Christmas day."

And it was. At one end, by a small shed, Santa Claus held court, with Mrs. Claus by his side. To the right, the live reindeer was in his pen, chomping a carrot. On the roof of the shed, someone had installed a lighted sleigh and eight painted fake reindeer. He bit back a laugh. "You weren't lying, were you?"

"I told you he was dressing up as an elf."

Earl Klein, in an oversized elf costume, looking more like the Jolly Green Giant than one of Santa's helpers, stood to the front of the small shed, handing out candy canes and greeting all the children. Throughout the park, a sound system played a jaunty, tinny selection of Christmas carols, carrying through the air with the scent of hot chocolate and peppermint. Hundreds of people milled around the Winterfest, chatting happily, visiting the petting zoo, greeting old friends, hugging family members.

"People really get into this thing, don't they?"

"I told you, it's a big deal."

"It's…unbelievable."

Sam laughed. "No, it's fun, that's what it is."

Everything Sam had promised him was here. The Riverbend Winterfest was, indeed, the perfect Christmas celebration, all in one place.

"Let's hit the games first. There's a prize every time." Sam pointed toward a set of dart games, with stuffed animal prizes dangling from the roof. "How's your aim?"

He chuckled. "Terrible."

"Good thing there's a prize every time then."

Before he could protest, or think twice, Flynn found himself plunking down a couple bucks to throw a trio of darts at some small balloons. A few minutes later, he was rewarded with a tiny stuffed Santa, which he handed to Sam. "Your prize, m'lady."

"Oh, it's all yours. A souvenir from your time in Riverbend."

He ticktocked the miniature jolly guy back and forth. "He'd be my one and only Christmas decoration."

Sam closed her hand over his, and over the toy. "Well, you gotta start somewhere, don't you?"

Did he? Flynn stuffed the toy in his pocket, more disconcerted than he could remember being before. And all over a Santa no bigger than the palm of his hand. This was crazy.

He walked through the displays, tasting the pretzels, riding on a few of the rides, with Sam by his side, telling himself he should be asking her questions, probing deeper for his article, but he kept getting distracted…by the one thing he'd never thought he'd find in this town.

A good time.

They paused by the Joyful Creations booth, manned by Sam's Aunt Ginny. "Well, hello there. Are you two having a good time?"

"We are," Sam answered, sparing Flynn.

"Would you like to try some cookies?" her aunt asked, holding up a platter. "The shop's specialty, perhaps?"

Sam shot her a glare.

"No, I'm good. Thank you." After interviewing that couple earlier, Flynn wasn't taking any chances on having those cherry chocolate chunk cookies. Not that he believed the rumors, but—

Just in case.

Turning his life upside down by falling in love would be completely insane. So he'd stick to the story, and avoid the desserts. Yep. That was the plan. Except...

He wasn't doing so well in that department thus far. He couldn't help but admire Sam's curves, the way her hair danced around her shoulders as he followed her away from the booth and over to the carousel, where they stood and watched some children ride wooden ponies in a circle.

"There's something I've been meaning to ask you," Sam said.

"Shoot."

"Boston's really far from Indiana. Did you really drive all the way out here, just to interview me?"

"Well...not exactly."

"What do you mean?" They started walking again, weaving in and out among the crowds, the scents of hot chocolate, peppermint and popcorn wrapping around them like a blanket.

"I drove so I had the freedom to make another stop." Assuming, that was, that he was welcome.

"To visit family?"

Flynn shrugged. "Something like that."

"Do you have much family back home in Boston?"

The fun moments they'd been having dissolved as quickly as snow under direct sunlight. "No." He paused. "Yes."

Why hadn't he stopped at no? Where had that compulsion to qualify his answer come from? Now he was opening a door he had kept shut for years. A door he had never opened to anyone else.

"Yes and no?" She smiled. "Now, that's an interesting family."

"My brother used to live there...but we don't talk." That was an understatement and a half. Flynn could have said more, but he didn't. Why and how he and Liam had drifted apart required starting at the beginning, and Flynn refused to go back there. For anyone.

"Oh. I'm sorry."

"Yeah."

Whoa, there was an answer, Flynn. He could see the question marks in Sam's eyes, the inevitable "why" lingering in her gaze, but she didn't voice the question, and he didn't volunteer the answer.

He paused beside a hayride station, watching the children in line, thinking Sam would let the conversation go. Hoping she would. But when he racked his brain for another topic, he came up with...nothing.

"Older or younger?" she asked.

"What do you mean?"

"Is your brother older or younger? I'm an only child, so I've never had a sibling." She sighed. "I always wondered what it would be like, though I had cousins around a lot when I was a kid. They were sort of like brothers and sisters."

"He's younger. In his last year of college."

"Wow. A lot younger, huh?"

"Just four years. He got a late start on going to Purdue." What was this, show-and-tell? He'd never told anyone this much about Liam—ever. Yet, Sam's openness, her friendly, easy questions, made talking about his brother seem like the most natural thing in the world. Like he had a normal background. A normal family. A normal personal story to tell. Like so many of the ones surrounding them.

When the truth was completely the opposite.

"He's at Purdue? But, that's not far from here."

"I know."

"You could stop and see him for the holidays. The drive isn't too bad, maybe an hour and a half..." Her voice trailed off as she read his face, which must have said he wasn't going to go down that conversational road, because he'd already visited it and turned around. "You probably know that, too."

"I do."

Let the topic drop, he thought. Don't press it. He didn't want to talk about Liam, because doing that would lead to a conversation about his past. And that wasn't a door he wanted to open.

But Sam apparently didn't possess mind-reading skills.

"If your brother is still in school, then he's probably not married, is he?" Then she paused, and a blush filled her face. "I never thought to ask if you were. I just assumed, because you kissed me…"

"I'm not married." They stopped at a snack stand and ordered two coffees to go. "Not now. Not then, and not ever. I'm not a marrying kind of guy."

She cocked an elbow on the counter and tossed him a grin. "What's the matter? Are you scared of the big, bad altar?"

"No. It's just…" This time, he did have the sense to cut himself off before he started opening any more painful doors. He handed her a foam cup, then took his and started walking again.

"Just what?"

He took a long gulp of the coffee. The hot caffeine nearly seared his throat. "Some of us are meant for settling down, and some aren't."

"The nomadic freelancer?"

"Something like that."

Sam tipped her head and studied him, apparently not put off by his short answers. "Funny, it's hard to see you as a nomad."

He snorted. "You think I'm some two-point-five kids, German-shepherd-in-the-suburbs guy?"

"I think…you'd fit into a town like this better than you think." Her green eyes pierced through the shell that Flynn thought had been like steel-plated armor, but apparently, around her, had a few unprotected areas. "And that you're secretly more of a golden retriever guy."

"You have the golden retriever part right." He got to his feet. "But I'd never fit into a place like this. And I know that from personal experience."

He knew the truth. And knew he couldn't keep on walking around this Winterfest and pretend he was part of that world. That he could be some normal family guy, like all the others he saw. Sipping cocoa, laughing, singing. Acting like this was just another merry Christmas, one more out of dozens.

Whereas Flynn had never learned to have one in the first place. He tossed his half-full coffee into a nearby trash can.

"I have to go. I have work to do," Flynn said. "Sorry."

She pivoted toward him. The tease was still in her eyes, because she didn't understand, didn't see what this would cost him. How he couldn't experience this, and then walk away from it at the end.

It would have been better not to go at all.

"Not so fast, mister," she said. "There's more to this than just you not wanting to play pin-the-nose-on-Rudolph, isn't there?"

Flynn glanced over his shoulder at the Christmas paradise. The music and the scents streamed outward, calling to him like a siren. "I'm just not in the mood for holly jolly right now. I have work to do."

Then he left, before he could be tempted into something he knew he'd regret, by a woman who was surrounded by a cloud of cinnamon and vanilla. A woman who made all of that seem so possible—when Flynn knew the truth.

CHAPTER TEN

SAM HAD TO BE CRAZY.

Here she was, walking the streets of Riverbend long after
the Winterfest had ended. Her breath escaped her in bursts of
white clouds, and though she had her hood up and her coat
zipped all the way to the neck, the cold still managed to seep
through the thick fabric. If she was smart, she'd go home and
go to sleep. After all, she had to be up bright and early
tomorrow morning to start baking, and begin the whole
vicious work cycle all over again.

Just as she had every day of her life for the past umpteen years.

But after leaving the Winterfest, still confused about
Flynn's early exit, she'd headed back to the house where
she'd grown up. Once there, a restlessness had invaded her,
and she'd been unable to sleep. She'd paced for half an hour,
then finally given up, slipped back into her coat and boots and
headed out into the cold.

The bracing winter air stung her cheeks like icy mosqui-
toes, while the dryness sucked the moisture from her lips, but
she kept walking, increasing her stride. Silence blanketed
Riverbend, with all the residents snug in their proverbial beds.
Sam loved this time of day, when she could be alone, with her
thoughts, her town, herself. Her steps faltered when she

noticed a familiar figure outlined under the warm glow of a porch light.

Flynn.

Apparently she wasn't the only one who couldn't sleep.

Sam hesitated, then strode up the walkway of Betsy's Bed and Breakfast. "I thought a good night's sleep was guaranteed."

He scoffed. "Guess I better ask Betsy for a refund."

"Well," Sam began, suddenly uncomfortable under his piercing blue gaze, "I suppose I should get back to my walk."

"At this hour? Isn't that a little dangerous?"

She laughed. "In Riverbend? Our crime rate is so low, it's not even a number."

He shook his head. "I didn't think places like that existed."

"Walk with me, and you can see for yourself."

What had made her offer that? She'd gone out with the express intention of being alone. And here she'd gone and invited Flynn MacGregor along. The more time she spent with this man, the more she revealed about herself. Too much time, and she'd be exposing secrets she didn't want in print.

He was in town for one reason—for a story, and nothing more. Tonight, after she'd gone home, she'd unearthed some back issues of *Food Lovers* that had sat in her den, unread for months and months. Sam had skimmed them and found exactly what Aunt Ginny had said—most of the articles were more focused on the personal lives of their subjects than their products or business.

Sam's heart had sunk. Even as she knew better, she'd hoped for something different. Many of the articles had had Flynn MacGregor's byline. The worst ones, in fact. The ones that were the harshest, the ones that had the most blaring head-lines about businesses rocked by divorces, by deaths of a partner or a hidden bankruptcy.

And now, she knew, she'd end up the same way.

He wasn't really interested in her. How could she think anything different? He was using the kisses, using his charm, for one reason only.

To get the story.

He was a reporter.

Not a friend.

Just because he'd kissed her, and she'd kissed him back, didn't change anything.

Except…it did. She found herself liking him, even despite knowing all this. She sensed something about him, a vulnerability. It pulled at Sam, and told her there was a story beneath him, too. The problem was whether she was willing to take the risk of getting close to him to find out what that story was.

"A walk sounds good," Flynn said, ending Sam's internal debate. "It'll let me see the town with new eyes."

Maybe this wouldn't be such a bad idea after all. Perhaps if she showed him a softer, quieter side of town, he'd feature Riverbend in his article—and not her.

Uh-huh. And maybe she was just some naive country bumpkin, after all.

Flynn rose, buttoned his coat tighter against the cold, then hurried down the stairs. "Promise not to drag me to any hometown festivals? Or force me to ooh and ahh over the decorations?"

Sam crossed her heart. "Scout's honor."

A slight smile played on his lips. "Were you ever a Girl Scout?"

"Four years. I had to drop out because I needed to help in the bakery after school." They began to walk, falling into stride together. The town was silent, save for the occasional car or barking dog. Beneath their feet, snow crunched like cornflakes in a cereal bowl. "How about you? Were you ever in Boy Scouts?"

"No. I never…had time."

The pause in the middle of the sentence made her wonder. What was he leaving out? But he didn't seem inclined to share, and she couldn't badger him when she didn't want him to do the same to her, so she let it go.

Just as he had at the Winterfest, Flynn's hand dropped down and sought hers again, and he held onto her as they walked. It seemed so normal, so wonderful, and yet, she tried not to enjoy the feeling, tried to remind herself that he wasn't staying and she didn't have time for a relationship.

And most of all, that Flynn had ulterior motives for getting close to her.

Above them, heavy snow creaked in the branches of the trees, threatening to break under the extra weight. An SUV passed them, its tires crunching on the icy roads, red lights winking when the car turned right.

"I love the houses when they're decorated for the holidays." Sam sighed. "It looks so…magical."

Flynn glanced up at the cascade of lights around them. Had he ever taken the time to notice Christmas lights before? The way they twinkled in the ebony darkness? The play of white and red against shrubs and siding, the dancing rainbow of bulbs running along gutters, edging the houses with an almost mystical brilliance? "They're…nice. I guess."

Okay, they were *very* nice, but he kept that to himself. He refused to fall in love with this town, because places like this—seasons like this—didn't last.

"When I was little, my father hated hanging the lights, or at least that's what he always said. I think it's because he took them down so fast at the end of the year, they were a jumbled mess every December. My mother would be out there, helping him, reminding him that he shouldn't curse in front of his daughter." Sam laughed softly. "But once they were up, he'd hoist me onto his shoulders and take me outside, even if I was already in my pajamas, to see them. And that's when I got to make a wish."

"A wish?"

"Yep. The first time the lights are turned on, my father said, was the most magical time, and he told me it was like birthday candles. Make a wish for Christmas and it would come true. I was a kid, so I was always wishing for a toy." Sam's smile faltered. "If I'd known…I would have wished for something else."

"Known what?"

"Known I wouldn't have had that many Christmases with him." She let out a breath, which became a cloud, framing her face in a soft mist. "I wish they were still alive."

"I'm sorry." And he was, because he knew her feelings.

She shrugged, as if she was over the loss, but Flynn saw a glistening in her eyes. "It's okay. My grandparents were there, and they were wonderful. The best substitute I could have asked for. What about your family? Did they hang lights every year? And curse their way through the process?"

"No."

They paused at a stop sign, even though there was no traffic. Sam turned to look at him, clearly surprised by his single-word answer. Flynn stepped off the curb and continued the walk.

"Did you live in an apartment? Is that why you didn't hang lights?"

What was with this woman? She was like a terrier with a new bone. She refused to give up on a topic. "No, that wasn't it. I just didn't celebrate Christmas much as a kid."

Sam halted on the sidewalk. "Really? Why?"

Flynn scowled. "I thought we were taking a walk. Not writing my biography."

The winter wind slithered between them, building an icy wall faster than a colony of ants could invade a picnic. Sam's hand slipped out of his and she stepped to the left, not a noticeable difference, but enough to send a signal.

He'd stopped getting personal, and she'd stopped connecting. He should be glad. He didn't want any kind of personal connection, anything that took him from the controlled path he'd always carefully maintained.

Then why did the bitter taste of disappointment pool in his gut?

"So, you said earlier you had some more questions to ask me," Sam said. "Did you remember what else you needed to know?"

Now that the time was here, and Sam was looking at him, waiting for him to ask the questions he knew he should—the kind he'd asked a hundred times before—

Flynn hesitated.

"Let's not talk business tonight. Let's just enjoy the walk."

She laughed, the sound as refreshing as lemonade on a hot summer day. "The intrepid reporter, getting sentimental? Dare I think the Winterfest actually got to you?"

No. *She'd* gotten to him. Every time he should be thinking about his job, he thought about kissing her. Every time he thought he was focused, he got distracted. And right now, when he was supposed to be taking the actions that would put his career back on top, everything within him started to rebel. For a man like Flynn, who lived life on a leash, that could only mean trouble.

"We have time anyway. It turns out my car won't be ready for another day or two." He thumbed in the general direction of Earl's shop. "So it looks like I'm stuck here."

She let out another little laugh. "You make it sound like you've been sentenced to a chain gang."

"Nah. Just Alcatraz."

She pressed a hand to her chest. "Flynn MacGregor, did you just make another joke?"

He grinned. "Not on purpose."

Flynn didn't know how they had done it, but their path had taken them to the park where the Winterfest had been held. On purpose? By accident?

He paused at the entrance. The lighted displays—gingerbread men, snowmen, Christmas trees, teddy bears—had all been left on, layering the grounds with silent, twinkling enchantment. The people were gone, Santa and Mrs. Claus back at home, the stands and games shut up for the night. Only the reindeer remained, chomping on some hay in his pen. The blanket of night gave everything a spirit of magic, as if anything could happen, as if, on this night, wishes could come true.

What would he have given to have gone to something like this as a kid? To have been able to bring Liam to Santa's Workshop, to let him sit on Santa's lap, and tell Santa what he wanted—

And even more, have Santa actually deliver what he and Liam really desired?

The one thing neither of them had ever had. The only gift ripped away, time after time.

A home. A family. A place he could depend on, knowing it would be there this December 25th and the next, and that there would be someone there who would hang the lights and string garland on the tree.

Flynn shook his head. Damn. He hadn't intended to think about those days. Ever.

He felt a soft hand on his back. "Flynn? Are you all right?"

Sam. Her voice so gentle it called to him like a salve.

Maybe it was the timing. The darkness, punctuated by the sparkling holiday lights. Or maybe it was something more. Flynn didn't pause long enough to question why, he just turned toward Samantha Barnett and gave in to the desire that wrapped between them as tight as a bow on a present, and kissed her again.

When Flynn's lips met hers, Sam nearly stumbled backward in surprise. Then a wave of desire rocked her, and she leaned into him, her mouth parting against his. Their tongues danced, their bodies pressed together, heat building in crashing waves, even through the thick fabric of her winter coat.

His fingers tangled in her hair and her hood fell down, but she didn't feel the bite of winter, only the whoosh of desire as Flynn gently tugged her even closer.

Had she ever felt this treasured? Like she was the only woman in the world? The most special gift he had ever held? When he released her, disappointment slid all the way to her toes.

"We keep doing that," he said. "And we probably shouldn't."

"Yeah." Though right now, Sam couldn't think of a single reason why. "Not that I'm complaining," she added.

"I'm not complaining, either," he said. "And even though I know I shouldn't, because it shoots my reporter's objectivity all to hell, I couldn't resist." He caught a tendril of her hair and let it slip slowly through his grasp. "You are a very desirable woman."

"Oh, yeah, I'm a totally hot beauty right now." Sam ran a hand down her puffy jacket and let out a laugh. "I mean, I'm a walking marshmallow in this coat and even without it, I'm no skinny-minny, not to mention I—"

He put a finger to her lips. "You're beautiful, just the way you are. Skinny doesn't automatically mean gorgeous. Nor was it your jacket that attracted me to you."

A shiver of pleasure ran down her spine. She hadn't been fishing for a compliment, but the words sent her heart singing.

"Good, because if you were turned on by this thing, I'd be worried about you." She let out a laugh, but still it shook at the end. Flynn MacGregor had unnerved her, without a doubt.

"Do you find it that hard to believe that I'd be attracted to you?"

Sam broke away from Flynn and crossed to one of the displays, silent and immobile, but still lit, giving the town an all-night Christmas picture. She ran a hand down the lighted gingerbread mother, then up and over the circular heads of the little gingerbread children, all of them plump and happy in their wooden splendor.

"No…" But her voice trailed off, into the cold. Because she did. Flynn, the charming city man, who had surely dated women miles away from Sam, finding her attractive, seemed so unbelievable, yet very, very heady.

Silence held them in its uncomfortable grip for a long time, then Flynn came up behind her. "Who broke your heart, Samantha?"

"Is this on the record?" she asked, without turning around.

"Do you think that little of me, that I'd actually put your personal life into the story?"

She pivoted. "Would you, if you thought it would add more depth? Get you on the cover?"

He hesitated for only a fraction of a second, but it was enough to give her the answer she needed. Had any of this been real? Had he wanted her for her? Or for the story?

She needed to remember the truth. Behind every move Flynn MacGregor made, was an ulterior motive.

Sam's heart shattered in that instant. And even as Flynn said "no," Sam was already heading out of the park and back home.

Alone in the cold.

CHAPTER ELEVEN

THE MAN WAS LIKE A VIRUS.

Okay, maybe not a virus, but Flynn MacGregor had a tendency to be everywhere. Just when Sam thought she'd have a moment to breathe without him, he showed up, and disconcerted her all over again.

Heck, she'd been disconcerted ever since that kiss last night, not to mention the one before that, and all the times she'd thought about kissing him in between. She'd gone home, gone to bed, then tossed and turned for an hour, alternately berating herself for getting swept up in the moment and reliving the way his lips had moved against hers. The way he had awakened something inside of her that she'd thought didn't even exist.

The way he'd made her feel not just pretty, but beautiful. And then undone it all with the way he'd hesitated in his answer to her question.

He'd been at Joyful Creations first thing in the morning, which had surprised her, considering the way they'd ended things last night—or rather the way she had ended the evening. She half expected him to get out his notepad and start asking questions, but instead he'd come into the kitchen and simply kept her company for the last few minutes.

Which had set her off-kilter, made her lose her concentration more than once.

What *did* he want?

"Uh, Sam, I'm not here to tell you how to do your job, but aren't you supposed to crack the eggs *before* you add them to the batter?" Flynn asked.

Sam looked down at the bowl, where three eggs sat, mocking her distractedness with their white oval shells. "Oh. Yeah." Her face flushed.

She fished the eggs out and cracked the shells against the edge, then turned on the professional-sized mixer, several times larger than one used in a regular kitchen. Instead of watching Flynn, she watched the dough turn and consume the yellow yolks.

"Why are you working today?" he asked. "It's Christmas Eve. How busy could you possibly be the day before Christmas?"

She turned off the mixer and reached for the sugar, measuring it into a large cup and pouring the crystals into the wide metal bowl. "You'd be surprised how many people have parties and need last-minute desserts. Or want Danishes for Christmas morning breakfast. It'll be busy in here. Though I do close early." She turned on the mixer and began incorporating the ingredients. "Technically, today's supposed to be my day off, but—" She shrugged, as if what he thought didn't matter. Sam turned away, feigning the study of a recipe in a book, before she started measuring her dry ingredients into a second bowl. She already knew the recipe by heart, but used the book as a way to avoid Flynn.

She'd do well to remember their roles. She was the story. He was the reporter. Getting any more personal with him than she already had would be a mistake.

If she did, she might end up spilling her personal beans,

and he'd use her grandmother's story to throw in some human interest angle for his story about the bakery, making it national news, which would spread Grandma Joy's personal info all over Riverbend. She'd seen it happen too many times to other people—they became news charity cases. Sam refused to become another headline on Flynn's wall.

Flynn MacGregor would be gone in a day, two at most. She could keep her secrets safe that long. Protect her grandmother's privacy. She didn't want people knowing what had happened, realizing that Joy had lost the very memories that had once made her such a treasured part of this town.

That wouldn't do Joy or the people who loved her any good. All it would end up doing was creating a stirring of sympathy and a rush to "do something," when really, nothing could be done.

Flynn leaned against the doorjamb, his arms crossed over his chest. "Bet you haven't taken a Christmas Eve off, in…"

Sam began dropping teaspoonfuls of cookie dough onto cookie sheets. "About as long as you haven't."

"Touché." He moved closer to her. "Then why not take the day off?"

She paused in making cookies and studied him. "Are you suggesting we play hooky?"

"Exactly."

"But that would be…crazy. I never do that."

"Me neither."

She stared at him, stunned by the thought. All these years, heck, most of her life, she'd been working here full-time—more than full-time—and she couldn't even imagine the thought of leaving here for no good reason other than because she felt like it, and here she was thinking of doing exactly that for the second time in two days. "What would we do all day?"

Flynn cleared his throat. "Well, seeing as I have two

choices—hanging out at Betsy's and listening to her struggle through Christmas carols or go to Earl's garage and hear his long-winded stories—both options painful in their own aural way," he said, wincing, "I thought I'd see if you…"

"What?" she asked when he didn't finish.

"Nothing. It's a crazy idea."

She tapped her lips, suddenly feeling game. It took her a second, but she put together the elements before her—guy, day of the year—and came up with what he'd been about to say. "Let me guess. You haven't bought a single Christmas present yet and wondered if I'd go shopping with you."

He shrugged. "Yeah."

Spending the day alone with Flynn would be a bad idea. She had enough work to do to keep her busy for a week, and he—

Well, he had this way of disrupting her equilibrium every time he entered a room. Sam prided herself on never letting those kinds of things happen. She was a levelheaded, practical businesswoman who made smart, well-thought-out decisions. Who put the right decision ahead of her personal temptations.

And Flynn could be dangerous if she let him get too close, a threat to everything she had worked so hard to build.

Yet, as she looked at his face, she saw a flicker—so brief it could have been a trick of the light—of vulnerability and her heart went out to him. Then the look was gone, and he was back to his stalwart, standoffish self.

Was it just because they had shared a kiss? Or was it because she thought, just for a moment, that she had seen a kindred spirit in him? The man who'd left the Winterfest, unable to stay around the Christmas celebration, the man who she'd noticed appreciating the lights last night even if he wouldn't admit enjoying the twinkles, the same man who could barely talk about his own family?

Could it be that there was far more to Flynn MacGregor than met the eye? And maybe she had misjudged him?

She thought of the few hints of his life that he had given her, the way he seemed to avoid Christmas like most people avoided friends with the flu, and wondered whether he, like her, had reasons behind it all.

"You need a day off, more than anybody I know," he said, interrupting her thoughts. "And I need to shop. Since you're not very good at taking time off, and I really stink at shopping, the only solution is to work together. I don't know about you, but I could use a break." He took a step closer. "What do you say, Sam?"

"I have cookies to—"

"There will always be cookies to bake." Flynn took another step closer. "Come on, take the day off. For no reason, other than you just want to."

"And help you shop."

Flynn moved a little closer still, his hand inches from hers, triggering the memory of his kiss. "Something like that."

She knew she should say no. Knew she should stay right here, running the shop, baking cookies, filling orders. Except she didn't want to.

The craving for normalcy rose inside Sam, fast and fierce, tempered by guilt that she should stay. But the yearning for a life outside this bakery, doing ordinary things like shopping and dating, overpowered her, and she found herself tugging the apron off and tossing it onto the counter.

"Well, to be honest," Sam said, as everything inside her rebelled against the idea of working one more minute, "I haven't finished all my shopping yet, either."

"Let me guess. Too busy working to get to the store?"

"Something like that," she said, repeating his words. She didn't tell him that Christmas had lost its sparkle a long time ago. When her grandmother started forgetting holidays, when every day at the Heritage Nursing Home ran in Joy's head one after another, like an endless stream of Tuesdays. Without a husband, or a family, Sam just didn't have the desire to shop and celebrate like she used to. She still put up the tree, and made the attempt, but it wasn't the same.

"Yeah, me, too," Flynn said.

But as the two of them cleaned up the kitchen, then left the little shop, while Aunt Ginny offered—with a knowing wink—to stay behind with the temporary workers and cover the day's customers, Sam began to worry that she'd just made a huge mistake.

What had he been thinking?

Flynn could name on one hand the number of people he needed to shop for. Mimi. Liam. Who probably wouldn't even open the gift anyway. Maybe his editor. Most years, Flynn just dropped off a fruit basket for the office, if he even thought of that.

Hey, he was a guy. Gift-giving wasn't exactly his forte.

He knew why he'd proposed the shopping trip. It hadn't been about escaping Betsy's piano playing. Or Earl's stories. He'd been looking for something to fill the day, the hours until his car was fixed, and spending that time with Sam had seemed like a good idea when he'd been standing in the back of her little shop, wrapped in the scent of cookies. The deep green of her eyes.

He could tell himself it was because he still wanted to get to the heart of his story, to find out about her grandmother. To finish those final pieces of his article.

But that wasn't it at all.

He wanted to be with her, craved her presence, in a way he'd never craved anything before. She represented all the things he hadn't thought existed. Small towns, with families where parents raised their children, made a life based on love and commitment.

The kind of life he'd dreamed of, and never imagined he could have. For just a little while longer, before he had to go back to real life, he'd hold on to that dream.

Now, they wandered the aisles of a cramped antiques shop, looking at trinkets he had no use for and furniture he'd never bring to his apartment, not that he was home enough to even use the furniture he already had. He picked up a white dish that looked like it had beads imbedded in the edge, then set it down again. Fingered the fringe on the edge of a lamp so gaudy, he couldn't even imagine what sight-challenged artist had designed it in the first place—or why.

"Finding anything?" Sam asked. Her arms were laden with purchases. A wide painted bowl, a leather-bound book, a hand-cut glass vase and an intricate wrought-iron wine rack. Everything she'd picked out looked tasteful and perfect, the kinds of things he could imagine in his own home, if he ever bought a house.

"Nope."

A smile curved across her face. "You're totally out of your league, aren't you?"

"Well…" He looked around the shop. "Yeah."

"And I bet this isn't exactly your kind of place, is it?"

"Not quite. I was thinking something more…fancy. Maybe a jewelry shop?" A bracelet or some earrings, he knew would make Mimi happy. Other than that, he had no idea which way her tastes ran.

It occurred to him that he had probably spent more time inside Sam's bakery than he had inside Mimi's apartment. He'd have an easier time buying Sam a home decoration than his own girlfriend, if that was even the label he could put on Mimi.

Sam thought about that for a second. "I know where we

can go. Let me just purchase these. Then we can head down to Indianapolis. There's civilization there. Meaning a mall." She gave him a grin.

"Civilization." Flynn drew in a deep breath, as if he could suck up the city from here. "That's the one thing I'd pay about anything to have."

He should have been excited, but for some reason, the expected lilt of anticipation didn't rise in his chest. Even the knowledge that his car would be ready tomorrow—meaning he could leave—didn't excite him like it should.

He attributed it to a lack of sleep, or too many renditions of "Jingle Bells" ringing in his ears from Betsy's overactive piano fingers. Because he certainly hadn't started to like this town. There was *no way* Riverbend was beginning to grow on him.

He'd feel better when he got to the city. Away from this overdone home of all things Christmas. Back to the cold, impersonal world he knew.

Flynn took several of the items from Sam's arms, earning a surprised thank-you, and a few minutes later, she had paid and they were inside her Jeep, on their way out of town. The snow had started up again, falling in thick, heavy flakes. "Does it ever stop snowing around here?"

"Welcome to the Midwest. Although this month, we are getting a record amount of snow, so you're getting a treat." She shot him a smile. "You're from the East Coast. Don't you get a lot of snow, too?"

"I live in the city. I guess I don't notice as much."

"This storm is supposed to stop tomorrow. And we should be fine. I have four-wheel drive on the Jeep. If not—" Sam looked over at him "—are you up for an adventure?"

Flynn glanced down at his dress shoes and cashmere coat. "I'm not exactly prepared for much beyond a dinner party."

"Well, then, Flynn MacGregor," she said with that laugh

in her voice that rang as easily as church bells, "you better hope nothing goes wrong on our expedition."

Sam should have kept her mouth shut.

Twenty miles outside of town, the Jeep suddenly got hard to steer. Sam attributed the stubborn wheel to the icy roads, until she saw steam coming from the hood. She pulled over, wrestling with the steering wheel to get the Jeep to come to a stop at the side of the road.

"Overheated?" Flynn asked.

"Maybe. I have no idea what's wrong. Are you handy with cars?"

"Are you kidding me? If I was, I would have fixed my own and been gone long before now."

Steam curled in twin vicious clouds from under the hood, spreading outward in a mysterious burst that spelled certain doom for the engine. Sam sighed. "Well. That doesn't look good."

"Let me take a look under the hood."

"I thought you said you weren't good with cars."

"I'm not, but considering we have zero options here, I figure I can't make it any worse." He gestured toward the windshield. "Pop the hood. Maybe I'll get some mechanical vibes from the engine."

Sam pulled the latch for the Jeep's hood, then waited inside while Flynn got out and went around to the front of the car. When the worst of the steam had cleared, Flynn leaned in to look at the engine. One minute passed. Two. She heard him tinker with something.

Finally, Sam climbed out of the Jeep and joined him at the front of the SUV. "Did you find anything?"

"Radiator fluid is fine. But your oil is low." He held up a dipstick.

Furious gusts of wind blew into Sam and Flynn, and snow drifts skittered across the highway in white sheets. Sam shivered and raised her voice over the howling storm. "I don't think that's the problem. Do you?"

"No." Flynn slid the long skinny stick back into place, then leaned farther inside. Another chilly thirty seconds passed. "I'm no expert, but I'd say *that's* your problem." He pointed into the dark depths of the engine.

"I don't see anything."

"Right there."

Sam moved over, until her shoulder brushed against his, and despite the cold and the bulky layers of her coat, a jolt of electricity ran through her. For a second, she forgot about the engine. Awareness of the man beside her slammed into Sam like a tidal wave.

"Do you see the problem?"

Oh, yes. She did. All six foot two of him.

"It's right there," Flynn said.

Get a grip, Sam.

They were stuck in the middle of nowhere, with a blizzard bearing down on them. This was not the time to go off on a hot man tangent, not when she had a major hot car problem.

"Uh, is it that what you're talking about?" Sam pointed at a frayed belt buried deep in the engine.

"Yep. Like I said, I'm no mechanic, but even I know a broken belt is a problem. Whichever belt this is, it's an important one."

The snow continued to fall, building up so fast, the engine was already covered with a fluffy white blanket. Flynn ran a hand over his hair, mussing the straight lines, and sending a spray of flakes to the ground. "We need to get out of the storm."

They hurried back inside the Jeep. Sam shuddered and rubbed her hands up and down her arms. "It's getting cold out there."

"And we can't stay in the car. It's not running and it won't hold whatever heat it has for very long." Flynn flipped out his cell phone, held it up toward the angry gray sky, then let out a curse. "Is there anywhere around here that has a cell tower?"

Sam gave him a smile. "We were driving *toward* civilization, if that helps."

"Well, we're going to need something approaching civilization or we'll become Popsicles pretty soon."

Sam looked out the window. The blizzard had picked up steam, and no cars were on the road. She should have checked the weather forecast before deciding on this impromptu shopping trip. Clearly, it had been a bad idea. And now, they were stranded, with nowhere to go.

Then, a little way down the road, she spied a familiar orange sign, tacked to a light pole. Serendipity, or a miracle, Sam didn't question which it was.

"My father used to hunt in this area when I was a little girl," Sam said. "I never went with him, but I know he and his friends used to stay overnight sometimes. That means there must be a hunters' cabin out here somewhere."

Flynn cupped a hand over his eyes and peered out into the white. "That's the problem. It's somewhere."

"It's better than staying here and freezing to death."

"True."

"Riverbend is twenty miles behind us. The next town is thirty miles south. Either we find the cabin or hope someone else was stupid enough not to check the weather before getting on the road."

"What are the chances of that?" Flynn asked. He took one more look down the road, in both directions. Empty, as far as the eye could see, visibility closing to almost nothing. "Well, you told me to be up for an adventure. I guess this is it."

CHAPTER TWELVE

IT TOOK THEM CLOSE to an hour to find the rustic cabin, nestled deep in the woods off the highway. By that time, Flynn's shoes were ruined, and the snow had soaked through his gabardine pants, all the way to his knees. His coat, which had seemed warm enough for the season when he bought it, turned out to be little protection against the biting winter wind.

But then again, when he'd bought the cashmere coat, it hadn't been with the intention of traipsing through the woods, searching for a hunters' cabin.

Sam was better prepared for the weather, in her thick parka and boots. Still, her face was red and she looked ready to collapse by the time they spied the small wood structure.

"Finally," Sam said, the word escaping with a cloud of breath. She hurried forward, pumping her arms to help her navigate the deep snow. "I can feel the heat already."

He grabbed her sleeve. "Wait. We should gather some dry wood so we can start a fire."

Sam drew up short. "Of course. I can't believe I didn't think of that. Maybe there will be some over there—"

"No. You go inside and I'll get the wood." He gestured toward the cabin.

She gave him a dubious look. "You are hardly dressed to go gallivanting through the forest looking for firewood."

"I'm not letting you go gallivanting through the forest, either," Flynn said as they continued through the woods, stopping when they reached the stoop of the cabin—if the few slats of wood under a one-foot overhang could even be called a stoop.

"Oh, I get it. This is you playing the gentleman. I'm supposed to wait inside, because I'm the girl, is that it?"

"Well…yeah."

"I can take care of myself."

"I have no doubt that you can. And that I can take care of you, too." This woman could sure be stubborn when she wanted to be. It was probably what made her such a good business owner, what had gotten her through those difficult years when she was young, but damn it, he wasn't going to let her go running off in the woods alone.

Sam laughed. "You, take care of me? I probably have more survival skills in my left foot than you have in your—"

He put a finger to her lips, and when he did, he became acutely aware that they were alone in the woods. That it had been twelve hours since he'd kissed her. And how very much he wanted to kiss her again. "You don't know me as well as you think you do. So why don't you go inside, and let me do this?"

She considered him for a long moment, then shrugged concession. "Do you want my boots?"

He grinned. "I think your feet are just a bit smaller than mine."

"All the more reason why I—"

"I'm not arguing this." He'd take care of her whether she liked it or not, not out of some macho need to be the guy, but because she was the kind of woman who deserved to have a man take care of her—and the first woman to tell him she didn't. Flynn reached forward and pulled open the cabin door.

The outside light spilled into the cabin, illuminating part of the interior. "Let's go inside, and I'll light a candle or something for you, then I can go looking for firewood."

Sam started to laugh.

"What's so funny?"

"Apparently, you don't have to go far, Superman." She pointed inside the small, musty building. Against the wall, a pile of wood had been stacked in a pyramid. "But at least I know you would have taken care of me, if I needed you to."

He would have, even if he'd had to go back into the woods barefoot, but he didn't say that. She might be great at the helm of her bakery, but out here, he knew what to do.

"Well, that's a start. I'll get a fire going, then load us up, in case we're stuck here for a while." Flynn stomped the snow off his shoes, then crossed to the fireplace. He rubbed his hands together to bring some feeling back into his fingers, then laid the kindling in the cold cavern. Flynn found a box of matches on the mantel, and a few moments later had a tiny flame licking at the edges of the small sticks.

He kept his back to Sam, feeding the flame, one piece of wood at a time. It was far easier to do that than to consider the fire brewing behind him.

One he hadn't counted on when he'd first arrived in Riverbend. One he hadn't counted on at all.

It wasn't the flames that had Sam amazed so much as how fast Flynn MacGregor coaxed them from the wood. Of all the people she would have listed as least likely to be able to build a fire, he would have topped the list. And yet, here he was, stoking the fire and building it gradually, like he'd been a Boy Scout all his life.

Flynn MacGregor. The same man who'd walked into Riverbend wearing expensive leather shoes and a cashmere

coat. The one who'd hated small-town life, and seemed like
he'd never been more than five minutes outside of a city. And
here he was, bringing in wood from the forest, laying it by
the fire to dry, then expertly tending to the fireplace, warming
the tiny cabin so fast, Sam could hardly remember being cold.

Well, it was Christmas. The season of miracles, after all.

The cabin was small, about a fifteen foot square, and not
exactly five-star accommodations. Rough pine walls had been
nailed together enough to block the weather, but not so well
that they kept out all drafts. There was no insulation, no
drywall. Nothing fancy that would make anyone mistake this
hunting cabin for anything more than a temporary stopping
place. A kitchen table and two chairs sat on one end of the
single-room cabin, and a threadbare cushion covered a log-
framed couch on the other. Against the far wall, a set of bunk
beds with plastic mattresses, apparently made for sleeping
bags instead of fine linens, waited for weary hunters. In the
kitchen, a shelf of canned goods sat beside two pots and a
couple of spoons. Sam suspected she wouldn't find much
more than a few forks and knives in the single drawer beside
a rudimentary dry sink.

As Flynn worked on the fire, she grabbed a few jarred
candles from the shelf, then lit them and set them around the
room. She also found a hurricane lamp and after a lot of
fiddling, got it to light.

Okay, so the whole atmosphere was oddly romantic, but
Sam ignored the flickering flames, the soft glow. They were
here to get out of the storm. A temporary place to get warm.
Soon, the storm would stop and they could make a plan.

When Flynn was done, he swung the sofa around to face
the fire. A cozy sitting place, just for the two of them. "It's
not the Ritz, but it should do until the storm blows over."

"It's great. Thank you."

"You're welcome."

They were quiet, the only sound in the room coming from the crackling of the logs and the occasional soft thud of a snow chunk falling from the roof. For the first time, Sam became aware that they were alone. Totally alone.

And as much as she hoped otherwise, it could be hours. Many, many hours, until the storm ended and she could get a tow truck to pick up the Jeep. That meant they'd be stuck here, for an indefinite period of time.

"You should come over here and get warm." Flynn took off his damp coat and draped it over the arm of the sofa. "And take off whatever is wet, so you don't get sick."

"I'm fine." Way over here. Bundled up. Not so tempted to kiss him then.

Flynn crossed to her and placed a palm against her cheek. The touch warmed her, not just because of body heat, but because every time Flynn MacGregor touched her, he seemed to set off some kind of instant thermal jump inside her. "You're freezing. Come on, sit by the fire. And don't argue with me."

Sam's protests were cut off by Flynn taking her hand and leading her over to the sofa. She stood there, her palms outstretched to greet the heat emanating in waves, still a human marshmallow, until Flynn slipped between her and the fire and began to unzip her coat. "What are you doing?"

"Your coat is soaked. I know it's waterproof, but that doesn't mean it's completely impervious to snow." He slipped his hands under the fabric and over her shoulders, sliding the heavy fabric off. His gaze caught hers, and heat rose in her chest. Desire quivered in her gut, then coiled tight against her nerves. Her breath caught, held. Flynn's thumbs ran over her collarbone, sending a tingle down her spine.

His gaze captured hers. A second passed. Another.

"What are we doing here?" The words whispered out of her.

"Getting out of the storm."

"Is that what we're really doing?"

Flynn released her and stepped away, bending to retrieve her coat from the floor. "Yes. That's all."

Sam moved closer to the fire, running her arms up and down her sleeves, warding off a chill she didn't feel. Behind her, Flynn pulled one of the kitchen chairs closer to the flames, and draped her jacket over the back, leaving it to dry in the heat. She expected him to join her at the fire, but he paused for a long second behind her, then she heard his footsteps recede.

A moment later, he was in the kitchen, going through the canned goods, pulling one after another off the shelves until finding whatever he was looking for.

Sam remained where she was, trying to calm the turbulent waters in her gut. What was it with this man? Was it just that he was a stranger? A sexy city guy who offered something new and different? Or had she simply been cooped up with that mixer too long?

Every time she was near him, she forgot the hundreds of reasons she shouldn't get involved with him. Most of all, she forgot reason number one. When Flynn drew near, when his gaze captured hers, she lost track of her goals—with the business, this article, her future, her family—and that was reason enough not to get distracted by him.

Flynn brushed past her, a pot in one hand, and a long-handled contraption in the other. He set up the handled thing near the fire, then attached the pot, swinging it out and over the flames. They licked eagerly at the bottom of the pan, heating whatever was in there as easily as they had Sam.

She watched him cook, stunned, speechless. He seemed to know exactly what he was doing, because a few minutes later, he swung the pot back, took it off the handle and brought it back to the kitchen.

Well. She hadn't expected that. Flynn *cooking?*

"Spaghetti surprise," Flynn said, returning and holding a plate out to Sam.

She bit back a laugh at the sight of canned spaghetti topped with crushed saltines. "You are very inventive, Mr. MacGregor. I had no idea you could do all this, or come up with a recipe for dinner, based on what was in there."

"Hey, I had to be inventive when I was—" He cut off the sentence. "There wasn't much to work with in the kitchen."

What had he been about to say? What personal tidbits was he leaving out? Every time she got close, he seemed to shut the door on himself. Because he didn't want her to get to know him? Or because there were things about himself that he didn't want to share?

She had no right to criticize him, Sam realized. She'd yet to tell him the truth about her grandmother. Heck, she'd yet to tell the town the truth about her grandmother, the same customers who patronized Joyful Creations every day, and asked about Joy just as often.

Sam thanked him, for the food, but deep down inside, she was even more grateful for the diversion.

They took seats on opposite ends of the sofa and began to eat. The odd dish turned out to be far more appetizing than it had looked. "Where did you learn this particular recipe?"

Flynn picked at his dish, but didn't take another bite. He let out a long breath, then put his plate down on his knee. He hesitated, as if warring with himself about the answer, before finally speaking. "Foster care."

"Foster care? You were in foster care?" Again, another major surprise. Not something she would have associated with him. At all.

"Let's just say not all the places I lived were the best, so I learned how to take care of myself. And sometimes, I was taking care of my brother, too."

"Sometimes?"

"Not every foster family wanted the two-for-one deal."

The words slammed into Sam. She may have lost her parents when she was young—far too young, she'd always thought—but she had grown up in a happy, two-parent home, first with her parents and then later with Grandma Joy and Grandpa Neil. She'd always had grandparents around, a town she'd known all her life, lots of people who loved her. Stability.

She'd never had to live with strangers. Never had to concoct spaghetti surprise.

Sam laid a hand on his arm. "I'm so sorry, Flynn."

He shrugged. "I turned out okay. And I learned some cooking skills."

At what price? Sam looked at Flynn with new eyes. Knowing his past, or at least the little he had shared so far, explained so much. The way he'd reacted to Riverbend. The way he held himself back from people, didn't engage, didn't connect. All along, she'd faulted him, thinking he was disagreeable, only after the story, when he'd simply been someone who probably hadn't had a chance to find a home. To find people to connect with. Sympathy rode through her in a wave, and she made a vow.

A vow to give Flynn MacGregor the best darn Christmas ever. Assuming, that was, that he let her. And they ever got out of this cabin and the storm.

"What happened to your parents?" she asked.

He made a face, as if he didn't want to talk about the subject, then let out a long breath. "I've never talked to anyone, besides Liam, about my childhood."

"Oh." She didn't know if that meant he didn't want her to

ask, or if he meant the opposite. She simply waited, allowing Flynn to call whatever shots he wanted.

"It's not an easy topic for me." He picked at his food, but didn't eat, as if the twist of noodles on his plate held some answers she couldn't see. Before them, a log split, the fissure hissing and spitting sparks. "My mother was…not the most responsible person on the planet. She never knew who my father was. Mine or Liam's."

Again, Sam reached out a hand to Flynn, laying her palm gently on his wrist. She was here, and she would listen. That, she suspected, was what he needed most right this second.

"She was an addict. Nothing too heavy when I was born, but by the time Liam came along, she was doing cocaine. Nothing could get her to stop, not even getting pregnant. They tested him for drugs in his system at birth, and that was it. We were yanked out of the house, and even though she made a stab at getting clean a few times, it never stuck. So we bounced around the foster care system all our lives. She overdosed before we were in high school."

Sam gasped. "Oh, Flynn, that's awful. I can't even imagine."

"Don't. Because whatever picture you come up with, it's probably not half as bad as the reality. I'm not saying all foster care is terrible, because there are a lot of good foster families out there, but Liam and I never seemed to hit the family lottery. We were…" He shrugged. "Difficult."

"You were traumatized."

"Yeah, well, in those days, that wasn't what they called it."

Her heart broke for him, and even though she knew it was impossible, Sam wished she could go back in time, and make up for all those years. Take away all the rejections, the shuffling from place to place. Somehow give Flynn and his brother the home they'd never had. "And Liam? Did he do okay?"

A smile filled Flynn's face. Clearly, he loved his brother. "He's at Purdue University, going for a master's in engineering. He's smart as hell. And thank God, he's turned out just fine."

"Because you were there for him."

"Not enough," Flynn said quietly. "Not enough."

She heard the guilt in his voice. That was an emotion she understood, too well. "Are you still planning on seeing him before you go back to Boston?"

Flynn rose and grabbed a log, tossing it onto the fire. He watched the flames curl around the wood, accepting it and devouring the bark, then eating into the wood. "No."

"Why not?"

"We lost touch when he went away to college. It was always hard for Liam, and he was younger, so he didn't always understand. I tried my best…" Flynn rose, dusted his hands together. "I just tried my best."

"I'm sure you've done plenty, Flynn."

He shook his head. "I watched out for Liam when I could, but we weren't always together. That hurt him, more than me. It's made him…distant. It's like an old joke. You think I'm detached?" He looked up at her, his face no joke, but filled with the pain of separation, of losing the sole family member he had. "You should meet my brother."

"Oh, Flynn," Sam said, reaching for him where he stood, but he didn't want the comfort, not yet. It was as if he needed to say the words, get them out in one painful pass.

"Everything we went through was so much harder on him because he was younger. I can't take those years back. I can't undo the damage." Flynn ran a hand through his hair and sighed, the sound pouring from him like concrete. "All I can do is make it up to him the best way I know how. Keep taking care of him, but this time with dollars."

Guilt lined Flynn's face, and his shoulders sagged beneath

a burden only he could feel. For a moment, she wanted to reach out, to tell him she shared that burden. That she felt that pain every time she brought her grandmother cookies, a new sweater or simply made sure the nurses and staff had her favorite blanket on her bed. Instead, Sam kept her secrets walled inside. "You pay for everything for him?"

Flynn shrugged. "Yeah. But he…won't talk to me."

"Maybe…" She paused. "Maybe he wants you, not the money."

"Maybe. Maybe not." Flynn returned to the sofa and picked up his plate again. "Fire's doing well, don't you think?"

"It is." The heat was so good, it was making her drowsy. Sam tucked her legs beneath her, and leaned closer to Flynn. She let the subject of his brother drop. She certainly didn't have a right to tell others how to handle their relationships with loved ones when she wasn't taking anyone's advice, either. "Who taught you to build a fire?"

"There was one house," Flynn said, stirring his food, "we stayed at for almost a year. The father there, he was into camping. Loved the outdoors. He took my brother and me a few times, and made sure we knew how to survive." Flynn scoffed, then his voice softened, going so quiet Sam had to strain to hear him. "Turned out, that was the one skill I'd need the most."

"What do you mean?"

Flynn rose, forcing her touch to drop away, and crossed to the kitchen, depositing his plate on the counter. "Considering how well you bake, I'm sure you're a hell of a cook, Sam. You probably would have done a better job than me."

The subject of his childhood was closed. He couldn't have made that any clearer if he'd hung up a sign. Sam could hardly blame him. She'd been hanging No Trespassing signs around her own heart for years.

But for the first time, she began to wonder if maybe the time had come to take a few of the signs down. And take a chance again.

CHAPTER THIRTEEN

WHAT HAD HE been thinking?

For five minutes there, Flynn had lost control. Had opened the door to a past he'd vowed never to visit. Not again. Instead of continuing the conversation, he melted some snow over the fire and used it to wash the dishes and put them back.

But that only killed a few minutes.

Long, potentially endless hours stretched before him. Alone with Samantha Barnett. A woman he told himself, over and over again, that he wouldn't get involved with. Wouldn't open himself up to, emotionally.

Except for those kisses. Yeah, there had been that. And the fact that he wanted to repeat those. Again and again. Wanted still to take her in his arms, even as he knew he shouldn't.

What he should really be doing, instead of spilling his guts over some lousy canned spaghetti, was getting the story his editor was paying him to find. Start probing *Sam* for answers instead of spitting out his own every five seconds like some crazy self-pity candy machine.

"Do you need some help?"

Sam's voice, soft as silk, over his shoulder. "No, I've got it."

"Listen, I didn't mean to intrude earlier. If you don't want to talk about your childhood, I understand."

"Like I said, it's not my favorite subject."

"Then how about we spend the rest of our time here doing something else?"

The invitation in her voice brought the roar of desire, one he'd barely been holding back, to life again. Flynn laid the last dish on the shelf and turned to her. "I don't think—"

And saw that Sam was holding a deck of cards. "I found these in one of the drawers. Are you up for some gin rummy?"

She'd meant card games. Not kissing. Not anything else. He should have been grateful, but, damn it, he wasn't.

What did he want? Flynn crossed the room, following behind Sam's curvy figure, and knew, without a doubt what he wanted. Everything.

He wanted to get the story, get out of Indiana, go back to Boston, keep his job, and—

Have this moment with Sam. To forget that he was Flynn MacGregor, a man who'd never known this kind of sweet simplicity, the kind that she believed in as devoutly as children believed in Santa Claus. To surrender to the same beliefs, and just…

Have a merry Christmas.

In the last few days, that Christmas spirit had started to rub off on him, as silly as the thought was. The possibility that Flynn, of all people, could have what Riverbend offered began to feel…real. It sounded so easy. But for Flynn, nothing had ever been that easy.

Still, he ended up at the kitchen table with Sam, who dealt the cards. He vaguely remembered how to play gin rummy, and fanned his cards in front of him.

"Flynn? Your turn. Lay down or discard."

"Oh, yeah. Sorry." He discarded an ace he'd really wanted to keep, which Sam promptly picked up and used to make her own triplet of aces, crowing with delight over the find. Three minutes later, Sam had trounced him at cards.

She leaned forward to collect his cards, getting ready to deal again. "Your mind's not in the game, MacGregor," she teased. "You keep playing like that and—"

Flynn leaned forward, cupped a hand around her neck, and kissed her again. The fire crackled softly, sending quiet waves of heat over them, but there was already plenty of heat brewing in the kitchen. Flynn's fingers tangled in Sam's blond mane, dancing up and down the tender skin of her neck, while his mouth captured the sweet taste of hers.

Her tongue darted into his mouth, dancing a slow, sensual tango, which only served to inflame the desire in his gut. Flynn groaned, sliding out of his chair to get closer. His hand drifted down, over her shoulder, along her arm, sliding around to cup her breast through the thick fabric of her sweater.

Sam arched against him, responding with a fervor that matched his own. She whispered his name into his mouth, and Flynn nearly came undone.

Had he ever known anyone this sexy? A woman who could make him fall apart with a kiss, the mere mention of his name?

Sam curved into him, her arms going around his back, holding him tight, as if she couldn't bring him close enough. His kiss deepened, wanting more of her, so much more than he could have.

Finally, reluctantly, he pulled back. "If we, ah—" he caught his breath "—don't stop, we'll probably end up finding ways to pass the time that we hadn't intended."

Sam's green gaze was steady on his, deep, still filled with desire. Against his chest, her heart hammered a matching beat. "And that would be bad."

"Very." Though he was having trouble thinking of very many reasons right now.

"Because…"

"We don't know each other very well."

"There is that."

He traced a finger down her cheek, along her jawline, fighting the growing desire to kiss her again, to taste that sweet skin. "And we should probably be thinking about ways of getting out of here."

Sam sighed. "Yeah, we probably should."

And he should be focusing on his job. On what was important. Kissing a woman he had no intention of staying with didn't even make the list.

So, he tried. He picked up the deck of cards, dealt them out again and tried to concentrate on the game.

And failed miserably.

A rock band drummed in Sam's head. Pounding, pounding, calling her name…

"Sam! You in there?"

She jerked awake, just in time to see Earl stumble into the cabin, along with a flurry of snow and a barking dog. Beside her, Flynn popped to his feet. The two of them had fallen asleep after playing cards, the heat of the fire and the exhaustion of the day finally catching up with them. "Earl?"

"You're alive! Well, thank the Lord in heaven. I thought sure I'd be finding myself two Popsicles in the woods." Earl brushed a load of snow off the top of his hat. The golden retriever started running around the cabin, sniffing every corner, his tail wagging, as if he'd just latched on to his own personal treasure trove.

"What are you doing here?" Flynn asked. He had already disentangled himself from Sam, and gotten off the sofa.

Had Earl seen them like that, lying in each other's arms? And how had they fallen asleep like that? Sam remembered sitting on the sofa, talking lazily with Flynn about when the storm might end…

And then nothing.

Earl stared at them like they were idiots. "Looking for you."

"How did you know we were here?" Sam said.

"Ol' Earl's not as dumb as he looks. Plus, your man here told Betsy he was going shopping. And you, Sam, told your Aunt Ginny you'd be back this afternoon. She called Betsy, looking for you, all worried that you weren't back yet. Me and Betsy, we were gettin' cozy—" Earl paused, cast a glance at the sofa, then cleared his throat "—we were talking, just talking, and we put two and two together, and got thirty-one."

Earl had seen them. Great. He'd tell Betsy, and the next thing Sam knew, the whole town would be planning her wedding.

Flynn shook his head. "Two and two adds up to four, Earl."

Earl removed his cap and gave Flynn a grin. "Not when you and Sam are on highway thirty-one, it don't."

"Whatever math you're using," Sam said, crossing to give Earl a hug, "I'm glad you found us. We were worried we'd be stuck here forever."

Earl's face reddened, from collar to hairline. "Aww, it was nothing, Sam. Really." He stepped out of the embrace, twirling his cap in his hands.

The golden retriever, done with his search of the cabin, came bounding over to them, pausing by Sam for an ear-scratch, before heading to Flynn and jumping on him. Flynn looked surprised for a second, then patted the dog. In response, the golden retriever licked Flynn's face then jumped down again. Flynn swiped at his jaw. "What's the dog for?"

"That's Paulie Lennox's worthless mutt. Supposed to be good for tracking, but Gracie there, she didn't find nothin' but two black squirrels. If I'd had my shotgun, we'd all be having squirrel for dinner—"

Flynn blanched.

Earl chuckled and clapped him on the shoulder. "Just kidding there, city boy. I draw the line at animals that climb trees."

"We have that in common."

"See? Told you that you'd fit into this town." Earl plopped his hat back on his head. "Are you two about ready to leave? Or you thinking of moving in here? I gotta admit, it's mighty cozy here. Maybe this summer me and my Betsy…" He colored again. "Well. Time to go."

A flicker of sadness ran through Sam. She should be glad to be getting out of the cabin. Back home. Her Aunt Ginny was undoubtedly worried sick, and things at the bakery were probably insane without her there.

But as they doused the fire, tidied the cabin, and headed out the door, Sam couldn't help but feel a little regret that the small oasis she'd found with Flynn MacGregor had come to an end. They were going back to the real world.

And soon, he'd be going back to his.

"Good news," Earl said, while he drove them back to town, in a pickup truck that had been built long before Flynn had been born. "Your part came in while you were out traipsing through the woods."

"My part?"

"My goodness, boy, I think the snow has damaged your frontal lobe." Earl looked over at him. "For your car. I put it in and your car is running like a dream again. I told you ol' Earl would take care of you. Now you can hightail it out of town. And just in time for Christmas tomorrow."

Christmas.

He'd be heading back to Boston. To his apartment. Alone.

He should have been happy, but he was inexplicably disappointed. Irritated, even. Like he wished the part hadn't arrived. That his car would remain on Earl's lift for a couple more days. What was up with that?

Mimi would have already flown to Paris, or Monte Carlo, or wherever it was that she had chosen to spend her holiday this year. Mimi didn't do holidays—except New Year's Eve, which was an occasion to host a social event, and get noticed by people in the business. Flynn tended to avoid Mimi's parties, the crush of strangers, because they were always more of a networking tool than a celebration.

And Liam? Liam was probably with his friends, or a girlfriend. Flynn hadn't talked to his brother in so long, he wasn't quite sure. The chances of Liam still being on campus tomorrow were about zero.

Most years, Flynn didn't mind that his Christmases were anything but conventional. He couldn't remember the last time he'd had anything even remotely resembling a traditional December 25th.

In fact, most years, Flynn *preferred* to be alone on holidays. It gave him time to catch up, to clear out his desk, go through the backlog of e-mails, and most of all—

Pretend he didn't care that there was no one's house to drive to for a turkey dinner and a slew of presents to open. That it didn't matter that Liam hadn't returned his calls. Or that he hadn't called Liam, either. Because for a while there, the brothers had lost touch and stopped relying on each other because it was easier than connecting and being torn apart again and again.

It was this town. And most of all, Samantha Barnett. The two of them had gotten him dreaming of something he'd never really had—a real Christmas.

He fished his cell phone out of his pocket and flipped it open. He scrolled through the list of contacts until he got to Liam's name. The four letters stared back at him, simple and plain.

"Oh, look," Sam said from her position in the backseat. "You finally have a signal. If there's anyone you want to call." Her gaze met his in the rearview mirror. "Tomorrow's Christmas, Flynn."

He had a signal. He could make a call, if he needed to, as Sam had said. The phone weighed heavy against his palm. He ran his thumb over the send button, but didn't press the green circle.

"Gas station coming up in a few miles," Earl said. "I need to stop and fill the ol' bucket up."

"Great," Sam said. "I could really use a cup of coffee. Flynn? How about you?"

"Huh?"

"Coffee?"

"Yeah. That sounds like a good idea."

But when they finally did pull over, Earl got out to pump gas, and instead of staying behind to make a call, Flynn offered to head inside to get the coffee, leaving his phone on the dashboard.

CHAPTER FOURTEEN

SAM WAS FORCED to go straight home. Earl refused to drop her off at the bakery. He told her in no uncertain terms that it was Christmas Eve and no fool in her right mind worked the night before Christmas. "And you, my dear Sam, are no fool," Earl said. "You have yourself a merry Christmas. I'll get your Jeep on December twenty-sixth, and fix it up, good as new."

"Thanks, Earl." Sam left the truck, and traipsed up her stairs, Flynn behind her. She unlocked the door, then paused. "Do you want to come in for a while?"

Earl tooted his horn, then pulled away, tossing Sam a grin and a wave as he did. "Looks like my ride has left me," Flynn said.

"Everyone in this town is a matchmaker," Sam muttered.

"What?"

"Nothing."

Flynn cast a glance at the dark sky. "I should probably get back to Betsy's. Finish my article, get packed…" His voice trailed off. He toed at the porch. "Earl's got my car ready, so I can get on the road."

"It's Christmas Eve, Flynn. Surely you aren't thinking of driving home tonight."

Flynn flicked out his wrist and checked his watch. "It's a fourteen-, or fifteen-hour drive back to Boston. The longer I stay here, the longer it is 'til I get my article turned in. I could take a chance on getting it e-mailed from here, but the Internet connection is too spotty. So I should—"

"Should what? Hurry home for a Christmas that's no Christmas at all?" She leaned against the open door and faced him. No way was she going to let him go without making a good attempt to get this man to enjoy the holiday. Not after what he'd told her back in the cabin. He, of everyone she knew, deserved more than that. "What's waiting for you back in Boston? An empty apartment? A half a bottle of wine in a refrigerator filled with take-out boxes?"

"I doubt my fridge is filled with anything. I don't eat at home often enough to even leave the leftovers in there."

"Exactly my point."

He thumbed in the direction behind him. "My car is—"

"Still going to be ready the day after Christmas. You should stay here. And have a Christmas, a real one, for once. Look at this town. It's Christmas personified. Where else are you going to find a bed-and-breakfast owner wearing jingle bells, for Pete's sake?"

He quirked a grin at her. "Are you trying to convince me to stay?"

"I'm offering you the deal of the year. A holiday you won't forget." She'd do whatever it took tomorrow—bake a ham, light the candles, sing the carols—if it would give Flynn the Christmas she suspected he had yet to have.

He shook his head, the slight smile still playing at his lips, as if he could tell he was being beaten at his own game. "And what will *you* be doing this Christmas?"

"Spending the morning with my Aunt Ginny and then…" Sam's voice trailed off. She may want to give Flynn MacGregor a Christmas, but in the end, he was still a reporter, and she was still a woman who wanted to keep a few personal details private.

"And then what?"

"I visit other family members."

He studied her. "You don't trust me."

"Should I?"

"Why shouldn't you?"

"Let's be real here, Flynn. You want me for the story, not for me. And you'll be gone after the holiday. I can't afford to have my heart broken."

"So instead you don't risk it at all."

She met his gaze, seeing in him the same distance that he had maintained from the minute he'd pulled into town. Every once in a while, Flynn had let down his guard—like he had back in the cabin—but most of the time, he had a wall up as unscalable as Alcatraz. "I say what we have here, Mr. MacGregor, is a clear case of the pot calling the kettle black."

He chuckled. "Touché, Miss Barnett." Then he took a step closer, winnowing the gap between them into inches. "Perhaps we should just say goodbye now, rather than delay the inevitable."

"Maybe we should."

"That would be the wisest course."

She didn't move. Didn't breathe. "It would."

"And yet…" He paused. "I'm not leaving."

"You're not?"

"I want what you're offering." A shadow flickered in his eyes, like he'd briefly wandered into a bright room that exposed every vulnerable corner of his soul. "I want a Christmas. Just this once."

Resisting those four words was impossible. Even if it meant opening her heart, being vulnerable and maybe being left alone—and sorry—at the end of all of this.

She'd do it for the boy who hadn't had a Christmas. She'd

do it because she saw something in his eyes that bordered on the same longing she had felt ever since Grandma Joy had left.

"I can give you that," Sam whispered. "I can."

Flynn MacGregor had stepped into the one fantasy he'd never allowed himself to have.

A seven-foot Christmas tree stood in the living room, hung with unlit multicolored lights. A string of gold beads draped concentric festive necklaces down the deep green pine branches. Not a single ornament matched. Every one of them, Flynn was sure, from the tiny nutcracker to the delicate gilded bird, was the kind that had a history. A story behind it. An angel held court over the tree, a permanent patient smile on her porcelain face, arms spread wide, as if welcoming Flynn to the room.

Beneath the tree, dozens of wrapped presents waited for tomorrow. For loved ones, for friends. There wasn't one, Flynn knew, for him, but for just a second, he could pretend that this tree was his own. That he would wake up tomorrow in this house and the sun would hit those branches, gilding them with a Christmas morning kiss. That Sam would flick on the tree lights, he would make a wish—

And it would come true.

Damn. He was getting sentimental.

And most of all, forgetting why he had come to this town in the first place.

"I can make some coffee," Sam was saying, "or if you're hungry…"

"Do you have…" He paused. This was insane. He was a reasonable man. A man who never, ever, got emotional. Out of sorts. But something about that tree, that damned tree, had him feeling—

Nostalgic.

Craving things he'd never desired before.

"What?" Sam asked.

Flynn swallowed. Pushed the words past his throat. "Hot chocolate?"

She laughed. "Of course."

He followed her into the kitchen and found this room just as festive as the other. Instead of annoying him, as the town and Betsy's house had when he'd first arrived, Sam's home seemed to wrap him with comfort. Her kitchen, warmly decorated in rich earth tones of russet brown and sage green, held a collection of rustic Santas, marching across the top of the maple cabinets. A quartet of holly-decorated place mats waited for guests at the small oval table, which was ringed with chairs tied with crimson velvet bows. It was beautiful. Picturesque, even.

Oh, boy. He was really getting soft now. Next, he'd be breaking out into song.

Outside the window, a light snow began to fall, the porch light making the white flakes sparkle against the night like tiny stars. Flynn shook his head and let out a soft gust.

"What?" Sam asked, handing him a mug of hot chocolate.

Flynn looked down. Whipped cream curled in an *S* on top of the hot liquid. In a snowman-painted mug. "Of course."

"Of course, what?"

He turned toward her. "It's like you ordered up a Christmas, and it arrived straight out of the catalog, and into your house."

"This? This is nothing. I didn't have enough time this year, because the publicity from that article has kept me so busy at the bakery, to even put up all the decorations. I haven't even turned on the lights once yet. You should see my house when I really—"

He cut off her words with his own mouth, scooping her against him with his free arm. Just as fast, he released her.

What had come over him? Every time he turned around, he was kissing her. "Sorry."

"Sorry for kissing me? Was it that bad?"

"No. Not for that." He turned away, heading for the back door. He watched the snow fall and sipped at the hot cocoa. Perfectly chocolately, just the right temperature.

Suddenly, guilt rocketed through him. Here he was, standing in the perfect kitchen, enjoying the perfect cup of hot cocoa, with a woman who could be anyone's wife, when he was far from the kind of man who would make a good husband.

For a moment there, he'd actually pictured himself staying. Enjoying the holiday. Being here, in this crazy town for longer than just one more night.

Who was he kidding? Flynn MacGregor was a nomad. A man who didn't stick, any more than the flakes falling to the ground. In a month or two, or even three, they would melt and be gone, as if they had never existed.

He would be wise to do the same. Instead of thinking he could have what he'd never even dared to dream of.

Especially when this was his last chance to get what he had really come for. What he needed, if he hoped to make that final payment on Liam's tuition, and do what he'd promised Liam he'd do since that day on the beach.

Take care of his brother for as long as he needed him.

Flynn took another sip of hot chocolate, but the drink had lost its sweetness. He shifted position, and something poked him in the chest.

His notepad.

His job. He was supposed to be asking questions. Somehow, he'd lost his compass, forgotten his focus, and Flynn knew exactly when that had happened.

When he'd lost the tight hold on his emotions, let down his

guard and kissed Samantha Barnett. He cleared his throat, tugged the notepad and pen from the breast pocket of his jacket and flipped to a clean sheet. Back in work mode, and out of making-mistake mode. Hadn't he learned his lesson back in June? He couldn't afford another mistake like that.

He turned around, back to Sam. "You owe me a few answers, Miss Barnett, remember?"

He worked a smile to his face as he said the words, but he knew Sam caught the no-nonsense tone, the formal name usage. Shadows washed over her features.

Flynn had done what he wanted. He'd erased those kisses, undone them as easily as if he'd painted over the past with a wide brush. Leaving this room, filled with so many rich colors, as pale as an old sheet.

He was so tempted to put the notepad back, to leave the subject alone. Just walk out that door and write a nice, sweet article about a happy baker in the middle of Indiana making cookies that had made dozens of couples fall in love.

And watch his career go right down the toilet.

"Yesterday," he began, clicking his pen on, "I wrote up a draft of my article, and when I finished the piece, I realized there were a few holes."

"Holes?" Sam crossed to the refrigerator, pulled out a selection of cold cuts and condiments, then headed for the breadbox. "Like what?"

"I wanted to ask about your grandmother."

Sam bristled. "I told you. She doesn't work at the bakery anymore."

"Because she lives in a rest home now?"

Her features froze, and a chill whipped through the room. "How do you know about that?"

"This is a small town, like you said. Everyone knows everything." A flicker of regret ran through him. Maybe he shouldn't have said anything. Clearly, this was a subject Sam wanted him to leave untouched.

But he couldn't. Every instinct inside him told him this was where his story lay. If he didn't pursue this line of questioning, he'd surely run his career into the ground.

"I don't want to talk about my grandmother," Sam said. She opened the package of ham, unwrapped a couple slices of cheese, all the while avoiding looking at him.

"She founded the bakery," Flynn said. "She's where everything began. I think people would want to know—"

Sam wheeled around. "I don't give a damn what people want to know! Let them remember her the way she was, not as this—"

She cut off the words, as if realizing she'd let too much slip already.

"As this invalid who doesn't remember the very dream she helped create?" Flynn finished.

And hated himself.

Tears pooled in Sam's eyes. "Don't. Don't print that."

"It's the truth, Sam. It's—"

"I don't care what it is. I don't care if this is the story that gets you the big headline." She snorted, disgust mixing with the beginnings of tears. "That's all I am to you, isn't it? That's all this was about? A headline?"

"No. That's not it. There's more to this story than that."

"Right." She shook her head. "Tell me you weren't planning on writing some dream falling into a tragedy? Or are you going to pretend that you had something else planned from the beginning? Some happy little piece? I read your articles in the magazine, Flynn, but I kept thinking—" her voice broke and damn, now he really hated himself, really, really did "—you'd be different, that you wouldn't do that to *me*."

The man in Flynn—the one who had kissed Sam, had held

her in front of the fire in that cabin—wanted to retreat, to end the conversation before he hit at the raw nerves he knew ran beneath a difficult subject. Hell, he could write the book on raw nerves. And he could see, in Sam's eyes, in the set of her shoulders, that this wasn't something she wanted to talk about. But the reporter in Flynn had to keep going. "I'm not trying to hurt you, Sam. I'm just trying to get to the truth."

Sam wheeled back to face him. "Why? So you can get your headline by dragging my family's personal pain onto the cover? Blasting that news all over town, so people can pity her, pity me? No, I don't think so." Sam slapped the bread onto the counter, twisting off the tie in fast, furious spins, then yanked open the drawer for a butter knife.

Damn. He should have trusted his gut. Should have let this go. But he'd already asked the question, he couldn't retrace those steps. "Trust me, Sam. I'll handle the story nicely. I'll—"

"Trust you? I hardly know you." Sam began to assemble a sandwich, layering ham and cheese, spreading mayonnaise on a slice of bread.

The words slapped him. Although, it seemed like he knew Sam better than he knew anyone in his immediate circle. How could that be? He'd been in this town for a matter of days, and yet, he had shared more with her—and felt as if she had opened up to him—than he had shared in his life.

"Nor do you know my family, or what I've been through," she went on, "so I would appreciate it if you would stick to the cookies, the bakery, and nothing else."

Defensiveness raised the notes in her voice, and maybe if he didn't have someone else depending on him, he would have retreated, would have let the subject drop. But that wasn't the case. And he couldn't afford to let emotion, or sympathy, sway him.

"I need more than just the story of the cookies," Flynn said, deciding he had to push this. He had no time left, and no options. He knew what he had for an article already—and knew what his readers and his editor expected. And it wasn't what Flynn had written. "My editor sent me here to get the whole story, and I'm either getting that, or no story."

"What is that supposed to mean?"

"That I'll go find another bakery to profile in the Valentine's Day issue. You're not the only one baking cookies."

The icy words shattered any remaining warmth between them and Flynn wanted to take them back, but he couldn't. He'd played his trump card, and now it lay heavy in the air between them. Her gaze would have cut him, if it had been a knife.

They had done what he'd expected. Severed the emotional tie.

"You'd seriously do that? Just to get the story?"

"Listen," he said, taking two steps closer, "I'm not here to write some kind of mean-hearted exposé. I know you love your grandmother, I know you want to protect her privacy. But readers want to know what happened to her, too. Heck, the *town* wants to know. Don't you think people worry, care? Want to help?"

"Why? The people who love her already know. That's all that matters."

He moved closer, seeing so much of himself in the way she had closed off the world, insulating herself and her grandmother from everyone else. As if she thought doing so would make it all go away. He knew those walls, knew them so well, he could have told Sam what kind of bricks she'd used to build them. "Did you ever think that maybe people worry and wonder because they care about you, too? That they'll want to help if they know?"

"Help how?" Sam shot back, her voice breaking. She stepped away from him, pacing the kitchen, gesturing with her hands, as if trying to ward off the emotion puddling in her eyes. "What are they going to do? Send in their best memories to my grandmother, care of the Alzheimer's ward? It's not going to work. She's forgotten me. Forgotten her recipes. Forgotten everything that mattered." Sam turned away, placing a palm against the cabinets, as if seeking strength in the solid wood. "Seeing her is like ripping my own heart out. You tell me why I'd want to share that pain with the rest of America." Her voice broke, the rest of the sentence tearing from her throat. "With *anyone*."

Tears threatened to spill from Sam's emerald eyes. Flynn told himself he didn't care. He told himself that he needed to write down what she'd just said, because they were damned good quotes. Exactly the kind his story needed.

Instead, he dropped the pen to the counter, crossed to Sam and took her in his arms. When he did, it tipped the scales on her emotions, and two tears ran down her cheeks. She remained stiff, unyielding, but he held her tight. "Don't," she whispered. "Don't."

"Okay." And he held her anyway. She cried, and he kept on holding her, her head against his shoulder.

"She doesn't know me," Sam said, her voice muffled, thick. "She doesn't know who I am."

"And you're carrying this all by yourself."

"I have my aunt Ginny."

"Sam," Flynn said, his voice warm against her hair, "that's not sharing the burden, not really. And you know it. You carry this bakery, this house, your grandmother, all on your shoulders. Why?"

She turned away, spinning out of his arms, crossing back to the sandwiches, but she didn't pick up the knife or top the ham with a slice of bread. She just gripped the countertop like a life preserver. "Because I have to. Because if I rely on anyone else…"

Her voice trailed off, fading into the heavy silence of the kitchen.

And then Flynn knew, knew as well as he knew the back of his own hand, what the answer was. Because Sam was him, in so many ways. His heart broke for her, and he wished he could do something, anything to ease her pain. But Flynn MacGregor couldn't fix Sam's situation any more than he could fix his own. "Because if you rely on anyone else, they might let you down."

"I…" She stopped, caught her breath. "Yes."

He let out a half laugh. "We're two of a kind, aren't we? Neither one of us wants to put our trust in other people, just in case things don't last. Only, you have more faith than me."

"Me?"

"You still live in the fairy tale," Flynn said, waving at her kitchen, at the Christmas paradise that surrounded them. "And I…I gave up on that a long time ago."

"You don't have to, Flynn. It still exists."

"Maybe for you," he said, a smile that felt bitter crossing his face. "You can reach out, to the town, you can lean on other people, and you can try to connect with your grandmother, and try to build that bridge."

"How am I supposed to do that?" She swiped at her face, brushing away the remaining tears. "Last time I went there, she thought I was the maid."

Flynn might not be able to fix everything for Sam, but he could help with this. A little. Maybe. "This fall I did a story on a chef whose wife had Alzheimer's," he said. "It was heartbreaking for him, because the restaurant, everything, had always been all about her. His whole life was about her. When I interviewed him, he didn't want to talk about the restaurant at all. He only wanted to tell me about this photo album he was making. It had all the moments of their life. From the day they met through the day their kids were born, through every day they spent in the restaurant. He'd go over to her room, every single afternoon and flip through that book. It didn't bring her back all the way, but there were days, he said, when she would look at him, and know him."

Sam glanced up at him. "Really?"

Flynn nodded. Even now, months after writing the story, it still moved his heart, and tightened his chest. He remembered that man, the tender way he'd loved his wife, as if it were yesterday. *That* had been the kind of article Flynn wanted to write, but it wasn't what he'd ended up writing.

Instead, he'd done the kind of piece he'd always done. A story on how a dream had died, along with the woman's memories, and the man's inattention, because he wasn't at the restaurant as often as he should be. Because he was with his wife.

How would it have felt to write the other story? The kind he'd written a few days ago in the back of Sam's shop?

Sam's gaze, still watery, met his. "And what kind of story will you write about me? One as sweet as what you just told me?"

He swallowed hard. What could he tell her? The truth would hurt, and lying would only delay the inevitable. So he just didn't answer at all.

"Thanks for the hot chocolate," Flynn said, placing the mug on the counter before it got too comfortable in his grasp. "But I have to go."

Then he grabbed his coat and headed out the door. Because the one thing he couldn't do was break Samantha Barnett's heart on Christmas Eve.

CHAPTER FIFTEEN

"MERRY CHRISTMAS," Sam whispered, pressing a kiss to her grandmother's cheek.

Joy stirred, then swung her gaze over to Sam's. "Is it Christmas?"

Sam nodded, then pulled up the chair beside her grandmother's bed and took a seat. On the opposite side of the room, Grandma Joy's roommate snored loudly, under a red-and-green plaid blanket. Sam reached for her grandmother's hand, then pulled back, not wanting to scare her by becoming too familiar too quickly. "Yes, it's Christmas."

"Oh, that's my favorite day of the year." Joy sat up in the bed, pushing her short white hair out of her eyes.

"I know." Sam smiled. God, how she missed those days, when her grandmother would decorate the house and pour every ounce of energy into making the holiday merry. The house would ring with the sound of singing, the halls would be filled with the scents of baking. Both generations of Barnett woman had loved Christmas, and passed that holiday spirit on to Sam. "They're having a piano player come today, to play for everyone here. For the holiday party."

Her grandmother smiled. "That will be nice."

"Do you want me to help you get ready?"

"Of course. I'll want to look my prettiest for the party."

Sam tried to keep her spirits up, to not let the lack of recognition dampen her Christmas, but every year she came to Heritage Nursing Home and every year, it seemed to be the same story. There had been holidays, in the beginning, before the Alzheimer's had gotten so bad that her grandmother had to be hospitalized, when Joy would remember, but then, it seemed as if the entire world became strange, and though Sam kept praying for a miracle, for a window to open, if only briefly—

It didn't.

But was it possible, Sam wondered, as Flynn had told her, to help push that window open? For a long time, Sam had tried, by bringing in her grandmother's favorite things from home, and hanging pictures of loved ones around the room, but then she'd given up, frustrated and depressed. Maybe it was time she tried again. In a bigger way than ever before.

"I brought you a gift," Sam said.

"For me?" Grandma Joy smiled. "Thank you."

Sam held her breath and put the wrapped package into her grandmother's hands. What if Flynn had been wrong? What if this was the worst idea ever?

Joy removed the bow, smiling over the fancy gold-and-white fabric decoration, then undid the bright, holiday packaging. She ran a hand over the leather album. "A book?"

"Of sorts. It's a story." Sam swallowed. "About you. And…" She took in a breath. "Me."

"Us?" Confusion knitted Grandma Joy's brows. She looked down again at the thick brown cover, then opened the book and began to turn the pages.

Page after page, Joy and Sam's lives flashed by in a series of images. A young Joy working at the bakery with her husband in the first few days after it opened. More pictures of her, as a new mother, with baby Emma in her arms, then handing out baked goods at a church fund-raiser, then, at Emma's wedding. Joy paused when she reached the picture of herself holding a newborn Sam, her face beaming with pride. Her fingers drifted lightly over the image of her grandbaby. "So beautiful," she whispered.

Sam could only nod. This was too painful. Flynn had been wrong. How could she possibly sit here and watch her grandmother not remember the most important days of her life?

Joy turned another page, to images of Sam in kindergarten, then the second-grade class play, then to older pictures of Sam, after her parents had died and she had gone to live just with her grandparents. Middle school science fair, high school awards nights, and so many pictures of Sam working with Joy at the bakery, others at church on Easter, in front of Christmas trees. Joy paused, over and over again, mute, simply tracing over the pictures, her fingers dancing down faces.

Sam shifted in her chair. She was tempted to leave. She couldn't watch this for one more second. She half rose, opening her mouth to say goodbye, when her grandmother reached out a hand.

"This one, do you remember it?"

Sam dropped back down. "Do I remember…?" She leaned forward and looked into the album. It was one of the last pictures of her and her grandmother, before her grandmother had been admitted to Heritage Nursing Home. They stood together, arm in arm, in front of the bakery, beaming. Still a team then, thinking they'd run things together. A good day, one of the few Joy had had left. "Yes."

"My sister Ginny took the picture."

Sam's breath caught in her throat. "Yes, she did." Six months before everything had changed, when Aunt Ginny had come up for a visit, not realizing that things would get so bad so fast later and Sam would be forced into taking over the bakery, but Sam didn't mention that part. There were certain things she was glad her grandmother had forgotten.

Her grandmother smiled. "It's a beautiful picture."

Sam exhaled, deflating like a balloon. "Yeah. It is." And now she did rise, tears clogging her throat, burning her eyes. She couldn't spend another Christmas being mistaken for a stranger. Her heart hurt too much.

This was why she couldn't stay in Riverbend. This was why she couldn't give her heart to anyone else. Because she didn't have it in her to see it fall apart, crumble so easily. Not again.

"It's so beautiful," Grandma Joy repeated, "just like my granddaughter." She reached out a hand—long, graceful fingers exactly like Sam's—and grasped Sam's wrist before Sam could walk away. She stared at Sam, for a long, long time, then she smiled, her eyes lighting in a way Sam hadn't seen them brighten in so, so long. "Just like you, Samantha."

"Did you…did you just say my name?" Sam asked.

"Of course. You're my granddaughter, aren't you?"

Sam nodded, mute, tears spilling over, blurring her vision. She sank down again, this time onto the soft mattress, and reached out, drawing her grandmother into one more hug.

And when Grandma Joy's arms went around her, fierce and tight, Samantha Barnett started believing in Christmas miracles again.

Betsy was singing.

If Flynn didn't know better, he'd have sworn a cow was dying in the front parlor of the bed and breakfast. He headed downstairs on Christmas morning, going straight for the coffeepot. In the parlor, the few remaining guests were gathered around the piano, joining Betsy in a rousing and agonizingly off-key rendition of "O Little Town of Bethlehem."

From the dining room, Flynn watched the group. He stood

on the periphery, never more aware he was on the outside. How long had he lived like this? Outside of normal people's lives?

Living another kind of normal. One that he now realized was far from normal.

The front door to Betsy's opened and Sam walked in, her arms laden with boxes from the bakery. Flynn put down his coffee and hurried over to help her. "I thought you were under Doctor Earl's orders not to work on Christmas Eve."

"I baked these ahead of time. And besides, it's not Christmas Eve anymore, it's Christmas Day. So merry Christmas." She gave him a smile.

A smile? After the way things had ended between them yesterday? Flynn didn't question the facial gesture, but wondered. Why the change?

"But you *are* working, even on Christmas?" he said.

"I'm delivering, not working." She thought about it for a second. "Okay, yes. But only for a little while. And, I had an ulterior motive."

He unpacked a box of Danishes, laying them in a concentric circle on a silver-plated platter. It reminded him of the first time he'd done this, right after arriving in town. That seemed like a hundred years ago, as if he'd met Sam a lifetime ago. Before yesterday, he'd thought…

Thought maybe there was a chance they could have something. What that something could be, he wasn't sure, because he lived on the East Coast and she lived in the Midwest, and their worlds were as opposite as the North and South Poles.

And then he'd gone and driven a wedge between them yesterday. Had made it clear where his priorities lay—with his job.

If there'd been another choice, Flynn would have grabbed it in a second. Another choice…

He looked at Sam, her face bright and happy, her hair seeming like gold above the red sweater she wore, and wished for a miracle. It was Christmas, after all. Maybe a miracle would come along.

Uh-huh. And maybe Santa would just sweep on through the front door, too. Best to abandon that train of thought before it derailed his plans to leave.

"Ulterior motive?" he asked.

"You left last night before I could give you your Christmas gift."

That drew Flynn up short. "You bought me a *Christmas gift?*"

"Well, I had to sort of improvise, and your gift is, ah—" she looked at her watch "—not quite here yet, because what I bought you is still in my Jeep, which is on the side of the road."

"You bought me a gift yesterday?" He couldn't have been more surprised if Santa himself had marched in and handed him a present.

"Of course. It's Christmas. Everyone should have a gift on Christmas. I was going to give it before you—"

Even though he knew he shouldn't, even though he'd just vowed a half second ago to stay away from her, Flynn surged forward, cupped her face with both his hands and kissed her. "Thank you."

She laughed. "You don't even know what I got you. You could hate it."

"It doesn't matter. It's the thought that counts." She had thought of him. Thought about whether he would have a merry Christmas. Who had worried about his Christmas? Ever? Flynn couldn't remember anyone ever doing that. Most holiday seasons, he and Liam had been between homes, shuffled off by the system to some emergency place, a temporary landing, before they'd be off to the next family. But no one had latched on to the boys who rebelled, who didn't connect, fit in with their little blond-haired boys and girls.

The fact that Sam, a woman he had met a few days ago, would go to so much trouble, for him, blasted against him.

He might not be a little kid anymore, and no longer cared if there was a gift under the tree, or heck, a tree in his living room, but to know that someone had taken the time to plan a gift like that…

It touched him more than he had thought possible.

A fierce longing tugged at him, and the urge to leave dissipated. Instead, he found himself wanting to stay. Here, in this town. This crazy, Christmas-frantic town.

"Are you speaking in trite phrases now, Flynn MacGregor?"

"I, ah, think this town is rubbing off on me."

Sam laughed again. "You must be catching pneumonia or something."

"I've caught something," Flynn said, tracing Sam's lips with his fingertips. Wanting to kiss her again. Wanting to do much more than that, but painfully aware that they were in Betsy's dining room.

"Come on in, Flynn, Sam!" Betsy called. "And join us!"

Sam's eyes danced with a dare. "Are you feeling truly festive?"

He cringed. "Singing with Betsy might be pushing it."

Sam grabbed one of his hands and pulled him toward the parlor. "It'll be good for you, Flynn."

And as he stood by the piano a moment later with an assortment of strangers, his arm wrapped around Sam's waist, joining in on "Jingle Bells," a swell of holiday spirit started in Flynn's chest and began to grow, as if the music itself was pounding Christmas right into him. Somehow, he seemed to know the words, or at least snippets of them, to every song. Perhaps he'd absorbed them over the years, some kind of holiday osmosis, and he added his baritone to the rest of the singers. Sam leaned her head against his shoulder, and for those moments, everything seemed completely perfect in Flynn's world.

A truth whispered in his ear, one he wasn't prepared to hear. He loved this woman.

Loved her. It didn't matter that it had happened in four days, four weeks or four years. The feeling ran so deep, and so strong, Flynn could no longer ignore it.

For the first time in his life, he wanted depth, he wanted a real relationship, no more convenience dating, the kind of flighty relationship he'd had with Mimi. She was surely off in some foreign country, probably flirting with someone else, which didn't bother Flynn one bit.

He had everything he wanted right here with him.

Never before had he fallen in love, but he recognized the emotion as clearly as his own name. His arm tightened around Sam's waist, and he vowed that as soon as the song ended, he would pull Sam aside and tell her.

Another set of chimes joined in with the piano. It took a moment for anyone to realize the sound was coming from the doorbell, and not Betsy's feet. "Oh, someone's here," Betsy said. "I hope whoever it is, sings tenor!"

"I'll get it," Flynn said, releasing Sam to cross the front parlor, head into the hall and down to the door. He expected one of the guest's relatives. Or maybe Earl, here to chide Sam about making a delivery on Christmas Day.

But when Flynn pulled open the door, he found a gift no one could have fit under a tree. And one he wasn't so sure was glad to be here.

His brother.

"What are you doing here?"

"I was invited," Liam said. He picked up a suitcase that had been sitting by his feet. A suitcase? Why? Was he intending to stay a while?

Confusion waged a war in Flynn's gut. Who had called Liam? Why? And what had made Liam drive all the way up here?

The tension between them ran as thick as syrup. Flynn knew the choice was his. He could step aside, let Liam pass and leave the moment as it was, or he could do something about it.

Liam hoisted the suitcase higher in his grip and moved forward, making the decision for him. Before his younger brother could pass, Flynn reached out and drew Liam into a tight embrace. "Hi, Liam."

Liam stiffened, then patted Flynn's back in a gesture meant more for a stranger than a relative. "Hi, Flynn."

Damn, how he had missed his brother. It didn't matter if two years or two minutes had passed, whether they were in their twenties or still in elementary school. A fierce love rose in Flynn's chest, and he held tight for a long moment, his mind whipping back to the beach, to the two of them together against the wind, swearing to always be together. Always.

Flynn clapped his brother hard on the back, then released him. He swept his gaze over Liam, who was thinner than Flynn remembered, but still had the same tall, dark good looks. His hair was curlier, his eyes tended more toward green than blue, but otherwise, the two shared a lot of the same characteristics. "It's good to see you."

Really good.

"Yeah. Same to you." Liam came inside and shut the door behind him, then dropped the suitcase to the floor. Behind them, the caroling continued, segueing into "We Wish You a Merry Christmas." Liam shuffled from foot to foot, ran a hand through his hair. "Singing, huh?"

"Yeah."

Some more silence extended between them. If one of them

didn't say something, Flynn knew they never would. There'd been too many phone calls, too many visits, that had been filled with awkward small talk and anguished pauses, and nothing of substance. He cleared his throat. "Listen, Liam, about the last time we saw each other—"

"You don't have to say anything."

"Yeah, I do." Flynn ran a hand over his face, then met his brother's gaze. "All I've been trying to do is take care of you. But you make it damned hard sometimes."

Liam shook his head, and a flush of frustration rose in his cheeks. "Flynn, I'm all grown up now. I can take care of myself."

"I know, but…" Flynn let out a breath.

"There's no buts. You keep on trying to throw money at me. I don't want that, Flynn. I want—" Liam cut off his sentence and let out a low curse.

"You want what?" Flynn prompted when Liam didn't continue. Behind them, the group had moved onto "O Little Town of Bethlehem."

Liam stared at his shoes for a long while, then finally looked up and met Flynn's gaze. "I want you, big brother. Not your damned money."

There. It was out. The truth. Liam needed the one thing Flynn had always held back, kept tucked away. His heart. His emotions.

And what good had it done him? Left him alone, estranged from his brother, living one holiday after another without anyone.

Flynn ran a hand along the woodwork, fingers tracing the thick oak. "I was wrong, Liam. I pushed you away…."

"Because I was a reminder of all we went through," Liam said, finishing the sentence.

"Yeah." Here he'd thought he'd been controlling his life. Controlling his emotions. When all he'd done was shove them in a closet and ignore them.

Liam's gaze met his older sibling's. In that moment, a

shared history unfurled between them, a mental *This is Your Life*, that played in an instant, then came around full circle to the two of them, together then, together now. "Yeah, me, too."

There was no need for words, no need for anything other than that assent. They knew, because they'd been there. Because they shared the same DNA. And heck, because they were guys. Blubbering for hours simply wasn't the way they handled things.

Flynn reached out, and drew his brother to him again, in an even tighter embrace this time, one that lasted longer, and made up for the last two years. "Merry Christmas, Liam."

Flynn couldn't hear his brother's response, because he was holding him too tight. But it didn't matter. He didn't need to hear the words to know his little brother felt the same.

Because this time, Liam hugged him back.

"Oh, we have another guest!" Betsy exclaimed from behind them. "At Betsy's Bed and Breakfast—"

"There's always room for one more," Flynn finished for her.

Betsy grinned. "Absolutely!"

Flynn picked up his brother's suitcase. "Come on in, make yourself at home."

Liam gave Flynn a dubious glance, as he watched Betsy hurry forward, her house slippers jingle-jangling, her mouth going nonstop about the town, the Christmas activities planned for the day, the dinner menu, the local call policy. "Is it always like this here?"

"Yep. And that's the beauty of the place. Hang around for the Christmas carols," Flynn said. "They're the best part."

Liam glanced over at him, eyes wide. Flynn just laughed, and it felt damned good to do so.

CHAPTER SIXTEEN

SAM SLIPPED OUT Betsy's back door. She'd seen Flynn greet his brother and knew she had done what she wanted to do. She had given Flynn the merry Christmas she had intended.

The wind stung her face as soon as she stepped outside, and at first, she couldn't understand why the cold hurt so bad, until she realized her cheeks were covered with tears, and winter's wrath had turned them to ice. She swiped at her face with her glove, then walked the few blocks to the bakery, opting for the peace of the shop, instead of heading to Aunt Ginny's house.

She let herself inside Joyful Creations, turning on a single light. Then she headed to the case, filled a plate with all the treats she never had time to eat, put on a pot of coffee, and when it was ready, she took her snack out to one of the café tables, as if she were a customer.

She sat down, and for the first time in a long time, enjoyed the fruits of her labor. Outside the window, a soft snow began to fall, a dusting, really, just enough to sparkle for the holiday.

The door opened and Earl poked his head in. "What on earth are you doing, Sam? It's Christmas."

She smiled. "I could say the same to you."

"I'm on my way over to Betsy's. I've got her Christmas gift out here."

"Out there?" Sam rose out of her chair and peeked through the window. "You bought her a truck?"

"Hell no. I bought her what's in the back of my truck." Earl beamed with pride at his thoughtfulness. "A new washer machine."

"Oh. How romantic."

"My Betsy is practical. She's gonna love it. You'll see." He adjusted his hat, then gave Sam another disapproving glance. "You aren't planning on spending your holiday in here, now are you?"

"No. I'm going to my Aunt Ginny's."

"Good. You need to do more for yourself. You don't want to make this place your life, Sam. We need you around this town more than we need a bakery." He tipped his head toward her to emphasize the point. "If you see Joy today at that fancy retirement place, please give her my best. I sure do miss seeing her 'round here."

Sam drew in a breath. Flynn was right. It was time to tell the people of this town about Grandma Joy. Everyone in Riverbend cared about her—hadn't they made that obvious a hundred times over? And they'd cared about her grandmother, and would continue to care—regardless of what had happened, and whether Grandma remembered them or not. "No, Earl. My grandmother doesn't live in a retirement village. She never did." Sam paused. "Grandma Joy lives at Heritage Nursing Home, in the Alzheimer's unit."

Earl looked at her in shock for a long moment, then he nodded somberly, as if he'd expected to hear that. "I saw her mind going, long time ago. I wondered how long it would be. I'm sorry, Sam. But you made the right decision." He ambled into the store, and gave her a hug.

Sam's heart filled, the love of the people of Riverbend bursting in her chest. "Thanks, Earl." She brushed away a few tears, but this time, they weren't tears of sorrow, just tears of gratitude for the comfort of others.

"Don't think nothing of it. Maybe me and Betsy, we'll head on over there, see her today."

"She probably won't remember you."

Earl waved a hand in dismissal. "That's okay. Half the time I don't remember my own name." He grinned. "And if your grandma doesn't know me, it won't bother me none. Why, it'll be like making a new friend every time I go up there."

After a final warning not to work all day, Earl wished her a merry Christmas then headed out the door. Sam watched him go, feeling lighter than she had in a long time. Flynn had been right. Sharing the burden suddenly made it a lot easier to bear.

Now if she could only find a way to have it all—a life and carry on her grandmother's legacy, she'd be all set. Sam sighed, then took Earl's advice, and turned out the lights.

Flynn paused on Sam's doorstep, shifting the scratchy gift in his hands to his opposite arm. He rang the bell and waited. What if she wasn't home? What if she'd gone to her aunt's house? What if—

But then the door opened and Sam stood on the other side, a roll of wrapping paper in one hand. "Flynn."

"You're still here. I thought you might have gone to your aunt's already."

She held up the wrapping paper. "Working too much, not enough time to wrap gifts. So, I'm running late. What are you doing here?"

"I came here to say Merry Christmas."

"Merry Christmas, Flynn." A smile crossed her lips. "I think we already had this conversation this morning."

"It worked pretty well the first time, didn't it?" He grinned. "This is for you. It's, ah, not much, because there's not exactly many shopping options on Christmas Day, and yesterday's shopping trip was ended prematurely."

She laid the wrapping paper against the door, then took the wreath from his hands, the smile on her face widening. "A Christmas wreath?"

"I noticed you didn't have one on your front door. There was this guy selling them on the corner of Main this morning, and when I saw them, I—"

"*You* noticed I didn't have a wreath?"

"Is that so unusual?"

She hung the wreath on her front door, straightened the red velvet bow, then turned back to him, shutting the door behind her. "For one, you're a guy. For another, of everyone in town—"

"I had the least Christmas spirit."

"Well, yeah." She arched a brow. "Had?"

Flynn crossed to Sam, taking her hands in his. "I changed my mind about the holiday."

"What changed your mind?"

"Well, it sure wasn't Betsy's singing. Or her jingle bell slippers." He grinned. "It was you."

"Me? How could I do that?"

He reached up and cupped her jaw, tracing her bottom lip with his thumb. "Thank you for bringing my brother here. When you did that, you showed me what was important. That I had my priorities as backward as a man could get them."

Confusion warred in her green eyes.

"I wrote my article early this morning, and sent it in to my editor. Turns out one of the guests at Betsy's had a national broadband connection on his laptop, and we got it to work by sitting in the backyard, freezing our butts off." He chuckled. "Doesn't matter. The article is done, and gone. No going back. But I still wanted you to read it.

Either way, no matter what happens, I'm not changing a word."

Her face fell, and she stepped away. "Just be kind, Flynn. That's all I ask."

He fished the papers he'd printed that morning on his portable printer out of his pocket and handed them to Sam. "Read it, and then judge, Sam."

She took the sheaf of pages, then turned away from him, crossing into the living room. She sank onto one of the sofas, flicked on a lamp and began to read.

Flynn already knew the words on the page. It hadn't been all that hard to recall them from the first draft. His heart had committed those earlier pages to memory, and when he'd sat down to write, the article had poured from him, as easily as water from a faucet. *Visions of sugar plums dance…*

Long minutes passed, without Sam saying a word. She read, turning the pages slowly, while Flynn's breath held, his lungs tight. Finally, she looked up, her green eyes watery.

Damn. Had he written the piece wrong? Had he, despite his best intentions, still ruined everything?

"Flynn. It's—" she drew in a breath, searching for words "—wonderful."

He exhaled. "It's not what my editor wants. Or what my readers expect. It's not, in fact, at all what I was paid to write. I'll probably be fired." He grinned. "So if you're looking for a little help making cookies…I might need a job on the twenty-sixth."

"But…why? Why would you do this?"

He crossed to the sofa and sat down beside her. "I realized that my career didn't matter if it cost me peace of mind. Happiness." He drew in a breath. "Happiness with you, Sam, because…I love you."

Her eyes widened. "You love me?"

Flynn felt a goofy grin take over his face, the kind that made his jaw go slack with happiness. "Yes. I do. And I know it sounds crazy because I've only known you for a matter of days, but one of those days was spent stuck in a cabin in the woods, so that's like triple time, because we were alone so much, and—"

She surged forward, the papers on her lap falling to the floor, and kissed him. "Oh, Flynn. I love you, too."

Joy exploded in his chest. She loved him, too. Holy cow. This was what other men felt when a woman said those words? This was what made them settle down, have kids, buy a house in the suburbs? No wonder.

And what the heck had he been doing all this time, denying himself this? Thinking he was happier alone?

"All my life," he said, "I've controlled my emotions, held them back, because I thought it was easier not to feel, not to open my heart to other people—"

"Because protecting your heart kept it from getting it hurt," Sam finished. "But in the end, all it did was leave you alone. And unhappy."

He nodded. He placed a hand against her cheek, seeing so much of himself in her eyes. "You did the same thing."

"And got the same result." She worked a smile to her face, but it fell flat. "I don't want to be alone anymore, Flynn."

Flynn opened his arms, and drew Sam against his chest. "You won't be, Sam. And neither will I."

They held each other for a long time, while the snow fell softly outside, and the fire crackled in the fireplace. In all his life, Flynn could have never imagined a Christmas gift as wonderful as this.

Sam drew back, her gaze going over Flynn's shoulder. "I forgot to turn on the lights for the Christmas tree." She rose, pulling Flynn up with her, and they crossed to the seven-foot spruce.

Flynn ran a hand down the tree, his touch skipping over the history of Sam's life contained in the dozens and dozens of ornaments. Someday, he'd know the story behind every one of these. Because he would be with her for next Christmas and the one after that, and they would hang these ornaments together. He could hear her telling him that her grandmother had baked those salt dough gingerbread men, and her Aunt Ginny had made those macramé birds. That she'd bought the cable car on a trip to San Francisco, found the pinecone on a long hike in the woods. The joy in his heart tripled, for the future he could finally see, one with Sam by his side.

"Here," Sam said, handing him a switch. "You can do it. And don't forget to make a wish."

Flynn smiled. "I don't need to. My wish already came true." He pressed the button for the lights into Sam's palm. "You make the wish."

She closed her eyes, whispered a few words, then pressed the button. The lights came on, illuminating the tree with a burst of tiny white lights. A second later, they began to blink in a synchronized dance. "My favorite moment," she said. "The first time. It's like that's when Christmas really starts."

"What did you wish for?"

"If I tell you," she said, grinning, "it might not come true."

"If you wished for me to marry you," Flynn replied, swinging Sam back into his arms, "then that's one wish that's going to come true, because there's no way I'm letting you get away, Samantha Barnett."

Surprise arched her brows again. "You move fast, Flynn MacGregor."

"There's another thing you should know about me. When I see something I want, I go after it."

She smiled, then a moment passed, and the smile fell from her face. "I can't marry you, Flynn. It wouldn't be fair to you."

"What do you mean, it wouldn't be fair? We can find a way to make anything work, Sam."

"Do you want to know what I wished for?" She leaned her head against his chest. Flynn inhaled, catching the scent of sugar cookies. For the rest of his life, he'd associate that scent with Sam. "I wished for a way to have everything I wanted."

"I'm not enough?" He chuckled.

She looked up at him, sorrow filling her gaze. "I can't afford to pay for the treatment my grandmother needs, not without expanding Joyful Creations beyond the bounds of Riverbend. To expand, I have to work more hours. And if I'm working more hours, I won't be much of a wife, or a mother, if we ever have children."

Children. He hadn't thought of having kids—had never pictured himself with his own children at all—but now that Sam had said the word, he realized he did want a family.

A big family. A dog. A house. The whole enchilada.

But Sam was right. She couldn't have a life, and run multiple locations, not in such a demanding field. Hadn't he seen that when he'd went to live at Mondo's house? The chef and his wife had never been home, and eventually, called children's services to give back the foster children they'd taken in. Their best intentions had been undone by a work schedule that didn't allow for a family. He'd heard the same story over and over again. So many families tried to make it work, but in an industry that required early mornings and late nights, it was almost impossible. Some could work it out, but so many were forced to choose between business and home.

And as for Sam, if she had more than one location, along with the demands that came with those early years of still building her business?

He didn't see how she could have it all, either. Not unless…

"What if there was another way to expand Joyful Creations beyond Riverbend?" he said.

"Another way? What are you talking about?"

"It would require having Internet service," Flynn said with a grin. "Reliable postal service."

"Now *that* we have."

"Good." The idea exploded in his head, all those years of covering the food industry, and learning from chefs and experts coalescing at once. "What if you started a Web site? To sell, not just the regular cookies and desserts, but also the 'love cookies'? They already have a national reputation, and once my article runs—"

"I thought you said your editor would hate it."

"If he does, I'll just sell it somewhere else. It's a good article, Sam. A damned good article. I'll sell it, and in the process, make Joyful Creations even more famous."

"Ship the cookies. And stay here." Sam thought about that, pacing as she talked aloud. "It could work. I wouldn't have to move away from my grandmother or my aunt, and if I needed to increase production, I could always rent more space from the shop next door. They have a back room they don't use. My overhead would be low, the hours I'd have to put in…" She spun back toward him. "It could work."

"And you could have it all, Sam. Stay here, have a family." He grinned. "Have me, if you want."

"Of course I do." She crossed back to him, slipping into his arms as if she had always been there, fitting as easily as a link in a chain. "You're part of the package, Flynn MacGregor."

He leaned down and kissed her, capturing the taste of vanilla, the scent of cinnamon, the sweetness of Sam. Everything he'd ever wanted, in one beautiful, wonderful Christmas gift. "You know what people are going to say, don't you?"

"Hmm…what?"

"That we fell in love because of those cookies."

"But we never even ate any."

"No one knows if we did or not. And if it's rumored that we did…"

Sam grinned. "It'll be good for business."

"As long as it's good for us, I'm okay with that." Then Flynn kissed the woman he loved again, while the lights from the tree cast their golden light on her face. For the first time in his life, Flynn MacGregor believed in Santa Claus, because the jolly man had finally listened and given him the perfect gift.

The *only* gift he'd ever really wanted for Christmas—
A home.

* * * * *

A sneaky peek at next month...

By Request

RELIVE THE ROMANCE WITH THE BEST OF THE BEST

My wish list for next month's titles...

In stores from 21st December 2012:

3 stories in each book - only £5.99!

❑ Swept Away! – Lucy Gordon, Daphne Clair & Joanna Neil

❑ Her Amazing Boss! – Barbara McMahon, Nikki Logan & Anna Cleary

In stores from 4th January 2013:

❑ The Saxon Brides – Tessa Radley

Available at WHSmith, Tesco, Asda, Eason, Amazon and Apple

Just can't wait?

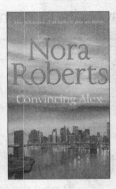